Just Call Me Rowdy

A Novel By Frank Farmer

ISBN-13: 978-0-578-03005-0

Published by *Ozarks Farm & Neighbor,* Inc.
Edited by Lindsay M. Haymes & Stanley E. Coffman

Contents

Trouble with Pa....5
Hear thatLonesome Train....13
Toby and Polecat....19
The Rabbit Habit....25
All Alone....31
A Saddle, A Rope....37
A Horse anda Jackrabbit....43
Headed for Texas....51
How Not toCross a River....55
How to Teacha Rooster Manners....59
Salt River Sally....65
Seeing the Wrathof the Lord....77
Sunday School Sport....85
Hog Trouble....95
Quail, Hot Biscuitsand Gravy....103
Wishin' For Home....109
You Lead aSow by the Tail....115
Tradin'....125
A MuleCalled Houdini....135
Booger Joe....143
Up the Creekand Canyon....151
Booger Joeto the Rescue....157
Saddle Up,....169
Cowboy....169
The Grand Rescue....173
Love and....179
Black Bulls....179
The Ride....183
Back at Sally's....187
Olivia Makesit Better....191
How toBreak a Mule....195
Fittin' JJ In....199
Letters Home....203

The Surprise....207
The Trap....211
The Rules....215
The Descent....217
Pieces of the Past....221
The Magazine Men....225
Family....231
The Monument....235
Time Standing Still....239
The Party....243
The Release....249
JJ's Big Surprise....253
Getting Acquainted....257
God Bless Texas....261
The Plan....265
The Tour....269
A New Family....275
The Scouts Return....279
Pigan's Miracle....285
Wrapping It Up....289
The Beginning....297
The Bull's Down....303
The Deal....313
Longhornsand Licenses....323
Preparing....333
Gettin' Hitched....337
Negotiating....351
Heading Out....355
The Reunion....363
New Beginnings....369

1

Trouble with Pa

Oh, Lordy!

I was lying on my back in the hay loft, just at the most exciting part of my Ace Western Story Magazine, when Pa caught me.

I hadn't heard him slipping into the barn loft, because if I had, I'd of slipped that magazine under a bale of hay in a hurry.

Pa ambled toward me, a raw-boned man, six foot tall, 220 pounds or so. He wore overalls and a blue work shirt, a straw hat – and no smile. In fact, he seldom smiled. All he cared about was working on our Missouri farm dawn to dark and seeing I did the same.

I didn't move. Wasn't time to, anyhow, Pa grabbed my magazine and ripped it in two and gathered up the front of my overalls in his big hands.

"Rowdy Farmer, I told you once what I'd do if I caught you loafing. I also told you not to read that trash. You know what you are going to get?"

I knew. All my 16 years – almost 17 now – Pa told me once. After that, look out. But I told him the last time he whipped me it was just that – the last time. Said I'd fight him if he tried. After all, I just lacked an inch of being six foot, near tall as Pa, and was nearly as heavy, being raw boned, long legged and big footed. Folks said I looked like Pa, big ears and all, 'cept I was uglier.

"Figure I got a right to be treated like a man, Pa."

"Rowdy, you'll be treated like a man when you act like one. Right now you are going to be treated like what you are, a lazy kid. You didn't hoe the strawberry patch for your mother like I told you to do."

That did it. I wasn't going to take that from my Pa or anybody else, and I had already licked two guys at the Cave Spring store who called his wife my mother. "She ain't my mother," I shouted. "She's just an ol' floozy with two kids you picked up after you and mom broke up."

And that was enough. Pa slapped the side of my head with his big raw-boned hand.

I screamed. I kicked. The more I did, the more he did. Finally, I busted out crying and laid down on the straw, crying in both anger and shame.

He said, "When you get through blubbering, remember I don't tell you twice what to do. Drive in the cows and have old Betty milked in time for supper. Your ma works hard, too."

There! He did it again, called "that woman" my ma again. I had put up with that for two years now, and I wanted to go live with my mother. But she had gone to Washington D.C. to take a job with the war department, since it looked like World War II was about to break out sooner or later. She couldn't take care of me in an apartment. And besides, I'd rather have died than take a job cooped up in a city like a dog or cat.

But I knuckled the tears out of my eyes and blew my nose. I didn't mind the sting in my rump. I was being treated like a kid, and all on account of him bringing another woman into my life. And also, how was a guy going to find out about women if he didn't read a good story like "Guns and Gals" once in a while?

But still, I was helpless as long as I had to live here. I grabbed a pitch fork, jabbed it into the bale of hay and cracked the handle. That gave me a savage satisfaction. Pa would be furious, and I'd catch it again in the seat of the britches. Suddenly I had the urge to get even with him, but how?

That black thought I had in my mind for a long time came boiling up again. Why not run away from home? I had always thought about running away from home these last couple of years. I always wanted to be a cowboy. And my mother's brother, Joe had run away from home many years ago. It hurt my mother's family awful bad, and they had searched and waited for word from him, but had all but given up.

All they knew was that he had talked about going to Texas.

The thought grew in my mind, but I knew I had to do the chores as Pa told me, so I jumped down from the loft and ran to the spring house to get my milk bucket. I whistled for my border collie, Moochie, the best dog anybody ever had. He slid up to me, nearly knocked me down, and kind of swallowed me up with his slobbery tongue. Ol' Moochie was deep brown in color, with four white paws and a white ring of hair around his neck, just like a collar.

"Dang it, Moochie, get off me. Go fetch old Jersey." And just as if he could understand human language, he tore off toward the pasture. I locked the cows in the stanchions, fed Betty her gallon of wheat bran, and began squirting the blue-john – the first milk to come out of the udder, the milk, and the cream from which my grandmother churned butter.

It had been a hot day in Missouri for early May. School was just out, and I had looked for free time to fish and swim in Asher Creek, which poured out of a cave two miles northeast of our farm. In fact, the early settlers, which included members of both my mother's and father's families, had given their new town the name of Cave Spring. That's where my mother's family stayed.

Most evenings after chore time, I'd run across the fields to the river, stopping along the way to get my friend, a black orphan boy named Jimmy Joe - JJ for short - and we'd catch a few perch for supper. After the fish quit biting, we'd strip off naked and swim until sundown. When it would get too cold, we'd climb out, dry off and go about our way, always hearing the whippoorwills singing their sad song just at dusk. Their song always gave me the creeps, and made me homesick.

Tonight though, there wouldn't be any swimming. If I was going to leave, then there was packing to do. I'd go get JJ and tell him what was up, and we'd hop the 10 o'clock freight that stopped at the little crossroad town of Pearl – a mile east of Cave Spring – and be on our way.

I was daydreaming long, the milk foaming to the edge of the bucket, when Jersey switched the flies off her back. "Dang you Jersey, that hurt." I slapped her side and she swatted again. So I slapped her with my hand. Moochie ducked, darted in and nipped her heel.

That did it. She lifted her hind foot, knocked me backwards and the bucket on top of me. She sailed out of the barn with her tail over her head, bawling like mad. I had hot milk all over my front side and cow dung on my hind side. I threw the milk stool at her and cussed her plenty and sat up to contemplate what I was going to catch from Pa.

We always fed the milk to the pigs and calves of a morning, and got our drinking milk, cream and butter from the night's milk. I'd take it down to the spring house, strain it through a clean cheesecloth and set it where the cool water against the sides of the bucket washed out the heat. The next morning, grandma would skim off the cream and churn it. Nothing beats sweet cream butter.

Now, if there was any doubt in my mind about running away from home, losing the milk chased them away. I had to leave now. Besides, how could a man call himself a man when he had to sit on a milk stool, prop his head into a cow's flank and pull on her teats to get milk? And like as not suffer the indignity of being hit in the face with her tail and kicked backwards into a cow pile.

Heck, out west a man didn't handle cows that way. The calves did the milking while the cowboys sat on top their horses with big hats and high-heeled boots and a six-shooter hanging at their waist. When they went to town everybody stepped high, wide and handsome and by dang that's where I was headed, the quicker the better.

Well, I had to act out my part, so Moochie and I went to the spring house like nothing was wrong, carrying the bucket like it was full of hot milk just in case pa was watching me. To kill a little time, like I was taking care of the milk, I caught a few crawdads and peeled their tails and walked down to where the spring emptied into Asher Creek and fed the big old perch in Blue Hole. Then I washed up and went to the house, knowing it was about supper time.

My step-mother met me at the kitchen door, a heavy spoon in her hand and said, "You don't come in, not until you take off your shoes. And go back out to the well house and wash your face and hands, they are grimy. And comb your hair before you come to the supper table."

That just burned me up. My mother didn't talk that way to me before she and my dad got a divorce. It seemed like I was a stranger in my own home, where I was born. Her two boys had rooted me out of my bed and bedroom, and I had to sleep in a little alcove by a chimney. If there was a big piece of cake left over on the table, guess who got it? Not ol' Rowdy, no, her boys got to split it. If I got anything extra, I had to walk across the country road to my grandmother's house. There, I was more than welcome. But my dad wouldn't let me stay with her, in spite of the fact she needed me to help care for her own father, who had broken a hip in a fall and was bedfast.

It beat all how this had to happen, and all because the old preacher at Cave Spring died, and a new one came in from another state.

I remember well, how all the town people waited for the new preacher to arrive with his family – a wife and the two boys – that had been assigned to our church. They got there just at sundown. The new man was "Mr. Personality." Something about him didn't strike me right, from the start.

As time went on, it seemed like his family got along well with everybody. Then, the new preacher decided to take some college courses in Springfield during the summer break. One day, he brought home a pretty girl who he said was a freshman student at the college and she was given a bedroom and stayed at the manse.

Some people thought it was a little strange, and whispers started going around, and one day the church elders cornered the preacher and he admitted he was in love with the girl.

Said he was planning to divorce his wife and marry the girl, but his wife asked him to not make up his mind right away. Said she told him to come into their home and let her live there before he made up his mind.

Well, that information brought about a rude awakening to the elders, and they fired him right on the spot. That made the preacher decide who he wanted right away – the mother of his two children, or the girlfriend.

He chose the girlfriend, and one day his wife drove him and his 18-year-old girlfriend ten miles south to old Route 66, dropped them off with a suitcase full of clothing, and the last she saw of them they were thumbing a ride from a motorist.

It didn't take long for the word to spread, and a reporter tracked them down for a story. The preacher told the reporter to "Go to Hell," and that hit headlines. So the reporters dogged them from Missouri to Arizona.

The preacher's wife bravely took the pulpit, was hired to be the new preacher, and it looked like everything had settled down.

Then one day my pa drove to Cave Spring and asked me to go with him. He stopped a block from the preacher's house, handed me a sealed envelope and asked me to carry it to the woman preacher, which I did.

I learned a few days later that the letter contained a note asking her for a date.

To make a long story short, a few weeks later, after the divorce from, my mother, dad married the woman and she and her two kids moved into what I had thought up until then to be my home.

I went to pieces with my temper, my obedience, my happiness and desire to live, except in my dreams. And the main dream was that I would just run away from home and go to Texas to look for my mother's brother, Joe. Last people heard of him, he had hopped a freight train at the nearest railroad station, Pearl, just two miles from our farm. He told the agent he was fed up with Cave Spring and was going to Texas to get a job on a cattle ranch.

I was just a little boy at that time, about five years old, but that had impressed me all of my life, especially after dad bought me a set of the "Frontier Boys" books. And whenever I got mad and pouted, I always threatened to go look for my uncle Joe.

But of course, nothing of the sort ever happened.

But the more I thought of it, after I was displaced by strangers in my own home, the more I thought that was what I would do some day. I had even stashed away a knapsack of things I would need to take with me, hid them in a hollow tree near the old fishing hole in Asher Creek.

It was time for me to go to Texas and find my uncle Joe. But I needed a friend to go with me, and I already knew who that would be, JJ.

I knew it was now or never. And this day, the more I thought about it, was the day.

I went back inside, through the living room, with its old fashioned fireplace at one end, and the wicker furniture and flowered rug on the floor. Out on the front porch was Pa, reared back in a chair with his feet propped up on the railing as he gazed out across the wheat field. The big heads the last couple of days had begun to show and I knew that in a couple of weeks, they would be in full flower and soon be ready to harvest.

Pa said, "Rowdy, reckon tomorrow we'll get the binder out of the shed and get it greased up. Looks like a bumper crop this year."

"Supper's ready," I jumped, and slammed the screen door behind me as I headed back to the kitchen, muttering, "But I won't be here to cut the danged stuff and get chaff down my neck. I'll be in a saddle on a cow pony about the time you are sweating those shocks of wheat."

I dug in for supper, thinking I'd better eat as much as I could, for no telling when I would have my next meal. I hadn't got all of that figured out yet, but I knew my camping experience in the woods would come in handy. For I could make a meal out of most anything, be it ripe wild berries, a handful of wild greens or even dig honey out of hollow trees. That is, if I could smoke the bees out before they stung me.

Dad said, "Better eat all you can hold and get to bed early, for you will need all the rest you can get tomorrow."

That was good news for me. I had to get my things packed and walk across the fields to Cave Spring to see JJ and tell him I was finally going west. I knew he would think it was just talk again, like I had done in the past, but this time it was for real, and I sure was going to try to get him to come with me.

As I walked past Pa he touched my arm and said, "Forget something?"

"Aw, Pa, I'm too danged old for kissin', ain't I?"

"Not for your pa, you aren't. He pulled my head down but I managed to slide sideways so his kiss landed on my cheek and he laughed and spanked my rear. Dang it, I was nigh onto a man. Couldn't he see that? By jinks, he'd know it come morning. And some day, I'd come back riding my horse, with my hat and boots on and spurs and chaps, and a big six-gun on my belt, and they'd all be sorry they didn't take me for a man sooner. I'd show 'em.

The stairs creaked under my feet. They always creaked when it got dry. In rainy season though, they tightened up and you could get up and down the stairs without waking up the whole house, but not now.

Once in my room, I dug out an old duffle bag, piled in a change of clothes, a fish line and some hooks, my hunting knife, my razor I didn't really need, $5.10 I'd saved from rabbit trapping last winter, my five-bladed knife and a bunch of matches I'd waterproofed with melted paraffin.

I stuffed as much as I could in my pockets and the rest in my bibbed overalls.

Overalls! Lordy, how I hated overalls. I wanted tight legged pants without bibs, like cowboys wear. But that woman never would buy me none. I had a big blue handkerchief, though, and tied it around my neck. Might's well start looking like a cowboy now, I thought even if I didn't have no hat or spurs.

After I had done my packing, I laid belly down on the bed and watched the sun go down and dark start to sneak up from the edge of the fields. The whippoorwills down by the creek started calling, so sad I could hardly stand it. A cow bawled her calf up to her and chewed her cud while it suckled. Once in a while the calf nudged her so hard she'd turn around with her head as if to say, "Hey, buster, take it easy." The old windmill creaked and I could hear the water pouring into the horse tank, and downstairs pa's rocking chair creaked on the front porch. I could hear the heavy tone of his voice, like a swarm of bees, and once in a while his talk of rain, drought, wheat, corn, alfalfa and "my boys" drifted up to me. Two of the boys he was referring to, as far as I was concerned, belonged to somebody else.

He just had one, and that was me, Rowdy. It made me grit my teeth until they hurt. If my mother was still here, my life would be perfect. But she was not, and I didn't want to be here without her and with another woman and her kids.

My eyes burned and a lump got in my throat. It made me so mad I got up and looked into the mirror and cussed myself good. By gum, I had to get out of here, fast.

I couldn't see the ground outside. It was time. I shimmied down the trellis beside the back porch, the honeysuckle perfume near suffocating me. I set off across the pasture toward Cave Spring, not looking back and running hard until my breath choked me. I knew the old house would be a tall rectangle against the skyline, with kerosene lamps throwing a yellow glow against the skyline through the downstairs windows. The barn, silo and windmill would just be silhouettes of the structures I had climbed to the top of many a time.

I sure wanted to go to Texas and be a cowboy. But just as much, I wanted to find my uncle Joe. Maybe he was a cowboy now, and I wanted to find him.

I hated to leave the farm. I bit hard on my tongue and shouted, "sissy, sissy, sissy," as loud as I could, and started running again. I didn't even stop when I got to Asher Creek, but splashed through and got wet. I went on to where I figured JJ would be staying that night, right over behind the field-rock store with the high board front, and next door to my grandma McLin's house.

2

Hear that Lonesome Train

JJ didn't have a real home, him being sort of an orphan. At least, nobody claimed him, although different people had different ideas about who his mother and father were.

So as a result, he just slept around; first with one black family, then another. Everybody suspected the whole black community, which numbered about 50 or so, knew who his parents were, but nobody would tell.

But folks didn't make a big deal out of it. People were accepted for what they were, not for who they were.

At the moment, JJ was staying with the Charley Rollin family, which was next door to the home of my mother's mother and my aunt Winnie. It was really little more than a barn that had been turned into a four-room house, but the roof did not leak and it was warm in the winter time.

Charley Rollin was a bull of a man and it was said it was lucky he was a gentle man who didn't get mad at anybody. His wife was a nice woman named Tilda. She was the opposite of Charley, because she was a pigmy. And they had triplet daughters, named Ruby, Tina and May. They were short like their mother, and hefty like their father. They could play baseball better than any of the Cave Spring boys. Also living with them was Charley's younger brother, Sherman.

But he was nicknamed "Monk." Once I asked him why he was called Monk, and he said, "When I was born, they said I looked like a monkey, so that's how I got the nickname. But I don't like it."

"Then what's your real name?"

"Sherman," he said. And so from that moment on, I called him Sherman, and he would do anything I asked him to do, because I respected him, and he respected me.

But this night, I only wanted JJ, and I found him sleeping on a pallet on the back porch.

I hid in a bunch of spirea beside the porch, and gave him our signal. "Whoo-hooo-whoo-hooo," just like an owl.

"I knowed you was there, Rowdy," he laughed. "You don't sneak very good. What you want?"

"I want you to slip out of bed real quiet and go with me next door to my grandmother's. I want to tell you something, real confidential."

He slept in his overalls, so it didn't take but a second for us to be in my grandmother's back yard. The lights were out, so I knew my grandmother and aunt were already in bed. That was even better, because I didn't want them to know what I was up to.

I guided JJ to the cellar door, found the lantern hanging inside the cellar door, and lighted it with matches grandma always kept handy. I closed the door and we got a couple of apples and sat down on the inside steps, like we always did when a storm came up and we thought we might get hit by a tornado.

"What's up, Rowdy? You're sneakin' around like a chicken thief."

"Well, I wanted to tell you I'm leaving home. Gonna go to Texas and be a cowboy. Maybe even get my own ranch."

"Sure you are. And I'm gonna fly over the moon just as soon as I get wings."

"Don't get smart with me. I mean it. Just wanted you to know."

"When you gonna do this?"

"Tonight, this very night. Got my bags packed, and gonna hop the puddle-jumper at the Pearl station when she slows down at midnight."

He jeered at me. "You're a coward. You won't do it."

He ought never to have said that to me. I grabbed him by the shirt front and said, "What you mean, calling me a coward. Take it back."

"Nope. Ain't gonna."

"Take it back. I'll twist your ear." I grabbed his ear, which he was always sensitive about, and he said, "All right, don't get sore. I take it back."

I let go his shirt. "Well, I best get going. Just thought I'd let somebody know, so the folks wouldn't be looking all over, thinking I was dead."

"I'm going, too," JJ announced much to my surprise, but that was what I hoped he would do. But I played it cool, "Don't know about that, JJ. Takes a he-man to be a cowboy. You're just a kid."

"Devil I am," he said. "I'm as old as you, almost."

"Shoot, JJ. You just turned 16. I'm nigh onto 17."

"Don't make any difference," he argued. "I'm 16, same as you." I turned to walk away but he caught my arm and said, "Besides, we always made it up that we would go to Texas together. It's not fair for you to go without me."

"Aw, you'd just get homesick. Besides, I don't want nobody slowing me down. Well, so long, JJ." I held out my hand. He wouldn't shake it and a scared look came into his eyes.

"Doggone you, Rowdy. You just wait until I get my things. I'll show you how homesick I get." He jammed up the lantern globe and before I knew it, he had blown out the light and ran into the house. I stuffed my pockets full of apples and called after him, "Hurry up. Ain't got all night. The train's due about an hour from now. We got to get in a boxcar on the siding before she gets there."

I kept to the shadows until JJ slipped back out of the house with his sack of belongings and we hustled down the road toward the creek. We stopped at the little cave and spring which gave its name, "The Cave," and where a spring roared out and ran into Asher Creek. I belly-flopped down and drank, thinking of all the fourth of July picnics I'd attended across the creek, and of all the times I'd caught perch and a bass or two from under the bridge across the road that lead to home. And I could just see myself coming home some day, riding down that big hill on my horse, splashing across Asher Creek right at the highest time of the picnic, rearing my horse up on his hind legs and waving my big hat at all the folks I used to know and who thought I wasn't nothing but a little old farm kid.

Directly, I heard a whistle from JJ, and I whistled back at him. "Better get yourself a drink, because it may be a long time before you have another chance."

JJ did as I suggested, and we heaved up our sacks over our shoulders and headed towards Pearl, two miles west. Pearl didn't amount to much... a one-room store and three houses, but it had a railroad depot, and every night the train stopped at the siding to pick up box cars loaded with hogs, cattle, wheat, strawberries, or whatever else was in season.

The cinders scrunched under my feet as I stepped on the right of way and I said, "Step on the ties JJ, so's we won't be heard,"

We walked along the siding, looking inside cars until I found a car with some dry straw on the floor. We threw in our sacks and crawled inside. "What time does the train come?" JJ asked.

"About 10 o'clock."

"How long will it take to get to Texas?"

I did some calculating. "Pa used to ship in sheep from San Angelo, and I've seen the bills of lading. I reckon four, maybe five days. Takes a car of sheep longer because they have to lay over and unload, rest, feed, and water."

"How will we know which train to take?"

"Why, just take every westbound train we come to."

"Well, I suppose we are already started wrong."

"All right, stupid. Why?"

"These tracks run east and west, but for only about a mile. Then they go north and south."

He had me there but I wasn't about to admit it. "Well, we'll just take it until we come to a westbound train. Ain't nothing to it at all." But I tell you, I was some worried, sitting there in the doorway of the open car, watching the stars and listening to the frogs croaking in every little pond. There sure had to be a way of getting to Texas from here, even if the tracks did run the wrong way. If the train that brought in sheep got here, there was bound to be one going back.

One by one the lights went out in the houses in Pearl and JJ and I were left all alone. The wind whipped around the cars and made a spooky noise that made shivers run up my spine. But it didn't bother me much. I tried not to think of ma, because that bothered me some. I knew she'd cry when she heard I had gone. But that was just the way it was. Every mother had to give up her son when he became a man. I'd write her when I got to a ranch, so's she wouldn't worry. If it bothered me thinking about pa, I just thought about the licking pa had given me, and I got mad all over again.

All of a sudden, I saw a shadow moving along the tracks toward us. JJ saw it too, and he grabbed my arm. "What's that?" His teeth chattered. I started to say it was a wolf, but I'm glad I didn't, for it was my dog, Moochie. He had smelled out my trail and followed us there. Why hadn't I thought to tie him up?

Moochie heard JJ's voice and came running. He jumped into the boxcar, whining and licking my face. "Dang it, Moochie," I said. "Go home." I shoved him out of the car. He thought I was playing and jumped in again. "Let's take him, Rowdy," said JJ urgently.

I would liked to have taken him, but a ranch wasn't any place for a farm dog. Why, like as not he'd get bit by a rattlesnake and die, or else lost, or kicked by a horse and killed. "No JJ. We'll just leave him here until the train comes. Then I'll shove him out when we pass our farm."

Now, away to the north, I heard the lonesome whistle of the train and it wasn't long before its headlight showed up on the prairie, and then here she came, huffing and puffing. Seemed like she always moved slowly until she got close to you and then she got in a hurry. The engineer stopped on the main tracks and the brakeman, back in the caboose, got off with his signal lantern and uncoupled a bunch of cars. The engine pulled onto the siding, backed up and coupled onto the cars, including the one we were in.

I heard the loud "clang" and then, like an echo, the noise rolled down the line to each car and it suddenly took up all the slack. When our car jerked, the force nearly knocked us over. Old Moochie wasn't braced and he fell plumb down and rolled over and over. He just got up, laughing with his tongue out, and barked real loud. I grabbed his muzzle and choked off another bark so the brakeman wouldn't hear him. He licked my face and whined. Then the engineer whistled twice and the slack was taken up with a bigger jerk than before. We pulled out on the main track, coupled on to the rest of the cars, and the whistle tooted again.

"Texas, here we come," I said. JJ's face was white in the starlight and his eyes big and round. He was scared, and I bet if it hadn't been for me, he'd have never had a chance to be a cowboy.

We rolled southward, passed the west side of our farm and when we cleared the timber, I saw the outlines of the house, barn, silo, windmill, and the tall maples around home. There wasn't a light on any place, so I knew they hadn't missed me. I tell you, I had to bite my tongue to keep from crying, and if that train hadn't moved so fast, I reckon I'd have backed out. When we got opposite to our house, I shoved Moochie out the door and he rolled head over heels. He scrambled up, started barking and then ran after us, but we had picked up speed and he got left behind.

"So long, Moochie, old boy," I called, choking some.

Every mile from here to Willard there was a crossing and the lonesome whistle of the engine rolled and echoed above the clickety-clack of the wheels on the rails. Pretty soon the lights of Willard showed up and we slowed down and chuffed to a stop and the engine wheezed and smoked, cause I could smell the smoke and feel its bite in my eyes.

"What are we stopped for, Rowdy?"

"Get water for the boiler, stupid. What else you think this train runs on?"

"It runs on water?"

"JJ, I swear. I don't know if you ought to go with me or not. Boy, are you dumb. The engine heats the water and forces it through the hydraulic pistons and that makes the wheels go around. Boy!"

"You mean it makes steam, don't you?" he said.

I didn't bother answering. I just wanted the train to hurry and take me to Texas.

The engineer pulled the rope and the whistle tooted twice and the cars clanged up and down the line. Just then, I heard a dog bark. It sounded like old Moochie, and I stretched my neck out the door of the car.

Sure enough, there was Moochie, stretched out and running fit to kill. He tried to jump into the car, but was so tired he fell back. JJ got on his knees in the doorway and said, "Good old Moochie come on, come on."

All of a sudden, I never wanted anything more than old Moochie in my arms. I'd had him since he was a puppy, and I wasn't much more than a pup when I got him. I jumped out of the car, hoisted him inside and by that time the train was moving a good clip. But with JJ pulling my arms, I managed to get a knee up, and got inside. JJ laughed and Moochie barked in fits and all of a sudden, JJ buried his face in Moochie's fur and bawled like a baby.

Boy, did I get mad. But then, I felt a bit of salt water sting my eyes and I bit my tongue and let him cry. I'd just have to look after the both of them to keep them out of trouble.

Directly I said, "Well, JJ, let's hit the hay. Got to rest up so's we can ride, soon as we get to Texas." We scratched up a bed of prairie hay that was littered around the car floor, spread out a blanket and laid down. Moochie snuggled down between us and we each had an arm thrown over him. The train settled down to a steady gait and the boxcar swayed gently from side to side and the wheels clickety-clacked. I don't know when we went to sleep, but after a while I sat up and wondered where the devil I was.

3

Toby and Polecat

"JJ, wake up."

Moochie jumped up at the sound of my voice and padded to the doorway of the car. He began whining.

"Where are we, Rowdy?" We went to the door of the car. "Are we in Texas?"

"Of course not, stupid."

"Well, where?"

"Anybody ought to know that."

"Where are we, then?"

I didn't bother to answer. Truth is, I didn't know, but I didn't want to admit it. Didn't matter, I figured we had to change trains unless we wanted to end up someplace besides Texas. I figured we must be in Springfield. I knew the tracks were running east and west, by looking up at the stars and finding the Big Dipper. We had come in headed east, so I had to find a train headed west.

As I looked across the yards, there seemed to be a hundred sets of tracks. I couldn't tell which was the main set to Texas.

JJ's teeth chattered. "What'll we do?"

I grabbed my sack of stuff. "Get out of here," I said, "and find us a westbound train." I jumped out, kept to the dark side of the cars and started walking. Boy I tell you, I didn't know which way to look. As we slipped from shadow to shadow across the yards, I heard a train whistle to the east of me, saw an engine headlight and a train headed toward us, picking up speed. It was westbound, looked like a mainliner to me, and I yelled, "Come on, JJ," and we ran for it. I jumped into the first open car I saw, with Moochie right beside me, and helped JJ inside.

Boy, was it dark in there. Moochie was the first to sense there was someone in there, because he growled and rubbed up against my leg. I put my hand on his neck and felt the hair standing up. JJ grabbed my arm and I heard his teeth chattering.

Then I saw two dark figures at the end of the boxcar and I said, "Who's there?"

A raspy voice came out of the black. "Shut your face, kid."

But an easy drawl followed the raspy voice. "Pay him no mind, boy. Ease on in. Who's your pard?"

"I'm Rowdy Farmer," I said. "This here's my dog, Moochie, and my pard, JJ."

"Well, howdy, Rowdy," chuckled the one with the soft voice. One of the guys lighted a match and its yellow flare made me blink. Then I got a glimpse of their faces. They looked to be 20 to 22, and the one holding the match, his eyes glittered like a snake. The other's eyes sort of smiled without meaning anything, and I decided it was him that'd been talking nicest. He said his name was Toby and I sidled over toward him before the light burned out.

He said, "You kids better get home before somebody chews you up and spits you out. And hold that there dog off of me or I'll slit his throat."

Moochie growled and I felt the fur stand up on his neck again. I could see better now that my eyes were used to the dark, and I saw Toby reach out and pet Moochie on the head. "Nice old dog," he said. "You wouldn't hurt me, would you?" Moochie stopped growling and sniffed at Toby. His tail beat the side of my leg. Toby said, "Where you boys headed?"

"Texas," I said. "got a job as cowboys." JJ digged my side with a thumb and whispered, "No, we haven't."

"Have you now?" asked Toby. "What ranch?"

"Uh... ain't decided which job we'll take yet," I said. "Got several offers."

"Ain't that strange now," he laughed. "I sort of got the impression jobs was hard to come by these days. What kind of cowboying you do?"

"Well," I said, "I'm a bronc rider, myself. My pard here, he is sort of a tenderfoot and ain't decided what angle he'll take up."

Toby chuckled. "Well, you boys better bed down and get some shuteye. You'll need it, come day. Walking is rough."

"Walking?" We ain't about to walk. We're riding the rods," I said.

Toby laughed again. Seemed he didn't do nothing but laugh. "Ever see a brakeman seven foot tall with a ball bat in his hand? You'll walk, all right, or lay over until dark."

That bothered me some. "I'd have to think on it," I said, "Where you guys headed?"

"Kansas," Polecat snorted. "To work in the wheat harvest."

"Wheat?" I asked. "Wheat's the reason I'm going to Texas. I could have put up wheat at home. Who wants to ride a binder and shock wheat when he can ride a horse? Not me."

He snarled, "I can make 50 cents an hour in wheat. Best you can do on a ranch where we came from is $20 a month and your keep, and you furnish your saddle. Kid, you ain't even got a saddle. You best go home."

Well, there wasn't any use wasting time arguing with anybody dumb as Polecat. Me and JJ laid down, Moochie's tail between us, and went to sleep. Once in a while that lonesome whistle moaned and woke me up, like out of a nightmare, but the swaying of the boxcar rocked me back to sleep. I kept dreaming of rounding up cattle and eating at the chuck wagon and going into town on Saturday nights on a white horse and whooping it up with the cowboys.

Moochie's growling woke me up. I sat up, seeing Polecat standing over me. He shoved me back down and grabbed my sack of belongings. Moochie snapped at his arm, got a mouthful of coat and he yelled, "Get him off of me, kid."

Moochie gave another snap and jumped to his feet, trying to eat Polecat up. Polecat ran for the door and, looking around wide-eyed, yelled at Toby, "I'm getting out of here," and jumped. The train was moving pretty fast and Polecat rolled over and over. I looked back to see him sitting beside the track, blood running down his forehead and shaking his fist at me.

Toby stood beside me, laughing, and he yelled out, "See you in Wichita at the Long Horn Cafe," and he turned around and went back to the end of the car, still laughing. JJ was still asleep, his long legs curled up and his arms folded across his chest like he was trying to hug himself to death.

"Well, kid," said Toby, "you learned some of the rules of the road, didn't you?"

"If stealing's a rule," I said, "I'd just as soon not know the rules."

Toby spread his hands in a gesture of helplessness. "Man's got to get by best he can."

I took a good look at Toby for the first time. He was a little bit of a squirt, wouldn't have weighed 115 pounds, soaking wet. He wore a denim jumper that'd seen better days and blue jeans and run over cowboy boots. A red flannel shirt that was buttoned at the neck below his skinny adam's apple and he wore a greasy, tattered cowboy hat. But I sure didn't take him for no cowboy, just because he had on a hat and boots. He looked like pure bum to me.

Moochie whined. I knew he was hungry, cause he licked his lips. I dug into my sack and got out a can of pork and beans and got out my knife and opened the can. Toby crept closer. "What's that? Pork and beans?"

"Yeah," I said. "Got to feed my dog."

"You ain't going to feed them good beans to a dog, be you?"

"Sure," I said. "Nothin's too good for old Mooch. He kept Polecat from stealing my stuff."

Toby sat cross-legged, and his tongue flicked out and ran across his lips. He said, "That dog is wormy."

"How's that?"

"I said that dog's wormy."

"How can you tell?"

"Hair's rough. Eyes ain't bright. Got a penny?"

"Sure."

"Well, gimme it."

I fished a penny out of my pocket and Toby took it and petted Moochie on the head, worked his fingers into the side of his lips and thrust the penny down Moochie's throat. He gulped, yelped and ran to the far end of the car.

"What'd you do that for?" I asked.

"Copper in the penny," he said. "That'll kill worms. Now, best not feed him for an hour or so. Let him digest the penny so's it'll kill the worms."

Toby took the can of beans out of my hand. "Reckon that's about a fair trade," he said. "My dog sense for his pork and beans." Before I knew it, he had turned up the can and swallowed half the beans. I didn't know what to think, but I knew one thing for sure. Anybody that was good to my dog, he was my friend. "I sure do thank you," I said. "Ain't nobody ever showed me nothing like that before."

About that time, JJ woke up. He sat up, rubbed his eyes and looked at me, then at Moochie, then at Toby. Without a word, he doubled up his legs, hugged himself and lay down again bawling fit to kill.

"What's wrong, JJ?" I asked.

"Want to go home," he bawled, "right now."

Well, it made me feel right bad. I sure wanted him to come with me, but I hadn't exactly made him come, either. Dern cry baby. I had my dog and my new friend, Toby, and I sure didn't need no handy man's son crying on me. I should have known better than to take on a sissy like JJ for a pard.

Toby chuckled. He patted his stomach, handed me the empty can and said, "I'll give you a tip for one of the apples in your pocket."

I fished out a couple of Grimes Goldens and handed them to him. Toby tapped me on the shoulder and pointed to the can. "Keep that tin can. Best friend a man on the road can have."

"Why?"

"Well, you can dip water out of a spring and get yourself a drink. You can boil coffee in it. Or catch a cow's milk if you can find one in some farmer's field that will stand still. It will hold blackberries and wild strawberries. Or fishing worms and crawdads. Get it?"

Lordy, I hadn't thought of that. Back home, a tin can was something to take to the trash pile, but here, Toby had come up with all sorts of use for it. "I sure am beholdin' to you," I said.

Now the train began to slow up and I looked out the door. Gosh, I hadn't seen country like this before. There wasn't any trees at all, just grass and long, rolling hills, with cattle standing all over them, grazing. The sun was coming up back in the east and it cast long lines of light and shadow and sure made the tall, green grass look pretty. "Where are we?"

"Kansas," said Toby. "These here are the Flint Hills. That tall grass is bluestem."

I sure was disappointed. Hoped it'd be Texas, for all I knew we had been traveling long enough. But I sure would have liked to cowboy here. Toby said, "This here's cattle country. Kansas ain't all wheat and dust. Wheat's west of these hills."

Toby moved beside me and I suddenly realized he smelled like a goat. But then, reckon a man on the move like him couldn't always be taking a bath. "Better get your pard," he said. "We're about to leave this palace on wheels."

Whatever Toby said was good enough for me. "Come on, JJ," I said. "We're going to leave this palace on wheels." JJ shook his head, looked up with big tears on his cheeks and said, "I'm hungry."

Toby said, "So am I, kid. That's why we're getting off."

4

The Rabbit Habit

The train chuffed to a near stop and Toby slipped off, so neat he didn't even stumble. I tried it, but rolled along the ground with Moochie beside me. JJ stood paralyzed in the door as the train gathered speed.

"Jump, stupid." I grabbed him and he fell on top of me and we both got skinned up knees. "Why didn't you jump?" I yelled, wiping the blood off my palms on his shirt. But he looked like he was going to cry so I left him alone.

Toby was prowling the right of way and the train clickety-clicked westward. I hated to see her go. She was my ticket to Texas. But Toby wiggled a finger at me and I followed. "Got any matches?" he asked.

"Sure." I pulled the paraffin matches out of my pocket. Toby's face twisted into a grin. "Whew Lord, now. Ain't that something? Got them matches all fixed so's they won't get wet."

"Boy, you'll make a good man for the road, someday. Now, I tell you. You scrounge up some chips and grass and build a fire whiles I get us some meat. Then we'll have breakfast keen as anybody's."

"Grass I can get," I said. "But there ain't a tree in sight I can see, and I ain't got no ax, anyhow."

Toby chuckled. "Boy, you got lots to learn. Chips out here ain't wood chips. They's cow chips?"

Toby pointed to the side of the hill. "Manure, boy. Dried cow dung. Makes a hot fire, even if it stinks some. Cooked many a meal off'n it, I have."

"Boy," said Toby, "you ain't home now. You want me to learn you something or not?"

I didn't argue no more, but headed up the hill with Moochie to get some cow chips. "Come on, JJ," I said. "help me." He followed, not saying anything, but whimpering once in a while.

We gathered up all the dried cow dung we could carry in our arms and went back to the right of way. Toby was there, and by durn if he didn't have two rabbits, skinned out and spread apart on sticks. Toby rested on his haunches, his tongue flicking across his lips in anticipation as he looked at the juices dripping out of the fat little rabbit carcasses. His eyes fairly sparkled as he saw me looking wide-eyed at the rabbits. I got off the train here for what? Water, that's what for. Where there is water, there are rabbits and cow chips, right?"

I nodded, but I still didn't see no river, not even a pond. Toby pointed up the hill. "See down the bottom of that draw, where the two hills come together like folds in a cloth? See that dark green grass? See where the cow paths come off the hills and head together?"

I nodded again.

"There's a spring right there. Now hurry up, and give me another match."

"Come on, JJ," I said, and he hurried after me, his blue mood gone. He half ran to catch up with me and he said, "Gosh, that geezer is smart, isn't he?"

"Smartest man I ever saw," I said. "And quit saying 'isn't. That gives you away for a city kid. I bet my pa could learn a few things from him. Boy, are we lucky."

Sure enough, right where Toby said, there was a clear spring. It bubbled out from under limestone, and all around the grass was tall and green. We filled the innertube, carried it back to where Toby had smoke boiling up from the cow chip fire and rabbit juice dripping into the blaze, near making me crazy to taste it.

JJ hunkered down right by the fire and watched Toby turn the sticks a little at a time. Moochie sat down on his haunches and whined. He hadn't had anything to eat, either. Toby said, "Now boy, get your tin can and fill it with water and set it in the hot coals. Directly, we'll have us some coffee."

While we waited for the water to boil, we ate the rabbits. They had a crisp outer layer, where they'd got too hot, and inside was still raw and pink and juicy, but hot, and it was the best meat I'd ever had. Even without salt. When the water boiled, Toby put in a pinch of coffee from a bread sack in his pocket and after it bubbled a while, we washed down that rabbit meat with the coffee. I reckon it was just about as satisfying a meal as I ever had.

Toby scattered the fire, rubbed his belly and said, "Reckon it's time for a little nap." He squinched up at the sun, rising high and getting hot now, went to the north side of the tracks and laid down in the shade. First thing

I knew, he was snoring and JJ and Moochie and me felt all alone without him awake.

"Boy," whispered JJ, "I wish we could talk him into going on to Texas with us. I bet there isn't a cowboy in Texas half as smart."

"Reckon you're just about right," I said. "Thing I want to know is, how does he catch rabbits with his hands?"

"Maybe he'd teach us," said JJ. "Then when we get back home we could make lots of money trapping rabbits."

"What you mean when we get back home? You figuring on a vacation or something? Me, I'm out for a career. I ain't about to go back to the farm, close as I am to being a cowboy."

JJ just dropped his chin on his knees and his eyes took on a sick-chicken look. Well, I wasn't about to baby him. I laid down in the shady side of the right of way, like Toby. I reckoned if he had to rest up, I did too, so pretty soon the world got all drowsy and I went to sleep. When I woke up, JJ was asleep beside me. The sun got high enough to touch us and it made me prickly with heat and I wished Asher Creek was close enough to jump into and get cooled off. I saw Moochie lying at my feet, his eyes on me, and he wiggled his tail when he saw me awake. Toby squatted on his heels close by, eating an apple. I put my hand down to my pocket and didn't feel any bulge. He laughed and said, "Figured you wouldn't mind me taking your last apple. I sort of need the vitamins, but you look healthy enough to me."

"That's all right," I said. "But I sure would have liked the taste of one of those Grimes Goldens right now."

Toby said, "Reckon you'd best wake up your pard if you want another lesson, that is."

"What kind of lesson?"

"Kind of got you, the way I caught rabbits, didn't it?"

"Figure on showing you. Wake up your pard."

I shook JJ and he jumped up quick like, crying out a little. He sure was edgy. "Wake up, JJ. We're going to learn how to catch rabbits."

Toby finished off the apple core, even down to the seeds, and started down the tracks. "Boy," he said, "bring that tin cup. Leave all your things. We'll be back before dark."

We sort of moseyed along, me and JJ watching Toby and awaiting our lesson in rabbit catching. Only thing Toby did was say, "Kid, keep that dog back so he won't scare the rabbits." He took the tin cup and pretty soon he came to a dewberry patch and he picked some juicy black ones, feeding himself, putting some in the can. Me and JJ couldn't hardly feed ourselves fast enough and when Moochie whined, I dropped a couple in his mouth. He toothed them, spit them on the ground, looked at me, whined, and finally ate them and begged for more.

I never knew dewberries could taste so good. Back home they were something I had to pick so's ma could make jelly, and I sure got tired of getting chiggers on me and briars in my fingers. But here, I didn't mind a bit. This was for real. It made me feel like puffing out my chest. JJ whispered, "When are we going to catch rabbits?"

"Hush," I said. "Toby knows what he's doing." But I began to wonder a little, too. And get impatient. After all, I didn't have all the time in the world. I wanted to get on toward Texas.

About this time, Toby went to humming and he held his hand back to stop us. He started walking natural-like in a little circle, looking straight ahead and humming, and he kept getting the circle tighter, and then all of a sudden, one foot moved sideways and down. I heard a rabbit squeal bloody murder.

Sure enough, there beneath his boot was a rabbit, eyes bulging out, kicking like mad. Toby chuckled, reached down and picked up the rabbit by its hind legs, chopped behind its ears with the side of his hand and the rabbit stopped kicking. It was dead.

"What you think of that?" laughed Toby.

JJ ran around and around, laughing and jumping up and down. I'd never seen him so happy.

"Golly," I said. "How'd you know that old rabbit would be in that clump of grass?"

JJ said, "May I dress it?" Boy was I surprised. Back home, JJ wouldn't even gut a rabbit after he'd caught it.

"Sure," said Toby. "That's part of our bargain. Feed the guts to the dog. They are full of vitamins."

JJ borrowed my knife, gutted the rabbit and Moochie wagged his tail, jumped and begged for more. JJ laughed. "Boy, isn't this great?" By gum, maybe JJ would make a cowboy after all.

Well, that was the way it went. Toby showed us how to spot a clump of grass where a rabbit sat, how to look for his eyes looking bright at you. You never could see them if you looked for their fur, because it was the same color as the brown grass. But when we didn't look for anything but eyes, we learned to find them. He showed us how to act natural and walk in a circle so the rabbit would think you were going to pass him by and never move until you set your foot down on him. I got three that day and JJ got one, and old Moochie ate rabbit intestines until his sides bulged.

When we got back to camp, it was nearly dark and we cooked more rabbits and drank more coffee and I opened a can of peaches from my sack and we had a regular feast. And then Toby had us take a nap, "So's we can be ready for anything," and I hoped for a fast train to Texas.

5

All Alone

The sun went over the hills and the coyotes began to howl and the stars came out bigger and brighter than I ever remembered them back home.

We just sat there, Toby telling a story once in a while, waiting for a train. Directly, we heard that mournful cry away back east of us and Toby said, "She's about 10 miles out. Get all your things in a pile in front of you. When that old train slows down going up the hill, we'll make a run for an open box car."

By and by the train got closer and when it came down the hill east of us, I thought surely it would never slow down enough for us to hop on. But the hill was steeper than I thought and then I began to wonder how we were going to pick out a boxcar.

But Toby had already done it. "Come on, boys," he said, and eased up beside the rolling boxcars. As the car he wanted approached, he put out his hands on the door sill, ran alongside for a few steps, then just sort of stiffened his legs and rolled onto the floor of the car. Moochie jumped in, whirled around and barked for me and JJ to hurry up. I shoved JJ inside, threw my stuff after him and rolled in like Toby had done. Wasn't nothing to it at all.

Well, it sure felt good, having wheels under us again, but it was a little sad, too, leaving our camp. I crawled to the door and looked back as long as I could see the sparks of our last camp fire, and then we topped a hill and rolled west. The train whistled long and lonely and I shivered and was suddenly as sad as I'd ever been. I heard JJ crying and this time I didn't get after him. I just bawled a little bit, too, only I didn't let on to JJ. Old Moochie though, I couldn't fool him. He crawled into my lap and licked the tears away as they fell. I grabbed his fur and buried my face in it and let 'em rip for a spell and directly I fell asleep.

I don't know where we were when I woke up, nor how long I had slept. I only know it was sunup, for the sun was shining in the door of the car, and I couldn't get my senses around me for a while. Never had I slept so hard. My bones ached from it. I looked for JJ, and he was sitting with his knees pulled up under his chin, just staring. There were dark circles under his eyes. I looked for Toby but he wasn't in the car. Well I reckoned he was out rustling up breakfast for us. I'd just go help him.

"Where you going, Rowdy?" asked JJ.

"Reckon I'll hunt up Toby and help him."

JJ laughed nervously and waved a piece of paper, "Read this."

I grabbed it and found it was a note from Toby. It read: "Dear boys. I am headed for the wheat field and have to leave you now. I hope to see you in Texas. P.S. I left you my water bag and some fried rabbit. So long."

Well, dang his hide. Just run off in the night like a thief. And here I thought he was a regular fellow. "What the heck," I said to JJ, wading up the note and throwing it away. "We don't need him, anyhow."

"No," JJ said, "but we could use what he stole from us."

"Stole?" I echoed. "What do you mean?"

"He took your bag with all your clothing and the rest of our canned food. And he got his fist into my pocket and stole my $20 bill."

I tell you, I wanted to chuck my breakfast, but I couldn't because I hadn't had any. I didn't know whether to get mad or to cry. I saw old Toby had left us his old clothing and I knew he'd put on my good overalls and jumper. I felt in my pocket. At least he hadn't stole what little money I had left. I reckon the reason was because Moochie had been lying across my lap most of the night and he couldn't get to me without waking Moochie.

Well, there wasn't no use in crying about it, and getting mad wouldn't bring him back with our things. But I wished almighty hard that I could get hold of him about then to stretch his scrawny neck.

JJ just sat there, but that wouldn't get it done. "JJ, eat some rabbit meat and drink some water. Then we'll rustle about and see where we are. We may be in Texas."

"Nope," he said. "We are in Oklahoma."

"How do you know?"

"Look outside."

I went to the car door and looked around. There wasn't anything there but a big bunch of empty cattle pens and a few old buildings and sign that said,

'Tie Siding, Okla.' Well, I didn't know where Tie Siding, Okla., was, but I figured we'd passed out of Kansas and were well inside Oklahoma by now. One thing had gone right for us. We were still headed for Texas.

Then my spirits lifted considerably. There was a big windmill at the west end of the pens and in one of the sheds I heard a hen cackling. By gum, where there was a windmill, there was bound to be water, and where a hen cackled, there had to be eggs.

"Come on, JJ," I yelled, and jumped out of the boxcar, old Moochie running ahead and barking like a pup.

That old windmill sure whirled in the stiff breeze and the cold stream of water poured out of the pipe into the biggest danged tank I ever saw. I skinned out of my clothes and jumped into that water, and so did JJ, and Moochie did too, fur and all. We soaked and stuck our heads under the water pipe and drank until our bellies nearly busted. The sun came out warm and we climbed up on the edge of the tank and let it dry us and then dressed.

"Let's eat breakfast," I said.

"Great," said JJ. "But what will we eat?"

"How about eggs?"

"What eggs?"

"Tell you what, JJ. You go out in the cattle pens and gather up a big armload of cowchips and I'll furnish the eggs."

"Where you..."

"Don't argue. Ain't I got you this far safe and sound? Ain't we just a hop and skip from Texas and becoming cowboys? Now, just go on and do like old Rowdy tells you and you'll get along."

"Well," he argued, "I'm not going to get cow chips. There's plenty of old wood around these corrals. Give me the matches."

Sure enough, there were scraps of wood lying everywhere – I hadn't thought of that. I whistled to Moochie and went to tackle one of those sheds to see if I could find that old hen.

Somebody had lived here once, for there were the remains of an old two-room house. I didn't bother going in, for I was looking for food, fresh food. I guessed the old farmer had dried up and blown away, and that ranchers were using the place for a shipping point now. But I sure thanked that farmer for leaving an old hen or two.

Sure enough, I got around the far side of the pens and I heard and old hen clucking to a brood of baby chicks, and a rooster crowed. Dang me, if there wasn't a whole flock of red hens running around there, from frying size to baby chicks chirping after them. My heart just hummed. I went into a shed and an old hen cackled like crazy and ran off the nest. She left a whole pile of eggs. The only trouble was that they might have been partially hatched, but when I felt of them, they were all cool. I knew the old gal was just laying her clutch of eggs and hadn't started to hatch them yet. I took off my hat and gathered it full and hurried back to the windmill, where JJ had a good fire going.

"Look here," I said. "Ain't we fixed for eggs?"

JJ hopped about, first on one foot, then on the other. I saw he had my tin can filled with water and also the peach can, which we had saved. The water was beginning to boil and I dropped in a couple of eggs and laid back to wait until they got hardboiled. I tell you, I felt like a man for sure. Of course, it wasn't one of ma's roast beef dinners exactly, but it was food to keep a man alive. And I already planned how I was going to catch some of them frying chickens and have a noon feast. Why, shucks, there wasn't nothing to this business of making out for yourself. Anybody could do it.

After we ate our fill of boiled eggs, I decided we might as well take a nap. That's one thing I learned from Toby. A man never knew when he was going to need to be rested, and it paid to take a nap every chance you got. That's one thing I would have to learn pa, if I ever got back home.

But for some reason I couldn't sleep. I roused up JJ and said, "Let's look around and see what we can find."

"What is there to find?"

"Well, for one thing, we need some provisions. There ain't no telling what we might find around these old buildings. I got me an idea."

"What's that?"

"Wait and see. Let's go."

We went into the old barn first. It had a hay loft and box stalls on the outside of an alley down the middle. I climbed up the ladder into the hay loft and stuck my head around. The sunlight streamed in through the cracks in the boards and showed me a big pile of hay and a fork. "What's up there?" JJ asked.

"Just some hay and a bunch of junk," I yelled.

"Go on up. I want to see."

I climbed on up and looked around. Lying back under the eaves was a pile of old broken harness—leather and hames and collars and such—lots of baling wire, some pieces of rope and old covered wagon hoops. Couldn't see anything here that rung any bells with my plan.

"Let's see what's in the tack room," I said. There is always a tack room in every barn. It's always the first door on the left, don't ask me why, but that is where it is always located. It is never on the right, for that is where the corn crib is located. I opened the tack room door and couldn't see anything in the dark. "JJ, go outside and open the window so we can see."

Ol' Moochie slipped inside the room and started growling. I jumped back. "Who's there?" I yelled, and then Moochie gave a jump and knocked over a bunch of boxes and buckets and stuff and started fighting something.

"Hurry up with that window, JJ," I said, and about then he swung back the window and flooded the room with light. There was old Moochie, whirling around and around with a big old black snake in his mouth. "Give it to him," I yelled. "Give it to him."

Moochie jumped out the feed room door just as JJ ran back inside the gangway, and just then, old Moochie gave his head a flip and tossed the snake away from him. Danged if that snake didn't land smack around JJ's neck.

6

A Saddle, A Rope

JJ let out a squall that made Moochie yelp in fright.

JJ's hand tore at the snake and he kept screaming as he ripped it from him and threw it on the ground.

He just froze for a minute, looking back and forth at me and the snake and he stopped screaming. Then he saw the snake was about dead and he went over and jumped up and down on its head and started screaming again.

All of a sudden he turned on me and started acting wild as could be. He caught me a good lick under the eye with a fist, another in the stomach, before I knew what was happening.

"Dang you," he yelled. "Throw that old snake on me, will you. I'll show you."

"Well, I tell you, I was some surprised. I'd tried half my life to get JJ worked up to a fight and never could, and here he thought I threw that snake around his neck, and it made him mad, and he was really fighting.

I got to laughing, it seemed so funny, and JJ really pounded me good, and then he hit me on the end of the nose and that made me mad, and we both went at it then, rolling in the dirt, cussing and hitting and kneeing one another.

Moochie hopped around and around, barking loud as he could, and when we didn't pay no attention to him, he just jumped right on top both of us and started a fight of his own.

He saw we were into it and he didn't like it. That brought both of us to our senses and we fell apart and caught our breath in big gulps and then I started laughing again.

"What did you throw that snake on me for? I didn't do anything to you," said JJ.

"JJ, you take the prize. I never threw that snake on you. Old Moochie caught it in the feed room and was fighting it, like back on the farm. He just slings them away from him and then goes and bites them again and slings them away, until they are dead."

JJ's face fell. "You sure?"

"Double cross my heart," I said.

JJ walked over to the snake and kicked it out of the barn. "Dam' old snake," he said. I fell back laughing. First time I ever heard JJ cuss. Boy, what'd folks think of him if they could have seen him now?

I wiped the blood off my nose and went back to the tack room. Boy, stuff had piled here for a hundred years. Just about everything that ever had anything to do with homesteading, farming and ranching had a bit or a piece in here. JJ came in, and said, "Watch out for more snakes."

"Aw, don't be afraid of a black snake. They just eat mice and rats."

"They give me the creeps, anyhow," he said. He poked timidly at a pile of trash. "What the dickens you looking for?"

I figured it was time I filled him in. "Well, you want to be a cowboy, don't you? You don't want to spend the rest of your life riding a freight train, do you?"

"Well, out there by the water trough, I saw something you didn't see. Horse tracks. Yes sir, I said horse tracks. Well, they been coming to water. And they come at night. When they get here tonight, I aim to catch me a horse. I'm ready to become a cowhand."

"Balls of fire, Rowdy. You mean it?"

"Yep."

"But that's horse stealing."

Well, that was the dumbest thing I ever heard. "JJ, I've tried to be patient with you. But I'm just about to wear out. These here are wild horses. Mustangs, they call 'em. They belong to who catches them. And I aim to catch me one."

Well, that shut up JJ. He just couldn't argue with me about things like that. After all, I was the expert on cowboys and ranches. And soon as I got me a horse, I aimed to go to roping calves. Any calf I caught was mine, if I could get my brand on him. And I aimed to do just that.

I kept digging into the pile of junk and began to come onto things I hoped I would. First off, two old wooden stirrups tied together with a piece of wire. Then I found an old cinch. Some of the strands were broken, but not so many but what I figured I could patch them. All the while I moved that junk from one corner to the next, mice kept scurrying for hiding and Moochie kept barking and standing on his head, trying to catch them.

A set of old bridle bits came to light, then another set—and the last set was hooked onto a pretty good bridle, but without reins.

"Hot dogs, JJ. Lookit. I got me a bridle and set of stirrups."

"Then JJ let out a whoop and started dragging something from the pile. Dang me, if he didn't have a whole saddle. Course, it was beat up pretty good, but by gum I'd ridden many a mile back home on a worse one.

"Let me have it," I said.

"Derned if I will," he flared, thumping me on the chest. "I found it and it's mine."

Well, son of a gun. If old JJ didn't have some punk after all. I rubbed my nose where he had busted it during the snake fight. That kid might make a man yet. "JJ, I don't want to keep your saddle. I just want to look at it. It's your saddle, far as I'm concerned."

That relieved him and he carried it into the gangway. It was an old big horned Mexican saddle and had been a dandy in its day. The leather was curled and cracked from being so dry on oil, and the strings had been chewed off by mice and one of the stirrups was gone. But that could be fixed easy. "Leave her lay," I said. "Let's see what else we can find."

Well, we found a pair of mismatched spurs, and an old pair of shotgun chaps without any belt. The thing I really needed, and didn't find, was a rope. I went outside to think, squatting down on my heels and putting my back to the wall.

"What's the matter, Rowdy?" JJ asked. "Are you mad because I found the saddle?"

"Course not, JJ. It's just that I ain't found what I need worst. A lasso."

"Does it have to be a lasso?"

"Nope. Just a plain old rope would work. There was some pieces in the barn loft, but they are too rotten."

"What's wrong with a hay rope?"

"What's wrong with a hay rope," I mimicked. "There's nothing wrong with a hay rope, stupid. Except there is no hay rope."

"All right," he said. "If you are going to get smart about it, I'll just keep it to myself."

Well, JJ knew something I didn't know, and I had to figure it out myself. I made a mistake, talking to him like that. When he set his head, wasn't no use trying to change it. Hay rope. Where had he seen a hay rope?

I jumped up. The barn loft, of course. I hurried back up the ladder and looked up and sure enough, there was the track with the hay fork carrier and the big old rope that the old farmer used to hoist up hay into the loft. The rope had been kept dry and was tied up out of the way. There must have been a hundred and fifty feet of it. I shinnied up the rafters, hand over hand, hung on with one hand while I opened my knife blade with my teeth and one hand, and cut the knot and gave the rope a jerk. It fell out of the pulleys and thumped the barn loft floor.

Well, this sure wasn't a lariat rope. It was one inch in diameter and a lariat was only three-eighths. I couldn't throw it. But it was stout enough to hold an elephant. All I had to do was tie onto a horse and I could hold him. Just like that, then, I'd be a cowboy.

JJ and I spent the rest of the morning cleaning up and patching the equipment we had found. We ended up with a pretty good outfit for one horse and about half of an outfit for another. We scoured the old house and found a salt chest with a few chunks of salt pork in it. Lordy, it was salty. We could carry that pork the rest of our lives and it wouldn't spoil. But I tell you, after several fried rabbits and chickens without salt, that sure tasted good. We just chewed on it raw during the afternoon while we worked, then went down to the windmill to wash it down.

I found an old lard tin with some rancid lard and melted it down and worked it into JJ's saddle and the bridle. There was old sugar sacks and bedding in the house and we borrowed all that, too, so we could make a pack to carry our things.

"Well, JJ, I got me one other thing to do. I got to build me a branding iron."

"How?"

"Show you." I got a flat piece of metal off an old wagon wheel and took another piece of metal, heated it on our fire and started pounding. In about an hour, I had fashioned a rough "R." I heated it again, finally worried a hole through it, and riveted a handle onto it.

"What you think of that?" I asked. I heated her up again and put it against a board and it came out as pretty as you could ask for.

"Reckon all I need now is one of them wild horses."

"Rowdy, what you going to do if you catch one of those wild horses? How are you going to ride one?"

"Shucks, JJ, ain't nothing to it. I'll just break him, that's all. I've ridden a bronc back home on pa's farm in Missouri."

"I know where your pa's farm is. You don't need to tell me it is in Missouri."

"Well, I was just telling you. Anyhow, I'll sack him down until he gets used to that. And then I'll saddle him and blindfold him and just crawl into the saddle. I'll just ride him until he stops bucking and then spur him a few times and he ought to be broke in an hour or so."

"What are you going to saddle him with?"

"Why, your saddle, of course."

"Like fun you are. You put my saddle on an old wild horse and tear it up. That's the first saddle I ever had and you're not about to tear it up."

"JJ, I declare. I never in my life saw anybody so dumb. Boy what good is it going to be to you to have a saddle if you don't have a horse to ride? And how are you going to have a horse to ride if you don't loan me your saddle so's I can break him out? Boy."

"I don't care. You just aren't going to break any horse with my saddle. If there is any breaking to be done with my saddle, I will just do it."

If I hadn't been so mad, I'd have died laughing. "Why, kid, you couldn't even ride one of dad's old plug work horses back on the farm. How you figure to ride a wild horse?"

JJ's face got red. "I can. You just wait and see."

"Well, you are so all-fired smart, you can just catch your own wild horse."

I grabbed my five-bladed knife, whacked off a 40-foot piece of the hay rope and tossed it to JJ. He looked with a question in his eyes.

"Figure out the noose by yourself," I said, and built me a loop with my back to him, then waited for time for the horses.

7

A Horse and a Jackrabbit

In that period of long shadows between sunset and dark, the air cooled enough the sweat stopped dripping into our eyes. I had rigged up a platform of old boards halfway up the windmill and JJ and I climbed up, with our ropes, to be ready when the wild horses came.

I heard a bull bellow in south of us, where the country spread wild and fierce-looking, in long swells of grassland. Gradually, the commotion of a herd of cattle reached us.

Enough light still came out of the west to show us the cattle as they came to the tank. The old windmill kept cranking away and splashing water into the tank. The cows drank first, gathering head to head at the round tank so close they squeezed away the calves. They just stood off to the side, sticking out their little red tongues and bawling until they worked up a foam at the mouth.

Horns clacked against horns. Once in a while an old cow got mad and hooked another in the side, chasing her away and stealing her drinking place.

Now, trailing in behind the cows, their heavy-horned heads swaying side to side and nearly touching the ground, their anger a growl in their throats, came the bulls.

There were a half dozen of the old men in the herd and every once in a while they stopped to snort and sniff the air to bellow so loud it made the hair stand out on the back of my neck. A couple of them squared off to fight, pawing up clouds of dust and butting heads so hard it sounded like thunder.

A dozen bull calves capered around the bulls, mocking them. Once in a while a calf bawled and it ended up with a squeak, like my voice did when I was a little kid. Then he'd get up nerve enough to back off, make a run and butt an old bull in the sides. The old guy would just grunt and swat his tail, sort of like a horse fly had bitten him.

I knew from watching the herd back home that the old bulls seemed to like the calves around. I think half the time they were not as mad as they acted. They just liked to show off in front of the cows and calves. It sort of reminded me of back home in Cave Spring on the store porch on Saturday night, where the young bucks all pranced and talked big and loud while the girls giggled.

As soon as the old bulls got a whiff of water, they stopped fooling around. They lumbered to the tank, bellowing deep in their throat. The cows almost knocked one another down, getting out of their way. The calves, half starved for water, rushed in to drink with their pappies. The bulls seemed to make a place for the calves.

JJ punched me in the ribs. "I thought you said the wild horses would come to drink?"

Whew Lord!

"JJ, if you just knew how dumb you are. The cattle always come to drink first, then the horses. Just you wait and see."

He thought on that one a while. "What makes you think there is going to be wild horses? I mean, horses sure, but wild ones?"

I tried to be patient with JJ. "Well, old Rowdy will tell you, JJ. Ain't you ever heard tell of horseshoes?"

"Sure."

"Well, you can't ride or work horses unless they are shod. And there wasn't no shoe tracks around that corral or tank. So any horses that come in here are bound to be wild, understand?"

Gosh Rowdy, I don't reckon I will ever know as much about stock as you know. That makes lots of sense."

"Course it does. I can't help it if you are ignorant. I will try to learn you as we go along. One thing for sure, I don't want you making no fool out of us when we get to Texas. You just sort of watch me and you will get along all right."

He was quiet a minute. Then, - "Rowdy?"

"Yeah?"

"I'm going to tie my rope to the windmill. Is that all right?"

I thought on it. "I guess you better. You ain't had much experience roping, like me. You know how to build a loop?"

"I think so. Wouldn't it be best to drop the loop on the ground and let a horse step into it?"

I swear, I just didn't know what to think about JJ. He was beginning to aggravate the daylights out of me. But I just had to hold on to my temper. "JJ, I'm going to drop a loop over the head of the best horse that comes to water. If you will just do like me, we will both have horses, all right? Now, be still and watch for horses."

JJ didn't say any more, and that was a relief to me. I watched the bulls drink their fill and then the cows returned and slobbered some more over the water and then they all wandered over by the corral and settled down, except a couple of old bulls that worried the boards with their horns.

I reckon it must have been an hour or two and I had nearly dropped off to sleep, when I heard something like drumbeats off to the south, and then the high-pitched whinny of horses. An answer came from the north. What had answered was a whole bunch of donkeys. They dang near scared me out of my perch with their hideous braying. The cattle jumped to their feet and got the heck out of there. The last I heard, the calves and cows were bawling dimly south of us, going back to the heart of their range.

Oh, Lordy how my heart tried to climb right out of my mouth. I got so excited my ears rang and I couldn't think half right. A mass of bodies thundered in from the south and another mass came in from the north and they tangled right there at the water tank.

Didn't seem they were mad at one another, but just glad to be there. They pawed at one another, nipped at each other's necks and circled around until the dust got so thick I couldn't see nothing.

They all tried to drink at once, now and then I heard a set of hooves thud against a set of ribs, and a fight would start with the horses rearing up on their hind legs and fighting each other with their fore hooves. I still could not see a thing because of the dust, and because it was now so dark and I began to get frantic. I knew for sure, I wasn't going to let that bunch of horses get away from me without getting me something to ride.

I bent over to see what I could see and made out a head or two pretty plain. I dangled the loop of my hay rope, leaned out to see a little better and about that time felt the old windmill tremble. A horse down below let out a squall and the herd started to scatter. JJ yelled, "I got one Rowdy, I got one."

Well, of all the dang blasted idiots here, I hadn't even spotted me a horse yet and JJ had spooked the bunch. There was no time to waste now. I picked out a dim form, cast the rope and let it play out of my hand.

All of a sudden, I heard a snort and my arms felt like they were being jerked out of the sockets. I soared out of my perch in the windmill like a big bird. JJ yelled, "Rowdy, where are you going?"

And then I hit the water in the tank. That is all that saved my life. I didn't have sense enough to let go of the rope and whatever I had tied my loop on pulled me right through the water. When I hit the far side of the tank, it dragged me right over the top and I flipped onto the ground like a fish.

Why I couldn't let go the rope, I don't know. Reckon it all happened so fast I didn't have time to think and just held on because of reflex action. Anyhow, here I was being dragged, belly down across the ground, for I don't know how far. Pretty soon I realized I wasn't being dragged any more. I shook my head trying to get some of the stars out of it, and then JJ grabbed me and rolled me over.

"Rowdy?" JJ said. "You all right? Speak to me Rowdy. It's me, old JJ."

I sat up, groaning, still trying to figure out what all had happened. There I was, wet to the skin, with dirt and mud caked on me an inch thick, still holding to the hay rope, and JJ holding my head and trying to see if I was still alive.

Well by thunder I was, but that didn't matter. I had lost my horse. It had been a long time since I felt so down in the mouth. But I wasn't about to let JJ know it. "What did you catch?" I asked.

"Don't know," he said. "When you flew out of the windmill, I jumped down to try and help you. What did you catch?"

"What did I catch?" I stormed. "What the thunder do you think I caught? Nothing, that's what, he got away."

"Got away?" Like fun he did. He's standing out there at the end of your rope gentle as a dog."

Well I declare, I never felt so foolish. I peered through the star shine and sure enough, there was something four-footed out there. My old heart thumped against the bib of my overalls and I tightened up the rope until I felt the weight of him. I tugged and got a little slack, then hauled him in, hand over hand. Dang me, if I hadn't caught one that was already taught to lead. That was a break.

When we were eyeball to eyeball, I wasn't so sure I had a good catch. "He sure looks small," said JJ.

"Cow pony ain't supposed to be big," I said. "They got to be little and quick so they can stop on a dime and give you six cents change." I didn't make that up. I read it in Ace Western Story. I knew lots of good cowboy talk like that.

Anyhow, he did look sort of small. I got out my box of paraffin matches, struck one on my fingernail and held it up. What I had caught had a black face with a blaze of white between its eyes. I looked on up and there was the longest pair of ears I ever saw. JJ fell down laughing fit to kill.

"Dang it, JJ, I caught a danged donkey."

I was so mad I couldn't even spit. A donkey! Why, back home they were not even fit to kill for the dogs. And here out west, I was going to be a cowboy and I had caught a donkey! I just threw the rope at him and said, "Get out of here, you long-eared, overgrown jackrabbit. Come on JJ, let's go see what you caught."

We eased back to the windmill and for a minute, couldn't see a thing. Then I heard a horse choking and saw a shape writhing on the ground. "JJ, is that the horse you caught? He's choking to death." I felt around until I found the rope and ran down it to the horse's neck and loosened the loop. The horse began breathing normally and stood still as could be, quivering slightly under my hands.

"JJ, what did you do?" Put your loop on the ground like I told you not to do?"

"Nope, I threw it and missed. Guess that horse ran into the loop and got caught."

Of all the luck, I felt sick in part of me and happy in the other. "Well, JJ, you did good. Reckon I didn't do so good."

"You did all right, Rowdy."

"How do you figure that?"

"Look behind you." I turned around and there was that dang donkey. As if to mock me, he stretched his mouth and let out a hee-haw-hee-haw that shook my ear drums. I headed back for the corrals where we were camped, wishing a fast freight back home would come along. Right then, I sure would have hopped on. As it was, there was nothing to do but pull a blanket over me and go to sleep, which wasn't easy with JJ snickering and giggling and whispering over and over, "You caught yourself an overgrown jackrabbit that is all, just an over-grown jackrabbit."

I slept snuggled up to Moochie and woke up at down, full of disgust. I never had made such a fool out of myself as I had last night, and in front of JJ at that. Old JJ, he always looked up to me back home. But I sure had let him down out west. Well, I thought, as I got up and pulled on my shoes, we had us a brand new day. There was a cool breeze blowing from the southwest, the sky was clear and an old hen cackled in the shed. "Come on, Moochie," I said quietly. "Let's get us some fresh eggs."

It felt good to stretch my legs and be on the move again. I broke into a run and by the time I got up a good steam, I decided to run on down and look at JJ's horse. When I rounded the pens, I stopped short. Moochie ran on, barking and running a circle around the horse. "Gee, oh-gosh, but she is sure a dandy catch," I said out loud. It was a little black mare JJ had caught, clean legged, neat in the head, keen ears perched forward and head up and looking at me. She had gaunted up some, since there was no grass where she was tied. I walked to her and she snorted a little and jerked back on the rope, but she didn't go crazy like I half expected her to do. In fact, she let me scratch her ears.

"Little Lady Midnight," I said. "Old JJ sure got a winner." I untied a rope and lead her to some grass and she grabbed a few bites and looked up and nickered to me as if to say, "Thanks." Boy, the day got brighter in a hurry. Then, I got nudged from behind and heard that awful racket – "Hee-haw, hee-haw, hee-haw."

"Dang jackrabbit," I yelled. "Scat. Get out of here. Beat it." But it wasn't any use. The son-of-a-gun had adopted me.

I ran down to the shed, threw a couple of hens off the nest and grabbed a handful of eggs, then ran back to the camp beside the tracks. Moochie ran ahead of me, barking and jumping right straddle of JJ. He licked JJ's face, grabbed a blanket between his teeth and uncovered JJ.

"What's wrong?" JJ rubbed his eyes.

"Your horse, it's gone."

JJ tore out of there without stopping for his shoes. I laughed all the time I started a fire and by the time he got back, it was going good. JJ wasn't even mad at me for tricking him. "Boy is she pretty," he said. "Is she going to be hard to break?"

I had water boiling, and I dropped in four eggs. My stomach growled and my mouth watered. I would like to have had some lard to fry the eggs, but I used it all on JJ's saddle. "Naw," I said. "Nothin' to it, I'll just throw your saddle on her, spur her until she stops bucking and then run her for a while."

JJ thought a spell. "Rowdy?"

"Yeah?"

"What you going to do about a horse? You can't ride that donkey, can you?"

"Heck, JJ. You got one last night. We'll just hang around today, break out that little old mare and I'll catch one tonight. Tell you what I'd like to do. Been thinking about how I'd like to get me a big old stallion, you got a mare. We'd be in business. All we got to do then is rope some mavericks and get a piece of ground and we will be regular ranchers."

JJ screwed up his face. "Make those eggs in a hurry."

"I forked out an egg with a pair of sticks and tossed it to JJ. He peeled it and ate it. "Rowdy, what is a maverick?"

"Heck, everybody knows what a maverick is."

"I don't. What is it?"

"Well, I'll show you when we see some." Fact of the matter is, I hadn't never seen one, but I thought I knew. Nobody had ever asked me point-blank before what a maverick was. I had to have a little time to figure it out.

We ate all the eggs, waved to a train crew in a freight that rumbled past, then gathered our gear and headed for JJ's mare. I reckon this was just about the happiest day of my life. When we got to the mare, there was that dadgone donkey, just like he belonged. I threw a pile of dried cow dung at him and missed, and he brayed like he was laughing at me, ran over and nudged me with his nose.

"Rowdy, that donkey sure loves you," laughed JJ.

"I'll love him," I said. "I've been wanting some grease to fry my eggs in. If he messes with me, I will have some donkey grease for dinner."

I decided the best thing I could do was ignore the donkey. My real interest was in that little black mare. "Bring me the saddle JJ, easy now."

8

Headed for Texas

I eased up on Lady Midnight with the saddle, my heart thumping like crazy. A wild horse might do anything when the saddle was first put on. JJ said in a shaky voice, "Be careful Rowdy. I don't know what I'd do out here if anything happened to you."

"Ain't scared JJ, she can't hurt old Rowdy." So, wishing I felt as sure as I sounded, I walked right up beside her. She turned her head around and sniffed at the saddle and for a minute, I thought she was going to bite me. She opened her mouth wide. But she didn't bite. She just yawned.

"For gosh sakes JJ, you see that?"

"What? Her mouth open like she was going to bite you?"

I nodded. "And she just yawned. She don't care a hoot that I put that saddle on her back." I tossed the saddle on her and she didn't flick a hair. I reached under her belly for the cinch and she still didn't move. Even when I put my knee in her belly and pulled the cinch tight, she didn't budge.

"Rowdy," JJ said. "She's been broke to ride, hasn't she?"

"I reckon so for sure, JJ. Just can't figure it out. Here she's been running with wild horses. And yet, she's broke."

JJ came around and tested the saddle. "I'm not afraid to ride her," he announced. "She won't buck me." He put his foot in a stirrup and pulled himself up. Lady Midnight turned around to look at him as if to say, "Hang on." And when JJ took the reins, she moved out pretty as you please, neck reining and all.

"JJ, I think I got it figured out. Some rancher caught her and broke her, maybe when she was real young and before she got spoiled. Then she got away and started running with wild horses. And now, we have her. Aren't we lucky?"

JJ started giggling just like a little kid with a toy, and he rode that mare all around the pens and barns. He wouldn't even get off to let me try her out and rather than get into a fuss, I just let it go. While he played, I planned our next move.

I figured we must be right closed to the Oklahoma and Texas line and from studying the maps in Ace Western Magazine, I also figured that if we went south and west, we were bound to come to the Salt Fork of Red River. That was supposed to be big ranch country, and the first ranch we'd come to, why, we'd just ride up and get jobs.

But first, we had to make a living between here and there. I didn't have any idea where a town was, nor where roads to towns were located. I sure was tired of following that railroad, so I just decided if I could equip us well enough, we'd strike out, looking for a ranch.

I wandered all over that old place getting ideas and looking for things I needed. By the time I was finished, I had located a pair of old narrow-gauge wagon wheels, enough old boards to build a flat bed, some wire for a chicken coop and enough wire and nails and string to hold everything together. It took me the best part of the day and I wouldn't have got done then if JJ's tailbone hadn't got tired and he got off his horse to help me. By night, we had everything set – the chicken crate tied on the two-wheeled cart, a box for the rest of the salt pork we'd found in the old shack, and an old ten-gallon milk can filled with water.

JJ flipped up the lid on the chicken crate. "I'll just catch them right now," he said.

I grinned. "I'll wait right here while you do."

He creeped up on an old hen, dived at her and she cackled and flew away, taking her brood of half-grown fryers with her. The old red rooster crowed and ran away faster than JJ could run and old Moochie, with his barking, just made the rooster run faster.

Finally, JJ came back to where I had started a fire and was cooking supper. He panted and his face was red. "Rowdy, how are we going to catch them? They are faster than I am. And I am faster than you are."

"JJ, I declare, you're dumb, dumb, dumb. Just wait until the time comes. Old Rowdy'll show you how." JJ kept at me all the while we ate, but I just grinned and kept it to myself. It was kind of ornery, I guess, but it was fun showing JJ that I knew lots about things he didn't know. In school back home, he always rode me about my bad grades and when I got desperate enough, I would beg him to teach me my lessons. Now, it was sort of good to get even with him.

The sun dropped down, the old windmill creaked and I had a good feeling plumb to my toes. I noticed the chickens had got over being scared and little by little, as night grew on, they edged closer and closer to the shed. Just before the light disappeared completely, they went inside and I could hear them flying onto the roosts.

JJ and I talked about where we were going, and what we were going to do for an hour or more. "I may just start me a ranch," I said.

"It takes lots of money. More than you'll ever have," JJ said.

"Oh, I don't know about that. What did it cost us to catch our horseflesh? Just a little elbow grease and some old rope. And then look at the chickens we've got. They didn't cost anything at all. A man can take that old rooster and the hens and raise baby chickens. Then you can trade the chickens for calves – and you are in business."

"Yes, but what about land?" JJ said. "Where are you going to get money to buy land?

I just shook my head. "JJ, ain't you never heard tell of free range? Why, nobody in Texas has to buy land. He just takes what he needs. There's plenty for everybody."

"I don't think so, Rowdy. Don't you remember our teacher telling us that the free range days ended a long time ago, and that there is no more land to be homesteaded? And how fences have been strung up all over the west?"

"Heck JJ, you ain't gonna pay any attention to that dumb old Mr. Goswick, are you? Wasn't he born and raised right next door to your ma and pa? And where has he been in his life? Never been any farther east than Springfield and no farther west than Ash Grove. And I could skip a rock that far."

I spit into the fire and listened to it sizzle. "And you got gall enough to sit there and look at old Rowdy who's been farther west than your pa even, and mine, and tell me I don't know what I'm talking about. Boy, JJ, I just wish one thing. I wish I'd left you to home."

JJ tucked his chin between his knees and pouted for a spell and to keep him from getting too low, I said, "Come on. Old Rowdy's gonna show you how to catch wild, wild chickens."

He perked up some as I got an old pine board and held it in the fire until it was blazing good, for a torch, then I headed for the chicken shed, JJ beside me. We entered the old shed and the chickens whispered sleepy-like. They raised up their heads and their eyelids fluttered. I grabbed an old hen, tucked her head under a wing, and her under my arm. She went right back to sleep.

When I'd caught all me and JJ could carry, we went back to camp, put them in the crate and came back for more. We got eight old hens, a half dozen fryers and then old rooster. One old hen clucked angry-like over in the corner and when I reached under her to count the eggs, she pecked my hand three or four times before I could draw it back.

"That's about enough, JJ," I said. "Better leave some for seed. We might be back sometime."

We put the rest of the chickens to sleep and then we went to sleep ourselves and I was so excited I woke up well before daylight. The only thing left to do was fashion a harness so I could hitch Jackrabbit to the cart. But that didn't take long and by sunup, I had an old horse collar around his neck, the rope tied to an old set of hames with buckles around the collar, and I backed Jackrabbit into the shafts of the cart. He hee-hawed, swished his tail to knock off flies and went to sleep standing up.

Meanwhile, JJ had stirred up the fire and tried his hand at cooking. He burned the eggs but that didn't matter, for we were too excited to care if we ate or not. We stomped out the fire, JJ saddled up his mare, got in the saddle and I swear, I never saw him so happy. "Isn't it fun, Rowdy? I sure wish my friends could see me now."

Well, for a fact I did too. They'd never know him. He was grimy but under the grime, there were blisters on his hands, but I knew from experience they'd turn into calluses. Best of all, JJ had learned to spunk up to me when things didn't suit him, and he never used to do that at home. He'd just been beat down like a whipped puppy too many times.

Moochie ran around and around like a puppy and what with all the excitement, the old rooster stuck his head up through the slats of the crate and let out a big cockle-doodle-doo and flapped his wings so hard he broke the fastener. I made a dive for him just as he cleared the hole in the top of the cage and stuffed him back down again and tied the lid shut. He didn't like it and crowed and crowed in protest as we started out, the sun shining over our left shoulders.

I reckon we looked like a circus parade. It was a let down for me, in a way, not being able to ride a horse like I'd planned. But that was my luck, and I just swallowed hard and thought about what was ahead. At least JJ was man enough not to rub it in.

9

How Not to Cross a River

Best I could tell, I'd walked about ten miles when we came to a river. Now, I called it a river, because that's what it must have been. But it sure didn't look like any river I ever saw back home. There wasn't any clear-cut river bed, nor channel, but just a half-mile-wide gulch, dotted with sandbars and little islands of green trees out in it. What little water there was hugged up against the near bank and ran sluggish as could be, it seemed to me.

JJ got off his horse and we tied her and Jackrabbit to a tree and walked along the bank. "Gosh Rowdy, how'll we get across? Is that Texas over there on the other side? It doesn't look any different from Oklahoma. Is this the Salt River you've been talking about?"

"Thunderation JJ, stop asking so many confounded questions. Ain't I got things to do beside educate you? We'll just find us a ford and you ride over to make sure the footing is sound. Then I'll bring the wagon over."

"There doesn't seem to be any place for us to get down from the river bank even, let alone cross," he said.

We hunted up and down stream from where we tied up and finally found an eroded place upstream that led down to the river. We walked down and I waded out to my knees. By gosh, the current was swifter than it had looked. And the ground was so muddy with red sand I couldn't see my feet. I tested the bottom by stepping on it and it seemed solid enough. "Go get your horse," I said.

"We'll cross here."

We brought Lady Midnight and Jackrabbit up to the ford. JJ said, "Rowdy?"

"Well? What are you waiting for?"

"I'm scared."

"Scared, scared! For gosh sakes, what for? Go on so you can pick out a ford."

JJ shook his head. "I'm just scared, that's all. That's quicksand out there. I've read about quicksand before. It just swallows you up sometimes. Horse and all."

"Aw, JJ, you are just a big baby. Just like back home. Here. Give me your horse."

He didn't quibble but did say, "Be careful with her." I got into the saddle and reined Lady Midnight around. She walked up to the edge of the water and jerked the reins loose as she put her head down to sniff. "Go on, girl," I said. "Go on in."

She took a couple of steps into the water but when I spurred her with my one good spur, she whirled around, snorted and scrambled out of the water. I turned her around and around, trying to get her into the river. She balked. "Doggone it, JJ," I yelled. "Do something."

"Maybe she's got more sense than you, Rowdy. She knows that's quicksand out there."

I rode back up the bank and tied her to a tree and led Jackrabbit down to the water. "Come on, dumbhead," I said. "Let's show that mare a thing or two."

I waded into the river and Jackrabbit hee-hawed and waded right in, his nose poking around in my pocket like he thought I had a treat there. We got out thirty feet or so and I was walking along right confident, when I stepped into a hole. The current grabbed me and whirled me around and knocked my feet from under me. I lost my grip on the bridle.

Whew! Boy, I tell you, I was some scared for a minute when I opened my eyes. It was black as the inside of a billy goat at midnight. Back home when I dived into Asher Creek, I could open my eyes and see the bottom. I would catch crawfish and pick out pretty rocks and shells. But boy, here, it was different. I struck out for the top of the water and when I flailed out on top, I was happy. It didn't take me long to spot old JJ up there on the bank, safe and dry. He was yelling something at me but I couldn't hear. I just struck out for the bank and when I felt the bottom, I stood up and started to wade out.

"Rowdy," JJ yelled. "Help Jackrabbit, he's drowning."

JJ jumped into the water and I saw that poor old donkey with nothing but his head above the water. The cart was tipping over and pulling him down. The chickens rattled their wings against the slats and the rooster had his head out the top, crowing almighty loud. "Hurry, Rowdy, hurry," JJ screamed.

JJ and I reached Jackrabbit at the same time. But JJ didn't know where the drop-off was and just as he grabbed Jackrabbit's head, he stepped in over his own. Both went under water.

Well, I figured this just about finished poor old Jackrabbit, and maybe JJ, too. But I wasn't about to quit until I tried everything. As I ran, I reached into my pocket and got out my five-bladed knife and it didn't take but a jiffy to open the big blade, the one I kept honed for emergency.

And this was a sure enough emergency if I ever had one.

I splashed down where I figured the rope was tied onto the shafts and felt it hit and cut through. I cut for the other rope but missed and the surge of Jackrabbit against the shafts knocked me under the water for a minute. I scrambled back, felt with my left hand and found the rope and cut it.

The shaking of the cart stopped and the kicking and splashing went downstream a ways.

"Oh, lordy," I yelled. "They've drowned."

But old Jackrabbit's head popped up like a cork, and JJ's right with it. JJ was holding on to Jackrabbit's neck for dear life, his hair wet and plastered down to his skull. He coughed and sputtered for air, his eyes wild looking.

I lunged after them, fell into the hole again but found the top in a couple of strokes and swam hard to catch them. I grabbed the bridle and pulled Jackrabbit's head toward the near shore and he never missed a stroke until he hit bottom and scrambled out, dragging JJ and me with him. We just dropped and looked at one another. Oh, lordy, we sure were lucky to be alive.

"Is Jackrabbit all right?" JJ asked. He had scrambled up to Lady Midnight and looked around as if to say, "You guys coming or not?"

"That old boy saved our lives," I said.

JJ grabbed my arm and pointed at the cart. "The cart's sinking."

JJ ran to his horse, grabbed the rope off the saddle and ran back to the river and tied the rope on the cart. He pitched one end to me. "Tie it to the saddle horn," he said.

There wasn't enough rope to reach the horse and she wouldn't budge toward the river. So I grabbed Jackrabbit's bridle and let him to the water and tied the rope around his neck. He leaned against the rope. "Keep going," JJ yelled. "I'll guide the cart."

I slapped old Jackrabbit's rump and he strained and the cart rolled slowly shoreward, then onto dry and high ground. JJ and I lay a long time on the ground, glancing out at the water and edging farther and farther away from it. I'd never been afraid of water before, but I sure didn't want any business with this old river for a spell.

"JJ, why the devil did you risk your neck?"

"I don't know," he said. "I guess I couldn't stand to think about losing Jackrabbit and our chickens. I know one thing for sure."

"What's that?"

"I can't swim a lick."

JJ got up and opened the lid to the chicken crate and set them out on top one by one to let them dry off. Even the old rooster had the spunk taken out of him. But in a little while, his wattle quivered, he shook off the water and stuck out his neck and crowed. "By gum," I said. "You'd think he had saved you and me and old Jackrabbit all by himself."

10

How to Teach a Rooster Manners

After we dozed off and napped and got dry, JJ said, "Rowdy, I sure could use something to eat."

That made me think of my matches. I grabbed them out of my overalls to see if they had withstood the soaking. Yep, they had. That paraffin had kept them dry. I raked up a little pile of grass and sticks and struck a match. "What you want to eat?" I asked.

"I think we should celebrate. We almost drowned."

"That's a good idea," I said. "But what will we celebrate with?"

"Something special."

"Special!" I said. "What the devil is there special around here?"

Just then the old rooster made a mistake. He crowed again, loud and long, ruffled up his feathers and shook the last of the water off and jumped down from the crate. The old hens started to follow him and I jumped up just in time to slam the lid back down and keep them from getting away. No telling where they'd go before night if they got away.

"Old boy," I said. "You just became something special. Our celebration dinner is going to be roast rooster."

I made a grab for him but he was too quick. I dived at him – and he flapped out of reach and stood there with his head sort of cocked as if to say, "Hey, what's going on?" And then he must of got the idea, for he lit out running, his wings stretched and flapping once in a while to give him a good jump when I came close.

I chased him around and around the coop and finally reversed directions and ran right into him. But the old cuss ducked between my legs and left me holding a handful of feathers.

Moochie barked and made a dive and got a mouthful of feathers and that was enough for that old rooster. He sailed out over the river and landed 20 feet out. I waded in after him and came out holding our dinner.

"Heat up the skillet and put in some grease, JJ," I said.

"You got to kill and dress him first," JJ said.

"That won't take long," I said, and grabbed the rooster by the neck and twirled him around and around. When I figured he was dead, I sat down and started to pluck his feathers, but when the first feather came out, the rooster popped up his head, and eyelid fluttered up and he flopped around in my arms.

"Well, by dingies," I said. "He's tougher'n a boot. I can't kill him by wringing his neck. Well, I know how to fix him."

I got a stick from a dead mesquite and put the rooster's neck under it and stepped on both ends of the stick and grabbed him by the feet. I pulled and pulled and pulled. His neck stretched and stretched and stretched. But his head wouldn't come off.

I heard a noise over by the fire and looked around to see JJ rolling on the ground, doubled up like he'd been kicked in the stomach. I was so darn scared that he'd got kicked by the horse, or maybe even snake bit, that I dropped the rooster and ran over to see him.

"JJ" I yelled. "What's the matter?"

JJ finally sat up and there were tears in his eyes and his face was all twisted out of shape and he couldn't get his breath. Then it came to me. He was laughing. He kept pointing at the rooster, and then at me, and he'd double up again and laugh so hard he'd lose his breath and couldn't talk.

"Well, by dern," I said. "I don't think it's so funny."

And then I looked over at that old rooster. He'd come to from all that pulling on his neck. He shook himself, pulled his head out from under the stick and staggered around until he got his bearings. Then he took off like a shot for the crate, jumped up on top of it and tried to get through the slats to the hens. I went over and flipped up the lid and he jumped in and hid in a corner.

Then the funny part of it hit me, too, and I laughed just as hard as JJ. "There goes our special celebration dinner," JJ said. "And I don't even care."

"I'm blamed if I do, either. That old rooster's got more nerve than me. And besides, if he's too tough to kill, he sure would be long chewing."

All that excitement got to the hens, for all of a sudden, a couple cackled and dropped eggs. "By golly, JJ. The hens have cooperated, even if the rooster didn't."

I reached down into the crate and picked up a couple of eggs. We'll at least have an omelet," I said.

So that's what we had to celebrate being alive. And we fed the hens a lot of grass and berries and grasshoppers, hitched Jackrabbit to the cart and headed upstream.

We camped by the river that night, having traveled what I figured to be ten or fifteen miles. The country was growing more and more flat. The farther we went, it was also growing more and more brushy. There was a funny looking brush that just completely covered the ground. It looked sort of like our oak trees back home, but smaller, and ranged in size from three to eight foot tall.

"What is all that brush, Rowdy?"

"Best I can make out," I said, "it's some sort of oak. Seems like I've read in Ace Western Magazine that it's shinnery oak."

"Boy, you sure can learn just about anything from reading Ace Western Magazine, can't you, Rowdy?"

"Seems like it," I said. "That's just about a cowboy's best friend. Sort of a Bible of the range."

"Sure would like to read some stories in it," JJ said. "But I never learned to read that well."

"The best part's about the gals," I said. "It really taught me how to handle the gals."

"Tell me about it, Rowdy."

"Naw, reckon I best not, JJ. Some of it might make your face red."

"Aw, won't, either. I know lots about gals, anyhow."

"Well, just wait till we get to one of them Texas towns. I'll show you how to act around gals."

We bedded down around a cheery camp fire. I got to confess, first night or two we were away from home, I got pretty scared and homesick. But now, we'd come through so many scrapes and all, I just felt right at home around a camp fire. I felt like there wasn't nothing could happen we couldn't handle. And that's what I was thinking when I drifted off to sleep.

The next morning, I woke up before the sun came up and walked out to where we'd tied Lady Midnight and Jackrabbit by the shinnery oak. I rolled over leaves and sticks and logs and gathered up a bunch of beetles and bugs and such and carried to the chickens. They cackled with delight and the old rooster even perked up and crowed.

JJ woke up then, and we led the stock to water and tied them on fresh grass. I was running my hands over the little mare and admiring her when I suddenly thought of something. "Gee oh my gosh, JJ. We plumb forgot something."

"What's that?"

"Why, we plumb forgot to brand our stock."

JJ's mouth flew open. "What if somebody had come up on us and seen our stock without any brand? Why, they might just have taken them away from us, and there wouldn't have been a thing we could do about it."

"Well, we'll just rustle up a fire and heat the branding iron. While it's heating, we'll cook breakfast."

The hens had laid more eggs during the night, and we cooked the last slab of bacon with the eggs and washed it down with black coffee. By that time, the branding iron had turned cherry red. "Did you ever brand any stock before, Rowdy?"

"Nope," I said. "but I know how. I've read about it in Ace Western Magazine."

I didn't know how long you were suppose to hold the iron on an animal, though, so I thought I'd better try it out on a piece of wood. I stuck the iron on the side of the cart and the wood started smoking and I just held her there. All of a sudden the wood burst into flames and I had to beat the fire out with my hands.

JJ had another fit of laughing and I just ignored him. A feller had to learn by trying, didn't he?

I practiced until I learned just the right length of time to hold the iron down and still get a good brand, then I walked over to Jackrabbit and said, "Whoa, boy. This won't hurt." And stuck the iron on his hip. The little donkey humped up in surprise and then he let out a gosh-awful "Hee-haw," and kicked out with both feet. He caught me in the stomach and sent me rolling head over heels. The breath went out of me and I just lay there, gasping. But I wasn't thinking of being hurt. I was thinking of JJ and when he came over to look at me, I grunted, "JJ... if you so much... as snicker... just one time... I'm going to kill you. I mean it, by gosh."

JJ saw I was all right and he sucked in his lower lip and bit hard on it. He started to laugh and I doubled up my fist and said, "I warned you," and he turned and ran away plumb out of sight. I figured he just had to laugh. But he'd better not laugh in my face again. I was plumb fed up with being laughed at.

Well, I wouldn't make the mistake of trying to brand a horse without throwing and tying him but once. The brand I'd made on Jackrabbit wasn't too deep, but it wasn't smeared and I figured it'd do. It was a right good "R."

I got our rope and made a half hitch around Lady Midnight's chest and another in front of her flank and pulled hard on the rope. This cut off circulation in her stifle joint, and down she came. I tied up her legs, heated up the iron again and started to stick it on her hip when JJ ran up. "What are you doing?" he yelled.

"What's it look like? I'm branding your horse." And I stuck the iron on her. She squirmed some, but the minute I took off the iron, she quit, and I saw another pretty "R" on a piece of horse flesh. I tell you, I felt some proud. I felt just like a regular rancher.

But my pride went flying head over heels when JJ hit me and knocked me down. "You put your brand on my horse. What did you do that for?"

Well, I sure felt bad about that. I had forgot that "R" stood for Rowdy and not for JJ. "I sure am sorry about that, JJ," I said. "But fact is, you ain't got no branding iron. It was your idea to brand them in the first place, and now you go and get mad at me cause I done it. Heck, I know she's your horse. I ain't gonna steal her. But what about the first big-shot cowboy comes to feast his eye on her? How's he going to know it?"

JJ pouted. "Well... that may be so. But just the same, I'm going to make me a branding iron first chance I get. And I'm going to put my brand on Jackrabbit, too."

"Why, that's all right. Goshsakes, ain't we pardners, anyhow?

JJ thought on that a while and said, "I sure am sorry I got mad. Seems like I don't appreciate all you do for me."

We packed up and got going again and by noon, we topped a rise and spotted a little town a mile or so ahead of us. We stopped and talked it over. "You think we should go into town?" JJ asked. "Why not?"

"I don't know," JJ said. "I'd just feel better if we didn't. All this junk we're towing makes me feel sort of foolish."

"Foolish?" I shouted. "Foolish? Why, it makes me feel plumb proud. By dern, ain't every boy comes out of Missouri with his belongings in his pocket and in less'n a week's time ends up with a pretty good beginning to a ranch. No sir, by thunder. I don't feel foolish. I aim to march right down Main Street. I aim to tie my donkey in front of the first saloon I come to and walk in and say to the bartender, "Just call me Rowdy. And make it straight whiskey."

JJ's eyes got big as an owl's. He stuttered and finally said, "You aren't going to take a drink of whiskey, are you?"

"Why, by thunder JJ, don't all cowboys drink whiskey? Did you ever hear of a cowboy walking up and saying to the bartender, "Give me a bottle of sody pop?" Just like as if they was in Teague's Store back in Cave Spring? Why, heck no. If you ain't careful, you'll give us away as tenderfeet. Come on, let's go."

And so we started walking into town. I tell you, I never threw back my chest so far, nor stood so straight in my life, I felt so good. I just couldn't believe JJ was so chicken. He kept falling farther and farther behind, and him riding the mare. "Come on, JJ," I said. "Confound it, quit holding back on the bits."

"But Rowdy," he said. "I'm scared. What if we've stolen somebody's property?"

"JJ, I've told you for the last time, these are wild horses. Didn't see no brands on them, did you?"

"Well, no. But..."

"But, but, pigs in a rut. Course you didn't. But you see brands on them now, don't you?"

"Yes."

"All right then."

"Rowdy?"

"What is it, JJ"

He got off the mare and handed me the reins. "You ride her."

11

Salt River Sally

Well, that done my heart good. I can't tell you how bad I wanted to ride into my first Texas town instead of walking; but ride or walk, I was sure going into that town.

I swung up into the saddle and a king couldn't have been any happier. I just couldn't control myself. I jammed my one good spur into her flank and yelled back at JJ, "Bring Jackrabbit on in. I'll meet you at the saloon."

Lady Midnight ran full speed into town. I felt the wind bring tears to my eyes. Oh, lordy, how that mare could run. I guided her down the Main Street, looking for the saloon and didn't see one. I figured this was as good a time as any to put on a show.

I pulled hard on the reins, like I imagined the cowboys did in Ace Western Magazine. The little mare reared up on her hind legs and pawed the air with her forefeet. I felt so tall I could look over the world. I reached high into the air and waved to all the folks and sort of expected them to cheer.

Lady Midnight just hung there in the air, sort of waving her front legs in slow motion as if reluctant to come down to the ground.

There was a wagon of farmers starting to pull out of the feed store and they saw me and stopped. There were three old ladies with sunbonnets on their heads and baskets of groceries on their arms, and they saw me and stopped.

There was half dozen store porch loafers propped against the store front and they stopped whittlin' and squinted their eyes. And best of all two cowboys, wearing batwing chaps and neckerchiefs and ten-gallon hats that came out of the store and they stopped to stare at me.

And then it happened.

That rotten old cinch, the one I fixed in Tie Siding, it picked that time to break.

The saddle slid off Lady Midnight's rump and just sort of slipped off slow and easy like, and then I found myself in a heap, with Lady Midnight turning around and sniffing at me as if to say, "What the heck happened to you?"

Oh, lordy, I never felt worse.

I heard the people laughing fit to kill and it made my head spin like crazy. And all of a sudden a big mad busted out of my head and made me double up my fists. The first two people I saw coming toward me were the two cowboys and they held onto each other, laughing so hard their eyes were closed and tears were running down their cheeks.

I couldn't half see, what with anger and dust in my eyes but I yelled, "Come on, put 'em up. I'm gonna whip the tarnation out of you."

That got one down on his knees and the other leaned up against a wagon load of feed. Well, if they wouldn't fight, they wouldn't fight. Some of the mad left me and I knuckled dirt out of my eyes and then my eyes like to of popped out of my head.

All of a sudden I heard Moochie barking and JJ ran up and grabbed my arm and yelled, "Rowdy, look who those two cowboys are."

I blinked, and blinked and then I just had a hard time believing what I was seeing.

It was ol' Toby and Polecat. The guys we met on the train, now all dressed up in cowboy clothes. Before I could stop him, JJ ran over to them, and "Pow," he socked one of them on the jaw.

It bowled him over in the dust and then Moochie jumped onto him with both feet and a snarl and got a mouthful of checkered shirt.

"You low-down, ornery skunk. Take off and leave us in the middle of nowhere and steal our stuff to boot, will you."

And then Toby came to his senses and with a gleam in his eye, slung Moochie off and dived into JJ and the three of them rolled around the dirt before I could move a muscle and figure out what was happening.

Even though Moochie had a hold of one of Polecat boots and threatened to rip it off, they were giving JJ a pretty good thumping. Then I spit into the palm of my hand, took a running jump into the air and fell on Toby's behind hard as ever I could.

I heard him yell and he turned loose of JJ's ear with his teeth and rolled over. I lit right in the middle and hit him with both fists on the side of the head.

Then all of a sudden somebody grabbed my galluses from behind and hauled me up into the air like I was a fish and I saw JJ hanging next to me. The crowd had circled us while the men folks were laughing. Especially the two who were holding me and JJ, the women all looked mighty grim – especially one squaty, square-shouldered woman wearing bluejeans, a denim jumper and a greasy cowboy hat.

She waddled between Toby and Polecat, and JJ and me, and shook her finger at the cowboys. "You cussed loafers, leave them two boys alone. You ought to be home fixing fence. Now get on back to your work before I call up your pa and he wears out his neck yoke on your heads."

It was plain to see those old kids had tangled with that old gal before, and they didn't hanker to do so again. They wiped the laughter off their faces and looked like a couple of whipped hound dogs. They picked up their hats, dusted them off and didn't even look back as they hopped into an old stripped down Model-T Ford and ripped off toward the west.

The woman turned to me, her hair parted in the middle and braids hanging down from under her hat. Her face was red and creased like leather and two buck teeth kept her upper lip kinked into a perpetual grin.

She dusted off my head and shoulders and said, "You boys hurt? Well, you better not be or I'll skin Toby and Polecat yet. They didn't mean no harm. Just lazy, good-for-nothing louts. My brother's boys.

"It was sort of funny, the way you slid off that pony's rump and landed in a heap under the saddle.

"We've bumped into that pair before," I said. "I didn't know they were real cowboys."

"Just bums ridin' the rails." Her laugh was like gravel rolling down a tin roof. "I bet you seen them up in Kansas in the wheat field, didn't you?" Well, their pa found out where they were and went up and dragged them back to his ranch to help with the work. "You're not hurt, are you?"

"Just our pride, I guess. That wasn't exactly the sort of welcome I was counting on."

"You two come along with me," she said, grabbing JJ's arm and mine and wheeling up around like toothpicks.

"But Ma'am, I got other plans."

"What's that?"

"I was… I was…"

JJ blurted out, "He was going into a saloon to buy whiskey."

She let go my arm and grabbed my ear and pinched it until I cried. "Say you are sorry," she said fiercely.

"Whiskey's the devil's brew, bad for me and shame on you. Leave it alone and I'll stay home, swig a little liquor and I'll leave you quicker."

"Like the devil you are going into a saloon. Not while Salt River Sally's around. You're going to drink sody pop and cow's milk and lots of it. Besides, ain't no real saloons in Salt River no how. Unless you count what old man Keeper bootlegs from under the counter at his feed store."

Her fingers bit into my arm and she dragged me toward the feed store. Boy, here was a female cyclone in run over cowboy boots. There wasn't any resisting her grip. Besides, my mouth was pretty dry and a cold bottle of strawberry sody pop would taste pretty good.

Then I thought about our wagon and stock. "Hey, Miss Sally, what about our poor horses and chickens and stuff?"

"Oh, pshaw, they'll be all right. Wouldn't nobody dare touch anything ol' Sally's attached to. The people around Salt River don't mess with ol' Sal. She's a terror, that gal." And her laugh at her poetry was like a rusty gate hinge squeaking.

She latched onto my arm with one hand and JJ's arm with the other and marched us toward a sign that said F.G. Keeper's Grocery and Feed store. I whistled to Moochie and he wagged up close to me and whined as if to say, "What's next, boss?" And we marched up the board steps to the porch.

Just as I hit the last step, I glanced through the plate glass window and saw a pretty little face looking at me. She had pig-tails on either side of her yellow hair and her eyes were big as diamonds. She was sucking on an all-day sucker, and she had a little border collie about the size of Moochie, standing up at the window and looking out at us.

Moochie ran over to the window, put his front paws on the glass, and whined softly, then turned and looked at me and as if to say, "Hurry up and let's go inside."

Sally opened the screen door and herded us in like we were a couple of sheep, and before I knew it, she had put two bottles of strawberry sody pop in our hands.

I didn't dare look around at the little girl with the pigtails, but I heard Moochie paddle over to her dog. They did a little show-off dance like dogs do when they first meet. Then they each whined, and Moochie got a little too friendly, and the other pup growled and hid behind little Miss Pigtail's dress, and Miss Sally jerked me around and said, "Ain't you gonna open your sody pop, Rowdy?"

And so I popped the cap and about that time, a tall, lean lady with a severe look in her eyes grabbed Little Miss Pigtail's arm and said, "Let's go to the car, Olivia. Your father is in a hurry to get back to the ranch, as usual."

And so they left the store and left me staring at them, and left Moochie jumping up and down and trying to follow. I grabbed him and gave him a little sip of the cold sody pop and he settled down, but whined as if to say, "Why didn't you let me follow my girlfriend?"

Miss Sally went to the back of the store, where a pot bellied stove and a half dozen chairs showed where the loafing spot was in that store, and sat us down and looked severely into our eyes.

She studied us a while before she said, "Now I want to know something. Where you boys headed?"

"Texas," I said. "We're going to be cowboys. Maybe start our own ranch."

"That's right," JJ chimed in. "Already got some livestock to start with. Even going to homestead little bit of land."

She grinned. "Ain't you a little bit tender to homestead, honey?" You gotta be 21 years old first."

Well, I felt like somebody had kicked me. I knew back home everybody said you go to be 21 this and 21 that, but I thought out here in man's country you were just as big as you wanted to be.

"I don't care," I said stubbornly. "I'm gonna find me a piece of land anyhow."

Miss Sally didn't laugh. She was dead serious. "I been looking for a pair of strong, honest cowboys. Why don't you throw in with old Sal? I'll feed you good and won't work you too hard and you can learn cowboying from the word go."

I hesitated. There was something about taking orders from a woman that went against my grain and I told her so. She slapped me on the back and said, "Ain't you the rounder, though. Don't fret none. I ain't like these namby-pamby gals in skirts that toadies to a man. I can outwork, outsweat and outcuss any man in Texas, and don't you forget it. You just throw in with ol' Sal and you won't be sorry."

"Let's do it, Rowdy," JJ said.

I gazed off at the heat waves beginning to shimmer over the rolling land. "I had in mind working for a big outfit that runs a chuck wagon and brands cattle. I don't want to work for any greasy-sack outfit."

Salt River Sally jumped up like she was pecked by a settin' hen. "I ain't no greasy-sack outfit," she hissed. "I'll turn you upside down and get my sody back." She cackled and slapped my face gently. "I'll give you $1 a day and all you can eat, plus room and board."

I thought on that. A dollar a day didn't sound like much, but I knew many a man back home could raise a woman and ten kids on that much, if he had a big garden and was pretty handy with a fishing rod and a .22 rifle.

"Well," I said at last, "we will just throw in with you for a spell if you feed us good and pay regular, we will stay with you until we find a piece of grass for ourselves."

"Goody," JJ said.

"Goody," I mocked. "You sound like the girls back in Sunday School."

So I tied Jackrabbit to the tail of Miss Sally's wagon, got on the spring seat to drive. Miss Sally said, "Pull over there to the post office a minute. I got to mail a post card. You boys just wait out here for a minute."

JJ rode Lady Midnight and in about five minutes Miss Sally waddled out of the post office, accompanied by a skin-and bones man wearing a green eyeshade. The old geeser walked out to the wagon, peered up at me and grinned.

"Howdy, Rowdy. Gonna help ol' Sal a spell?"

I nodded and puffed out my chest. "Yep, she's got a lot of wild cattle to brand, and I reckon I'm just the cowpuncher to do that chore."

Miss Sally climbed up on the wagon. "Andrew, you best get out of the sun. And don't forget to take care of my little postcard, you hear?"

"I hear," he grinned. "The Pony Express ain't never been late yet."

"Let's go, Rowdy," Miss Sally said, and we ambled out of there on creaking wheels and a cloud of dust. Miss Sally complemented me on the way I handled the reins, and how strong I was for my age, and I got to half-way liking her by the time we turned off the main road and headed toward her ranch.

She wanted to know why we left home, and if our folks knew about it at all, and I told her and made her promise not to tell anybody about it or write home and tell our folks where we were.

"There just comes a time when a guy grows up and makes it on his own," I said. "It happens to everybody."

"Sure wish I had a couple of boys like you and JJ," she said.

"Well, you got 'em now, just so long as the dollar a day and the grub holds out."

The country road got wild looking and threaded our way down an old eroded dirt road. The shinnery oak and mesquite gave way to cedar and mesquite. I could see a river shining through the brush now and then and quail scurried in the short grass. They didn't look like our quail back home, and they had a little top-knot on top their heads. "Them's blue quail," Miss Sally said. "We got deer and wild hogs and all sorts of game back in the brush."

"I ain't seen any cows yet."

"That's the reason I need a couple of good stout boys," she said. "I ain't got any cows."

I like to have fell off the wagon. "No cows? What kind of ranch you got?"

"That's where you and JJ come in with your little horse. You see, the brakes along Salt River are plumb full of cows with brands, but are they ever wild. A mean old bull keeps them wild and out of sight most of the time, and he is a real old devil.

"All you got to do is to help me round them up and put my brand on them. Then I'll have a cow ranch again."

Before I got that figured out we left the brush and came to an open slope. At the foot of it, just above the river, was a high bluff with a big pool of water below it. "Here she is," Salt River Sally cried. "The Salt River Ranch. Biggest little outfit in Texas without any cows. But we're gonna fix that. You and JJ and ol' Sal."

Miss Sally showed her two big front teeth and her grin and I just nodded.

Numb-like.

"It don't look like to me there's any place to start," I said.

"Oh, yes there is," she said. "I got lots of my poor old daddy's tools, and there's rolls and rolls of barbed wire behind the shed. And there's enough cedar posts along the river to fence the world. 'Course, they got to be chopped down. And we got water enough to irrigate a little patch of feed for winter, and I've already canned a winter's supply of vegetables off my kitchen garden. I just need somebody that'll use some elbow grease."

I walked out in the shed and kicked around. There was an old forge and lots of scrap iron, and a heap of charcoal. There were axes and shovels, all rusty and dull, but nothing that couldn't be fixed. I walked on down to the pool of water and saw Sally's kitchen garden. It was the only neat, organized thing on the place, with okra and beans and potatoes flourishing in the rich soil and from the water in the pool she'd irrigated with. Sally said, "See that five-acre patch below the pool? We could plow that and plant some winter feed. That old team of plugs hitched to the wagon can pull a plow and harrow. Honest Rowdy, in a week, you'd never know this old place, if there was somebody like you and JJ to work it."

"Well," I said. "I feel like backing out. But my old pappy told me if I ever got stuck with a blind horse not to bellyache about it."

Sally hugged me until my ribs cracked and said, "Let's go have some good salt pork and beans and milk."

The house, in spite of its rough surroundings, was neat and clean inside. It was divided into two rooms by a burlap curtain. Sally had a fire going in no time and warmed up a pot of beans. She sent me to a spring house under the rock bluff where she kept her butter and milk. And for the first time since we left home, JJ and I ate with our feet under a table. And I got to admit, in spite of the fact it wasn't ma's cooking, it felt pretty good.

"Where'd you get the milk?" I asked.

"Got an old brindle cow out in the brush, somewheres," she said. "She comes in morning and evening for bran and to get milked. She had a pretty spotted calf, but the coyotes got it and ate it. That's the trouble. I ain't had nobody to cut brush in so long the animals just come right up to the edge of the place and kill my stock. I had a litter of pigs, too, but no feed so I just turned the old sow and boar out to rustle for themselves until fall. Maybe they'll come back in this fall and I can pen them up and raise me some more hogs. There's good money in hogs. Used to butcher, myself, and salt the bacons and hams and take them into town and trade for enough goods to make dresses out of and live in the winter time and have money left to boot."

My mouth dropped open. "Hogs?" I said. "You mean you have hogs on a Texas ranch? I thought Missouri, Iowa and Arkansas was the only places that raised hogs. I didn't know honest-to-gosh ranches had hogs."

Sally dished me out some more beans. "Why, course, honey. Whatever gave you the idea ranches didn't raise hogs? They taste as good to folks out here as they do to folks in Missouri."

Boy, I didn't know about that. In fact, I began to wonder if I was in Texas at all. The only two cowboys I had seen were driving a pickup truck instead of riding cow ponies, and they didn't have six shooters on their hips like Ace Western Story said they did. "Miss Sally," I said. "You ain't teasing old Rowdy, are you? I mean, is this really Texas?"

She slapped her thighs, threw back her head and laughed. "Yeah, this is Texas, all right. And it ain't a bit like the movies and the books say it is. It's just dirt and hard work and skin your neighbor before he skins you. If you ain't fighting drought and grasshoppers, you're fighting flood and snow. If you got fat calves, the market's low, and if you ain't got fat calves, the market's high. Same as Missouri, Rowdy. Only difference is, it's five hundred miles west of Missouri and a heap dryer. Sakes alive, how I wished we had some of that green Missouri grass and maple trees."

"But what about the roundups, and horses and such?" I said. "Don't you do that at all?"

"Shucks, Rowdy," she said. "The real roundups ain't been held in 35 or 40 years. Everybody's got fences on their places any more and they don't need roundups. They just go out with a couple of old plug horses and drive in their cows, except on some of the big rich outfits like the JA and the Pitchfork and the Four Sixes.

"But there's a heap more places like mine than there is like them. Places where the brush is so thick you can't ride through it and where the only rounding up to be done is like here – cattle that ain't been tended to and has gone wild back in the brush."

I chased a bean around my plate with my fork. "How do you get to those big places where they still have roundups?" I said.

"No sir, honey you ain't gonna go to one of them old outfits. Not while old Sal's heaving and breathing. They'd just put you to work chopping wood or washing dishes in the cook shack. They wouldn't let you get on a horse and chase cattle for most a whole year, until you caught onto things. It's not like old Sal's place, where you get to be a top hand the first day. Now, you and JJ don't want to wind up camp swampers do you?"

JJ said, "I sure don't. This suits me fine, right here."

"Well," I said, "there is something to what you say, I reckon. But I ain't making any promises past the next month or so. We'll help you catch a few old cows and put the place in shape. But then, if it's all the same to you, we'll just move along. I got a hankering to see one of them real cow outfits."

JJ and me didn't waste any time once we finished eating. First thing we did was rustle up some old rusty chicken wire and build a pen for our chickens. One old hen clucked a lot and wanted to stay squatted on her egg, so we fixed a special pen for her and a nest box and left her so's she could hatch some baby chicks. We let the old rooster roam around outside the pen so we wouldn't have to feed him, and we knew he wouldn't leave the hens.

We staked Lady Midnight out in a patch of grass where she could get water at the end of her rope, and Jackrabbit, well, we had to tie him up to keep him from stepping on my heels at every step. He hee-hawed when I tied him up and left him to go about the rest of the work. There was an old emery wheel in the shed and I sharpened the axes and then JJ and I cut cedar posts until dark. While Miss Sally piled up the old rotten corral poles and set them on fire so we could see, JJ and I dug post holes from the shed down to the pool of water. We wanted to fix it so's the calves could run in the pen and water themselves.

About midnight or so, Miss Sally said, "Boys, you just done fine. Let's quit now. Don't want to overdo it. There's just one little chore I want you to do before we bed down for the night."

"What's that?" JJ asked. "I don't know if I can do anything else or not. I'm wore out."

"Me to," I said. "Morning'll be here most before we know it."

"You deserve the sleep," she said, "but you deserve a feast, too." She went into the house and came back with an old double barreled shotgun and a kerosene lantern. She handed me a few shells and said, "You know how to use this, don't you Rowdy?"

"Sure," I said, although truth of the matter is the only time I got to shoot Pa's old 12-gage was when I sneaked it out. "But what am I supposed to use it on?"

She crooked a finger and grinned. "Follow me." She walked toward the pool of water and on around it and followed the river downstream for a half mile. Then she stopped so sudden I bumped into her. "Shh," she said. "You'll scare 'em."

"What's 'em?" I said. "It's so confounded dark I can't see nothing to shoot, no how."

She put her hand under my chin and tilted my face upward. I couldn't see nothing but an old dead tree with bumps on the limbs. "See 'em?" she said.

"Don't see no 'em nor anything else," I said. "What am I supposed to be looking for?"

"Turkeys, Rowdy. Don't you see 'em?"

"You mean wild turkeys?"

"Yes," she whispered. "There they are. Roosting on the limbs."

"I don't see nothing but some bumps on the limbs."

"Them's turkeys," she said. "Shoot 'em."

I drew a bead on one of the bumps on the limbs, pulled back the hammer and let her fly. The old gun kicked my shoulder so hard I bounced against JJ. The flash from the barrel lit up the countryside for a split second. Miss Sally shouted, "Quick, shove in another shell and get another shot." I broke open the gun and the empty hulls flew out and hit me in the nose. I shoved two more shells and looked up in the tree. Half of the bumps were gone but the other bumps were moving around and I got a bead on one and pulled the trigger again. The bump tumbled off the limb and fell to the ground.

The silence was back with us now, only after the thunder of the gun, it seemed to hurt my ears, things were quiet. Then I heard a quick threshing in the brush and a gasping sound. Miss Sally struck a match and lit the lantern. "You got one, Rowdy, you got one."

She ran in under the tree and the lantern light cast a yellow wedge of light on the ground. I saw a black shape on the ground and Miss Sally picked it up and held up the lantern so I could see it. "A big old gobbler," she said. "Ain't he a dandy?"

"But he shot twice," JJ said. "Where's the other one?"

"Reckon I missed," I said. "But let's look anyway."

We looked and looked, but there wasn't any other turkey to be found. Anyhow, one was enough. He must have weighed 10 or 15 pounds. We took him back to the house and scalded his feathers in boiling water and Miss Sally plucked him and then singed the pin feathers over a low fire. While she was doing this, me and JJ had got ready for bed – she'd fixed us a place on the floor by the fireplace – and some time later, while she busied with the turkey, I fell to sleep, old Moochie curled up beside me and his head resting on my legs.

12

Seeing the Wrath of the Lord

I woke up with the sun in my eyes. I sat up, smelling the turkey cooking and thinking I was back home, until I saw Miss Sally hovering over the stove. Moochie had gotten up before I did and was sitting beside her, taking a bite now and then from bits of scraps Miss Sally fed him. The room was beginning to heat up from the sun and the heat from the cook stove brought sweat and pink color to Miss Sally's face.

Moochie saw me rouse up and barked. Miss Sally turned around and grinned. "Howdy, Rowdy," she said. "Sleep good?"

"Too good," I said. "Sun's already up and I got lots of work to do. Got to get the corral finished so's we can catch cows."

"Not today, you don't," she said.

"Why not?"

"You forgot what day it is?"

"No," I said. "Sunday."

"Yep, Sunday, time we get up and do the chores and get breakfast over with and the turkey done, it'll be time to start."

"Start? Start what?"

"Start to Sunday school and church," she said. "Always go to Sunday school and church, come Sunday." Well, that did it. I didn't run away from home just to come to some place where they not only had hogs and fence post holes to dig, but church to go to just as well. I reached around for my pants but they weren't where I left them. Neither were JJ's. I reached over and shook him awake. "Hey sleepy head, where's my pants?"

"Ain't had your overalls," he said. "What'd you do with mine?"

"Miss Sally," I said. "You seen our clothes?"

"'Deed I have. They're out on the line, getting dry right now."

I held a blanket up to me and went to the door and sure enough, there were our clothes, hanging out on the line, still dripping wet. I don't suppose it hurt them any, being washed, but by the time we dug a few more post holes and set the posts we'd cut the day before, they'd be just as dirty again, and I told her so.

"Well, that may be," she said. "But they'll stay clean until we get to church and back." She started stirring eggs, flour, lard and chocolate powder together and she saw me looking at it. "Making a cake," she said. "Always bake a cake, come Sunday."

"Miss Sally. If you are figuring on me going to church, you're figuring wrong. That wasn't in our bargain. I ain't going."

"Oh yes you are, honey. Now don't argue with ol' Sal and get her riled early in the morning. You hear? Besides, we're going to take this turkey and this cake and have us a feast, right along with the rest of the folks after preaching. You never saw so many goodies. There'll be deviled eggs and all kinds of cakes and pies and maybe even a 10-gallon freezer of ice cream. Now, I ask you, ain't that worth sitting through preaching for?"

JJ said, "I wouldn't mind some homemade ice cream."

Well, the upshot of it was, they talked me into it. We did the chores, ate and I hitched the team to the wagon and about 9 o'clock we struck out for Salt Fork again. I remembered seeing the old church, sitting right there at the cross roads north of the bank of the river. It was like all churches I ever saw – a square one with white board siding that needed painting and a steeple tower with a big bell in it. We pulled up in the church yard just as the bell rang. There was already a lot of teams, wagons and buggies tied up at the board fence around the church. There were some nice looking saddle horses too, and a few old cars and trucks. The women folks, just like back home in Cave Spring, had already gone inside the church and the men folks had stayed around outside just so long as they could before having to go in. Some of them was dressed in blue shirts and wore starched white shirts, but most of the men wore overalls and blue work shirts and had their hair wet and slicked back.

The men all grinned when they saw Sally and started to joke with her. She said, "Can it, boys, can it. Preachin's done started. Ain't you got regard for the Lord?"

And she grabbed JJ's arm and mine and towed us on into the church. We sat down towards the back and the men filed in and filled up the back rows and the preacher, a long, gangling man with a grieved look like all preachers

I ever saw said, "Come right on up and fill the front rows, folks. Don't be afraid to face the wrath of the Lord." But nobody moved and he went on into a prayer that was like all the ones I'd heard back home. Full of hell fires and damnations and the like. It wasn't no wonder I didn't like to go to church. Why, the preachers scared me half to death of the Lord, talking like that. I could get out of the church house and see the sky and the grass and feel the wind and I'd begin to believe in the Lord. But get me inside a church and I felt like I was in a prison and the flames were going to lash out and burn me and my past sins in a flash.

On and on the preacher droned. I shut all but the buzz of his sermon out of my head and tried to see all of the people. There was a blond head down about three rows that looked pretty good to me. She had her hair parted in the back and braided down into two pigtails that hung over the bench a good foot, with red silk ribbons tied in the end of each. Her head was so shiny-clean you could see the pink of her scalp and her little ears peeked just around the edge of the pigtails.

That's about all I could see of her, so I concentrated on her mammy, sitting on her left, and her pappy, sitting beside her. Mammy was thin, patient-eyed and looked like she'd spent too much time hanging out clothes under a hot sun and having to split the kindling to heat her wash water to boot. But she held her back straight and her chin out, drinking in every word of the preaching.

Pappy was a thick-necked rooster who fidgeted on the seat until he near wore out the wood and his britches as well, and who finally couldn't stand that tie around his neck and he ripped it off and used it to mop the sweat off his neck. Mammy nudged him and whispered behind her hand, what, I couldn't hear, but it was plain to hear what pappy said, and it wouldn't bear repeating out loud.

"S-hhh," came plain as anything from mammy, and pappy grunted and shut his eyes. Directly, mammy had to nudge him when he grunted out a big snore. Finally, the preacher wore himself plumb out and after asking the Lord to "Forgive all them sinners sitting out there in front of me," he said, "dismissed," and you never saw a bunch of calves head for the rattle of the bucket like the feet that hit the floor.

Only thing was, hot and tired as I was, I didn't hurry. I figured to wait until I saw little Alice Pigtails some better. She got up and I could see the yoke of her neck wet with sweat in the back. Her red print dress was frilly on the bottom with what ma called rick-rack, and when she turned around, the first thing she set eyes on was – you guessed it, ol' Rowdy. And if it wasn't the very same girl I saw in the store, the day I first rode into Salt River town.

Well, I can't lie this time, although I figured I was pretty good at the little white kind. She was the prettiest thing I ever set eyes on. She reminded me of a bunch of hollyhocks in ma's backyard; it just seemed she was made up of pink and red and blue, her face was so alive and shiny. Lordy, her eyes must have been big as a cow's, and just soft and mellow. I hadn't never before had no use for gals – although I admit the stories in Ace Western used to get me stirred up somewhat. But this time it was a good thing I had on my shoes, 'cause my heart would have gone plumb through the floor if I hadn't.

I started to get up, but my legs got rubbery and wouldn't hold me, so I sat back down in the pew and stared at the floor while she passed me by. She smelled like honeysuckle, I swear she did. Her mammy passed me by too, and she smelled like lilac bushes, and her pappy, he passed me by too, but he smelled more like horses and cows and I imagined he'd be a heap more at home in a saddle than a church pew. He had a stomach on him that hung over the big belt buckle, but his back and arms looked hard as iron, and there was a mischievous look in his eye.

"Hey Rowdy," JJ said, "Ain't you gonna get out of here?"

"Get your fist out of my ribs, dern you," I said. But I couldn't move, because I'd looked into those big blue eyes of little Alice Pigtails. Boy, this wasn't at all the way a guy ought to feel about a gal. "Well, JJ," I said, "if you want to stay in this hot place, suit yourself. Me, I'm getting out of here."

And so I stalked out, trying to peer around pappy's backsides to watch the little gal. They went outside the church to a grove of pecan trees where somebody, whilst the preaching was going on, had set up some old vinegar barrels and placed some planks on top of them and spread white sheets over the planks to make tablecloths.

I don't know what made me do it. I guess desperation. But I sure had to meet that little Alice Pigtails. As the reverend passed by me, I reached out and grabbed his coattails and said, "Preacher, hold on a minute."

He turned around and said, "Yes, my son?"

"Preacher, I don't think I ever in all my born days saw as pretty a little old girl as that little gal over there with her ma and pa. What's her name?"

"Why, son," Preacher said, thrusting his thumbs inside his galluses and rising upon the tips of his toes, "That young lady is Olivia. She is the daughter of Mr. and Mrs. George Oliver. That's her parents, the big 'n over there in the shade and the lady getting the basket of food out of the truck."

"Yeah, I know that, reverend. I figured that out all right. I saw 'em sitting with Alice Pigtails - I mean, Olivia Oliver - in church. How do you reckon I'd go about meeting her?"

"Well, son. Are you a good Christian?" He laid a white hand, that didn't look like it'd ever milked a cow, on my shoulder.

"That depends on what you consider a good Christian to be, I guess. I never robbed nobody. I never beat up on nobody. Well, that is except on kids that was my size. And I never stole nothing. Well, that is, maybe a cookie or a cracker at the store back in Cave Spring. Yeah, I reckon I'm what you'd call a Christian."

"Now son, I could give you a lecture about those little petty stealings. One crime is just as big as another. Crime is of the mind. Crime is of the intent. Not just of the act."

Oh, Lord, why did I have to pick this man to ask to do something as simple as to introduce me to a girl. All I wanted to do was to meet the little thing. I didn't need no sermon. I just got through listening to one sermon. I said, "Preacher, never mind. I don't think I want to meet her anyhow. It's too hot."

He took off his hat and mopped around the sweat band with a dirty handkerchief and then swabbed his forehead. His eyes looked sober as a grave when he said, "My son, I think what you need to meet right now is a big plate of fried chicken, topped off with some bread and butter, some mashed potatoes, some homegrown peas, maybe a little pickle or two on the side. Tell you what I'm gonna do, I'm gonna see to it that you and your young friend -- what's his name --"

"JJ."

"I'm gonna see to it that you and JJ are the guests of honor today of our basket dinner. I'm gonna allow you gentlemen to go first. And if you promise me that you will clean up your plates like the good boys I know you are, then I'll introduce you, myself, to little Olivia. Now mind you boy, you must have honorable intentions, for Olivia is a Christian lady."

Well, that suited me fine. I didn't have no evil intent toward the sweet little old thing. Fact of the matter is, I was a little bit scared of her, I guess. If the truth was told, I hadn't hardly never looked at any girls back in Cave Spring. Oh, I'd looked at 'em. Sure, I can't deny that. But I didn't know what you did with girls.

I mean, them big old boys in Ace Western Story, they were rough on their women. Slam 'em down the stairs, drag 'em by the hair sometimes. And picking 'em up and slinging 'em over their shoulders and riding off with 'em. Sounded pretty good in a story, but you get to thinking about it, that's pretty rough treatment. I doubt if pa done that to ma. Fact of the matter, if ma was as big when pa started going with her as she was the last time I saw her, I know dern well he never. She was too confounded big. If anything, ma'd pick pa up and throw him down the stairs.

Well, first thing I knew, Reverend Dwiggins had a death grip on my arm and he guided me over to where JJ was gawking. It was little Alice Pigtails he was gawking at, of course, and that kind of made me sore.

The Reverend gathered up old JJ the same way he had hold of me, and he let out a whoop and a holler that would have called pigs from ten miles away. He said, "All right, brothers and sisters. The time has come for us to break bread together on these holy grounds, gather round now, ya'll. Bow your heads. Ladies, keep on your sun bonnets. It's a hot day. The Reverend will ask the blessings of the Lord on his children."

And I thought, oh, Lordy, have I got to go through another of his long-winded prayers? I just didn't think I could stand it, standing out there in the hot sun, and his fingers biting down in my arm. And then I got a glimpse of that table. There was old Salt River Sally. She was waving the flies away with a big mesquite branch full of leaves. Confound, if that food didn't look good. Big old platters piled up with golden brown fried chicken and mashed potatoes that looked like little white mountains, and bowls of gravy. I just knew what was swimming around in that gravy. Rich chunks of livers and gizzards. Oh, mercy. And my mouth started to water and my stomach to jump. Yeah, I reckoned I could stand another of the preacher's prayers.

Well, I reckon the preacher must have been about as hungry as me and JJ, for this was one prayer he cut pretty short. He just kind of let the Lord know we was there and he hadn't much more than got our heads down on our chests than I realized he was shoving me and JJ towards the table, and had already said, "Amen."

And, it kind of caught the other folks by surprise too, but it didn't take them long to get over it, and the little ones started whooping and hollering with their mothers chasing after them like cows chasing their playful calves. The Reverend shoved me and JJ in front of him, put plates and tools in our hands and said, "Boys, have at it. A man in this country eats all he can, every time he gets a chance. He don't never know when he's gonna have another meal."

I sank my fork in a plump chicken breast and put it on my plate and reached for another, but the Preacher wouldn't stand for that. He slapped my arm with his fork and said, "Ah-ah. Take a leg and move on. Other folks like white meat, too."

Well, that was all right with me. Hungry as I was, I could eat white meat or black meat or in-between meat. I moved on down and socked the mashed potatoes and gravy to it and a pickle or two.

I got down to the end of the table and saw cobblers and pies and cakes -- it made me wish I didn't have nothing else on my plate. "JJ," I said, "you reckon we ought to pile some of this stuff on top of our vittles. So we'll be sure we won't be without?"

"Rowdy, you know we were taught better than that, back home. We are supposed to clean up our food first, then come back for dessert."

"Yeah, I know JJ. Have you looked back behind you to see what's coming up? Them big old hungry hoot owls back there are liable to soak up this food like a sponge soaks up water. There may not be nothing left when we get back."

JJ had already started away from the table on his gangling legs, looked to me like he'd grown six inches since we left home. He said, "Come on Rowdy, if you'll shut up talking and come over and eat in the shade of Sally's wagon, we'll beat those other old boys back."

I saw a little sense in that. So I followed him and we got in the shade of that old wagon. Moochie was laying in under there, good old dog that he was, popping his tail against the ground and stirring up a little dust. He whined and lapped out his tongue when he smelled the food. He knew what was on that plate. So I pitched him a thigh, I didn't care much for thighs, and raked off about half my potatoes and green beans, figuring that'd help me hurry up and get back to that cobbler.

13

Sunday School Sport

We plopped down beside Moochie and wolfed down that food in nothing flat. I had just finished mopping up the last of my gravy with a piece of homemade bread and I glanced up and saw a pair of boots. I followed them boots on up to a big broad waist and a broader chest and a wider than that shoulders and a thick neck and a square face that was red from sun burn, and black beard stubble standing out. I saw a pair of beady black eyes staring down at us. "Well, howdy boys," he said. It was none other than "Ollie," father of little Alice Pigtails. I could just then see none of that little gal's charm in that big old boy.

He sure looked like a rough one to me, and I would have hated to tangle with him. He said, "What you boys figure on doing around these parts?"

"Well," I said, "we hired on with Miss Sally."

He squinched down with one eye and glared at us with the other, licked his lips soaked up the last of his gravy with a piece of bread and stuffed it in his mouth and swallowed it. Then he squinched down the other eye and said, "Did I hear right? You signed on with Miss Sally? Old Salt River Sally?"

"Yes sir. That is right. We are going to cowboy for her. We started fixing her fences and barns and are going to plant a little feed. We are going to catch wild cows and pen 'em up for her. That's what she's paying us to do."

And this old boy looked steady at me a long time and I began to wonder what he was up to. I don't mind telling you, I didn't like it too well. I felt like he was making fun of us.

Then he let out a whoop and a holler and slapped his thigh with a big hand and said, "Hey, Happy Jack, Dutchy. Hey you, Toby, Polecat. Come here a minute. I want you to get a load of this."

I looked at JJ and he looked at me. "What's he going to do, Rowdy?"

I couldn't answer him, for I didn't know. I started to crawl out from under that wagon. I sort of wanted to get on my feet. I didn't think I liked what I saw coming up. Somewhere else was where I wanted to be right then.

That old cuss, Ollie, sure bugged me. But we had waited too late. By the time we got out from under the wagon, there was this fellow called Happy Jack, with Dutchy beside him. Toby and Polecat were legging it toward us. They had us surrounded.

We backed up against the wagon. I never was one to back off from a fight, but I started looking for a way out of this. There we were, just two of us, and there were five of them. I had half a mind to get back under the wagon. But then I looked at Toby and Polecat and it came back to me how they hooted at me when I rode into Salt River and fell of my horse. And how they jumped on me and gave me a licking. Not only that, I felt old Moochie sidle up next to me. I reached down and felt the bristles come up on his neck. He growled a little bit. I handed my plate to JJ and said, "Here, partner. Hold this for me a minute. I think I'm gonna be busy."

I bowed my neck and put up my fists and Ollie let out a cackle. "Hold on there, boy," he said. "You are all the time wanting to fight. I heard about you jumping on Toby and Polecat yesterday in town. Was that very smart? They are older than you are. And they are bigger than you are. And they are on home territory. Now does it figure that you are going to whip somebody down here and get away with it? Now put down them fists. Put down them fists. Us old boys down here are friendly. We try to get along with everybody. We just want to talk to you a little bit."

Well, I reckoned maybe I had been a little hasty, so I put down my fists and said, "All right, but I thought you meant us harm. Rushing these old boys in here like it was Saturday night and you was gonna gang fight."

"Ah, no, boy. I'm your friend. I'm fixing to do business with you. Don't you know that?"

"Well," I said, "I don't know it. How would I know it?"

"Well, everybody knows that old Ollie is a pretty good old boy. And old Happy Jack here, he's Toby and Polecat's uncle. He's a horse trader and cow trader. He wouldn't cheat nobody, unless they tried to cheat him first. And this here's Dutchy. And boys, he's the man you want to get next to. Old Dutchy Schultz. He's the butcher in Salt River. Now you talk about catching wild cows, he's who'll buy 'em.

"Now I tell you boys what I'm gonna do. I'm gonna do you better than Salt River Sally. I gonna hire you boys to catch wild cows for me, too. And wild bulls, if you are man enough to. How would you like that?"

I had to think on that a bit. I looked at JJ and him at me. He said, "What do you think, Rowdy?"

"Well, JJ, we can't hire on to nobody else. We done give Miss Sally our word. We can't hire out to nobody else."

"Yeah, that's right. I forgot that."

Happy Jack had his fingers thrust down in the top of his trousers with his thumbs on the outside. He had a mustache that needed trimming and long black hair. He said, "Well, we are glad to find out that you are boys of your word. That's all right. We wouldn't want it any other way. What Ollie here was talking about was, maybe you could pick up some side money. Ain't that right, Ollie?"

"Sure, Happy. I wasn't trying to get them to break their word with old Sal. Sure, I wouldn't do that. You know how rough them old brakes are, up and down the river. And how wild them old cows are. We got more than we can do, you and me. And Toby and Polecat, they've got too much to do, too. Besides that, they wouldn't if they had the time.

"The important thing is that this town is starving for meat, and old Dutchy can't make a living without it, either. Don't you have in mind that these boys from Missouri could clean up the river on Sally's side? Do it in nothing flat, most likely. And then they can get over there and clean up on our side. We'd be able to use the canyon country for our range again, wouldn't we?"

Dutchy, a little round man with his shirt sleeves held up by rubber bands above each elbow and a mouth like a catfish, said, "He's telling you right, boys. Everybody around here is too busy raising crops any more. They don't catch any cattle. I have an awful time keeping my slaughter house going because there ain't no cattle brought in no more.

"Whenever they get their pen raised cattle fed up and ready to go to market, they won't sell them to me. They are too valuable. They drive 'em off to Fort Worth and put 'em on a train and take them to Iowa or Illinois. I have a dickens of a time. All I get are the cripples and the canners and cutters. I'd like to have some prime fat young cows and a few bulls to make bologna out of. I'd make a deal with you boys."

Well, I was about overwhelmed by their kindness. I said, "Well, gentlemen, that's plumb kindly of you. I'm put out at myself for lifting my fists quick as I did. I didn't understand what was going on."

Ollie said, "Aw, son, don't think any more about it. I know how you feel. You are in new country and you are surrounded by strangers. It's just natural to feel scared like you did. We wouldn't think about doing you old kids any harm."

And I said, "I'm obliged for the opportunity, but I plain don't see how we can do it. We are tied up with Miss Sally and we got our hands full."

"You fellers think it over," Ollie said. "If you change your mind, you let me know. Ask old Sal where we live. She'll point it out and you can come and see me. But I tell you what I'm gonna do. I don't know what old Sal offered you, but whatever she offered you, I'll just double it. And I'll even go one better than that. There is an old black bull longhorn that ranges on the south side of the river.

"Now that bull plumb infuriates me, tearing down my fence and busting up my gates with his horns, and driving off two or three of my good tame cows. And then I got to take time off from my work to look up them cows and mend my fences, mend my gates. I'm sick and tired of it. If you young 'ens will catch that bull, I'm gonna flat pay you one hundred dollars. That's right, I said, one hundred dollars."

"You catch that bull and carry him into old Dutchy's. Tie him up in Dutchy's pens by the horns when old Dutchy butchers him, you go in there and chop off his horns and bring them to me. There'll be a one hundred dollar bill waiting for you. Cash money. Now what do you think of that?"

By gum, I didn't have to think very long to think pretty highly of that. Man, I figured that was the easiest, biggest money I ever heard tell of. "Why, Mr. Ollie," I said, "I think that is downright generous. I assure you right now that my partner and I take you up on that offer. We are gonna deliver that bull to you."

At that, Toby and Polecat started snickering and I didn't like it, because they were the smart aleck kind anyhow. When I said I didn't like to be laughed at, they broke up, just like they did the day I rode into town. That rotten old saddle girth had to break just then and dump me down in the dirt in front of the Lord and everybody. They hung on to one another and dug their elbows into one another and poked their finger at me and called me a hick, and that got my hackles up again.

I thought I was gonna have to go after them. But JJ laid his hand on my arm and said, "Now, Rowdy, don't pay no attention to those dumb old boys. They got no more sense than to laugh and poke their fingers at other people. Don't let them get you riled. We got us a good deal and let's stick to it."

So I made my hackles lay down again and took Mr. Ollie's hand and shook on it. "I don't mind telling you, Mr. Ollie. I sure like the way you talk. I believe you are a square shooter. While I am on the subject, I want you to know too, that I been eying that little girl of yours. I think she's the prettiest trick I ever laid my eyes on. I would be proud to meet her."

Well, at that, old Toby and Polecat sobered up and I figured I'd struck a sore spot. I said to myself, "You don't reckon those two rascals are struck on her, do you?" Well, why not? They had lived here a long time and knew her and her pa. I reckon it was right natural. But I didn't think I had much to worry about, because that little old Alice Pigtails, she looked like a good girl to me. I couldn't believe she would have anything to do with two ornery birds like Toby and Polecat.

Happy Jack stuck out his hand and shook mine, and JJ's. Dutchy did the same, and I figured even though he didn't look like he had too good a sense, he'd make an honest deal. I shook hands with Ollie again on the deal I'd made.

So the three men wandered on back and took us to fill up our plates with pie and cobbler. There was Miss Sally dishing out homemade ice cream, looking happy as a cowbird on the back of a buffalo. She said, "How are my boys? Are you enjoying yourself? Did you get plenty to eat? Now, don't go away hungry. There's more where this came from."

She leaned over and whispered into my ear. "I'm going to give my boys some extra ice cream."

And boy howdy, did she. She piled it up on our plates. She said, "Now you boys hang tight around here. It's almost time to pack up and go home to do chores again. And we have lots of things to do tomorrow, so we want to get to bed early tonight. So you just go on over to the wagon and wait for me."

She hadn't much more than got that said than I heard the awfulest confounded yelping, barking and squawling I ever heard in my life. I looked around and down there beside the wagon were Toby and Polecat, leading a big cur dog that stood about six inches taller at the shoulders than Moochie. His hair was bristled up on his back and neck so it looked like a ridge of porcupine quills.

There was Moochie, standing under the wagon with his feet braced apart, and his head stuck out, his teeth showing, growling and barking and warning that old mutt to stay away from him. I'd seen dog fights around Cave Spring before. The smart-alecks like to bring dogs in and sic 'em on the town dogs. I never did go for that very much. I don't think it's very smart to pick on dumb animals, dogs especially. They can't help it 'cause they are dogs. They are just like anybody. They like to be left alone.

If somebody wouldn't egg 'em on all the time they couldn't fight one another. They'd like to be left alone and run together and be pals. But no, all the time some fool's got to be hissing 'em on one another, trying to stir up excitement. By gum, it gets dangerous, too. I've seen dogs break one another's legs and rip open their sides so their insides show.

I've seen 'em die, and if they didn't die, they might get their ears slit to ribbons or an eye bit out or an ear drum punctured so they ain't worth anything. Can't hear, so they don't know you are whistling and they can't even get up stock. Well, that's what that pair of cowboys were trying to do down there at that wagon with their mongrel. He weighed twice as much as Moochie. Heck, he could whip Moochie coming and going. Anybody could see that.

That set the fur on me. I didn't recall it, but I guess from what I found out later I dumped that plate of gooseberry pie and ice cream on the ground and took out running. I landed smack dab astraddle one of them danged cowboys just as he let the mutt go and he piled in under the wagon after Moochie.

I was flailing around, kicking and had my arm under his chin and choking him down. I don't guess I was conscious of it, but I caught on quick that JJ didn't think much more of that dog fight business than I did. He had the other old kid on the ground rolling him around. I want you to know we rolled in under the wagon, JJ on top of that old kid and him on the bottom, and then the other way around, and me and who ever it was I had a hold of doing the same thing.

That cur dog and Moochie were rolling around in there too, slashing at one another with their fangs, and growling like mad, slobbering. Every time I'd get on top and raise up to hit that cowboy, I'd bust my head against the bottom of the wagon and it'd daze me, and then he'd get me on the bottom and try to hit me.

It was the pure dickens for a little bit. Pretty soon I felt something hold of my leg and I found myself sliding out from under the wagon and this old kid - I saw by now it was Polecat - sliding out beside me, because somebody had hold of his legs, too.

The Reverend Dwiggins was shouting and praising the Lord and shaming us for breaking the Holy Sabbath. The only thing that didn't stop was the cur dog and Moochie. Didn't nobody get hold of their legs? Afraid they'd get their heads snapped off if they had any sense, and I guess they did. But when I shook loose from who ever had hold of me, I dived back under the wagon. I wasn't about to let that cur hurt my dog. Moochie'd been with me through thick and thin, and I had a picture bright in my mind just then of how hard he had run to keep me from going off to Texas without him. Why, it made me want to choke that cur dog with my bare hands.

I grabbed the cur by the scuff of the neck and dug into the ground with his front feet and I heaved and he let go. I fell backward and he came back on top of me and wiggled around in my arms.

I want you to know if that son-of-a-gun didn't rear back and come at me with his lips pulled back from his fangs and dripping like he was going to chew my gizzard out. His fangs looked yellow as an ear of corn and just as long. I tried to squeeze into the ground with my back, but it didn't give any.

The only thing that saved me was somebody's foot coming down in front of my face and landing against the side of the cur's head just as he was ready to sink his teeth into my throat. He fell off yelping and scrambled his legs up under him and tore out of there, still yelping.

I was never so glad of anything in my life. I was plumb tuckered. My head stopped ringing after while and I saw that whole picnic crew gathered around us. If I didn't hear the scolding of the year going on I hope to get tickled to death with a feather. There was Miss Sally. She had Polecat by the collar and Toby by the gallus and giving them what for.

"You ornery, lowdown, no good skinks," she said. "I done warned you once what was going to happen if you tangled with anything old Sally had her hooks in. I'm warning you one more time, I have any more trouble out of you scallawags, old Sally's going to load up her shotgun and it's not going to be with rock salt. I'm going to make you so sore, you're going to have to grow you a whole new behind before you can sit down to the dinner table again. Now you scamps get out of here."

I figured Miss Sally didn't have much business doing that to another man's boys, but Happy Jack didn't seem to mind. He was grinning as big as any man, looking like he was enjoying the show more than anybody.

That beat me, to think that fellows like Happy Jack, Ollie, Dutchy and the rest thought that a dog fight and a scrap between four boys was a sport on a Sunday afternoon. That would have been a sorry show back where I came from. Those fellows' stock fell about 100 percent with me right then. Of course, not enough to make we want to forget about that $100 bull deal. We'd already shaken hands on that.

JJ and me dusted ourselves off. "You got a lump on your cheek, Rowdy," JJ said.

"You don't look so hot yourself, what with a scratch on your nose and a chunk of hair pulled out by your neck."

"If they hadn't pulled me off," he said, "I'd had mine whipped by now."

"Yeah, me too. I reckon Moochie was the one that got the worst end of that. Look at him licking his flank. Gee gosh, a whole piece of flesh is ripped loose." I crawled in under the wagon and examined him, but he wasn't really bit deep any place. He'd been chewed on worse than that by coons back home.

I saw Miss Sally had Toby and Polecat taken care of so we wouldn't have to watch our backs any more that day. She waddled over to us, her arms stuck out like she had a half a mind to box somebody alongside the ears just for the fun of it, and gathered us up like a mother hen getting her chicks together. She rubbed back out hair and puttered over us and it made me feel good down inside to be this far from home and have somebody care enough for us to look after us that way.

"Poor boys, I'm so sorry. That ornery pair. Some day, somebody's going to skin them alive and hang them out to dry. Come on back to the table, you boys didn't get to eat your pie and ice cream."

I grinned at JJ. "How about you, partner. You got any appetite left?"

And JJ ran his tongue around his lips and said, "Got nothing left except appetite."

Miss Sally said, "Well, just eat the sweet stuff and leave room for a treat back home. We are going to have fresh sausage and scrambled eggs for supper, just to celebrate. And some fresh garden tomatoes."

So that's what we did. Sally hovered over us and saw to it we got all we wanted to eat without gorging ourselves. The other women clucked and tut-tutted about Toby and Polecat being so rude and sic'n their dog on my dog. It made us feel like we were part of the community.

The day was wearing on, long toward sundown, and Miss Sally tucked her basket in the wagon. I picked up Moochie and put him in the wagon. He whimpered some, but it was more from hurt feelings than anything else. Heck, it makes anybody feel bad to get whipped, so I sat him on the seat beside me and he nudged his head over in my lap and looked up at me and whined and licked my hand, and I picked up the reins and said, "Get up, Lady Midnight. Get along Jackrabbit," and we rattled out of the church yard and struck the road leading north out of town.

I looked around for little Alice Pigtails, but her mother had rustled her out of there. We waved at everybody and the preacher "Praised the Lord" and by the time we got home, it was time to feed the chickens.

The rooster was clucking around and scratching up worms and carrying them over by the pen to try and feed his hens, and they talked back at him so it sounded like the women back at the church.

The cow came bawling up with her bag full of milk. I fed her a gallon of bran and she stood still while I jerked the blue john out of her. Then I stripped the cream out in a bowl Miss Sally brought me and took it all to the spring house to cool.

It made me sort of home sick. This was just what I used to do for ma. Watercress grew so thick in the spring where is came out of the earth that you couldn't see the water unless you parted the watercress with your hands. There were little black snails lying all over the clear bottom of the spring and minnows darted every which way. There were big crawdads in there too, and I had a mind to catch a few one of these days and peel their tails. When they are fried, they tasted like fish meat, except more juicy and there isn't any bone to worry about.

I thought it would be real nice if I took Miss Sally a mess of watercress, and so I broke off a double handful, and swished it around in the water until I got all the grit washed free and took it in and she hoorayed over me for fifteen minutes for being so thoughtful. She sat us down for supper and after supper, I wanted to work on the pens some more, but she wouldn't have any of it.

"No, boys, it's been a long day and a good one. We are just going to sit here on the porch and watch the sun go down. There's plenty of time for work tomorrow, and if there isn't we don't need to work on the Sabbath."

So that's what we did, just rocked and listened to the whippoorwills call, and the quails whistle to one another down along the river. Toward dusk the coyotes began to yip-yip-yip and something rustled out in the brush by the spring.

"Probably some javalinas or that old sow and her pigs that got out on me. But never you mind. It's nothing that will hurt us. There's wildcats back in the brush but they won't come up where there's humans."

About dark I had to go to bed, not that I was tired. Didn't think I was homesick. It was just sort of lonesome. The quiet, still peacefulness of the place got to me and I wanted to be by myself.

14

Hog Trouble

I never liked to get up early back home, but for some reason, I realized I had been waking up early since I had left home.

I piled out of bed and pulled on my overalls and shoes. I reached over on the other side of the pallet and gave JJ a shake. "Hey, pard, wake up. Got lots to do."

JJ popped up, his hair down over his eyes and a few straws from the ticking in his hair. He yawned until his jaw bones popped and that woke him up. "Hey, Rowdy, what's on for today? Are we going to start catching wild cows? Hey, I could hardly sleep for thinking about that wild bull. Boy, one hundred dollars. Let's go."

He grabbed his pants and shoes, we both slept in our shirts, and moved faster than I ever saw him. What a change there had been in JJ. He had dragged his heels in the beginning, but he was all man and a yard wide now. He hadn't peeped a word about being homesick in several days now.

"Hold on, you ornery cuss," I said. "We got lots to do before we go to catch cows."

JJ looked mighty disappointed. "What do we have to do?"

"Well, for one thing, we've got to plant some feed. When we get those old cows caught, we've got to have something to feed them in the pens."

"I thought we'd sell them."

"Well, I reckon that's Miss Sally's decision, not yours and mine. But common sense tells me she's going to want to put some meat on those old hides before she sells them. I guess they'll have calves. She'll sell the calves and fatten the cows."

"But that's not cowboying, Rowdy. That's sort of like farming, back home, isn't it."

Well, that sort of hit me in the breadbasket. I hadn't thought of it that way. I just figured out what had to be done and went ahead and did it. "That don't make any difference JJ. What's got to be has got to be. Come on, now."

I went into the kitchen and couldn't find Salt River Sally, but it was plain she wasn't too far off, for bacon and pancake batter were on the cabinet. I moseyed to the door and saw her coming from the shed, a bucket in her hand.

"Well, good morning, Rowdy. Look what I've done. Already been out and milked the cow. Where's JJ? Breakfast's almost ready."

"He's dressed."

At breakfast I said, "Miss Sally, I figured to harrow up that five acres of black dirt down by the creek. You got any millet or cane seed?"

"Nary a bit Rowdy, but I'll tell you what, I've got a few ears of corn left. Why don't you just plant corn instead? That way I could fatten out some hogs this fall, along with having fodder for some cows."

Well, that suited me to a T. "That is, providing we can get enough water on the corn to make it grow."

"Oh," she said, "that's no problem. My daddy had it fixed so all we'll have to do is open the ditch with a shovel and turn on the water."

"I reckon if you want corn planted, I'll have to plow before I harrow. You got a plow?"

She grinned until the corners of her mouth near reached her ears. "'Deed I have," she said. "Even kept axle grease on the plow share. You'll have it shedding before you go one round."

Well, I got an old harness Sally had and put it on Lady Midnight. I'm proud to tell you she didn't move a hair when I backed her up to the plow. Lots of saddle horses would have thrown a ring-tailed fit. "Now, JJ, while I get the plow going, you hook old Jackrabbit to the harrow. As soon as I get the first few furrows plowed, you start following me around, breaking up the clods. The harrow is three times as wide as the plow, but Jackrabbit is slower. But you'll be able to make two rounds to my one. Miss Sally is going to shell the seed corn and by noon we can start planting and putting on the water. We'll plant and water as we go, and that way we won't have to work our ground again if it rains."

"Rain, my pain," JJ said. "It doesn't look like to me it's rained here since Noah parked his ark."

And that's the way it worked out. All that week we plowed and planted corn, and wet down the ground. Lady Midnight gaunted up considerably, pulling that plow by herself and with no grain to feed her at night, just grass. Most often, it takes two horses to pull a walking plow, and it would have this time if it hadn't been light soil that turned over easy. Jackrabbit didn't seem to gain or lose. He just pulled the harrow and seemed happy if he was near Lady Midnight, JJ and me.

Honest, the day I finished plowing the last acre and planting it, the first corn we planted had popped through the ground. I stayed out until after supper, putting water on the last ground, and I looked in the first new rows of corn before I went in to bed down. I swear, it seemed the corn had grown two inches the first day. The hot sun, the damp, rich earth, made that corn grow like nobody's business.

I went to bed tired, but happy as I'd ever been. I reckon before I fell asleep, my mind drifted back to ma and pa. I know they would be plenty proud of me if they could have seen what all I had learned to do by myself since I left home two weeks ago. I know one thing for sure, I had learned more on my own in two weeks than I ever had in two years before. And then I slipped off to sleep.

I woke up just before daylight and couldn't wait until I got my shoes tied before slipping out of the pallet and from the house. I ran as fast as I could out of the yard and down the path that led to the corn field below the spring and the irrigation ditch. There was something that had always excited me about putting seeds in the ground and waiting for them to sprout through the dirt. It was just starting to get daylight, it was sort of gray on the ground, like in a fog, but I could tell by the pink color in the east that it was going to be a clear day. The ground was still black, and I couldn't see when I first jumped the ditch.

I landed right astraddle of a confounded pig. Though I don't reckon I was any more surprised than that pig, for he let out a squeal louder than my yell, and then it seemed all tarnation broke out around me. I figured right quick I was in the middle of a whole litter of pigs and that where there was a whole litter of pigs, there was bound to be a mother pig.

I heard her right then coming to the rescue of her scared baby. I was at a disadvantage. The sow could smell me and probably see me too, against the skyline. I couldn't see her against the dark ground, but I could hear her all right, and what she was saying was, "Old buddy, if I can catch you I'm gonna sample that tender meat on your leg, and after that if I like it, I'll just take a few choice bites off any other places I come to."

I was more scared of a sow with pigs than any other farm animal and I didn't wait any longer to get acquainted. I fairly flew up the path to the yard, and jumped the fence and busted through the door.

"Miss Sally. JJ," I yelled. "Wake up."

I reached up over the front door and pulled Miss Sally's old shotgun down. Miss Sally appeared in the door of her bed room, her hair standing on end and her big tooth laying over her lower lip. She had on a long flannel nightgown. I guess my yell didn't faze JJ, the deadhead.

"What's wrong, Rowdy? What is it?"

"Hogs. An old sow and pigs in the corn field."

"Wait'll I get dressed. I'll..."

"Where's your shells? Gotta have shells."

"In my bedroom." She disappeared and ran back into the kitchen with a box of shotgun shells and pushed them into my hand. I fumbled a handful of shells out of the box and put them in my pocket and ran back as fast as I could toward the cornfield. As I ran, I broke open the gun and shoved shells in the chamber and pulled back the safety. Moochie came running from somewhere, the barn I guess, or maybe he had been out hunting all night. He barked every step at my heels, excited like I was playing with him.

But I wasn't playing, not by a dern sight. No doggoned old sow was going to root up my cornfield. I'd hang her carcass up for salting and smoking.

The day was light enough now I could see plain as anything. And as I topped the rise at the end of the path, I saw the old sow and pigs right in the middle of the cornfield, rooting fit to kill. It looked like my field had been plowed all over again. There wasn't a green spring of corn to be seen anywhere.

Moochie spotted the sow and pigs then and began barking in their direction. The old sow had heard a dog bark at her before, I'd say, because she never even threw up her head to look around. She just started running and her pigs caught the fever right away and passed her. They ran out of the cornfield at the far end where the river took a bend. I didn't even get one shot. It wouldn't have done any good to shoot her from this distance, for the pellets would have just bounced off her thick hide. To kill her I would have had to be right on top of her and almost stuck the shotgun down her snout.

But I was so mad I had to shoot anyhow, and I pulled down the old hammer and the gun shoved backward on my shoulder. The old sow didn't even squeal. She and her brood just disappeared in the brush.

I didn't know whether to be mad or sick when I walked down to the field and saw what that old devil had done. While I was mopping around trying to decide, Sally came running down, her big old work shoes on under her flannel gown, her stern broad as a barn door and her hair flying every which-a-way. JJ ran after her, his shirt tail flying, and one overall strap flapping behind him. He had a wild look on his face, and his hair stood on end as bad as Sally's and just as he started to take a jump to clear the irrigation ditch, he stepped on a shoe lace, tripped and fell head-first into the water. It splashed all over Miss Sally and she cried, "Oh, you poor dear," and waded into the ditch to pick him up.

JJ came up blowing and snorting and looking like a drowned rat and sputtered out something that sounded like something a mother would wash her boy's mouth out with soap for. I couldn't help breaking up over it. It was my turn to crack up at JJ now, and I got down on my knees laughing so hard. Moochie thought he should be in on the fun, too, and leaped up on my back and knocked me flat on my face. Before I could get up, JJ was astraddle of my back, thumping me good. That would have been even funnier if he hadn't been hitting so hard. By gosh, he had got stronger than he was when we left home.

"Hey JJ, cut it out. I ain't that old sow and pigs. She caused all the commotion. Take it out on her."

"Now boys, stop that," Miss Sally yelled.

She hauled JJ off me and he settled down. Then he began to look around at the ruined corn and I thought he was going to cry. He picked up a little corn sprout that had been rooted up and dug a little hole and planted it again. He pressed the earth down around it and reached for another one and then saw there was no use.

He looked at me with a face as long as a fence post and said, "Rowdy, what'll we do? That old fool ruined the corn crop."

"Replant it."

"That won't do any good. She'll bring that brood back."

"Good. That'll give me a chance to catch her."

"Why not shoot her?" Miss Sally asked.

"Well, I just figured out something. If I shot her, she wouldn't never know what for. But if I catch her and put her in a pen, she'll know why. Then I aim to fatten her up and butcher her. And I aim to sink a tooth in her. That's when I will get even with her."

"I've got a better idea," JJ said.

"What?"

"Catch her and sell her and all her pigs. I wouldn't eat that old fool."

"Well, for one thing," Miss Sally said, "we got to fence her out of the corn. If we don't, we might as well have never planted it. Come on, boys. Let's go eat breakfast, and then we'll figure out what to do."

After breakfast, we all went back to the cornfield and replanted that first batch of corn. The old sow and her pigs hadn't hurt the corn that wasn't up yet, except to track around in it some and tear up the ground. I dug in the hills and found the corn was sprouting, but it would come up all right. So we just lost about an acre, and after we replanted it, we turned the water on it again.

"Boy," JJ said, "I'm tired. Let's go eat."

"Nope," I said. "Can't."

"Why not?"

"Well, if we leave her before we get it fenced, the old sow and pigs'll be back here before you blink. We'll have to stand guard."

"Rowdy, I declare," said Miss Sally. "I don't know what I'd ever have done without you. That's a good idea. I'll tell you what. I'll go rustle up some grub and bring it back here. You and JJ just go over to the spring and lay back in the shade."

So that's what we did, and in fact I took a little nap and then woke up when Sally came with sandwiches and pie. I located an old woven wire fence back in the brush a half mile. Miss Sally said it had one time been around an orchard a settler had planted before he sold out to her father. In fact, there was a lot of apple trees still standing and some of the trees were loaded with apples the size of plums. If it rained any at all this summer, there would be lots of apples for Sally this winter. JJ had come along with me and we left Miss Sally to guard the corn field.

We had hitched old Jackrabbit to our two-wheeled cart so we could haul the wire back in it. I had an old double-bitted ax and I had filed one bit sharp to use to chop out sprouts and vines, and left the other bit dull to chop staples out of the posts.

Well, we found there was plenty of wire and more to go around our five-acre cornfield. The bottom six inches was buried in dirt and grass, but after we chopped out the vines and sprouts the sandy ground gave way easily. The old mesquite posts were crooked as a dog's hind leg but that didn't matter, because they were still stout and held the staples. I chopped them out and JJ rolled the wire and Moochie dug for mice in their hair and grass-lined burrows. Once he dug up a mole and spent an hour holding him between his paws, then letting him run away and stick that funny snout in the earth and start to dig his escape. Just about the time the mole thought he was free, old Moochie would grab him out with his teeth and the mole would squeal. I had to get after JJ for loafing and watching the mole show instead of rolling wire.

"Hurry up, JJ. I'm about dry as a bone yard. We forgot to bring any water. If we don't hurry up and get done, I'm going to have to leave and then come back. I don't aim to do that because you have been goofing."

"I never did see a mole before."

"Well, you're going to see my foot against the seat of your britches if you don't hurry up."

JJ got in gear and by 5 o'clock, we had the cart piled high with wire and posts. It was almost more than Jackrabbit could pull where the narrow wheels sank into loose sand.

But I guess Jackrabbit was thirsty too, because the closer we got to home, the faster he went until he was trotting when we entered the clearing by the barn. And when he smelled the water, he started galloping. I thought the wheels of the cart would collapse because of how they were held together, and then Jackrabbit ran in, cart and all, to drink. I waded in upstream from him and drank until I near busted, and then lay down in the water and sure liked that cool feeling all over me. Old Moochie splashed and lapped out his tongue as if to say, "Boy, we never used to have time for fun like this back home, did we?"

That made me stop and think that I sure had been working hard here in Texas. Even putting in more hours than I did for Pa, but I never minded it at all. I didn't even have to be woke up of morning's. Just woke up by myself. Well, it was hard for me to figure out why I enjoyed it and I reckon I'd have thought about it considerable more if Miss Sally hadn't come grinning around.

"It didn't take you very long," she said. "What kind of shape is the wire in? Was the posts all rotted and split?"

"Ain't nothing wrong with the wire that can't be patched," I said. "And the posts are too crooked to drive, but I reckon we can dig holes and set 'em."

"Did you see any apples?"

"Yeah. The trees are loaded."

"Hey, I saw a mole," JJ said. "You ought to have seen him trying to dig a hole with that funny nose. Just tried to screw himself down into the ground. Old Moochie, he wouldn't let him. Almost the time he'd get a hole started, old Mooch would grab him."

"We can make some pie," Miss Sally said.

JJ looked puzzled. "Mole pie?"

"Aw, shut up, JJ. She is talking about the apples. She don't care about your stupid mole."

A laugh shook Miss Sally so hard the fat under her arms jiggled as she waded in with us and put her arms around our shoulders. "Course I was talking about apple pie. Who ever heard of mole pie? And maybe there will be enough ripe apples so's we can stir up some apple butter this fall."

Miss Sally guided us out of the water like we were little boys and we didn't seem to mind. It just seemed like we were one big happy family, working hard to help each other. "Have you seen anything of the hogs?" I said.

"Nary a thing. She's too smart. She's laying out there in the brush waiting for us to leave."

"Well, I guess you'd better get us some supper and we'll work until dark on the fence."

"We ain't got no meat, Rowdy. Reckon you ought to take the gun out and kill us a rabbit?"

Well, a juicy rabbit and some gravy wouldn't taste bad I figured, and besides, I didn't exactly mind the thought of letting JJ start the fence. "Is there any special place they hang out?" I asked.

"All up and down the river. It's about time for them to come out and feed."

"Let me go," JJ begged. "You get all the fun."

"Did you ever shoot a gun, JJ? A 12 gauge?"

"You know I never."

"Well, do you think I'm going to let you learn to shoot a gun when we got to have meat on the table?"

"Reckon not."

"No, 'course not. Now you just get the shovel and start digging post holes. Dig the corners first and dig them deep. Then we won't have to dig the line posts in so deep."

JJ stuck his lower lip out and kicked a chunk of wood into the spring. "Dang it, I'm sick of doing all the work. You have all the fun."

"Yeah, like watching a dog play cat and mouse with a mole? If you want any supper you better wrap your hands around that shovel."

15

Quail, Hot Biscuits and Gravy

I grabbed the shotgun and went on down the river toward where I killed that wild turkey that night. I even secretly thought I might get to shoot another turkey, but I knew they were plenty smart, and likely I wasn't good enough a hunter to sneak up on them in the daylight.

I walked slow and looked hard for rabbits, but didn't see any I could shoot at. The brush was so thick. I kept a sharp eye out because I thought I might see the old sow and pigs. A fat pig would go about as good as anything. I walked a mile down the creek and still hadn't fired a shot, when I thought I saw a little brown shadow run across the trail ahead of me. I stopped real quick and waited, but didn't see nothing. I walked ahead a step or two and near jumped out of my hide when a bird jumped up right beside me like a bomb going off.

"A quail!" I said out loud. I lifted the gun, but he was gone before I could get a bead on him. I would of hated to pull the trigger even, because I had never shot at a quail before. My heart fluttered as I walked forward, wondering when another one would jump up and scare me half to death. But none did. And I stopped, disappointed, and turned around to look behind me.

Boy, it's a good thing I did. Those little old quail had just waited until I walked past them and then they ran out of the brush and headed back the way I had come. They just kept pouring out of the brush until it looked like there were 150 of them.

It suddenly occurred to me that these quail didn't look like the bobwhite quail back home. They had blue and brown feathers and had a higher topknot. They were bigger, and there was more of them, too. Heck, back home there wasn't more than 12 or 15 to a covey, and here they were still running out of the brush until it looked like as many as my ma had chickens.

Well, I knew then, that was my supper going down the trail. I'd always heard a man wasn't supposed to shoot a quail when it was running. But I sure was going to shoot one anyway, because they were not about to stop.

The old gun went "blooey," and the quail flushed with a sound like a hundred rockets taking off. When my head cleared from the recoil, I saw quail fluttering all over that path.

I ran up there and started counting and wound up with eleven. Then I got to laughing at my good luck, and danced a jig. I gathered up the quail and they wouldn't all go in my pockets, so I stuffed them inside my shirt and felt their warm bodies and feathers tickling me.

I ran hard as I could, and it seemed the path would never end, I was in such a hurry to get back and show off my good luck.

"Hey, JJ. Come running."

"What is it, Rowdy? Anything wrong?" JJ hollered back.

I burst into the clearing by the spring and there was JJ and Miss Sally running to meet me.

"What you grinning about, Rowdy?"

I laid down the shotgun and pulled a quail out of my pocket. "What you think of that?"

"A quail," squealed JJ.

"Oh, Rowdy, you are sure some hunter. First a turkey, now a quail. Didn't you see no rabbits? One quail ain't enough meat for three of us."

"Oh," I said, "I got more than one," and started pulling them out one at a time and laying them down in a row on the ground. JJ laughed and jumped around for the first four or five, and then he stopped and when I laid the eleventh quail on the ground and looked up at him, he was frowning.

"You dern smart aleck," he said.

I just puffed out my chest and strutted around the pile of quail with a grin. "Clean 'em JJ, while I get a little rest."

Miss Sally grabbed them up one by one and started ripping off the heads and feathers. I said, "Here JJ, run down to the spring like a good boy and wash their insides out."

He stuck out his lower lip and Miss Sally took up for him. "Rowdy, hush your face. These are my quail, ain't they? They grew fat on my beggerlice and spring water, didn't they? And JJ, don't get sore because you did go with him. Gun ain't got but one trigger."

I just grinned. "How many post holes you get done, JJ?"

Well, we had our quail and hot gravy and biscuits and JJ and me pitched our blankets by the spring for the night so we could guard the cornfield.

I sat propped against a rock with the shotgun across my knees until I reckon near midnight and must have dozed off. I woke with a jerk and it took a while to figure where I was. I didn't see or hear anything wrong out in the cornfield and I sure felt sleepy.

So, I decided I'd best lie down and sleep. Ol' Moochie sidled up and whined and I pulled his head up against mine and whispered for him to keep watch for me.

I don't know what time it was when Moochie's barking woke me up. I grabbed the shotgun, but it was too dark to see. But Moochie knew there was something out there. Then I heard the old sow grunting and her pigs squealing and Moochie took off through the brush. I grinned, old Mooch had got the word. He'd keep that old sow away until we got the fence fixed, so we went back to sleep.

We fixed the fence the whole next day. Never would have thought it could be done. Back home in rocky ground, we would have dug half as many fence post holes. But here, the ground is easy. The corn was sprouting in the warm, moist earth fit to kill, and Moochie stood guard all day like he hoped the old sow would return.

Well, I guess Moochie made a believer out of the old gal, for we didn't see anything of her the rest of the week, which we spent making the corrals stronger, in cleaning up the junk around the place and keeping water on the corn. All in all, the place looked as good as Pa's place back home. A little white paint on the gray boards would not have hurt anything and it would have been nice to have a gasoline engine to pump water instead of having to carry water from the spring to the corral. But I figured we could worry about that when the time came for it.

One morning while I was milking, Miss Sally came out to the barn. "You about finished? I need some milk for pancake batter."

"Got the blue john," I said. "Soon as I strip her, we'll have some cream for butter." I gave a few more squirts and waited for the white foam to settle so it wouldn't run the bucket over. I had to kick a couple of cats away to keep them from reaching up with their front paws, latching onto the top of the bucket and burying their snouts in the foam.

"Miss Sally, I guess we are about ready to start driving cows. Point me in the right direction."

"Did you say driving cows?"

"That's right. I'm middlin' anxious to commence."

"Law's a-mercy, Rowdy, if them cows could be driven they'd to have been gone long ago. They won't drive. They are too smart and wild. And the brush is too thick."

I was so startled I almost let the cow get her foot in the bucket. "How the devil are we supposed to corral them?"

"Why, I thought you knew. You got to rope them one at a time and drag them out. Less'n you find a bunch of cowboys and hold a real old-time roundup. And a fat chance we would have of that."

"You mean catch them one at a time? We got to lasso them one at a time and drag them out?"

"That's the only way."

I sat the bucket aside and got a pan to catch the cream, and studied a minute. "Ain't that awful slow?"

"That's the only way. Any other way somebody'd already have done it."

Well by thunder, I didn't know about that. Where I came from there was more than one way of skinning a cat. "Let me think about it a spell. Maybe I can figure out something." I finished stripping the cow, handed the milk bucket to Miss Sally and hung up the milk stool. "It'd help a lot if I knew where to start looking for cows."

We walked toward the house and Miss Sally stretched a clean cheese cloth over a big crock and poured the milk into the cloth. The weight of the warm milk made a little funnel shape in the cloth and the milk gurgled through, leaving the dirt and trash behind.

"Well," she finally said, "you won't find them running around all in a big herd like tame cows. They are in little bunches of two or three to a dozen, maybe. Sometimes, they gang up around a waterhole, and when they go out in the brush to graze, they split up. Sometimes an old mossy horn won't have nothing to do with anything else except her own calf.

"Once she kicked her calf off, she may hang around with a bunch of cows or a bull some. The old bull, he'd like to keep 'em all together. But the brush is so thick he can't do it. They scatter on him like quail."

"I hear there is a mean old bull among 'em."

"Were'd you hear that?"

"Last Sunday at church. Mr. Oliver told me about him. Offered me and JJ one hundred dollars to catch him."

Sally was in the middle of pouring some of the fresh milk into the pancake batter and her round face looked up at me right quick. In fact, she missed the bowl and poured the milk down her shoe top. I'd seen that same look on ma's face when she wanted to shake me real good.

"That skunk," she said, putting down the crock of milk and mopping up that she spilled. "Don't you pay no attention to him. He was pulling your leg. And mind you, leave that old black bull alone. There's lots of old bulls running loose in the brakes, and they are all mean as a hog with a toothache. But there is just one old black bull. He'll kill anybody gets near him, or a horse too. He's been known to lay in wait behind a bush for a stray horse grazing and bust out and gut him. Don't nobody with sense go in the arm of the canyon where he hangs out. You hear?"

That nettled me some, her talking so bossy to me like that. "Well, I don't know, that's a lot of money. I had in mind to use that hundred dollars to set me up in business."

Sally stirred up the batter and poured some in a greased skillet smoking over red hot mesquite coals. Ain't nothing this side of coal gets as hot as mesquite coals, I'd found out, less it is bois d'arc wood. Bois d'arc, that's hedge wood, or osage orange. Back home, we just call it "bodark," and leave off the fancy French saying of it. The pancake batter spread out and began bubbling up and turning brown and I felt my stomach call me to breakfast. By this time, JJ stumbled into the room, knuckling the sleep out of his eyes and yawning. Chasing Moochie and that mole around all the previous afternoon had tuckered him out, I reckoned. He slumped at the table and looked up like a hound dog at butchering. "What's for breakfast?" he said.

Miss Sally didn't seem to hear him. A frown lay heavy on her forehead and she said, "Rowdy, don't rile old Sally now. I ain't gonna say no more, and you ain't either. 'Cept you ain't trying to catch that black bull."

Well, I just walked right out of that kitchen, hot under the collar, and went out and kicked the woodshed door. I had in mind to go on to work, but then I caught a whiff of them browning pancakes and reckoned I hadn't ought to be that mad.

So I just made up my mind, I'd do like I did at home - keep my mouth shut and do as I pleased. I learned a long time ago it wasn't no use to argue with old folks. They were mule headed, all right. Whew!

I went back to the kitchen, the smell of bacon, hotcakes and coffee running through the house like a hound about to catch a fox, and Miss Sally flopped three cakes in front of me like I'd never huffed out.

After breakfast, I was at somewhat of a loss to know what to do and was too stubborn to ask Miss Sally after my little set with her, so I straightened up tools and junk around the shed. I reckon there was just about everything there, somewhere, that a body needed to operate a ranch, but it sure hadn't been taken care of.

Before the sun had much more than edged up over the mesquite and cut away the shadows of night, Miss Sally settled my problem.

She came out of the house dressed in a plaid cotton shirt and faded and patched blue jeans, a pair of run-over cowboy boots and a floppy hat on her head. She must of done up her hair, for it wasn't but a reddish wisp or two of it sticking from under the hat. Her face was flushed like a ripe tomato and she grinned. "Harness up the team."

"Where we going?"

"Law's a mercy, Rowdy. You'd have to ask a question if the devil was riding in on a freight train. You wanted to find out where the cows were, didn't you? I'm going to take you there."

I was anxious enough to go, but I didn't want to let it show, so I said, "I had in mind riding out on JJ's mare. Can't bring in cows with a wagon, can we?"

"No, you can't, but you ain't ready to bring them in yet. You'd just better get the lay of the land and find out where those cows run to when they are flushed."

"I don't..." I began, and then stopped. Miss Sally couldn't get it through her head I wasn't about to try and catch all those cows one at a time. Heck, even if I could catch them, how would I get them to the pen? They sure wouldn't lead like a milk pen calf, and Lady Midnight wasn't big enough to drag them all in. Why, back home, we had ways of getting cattle up in herds. I reckoned I could do the same with Texas cattle.

16

Wishin' For Home

So I shut up and caught the team and hitched it to Miss Sally's wagon cart and JJ, Moochie and Salt River Sally crawled in and I said, "Giddy-up" to the team and we rattled southwestward.

I'd never been in this direction of Miss Sally's ranch before, so she handled the reins, cutting around trees and up and down gullies. The rain had washed out an even trail leaving rocks and ruts – with maybe some the Lord had thrown in for good measure. It got rough real quick, I never saw such rough country. After we drove about a mile, all of a sudden there we were in the brakes of the Red River country. Miss Sally stopped the team at the rim of the canyon and I looked down – must have been a thousand feet to the bottom.

Nobody said anything for a while, just stared down in that awful, deep hole, and finally I said, "Gee, oh gosh. You could stand my pa's farm endways and it wouldn't touch the bottom of that thing."

South of us, we could see the far wall of the canyon, all black with shadows, and mottled green trees standing on top of it. Down in the middle distance was a creek that meandered and glanced the sun off of it.

"What made that big ditch?" JJ whispered.

Miss Sally laughed, and it rolled away and struck something and bounced back in echoing waves. "That little old river out yonder, that's what. That's the river that runs by my place. You know that?"

"You mean that tame little old creek we planted corn by is a part of this creek?" I said.

"The same, only don't think it's very tame. When there's been rain back in the canyon, that tame old creek gets plenty wild. You'd better hope it doesn't get wild. It'll take out our cornfield overnight."

Well, that distance stretched my eyes until they got tired looking. Besides, that wasn't what we'd come for. "Where's the wild cows?" I said. "Don't see nary a cow down there."

Miss Sally climbed down off the seat and waddled to the very edge of the canyon. She took off her hat and waved it in a way I took to mean a big stretch of country. "Down there," she said.

I felt a little pale around the gills. I didn't know what to say, so didn't say nothing. JJ looked at me innocent-like. I don't think he realized how I felt.

"Rowdy?" Miss Sally turned to me and the happy look was gone. "See? Sort of scary, ain't it? Now you got an idea why old Sally ain't got any cows? There's a hundred thousand acres down in that canyon ain't never been fenced. It's owned in part by me, and Ollie Oliver and half a dozen other ranchers. They got enough cattle they hardly ever bother about catching the ones that go wild. And if they do, it's just in the winter when their hands ain't got nothing else to do and they just go in and catch or shoot enough for the winter's meat."

"Why'd you let your cows get in there in the first place?" My voice sounded hollow in my ears.

"That was my pappy's winter pasture. There was plenty of grass and water and shelter from storms and pa turned 'em out of the fenced fields around the home place, always on Christmas day. And he went down in the canyon with a bunch of cowboys in the spring and branded the calves and drove the whole bunch home. He sold the calves and oldest cows and we just did that year after year."

She reached down and pulled up a couple of cockleburs and pitched them over the rim and stood there with her hands on her hips and stared off into space. The slack look on her cheeks and the gray in her eyes made me feel right sad.

"What happened then?"

She turned around and reached out her hand. "Help me up." She made the wagon wheels creak with her weight and she gathered up the reins and clucked to the team. "Well, one winter pa up and died. Then the war came on and you couldn't get no help. And then after that nobody would cowboy and finally I spent all pa left me. And I couldn't gather my cows. They just went wild in the canyon. And that's where they are now, them and all of their calves."

I chewed this a while, feeling mighty sorry for Miss Sally. "How many head you reckon are in there?"

"Lord only knows. I've wondered that myself. I've watched the water holes from up here many a time and tried to count 'em. But it ain't possible. There's so much country and so much brush you can't see more than a dozen, at any one time.

"If I guessed, I'd say two or three hundred, but there might be a thousand, for all I know. My pa had 50 head of cows when he died and they had calves. That's been 12 or 15 years ago. And the calves' calves are having calves by now. Besides that, there's no telling how many head of cattle belongs to others that have got out of pastures from time to time and gone wild. Even allowing for death loss, there's lots of cattle there."

"Where are we going now?" JJ asked.

"Thought we'd ride as far as we could until noon, then eat and turn around and go home."

"Ain't we going down into the canyon?"

"Can't from here," she said, waving her arm westward. "No way to get down for a hundred miles, I reckon. Leastways, none I know of."

"Why'd we come up here, 'stead of going into the canyon down below?"

"Because you can see more up here on top. Down there, it's just like up here. Mesquite and juniper so thick you can't see beyond the tip of your horse's ears. But up here, you can see a heap of country."

Well, that was a fact. Off to the south the canyon made a big swing west, then cut back north so that we came out on a point, stopped and saw a canyon on three sides of us. Way off to the northwest the canyon swept back west again, and it was all purple and smoky there, with distance. For the first time since leaving home, I felt a lump in my throat. I thought of pa's little square field all mowed, where a grasshopper couldn't hide if pa wanted to see it, except for 10 acres of woods where me and pa always cut firewood in the autumn, and the best red oak I split out for ma's cook stove. I closed my eyes and took a deep breath, trying to remember how sweet and juicy that oak smelled when I split it open, and how I'd press my nose against the inside of the tree which I had suddenly exposed, and how cool it felt against my cheeks. For a minute I could smell it, and hear the dry rustle of the leaves that hadn't fallen because of frost yet, and I had to bite hard on my tongue just then. I opened my eyes and turned and stared long and hard at the northwest, where I'd come from, let's see, how long had it been? I'd lost track.

I realized Miss Sally had been talking to me. "What did you say?"

"I said, when we get down to eat, beat out the bushes for snakes. Big rattlers thick as a horse's leg lay in here thick as ticks. They crawl out of the shale rock on the ledge and come back in here to catch mice."

So we got down and ate. We didn't see any snakes, and afterwards we drove back home. I learned from Miss Sally that the way to get into the canyon was to go down by the cornfield on the low side of the river bottom and ride due west. "Takes you straight into the mouth of the canyon," she said. "right where we been looking down on."

I couldn't hardly believe that we had driven all day long, most of it looking down into the canyon where they were supposed to be, and hadn't seen a head of cattle.

While JJ and me unharnessed and curried down the team, Miss Sally went to get supper ready.

"Rowdy," JJ said, "what you so quiet about?" I led Jackrabbit and Lady Midnight toward the creek, with JJ tagging along. The sun had dropped below the horizon in the west and I felt relief from the heat. The whippoorwills began their lonesome call, and down at the river I heard the quail calling one another. I reckon it must have been mates of those I shot the other night.

"JJ, I been pretty cocky about this business of running away from home. I ain't been scared, much. We had us a high old time and made out real good. But I tell you now, we've just about bit off more than we can chew."

JJ ran around in front of me and grabbed my arms and stopped me, his eyes spreading open. "Rowdy, dern you. Don't you scare me."

As if saying it scared him, he got a wild look and I realized how much he has leaned on me. That was reasonable. After all, I had got him through many a scrape. Well, I couldn't let him down now.

"What I'm scared of JJ, is that we can't pull off what we hired out to do. That was to go to work for Miss Sally and catch her cows for her. Did you see that big old country? All that canyon and how many cows did you see?"

"Nary a one, no sir. No wonder Happy Jack was so generous about that bull. And now I know what they all laughed at us for at the Sunday school picnic. They knew a couple of old farm boys couldn't catch the cows out here. Heck, we're just a couple of hicks and don't know it."

"Don't say that, Rowdy. We're cowboys."

"No we ain't, JJ. We're just farm hands. Look at us. What have we been doing? Plowing and planting corn, and digging post holes and stringing wire. Heck, we could of done that back home. And not missed the July fourth picnic."

JJ's face nearly broke then, and goose bumps came on his neck. We didn't talk any while the team watered, and we were plenty sober when we trudged back up the hill. I reckon if Pa had driven up at that moment in his V-8 Ford, I'd have hugged his neck and said, "Hurry up, Pa. Let's get back home quick as we can."

I tell you, that big country with its fierce, deep canyon had spooked me. It just about swallowed me up and I couldn't hardly keep up a conversation at supper. I excused myself as soon as I had my second piece of pie and went to our room and went to bed.

For once, JJ was more lively than I was, and he and Miss Sally stayed in the kitchen swapping stories until I don't know how long, because I went to sleep early, and had nightmares about falling off the top of the canyon and landing on the horns of a black bull.

I guess that's why I got up before daylight the next morning and went down to see about the cornfield. I felt comfortable down there, like it was home. Corn and the smell of fresh earth were familiar to me.

Moochie went with me, and when we got to the spring he let out a growl.

I dropped my hand to his neck and felt his hair bristled up and I knew what was wrong. The old sow and pigs were back.

17

You Lead a Sow by the Tail

This time, rather than let Moochie chase the hogs, I put my hand on his neck and dropped to my knees beside him. A growl died in his throat as I rubbed the bristly hair flat again. "S--hhh, Mooch. Let's slip up," I whispered.

Moochie could always tell, just by the sound of my voice, what I wanted him to do, seemed like. He sank to the ground and crawled a few inches on his belly and whined softly as if to say, "Yeah, but always before you sic'd me on them. Why not now?"

I answered by saying, "Let's sneak up and see what they are doing." That satisfied him and he licked my face with his wet tongue and pranced around me in circles as if to say, "All right, but hurry up."

So I got down on my hands and knees and Moochie crawled on his belly beside me, all the way down the path and around where the spring bubbled out of the ground at the base of the bluff. We crawled through the branch, and when we got on the down side of it, there was the river to cross. I still could not see the sow and pigs, because low like I was, the grass and brush hid them from view. But I could hear them all right.

The old sow kept up a steady, agitated "uhh-uhh-uhh," and every once in a while she'd let out a squeal that meant she was mad. I know, 'cause back home one of my chores was to slop the hogs. If a sow was in a pen and couldn't get out, she'd let out that mad squeal, and right now, I knew as well as if I could see her, what she was doing.

She was rooting around the edge of the corn field, puzzled because she couldn't get through, and her pigs were trailing her, quiet as mice because they didn't know why ma was upset.

I crawled into the creek until the water got up to my neck and then I walked on my knees and finally, I was able to get to my feet and cross the river. Moochie swam beside me and crawled out on the bank where we always crossed, and lapped out his tongue for me to hurry up. I followed him and pushed aside the brush and crawled until I came to the clearing. By this time, it was a gray morning and I could barely see across the corn field.

There, not 50 feet from me, was the sow, her pigs watching, then running up and nuzzling her. One pig decided he would run right through the fence, but he hit it and bounced back and let out a little protest. Old ma whirled around, her angry squeals turning into deep grunts that meant she was concerned about the hurt talk her baby had given.

He nudged her breakfast buttons a couple of times and when she found out he was all right, she stuck her nose under his belly and tossed him away and then tried the fence for herself.

Well, she wouldn't give up, and moved at a slow walk around the fence trying a half dozen times between each post, but no luck, for we had strung up the fence and stretched it tight.

Now this was a game I understood. Many's the time back home pa sent me out to catch an old sow and pigs, or a mule or a bunch of cows that had got out and pestered the neighbors. I learned a long time ago I couldn't out-wrestle them, because they were bigger than me. And I couldn't outrun them, because they are faster than me.

So I figured out quick I could trick them because they were not smarter than me. If they were, I sure would hate to admit it. Lots of times they fooled me the first time or two, but eventually I always got the stock back up. Pa said I beat all he ever saw, except his granddaddy, and that was different because he had been born in a barn and every time he heard a jackass bray he got homesick.

Now, I knew that just because this old sow was going around the fence wasn't any sign she wouldn't eventually get where she wanted to go. She just hadn't ever seen a fence in this spot yet, and didn't know how to handle it. But it wouldn't take her many days to start up her rooter and she'd go under that fence like she'd been greased.

This was as good a time as any, I figured, to catch her. How should I do it? Well, for sure, I couldn't catch her in the brush along the river. I couldn't even see her in that jungle, much less catch her. So it was pretty obvious I had to narrow down her territory, and the only place I could do that was on the inside of where I didn't want her, the cornfield.

"Stay here, Moochie," I whispered, pressing him to the ground. He whined and inched forward but I tapped him on the nose sharply and he dropped his head and covered his nose with his paws and looked hurt. He wasn't hurt, except his feelings maybe.

The old sow was down by the far corner now, and when she rounded it, I could just barely see the top of her back above the corn, which was about a foot high now and growing so fast you could almost hear it crackle. I crawled the ten feet from the brush to the fence, heaved on the wire until I popped the staple from the bottom wire, then pulled it up and hooked the bottom strand on a snag of the fence post. It opened up a hole on either side of the post and I knew the sow would find it as soon as she made her circle of the cornfield.

Hogs aren't spooky like deer, or dogs, or even cows or horses. They'd have known I'd been there by my scent and run away like they were scalded. But I knew that sow wouldn't bother to ask questions. She'd go through that hole like the Lord himself had opened it instead of just me.

I crawled back to the brush. "Come on, Mooch," I said, and he sensed my hurry. I rose to my feet, but bent low, and crossed the river and spring, and when I was out of sight behind the rise at the spring, I stretched my legs long on that trail and in a couple of minutes was pounding on Miss Sally's bedroom door. "Wake up, Sally. You up yet?"

I heard the rustle of corn shucks that filled her bed tick - it was a sorry substitute for the goose down ma used back home, but Miss Sally said a featherbed was too hot for her - and then her feet patted toward the door.

She swung it back and the bulk of her filled the door. She smelled sleepy and her red hair stuck up like bristles. She yawned and said, "Rowdy? Something wrong?"

"Not exactly," I said. "But there's going to be, directly. For that old sow, at least. Will you wake up JJ and get dressed? Don't go out until I get back."

"Why not? Where's that sow? Is she in the cornfield again?"

"No, she ain't yet. But if we are lucky, she will be, in a minute." I headed for the door, getting sort of prickly impatient. If this wasn't just like a grownup. Couldn't take a kid's word for nothing unless they first pried answers out of you.

"Hold on, Rowdy. Why will we be lucky if she's in the corn? That's what we don't want. I ..."

"Hurry and wake up JJ," I said, slamming the outside door and heading for the tool shed. Old Moochie jumped and barked softly and snapped at my heels with his teeth. He'd bear down on a cow or hog with those teeth, but just barely tickle me with them. That was his way of showing me he was feeling good, or was happy.

Well, I was happy too, and feeling a silly laugh bubbling up out of my stomach. That scary, empty feeling I'd had yesterday was gone now. I was back on familiar ground, doing things I knew how to do, well, better'n most anybody, I suppose.

I knew exactly where to go to get what I wanted. When I'd straightened up the junk, I'd driven nails on the rafters of the shed and hung up lots of stuff like buckets and pieces of chain and rope.

It was a bucket I wanted right now, a five-gallon bucket with a handle, and one of the ropes that JJ and I had caught Lady Midnight and Jackrabbit with. That, and a good stout two-by-four board about four feet long, and a couple of feed sacks. I turned the sacks wrong side out and ripped out the threads that made a feed bag out of a rectangular piece of burlap. That was all I needed. I put the sacks in the bucket, looped the rope over my shoulder, picked up the board and ran to the house, my face near splitting with a grin.

JJ was hopping around in the kitchen on one foot, trying to get his overalls on, one eye closed, his hair a tangle of straw, and Miss Sally was buttoning the red, checked, man's shirt she wore. She had her mouth set in a tight line and I figured I had some more explaining to do. Sure enough, she pulled a chair out from the table and reached out one hand and snagged JJ over to her and pulled his shoe out of his overall leg. No wonder he couldn't get his foot through.

"Rowdy," she said, "ain't you got time to explain to ol' Sal what you aim to do?"

"Sure, I said. "I done told you, I aim to catch that sow and pigs."

"How? Just how? I been trying to do that ever since she got out on me."

I held out the bucket, the board and rubbed my chin against the rope. "Got everything I need, right here."

She looked down in the bucket and reached in and pulled out the sacks and dropped them to the floor. She looked down again and didn't see anything else because there wasn't anything else in there except the bottom of the bucket. Then she touched the board and the rope. "Is that all?"

"Yep."

She was still a minute, her eyes boring through mine. "You ain't teasing old Sally?"

"Nope."

Then she started grinning and her fat shook with laughter. She slapped the table with one hand and said, "JJ, this here boy called Rowdy is about the funniest thing I ever saw. How's he expect to catch a 400-pound wild sow and her pigs with a hay rope, a five-gallon bucket and two old pieces of burlap? Can you tell me?"

By now, JJ had his galluses buckled and had pulled on his socks and shoes. He got a cold biscuit off the cabinet, and had it in one hand and a cold chunk of fatback in the other.

"Yes," he said, chomping the biscuit and biting off a piece of fat meat to chew with it.

"Well, how? Don't tell me he's going to rope her? You can't rope a hog. Don't you know that? They'll slip right through the loop. You could about as near rope a snake."

"Nope," JJ said. "He ain't gonna rope her."

"Well, how? Don't tell me he's done this before?"

"Yes, lots of times."

"Uh-huh. And what's the burlap for? To make her a dress after she's caught?"

JJ caught the spirit and lifted a finger and shook it at her. "Just you wait and see. Rowdy and I, we've caught lots of wild hogs, haven't we, Rowdy?"

I couldn't recollect any right at the moment but I didn't have time to think on it. But I didn't want to put JJ down so I said, "Oh sure, lots."

Miss Sally looked at me out of the corner of her eyes in disbelief. She sat straight upright with her feet flat on the floor, her legs apart and the palms of her callused hands braced on her knees like a man. "You boys are putting old Sally on, ain't you? Now what's a five-gallon bucket got to do with catching a hog?"

"You ain't never gonna know if you don't hurry," I said.

Miss Sally got up, shaking her head, a puzzled smile twisting her face. "I declare, you boys." She slapped her thigh, clapped her hat on her head and reached for the shotgun.

"You won't need that," I said. "I got all the tools we need." She put down the gun, a giggle squeezing out of her every once in a while, and she'd whack her thigh and we made our way down to the spring. Moochie bounced along, nipping our heels. I told them what I'd done while we walked. "Now, if the sow has found the hole in the fence," I said, "and if she's inside the field, we're all set."

"You're sure you know what you're doing?" Miss Sally asked.

This was getting a little aggravating so I didn't answer, just stretched my neck when we got to the hill above the spring and could look down on the cornfield. Sure enough, there was the old sow, wading right through the middle of the cornfield, with her brood scattered out around her. They were all so busy eating blades of juicy corn they wouldn't have heard us if we had been shooting cannons at them. So we didn't bother hiding and hurried on across the spring and creek.

I dropped the two-by-four and bucket, pulled the sacks out of the bucket and shook them out. I opened my knife, ripped out little strips on two corners and tossed one to JJ. "Tie that on the top wire," I said.

"What for?"

"Ain't you forgot? You said we'd caught wild hogs lots of times."

"What for?" Miss Sally said.

"For a blind," I said. "When I get ready, you and JJ and Moochie will go into the field and get after the hogs. They'll remember where they got into the field and they'll run right for the hole."

Miss Sally sat down on the bucket, shaking her head, her eyes leaking tears from laughter. "All right Rowdy, if you say so. How are you going to catch them? I can't for the life of me figure it out."

I grinned and tied the other burlap on the fence. "Break off a few tree limbs and stick them in the ground so they won't spook so easy."

So when we had a blind I could hide behind, I said, "All right, I'm ready. Get in there and bring 'em to me. Bring 'em in a hurry. If they have time to slow down, they might see me, the blind or smell me, and they won't come through."

JJ shinnied under the fence and we both held up the wire for Miss Sally and they skirted the field to come in behind the hogs. I surveyed my situation and was satisfied. I could stand straight up behind the blind, with the fence post and brush and burlap hiding me, and I could see the hogs without them seeing me.

Then I heard old Moochie let out a streak of barking and the sow grunted deep and mad. Her pigs squealed and then the sow stopped grunting, and I knew she was headed for the way out.

I picked up my two-by-four board and watched, and here they came. The pigs running ahead not knowing where to go, running back for instructions and getting knocked rolling. Moochie nipped the sows hind legs every step and every once in a while she'd whirl and drive Moochie away. Then she'd lope toward the hole again. JJ was about to catch her, yelling every step, and Miss Sally was so slow she hadn't much more than cleared the backside of the fence, but she was shrieking at the top of her voice and waving her hat in the air.

Well, by that time, I was about to have my hands full. A pig got to the hole but missed it and bounced off his feet. Two more over-shot the hole and got tangled up with the third, and such squealing you never heard. A fourth made the hole but found himself alone, got scared and headed back just as the sow lunged for the hole.

I lifted the two-by-four over my head and just as her snoot came under the wire, I swung.

I knew I had only one swing, but that didn't worry me, because I could always hit a baseball where I wanted on every swing. This was easy. That old sow's head was big as a coal bucket and it made a hollow sound when the board hit it.

I'd learned the trick by watching pa butcher hogs. It was called "stunning." It didn't kill, but knocked an animal senseless, and then pa'd cut the jugular vein. With the heart still beating, the animal's blood pumped out in a hurry and the animal didn't even know it had been hurt, much less killed.

The sow crumpled in her tracks, lost her momentum, and carried her under the fence. Her legs just gave way and she heaved a sigh and rolled over and lay on one side. JJ skinned under the fence. I dropped the board, grabbed the bucket and slapped it over her snout, pulled it up snug-- with the handle on top --"Grab the rope, JJ. Hurry."

JJ grabbed the rope, dropped it, picked it up and said, "Now what? What did you put that bucket over her head for?"

"Ain't you forgot? We caught lots of hogs before. That's what you said."

"You know I was kidding Miss Sally. What do you want me to do? Hurry up. She'll come to, won't she? Or did you kill her?"

"No, she ain't dead. And she'll come to. And she ain't going no where as long as I have the bucket over her head."

By now the pigs had found the hole. They hustled through, squealing fit to kill. They smelled their mother but when they investigated, they found something, namely me, astraddle their dinner bucket and one gave the word to leave. They oink-oink-oinked into the brush and I could hear their voices growing faint.

"They're getting away," JJ yelled.

"Don't worry about them," I said. "They'll be back."

Miss Sally waddled up like a fat duck, sweat streaming down her face. She peered over the fence, her eyes big as dollars. She looked at the sow, looked at me, clapped her hat on her head and disappeared behind the blind. She appeared again under the fence, and she crawled on her hands and knees beside me and said, "Rowdy, I'll be ding-busted. You did it, didn't you?"

"Yep," I said. "Wasn't nothing to it."

Well, I showed them how to loop the rope around the sow's body behind her forelegs. I drew it up tight, then tied the handle of the bucket to it and got up. By this time, the sow had come around. She was breathing all right and was grunting in a puzzled way. She didn't know what to make about it getting dark all of a sudden.

Suddenly she heaved to her feet.

"Look out," screamed Miss Sally. "She's getting away."

"No she ain't. Just watch," I said.

Just like I knew she would, the sow stood still as a mouse. Her flanks trembled slightly and she slung her head from side to side, trying to get the bucket off her head, but she couldn't do it.

"Well," I said, "I guess we are ready."

"For what?" Miss Sally said.

"To take her to the pen."

"How?"

"Well, you're going to walk and we are going to lead her."

Miss Sally let out a snort of disgust. "Lead her! You ain't about to lead her. She is too stubborn to lead and too strong to drag."

"You watch me," I said. "JJ, come around here in front. Put both hands on the bucket and push backwards."

JJ looked puzzled but kept his mouth shut. He didn't know what was going on, but didn't dare say anything for fear Miss Sally'd catch on he had lied to her.

I took my sweet time about walking around behind the sow. I got to admit, I liked this business of being in charge of something and seeing it come off right.

I grabbed the sow's tail, tugged on it and said, "Push on the bucket, JJ."

Well, what I knew that JJ and Miss Sally didn't was that if you put a bucket over a hog's head, they will walk backwards anywhere, and you can guide them by the tail just like you can steer a car. Miss Sally followed as I guided the sow backward to the barn, alternately laughing, slapping her thighs and shaking her head in wonder. "I can't believe it," she said over and over. "Never saw the beat of it in my life."

Well, it wasn't any trick at all, and fifteen minutes later I slammed the gate on that old trouble marker and wired the gate shut. I untied the bucket and the old sow was so beat she didn't even fight to get out. She went to the shady side of the pen, rooted out a hole and flopped down with a grunt of disgust. She was a brown sow, weighing about 400 pounds suckled down and with a long snout bruised up from rooting in the dirt and rocks for food. I hadn't even broken the skin when I hit her.

"Well," Miss Sally said, "we got the sow, but we lost the pigs."

"No we ain't," I said. "You just wait and see. When we get away and stay real quiet, and the sow gets milk built up in her udder, she'll start calling her pigs. They are laying down there in that brush right now, quiet as mice and twice as scared. They are waiting for word from ma, and when they get it, they'll hump it up here to her."

I kicked a board loose on the bottom of the pen. "Next time you see the pigs, they'll be in there suckling their mother."

We returned to the house for breakfast. I guess I strutted a little and acted pretty cocky, and JJ hovered close to me and couldn't quit grinning and every once in a while he'd say, "Boy, we did it, Rowdy, didn't we?" And Miss Sally would grin that toothy smile and pat me on the cheek and get right down in my face and say, "Rowdy, you do beat all."

"If you can just catch cows as good as you can catch hogs. I declare, never dreamt it could be done."

It was a fact that I felt sick in my stomach when we got back to the house from the trip to look at the canyon and I was about ready to give up my idea of being a cowboy. But catching the sow so keen returned my self confidence. I began to get an idea.

18

Tradin'

"Miss Sally," I said. "I need a horse if we are going to have any luck catching cows, we sure enough got to have two good cow ponies. We got one in Lady Midnight but it's precious few cows I can catch riding a burro."

Breakfast was over and I was stuffed with pancakes and bacon. Miss Sally sat down beside me with a cup of coffee and her face sobered. "I know it, Rowdy. But I was counting on you to come up with something. I got barely enough money to pay my taxes when they are due. All I got to live on is $565 a year that I draw for sale of a house and lot in Salt River. Daddy sold it on time before he died. When it is paid out, I won't have anything to live on unless you can catch my cows again and mend my fences so I can raise calves.

"Of course, it don't take me much to live on. I raise lots of my own food and can wild berries and stuff. But it does take some cash. For salt and sugar and coffee, plus a new pair of overalls and a shirt once a year. I ain't had a store-bought dress in over five years.

"The ones I wear to church I make out of chicken feed sacks. They come in flowered prints and are right pretty. But they ain't nothing like having a real dress right out of Sears and Roebuck's catalog. Who knows, if I had me a nice catalog-bought dress, I might catch me a man."

She dropped her chin and it made me a wish I hadn't brought up the subject.

But I felt so sorry that it sure made up my mind that I wasn't going to leave Texas unless I caught her cows. And I figured I could do it, with an idea I had in my head.

I patted her on the shoulder, light like, and felt sort of embarrassed. "Well, don't worry about money," I said. "I've got five dollars." I dug down in my watch pocket and pulled out the money I hadn't touched since I left home and put it in her hand. She looked startled and then smiled and pinched my cheeks.

"You and JJ are the best boys I ever saw. I can't take your money." She put it back in my hand and I laid it on the table.

"Well, if you will just give me permission, I'll make a swap. I'll swap that old sow and part of her pigs for a good horse, if I can find one."

"Why, sure you can, Rowdy. If you think you can, why go right ahead. But I don't know how. That sow and pigs ain't worth the half of a good saddle horse."

I'd figured that, all right, but it didn't bother me. All I needed was something to start bargaining with. I'd seen pa do this plenty of times back home. "You just say it is all right," I said. "And give me some time off. I'll make a trade, all right."

I figured I'd done my share of work for the day, so I told Miss Sally if it was all right, I'd go to town and sniff out a trade.

For once, JJ didn't argue with me. He was still so in awe of me for catching the sow and penning her he didn't argue when I said he had to stay, repair the fence and irrigate the corn. Miss Sally allowed as how I was man enough to be trusted in town alone, just so long as I promised not to get into a fight.

I harnessed Lady Midnight and Jackrabbit, hitched them to the wagon and set out for Salt River. The morning coolness was being pushed aside as the sun scooted higher, and big fleecy clouds loafed long overhead, seeming to watch me roll down the road surrounded by dust. Now and then up jumped a meadowlark and once a bobcat dashed across the road in front of me, followed by two kittens. I didn't stop to watch. I didn't want a mad mother bobcat in the wagon with me, no sir.

The clouds especially fascinated me, for they were drifting northeast, in the direction of home, it must have been 500 miles away, and I wondered if I'd ever see it again. Times like this, I got a big lump in my throat and visions of pa just now gathered around the breakfast table in the kitchen with his head bowed and asking the blessing - these visions passed through my mind like dreams. I could see pa taking those long strides from the house to the barn, leaning back on the reins when he drove the gray Percherons from their stable to the water tank where they sucked up the water with great noises, and I could see him standing in the bouncing wagon headed for the wheat field with hired hands dangling their feet from the sides of the wagon, probably cussing under their breath because they had to stack wheat instead of being off in the woods hunting squirrels.

And I wondered if the folks back home ever had things like this go through their heads about me. Likely not, I supposed. They'd probably forgot all about me by now. I watched the clouds and wondered if when they got to Missouri, they'd rain and get pa's corn wet. It'd need it about now, being head high and the tassels growing out the tops of the stalks like little flags. They had to come out before the ears could form. I'd helped pa plant that corn, stayed out of school two days in May to do it, and had to make up a history test. It made me shudder to think about it. But school now? Heck, I was free. No more being cooped up in a school house now. School houses reminded me of the inside of a jail.

It took about two hours to ride to Salt River. I didn't know how it was in Texas, but in Missouri, if you wanted to strike a trade, you started by going to town and hanging around the feed store or mill and listening to the gossip. I clucked Lady Midnight into a little faster pace so she'd look sharp and rode into the north end of town, past the shacks on the outskirts, past the neat painted frame houses next to them, past the garage and filling station, past Dutchy's butcher shop and stopped at the crossroads.

Keeper's General Store sat on one corner, across from the Salt River County Bank and Post Office, and if I'd rode past here I'd have been riding out of town, past the blacksmith shop "under the spreading mesquite tree," I said to myself, and then past the saddle shop and a bunch more houses and shacks. At the south edge I could see a dairy farm, with a bunch of Jersey cows being driven up from the creek bottoms to be milked.

The screen door banged at the store and old man Kepper stomped out with a broom in his hands. He made no mind to me as I pulled up to the hitch rail and tied up.

"Howdy, Mr. Keeper. Remember me?"

He didn't look up from his fog of dust, just grunted, but that didn't bother me too much. Lots of old folks ain't got time to mess with young ones. I stepped up on the porch, tripping on a loose board, and sat on a nail keg. Every store porch in the world, I guess, had a couple of nail kegs on it for seats, plus a battered chair or two held together with baling wire, and a bench made out of a plank nailed to a couple sticks of wood. They were usually occupied by loafers. This store porch was no different, except the loafers were still loafing in bed.

It was still early. I'd got up about 3:30 and it hadn't taken over an hour to catch the sow. Another hour to eat and talk and about two hours to ride to town, so I judged it to be around 7:30. I reckoned that was why Mr. Keeper was so grouchy.

"Ain't seen you for a spell, Mr. Keeper." I said it as kind as I could.

He thumped the broom on the porch and looked sharp at me over the rim of his wire-edged glasses. He had an old flour sack tied around his waist for an apron and he wore faded khaki britches and a shirt buttoned at the collar. His skinny neck stuck out from the collar like a buzzard's, all wrinkled and red, and his pink skull showed through his gray hair. "Humpf," he said, thumping the porch with the broom. "Humpf. Reckon not since you had a fit at the church basket dinner. Humpf."

He took his skinny frame to the door, caught his toe on the loose board and almost fell. He thumped the broom again, like a jackrabbit thumps his hind legs when he's in love, and said, "Confound it," and stormed into the store.

He slammed the screen door unnecessarily hard and the screws fell out of the top hinge. The door flew cockeyed.

Mr. Keeper turned around and glared at me like it was my fault and I said quickly, "I didn't do it," and bit my lip for saying it.

"Humpf," he said, and disappeared behind the counter.

Well, Mr. Keeper hadn't changed none since the day JJ and I got to Salt River. He sure enjoyed being grumpy. I got up and felt the door facing with my fingers. The wood was solid enough, but it hadn't rained for so long the wood was dry and had shrunk away from the screws.

I had a mind to fix it, thinking Mr. Keeper might be more friendly, so I pulled out my five-bladed Barlow, whittled several slivers of wood off a floor plank and stuck them into the screw holes. I pulled the door into place, replaced the screws and tightened them up and popped the door a time or two. Old man Keeper dashed to the door to see what was going on and said, "What you doing, boy?"

"Fixed your door," I said.

"How'd you do it?"

"Filled up the holes with splinters. That made the screws tighten up."

He slammed the door a time or two and satisfied himself it would hold, then said, "Humpf," and returned to the store, but not so mad like. I reckoned I'd made a point and when he called out, "There's a bottle of lemon sody in the cooler, boy."

The store smelled like spicy lunch meat, raisins, dust and kerosene all at once. The pop cooler was just inside the door and I said, "Thanks, Mr. Keeper," and pulled the cap off and sucked out the cold pop. I walked down the long counter to where Mr. Keeper sat at a ledger book figuring. "I'd buy a couple of crackers and slice of bologna," I said.

"Don't bother me." He waved a hand without getting up. "Butcher knife's back of the meat counter. Crackers in a barrel. Three cents a slice for meat and penny for crackers. Don't bother me."

I whacked off what I figured was three cents worth of lunch meat, got a couple of big old soda crackers and leaned against the counter, hearing Mr. Keeper's pen scratching against the paper like a cat trying to get out of a rain barrel. Outside somewhere, an old car chugged into town and stopped by the butcher shop and I saw a team pulling an empty wagon past the door, guided by a bent-over old man in overalls and a straw hat, puffing on a pipe and sitting on the seat guiding the horses. He drove around back where Mr. Keeper loaded out feed.

"Looks like you got a customer," I said.

"Humpf," he said, slamming the ledger book shut. I caught him looking over the rim of his glasses at me. "You want to make yourself useful as well as ornamental?"

"Reckon so. Why?"

"Then quit feeding your face long enough to load old man Founder's wagon with whatever he wants. And hurry up about it."

Mr. Keeper had a funny way of being friendly, but I didn't mind, so long as he let me hang around the store so I could learn who had what to trade.

I swigged the last of my soda pop, crammed the last bite of lunch meat in my mouth and went into the feed room and met the little old man in the overalls, still puffing his pipe.

"Howdy," I said, friendly as a pup. "Mr. Keeper said for me to wait on you. What do you need?"

"Howdy yourself, young feller. You're the boy from Missouri, ain't you? The one that broke up the church social with a dog fight? Thought I recognized you. Give me a bag of shelled corn, one hundred pounds of egg mash and a bag of shorts for my hogs. And mind you, don't tear the bags. My old lady wants the egg mash in the purple bags with the little flowers in them. She's making pantry curtains. Right purty, too."

"Yes sir," I said, watching him shuffle into the store.

He'd parked his wagon sideways to the dock so it wasn't any trick at all to load him. After that I got down to inspect his team. One was a Percheron mare with a bog spavin and the other an old saddle pony with the fistula. Their bones stuck out of their hide at the hips and shoulders and they sure were a sorry pair to look at. But I figured a fellow had to start trading somewhere, and this might be the place.

I went back to the store and found it getting crowded now, with three women I'd seen at the church social in the front turning bolts of dry goods over so the sun would shine on it, and chattering like hens in a corn bin. Mr. Keeper was bent over a ticket book with Mr. Overalls giving him an order for salt, bacon and such, and old Dutchy himself was leaning on the meat counter, writing out a ticket for meat he'd delivered.

"Hey, boy," Dutchy called. "How come you ain't down at Salt River Sally's catching wild cows? Got any caught yet?"

I felt like I'd found an old friend. "Nope. Ain't caught one yet. But I been looking over the lay of the land. Caught something else, though."

"You have? What?" His interest lighted up his eyes like he could smell a profit somewhere.

"Well, Miss Sally had an old sow get out on her a year or so ago. Wouldn't doubt but what she's a purebred Duroc. She got bred, I reckon to a wild boar out there in the brush, and she brought in a litter of pigs. Well, Miss Sally couldn't pen her. But I did. Got her this morning."

Dutchy thumped me in the chest with his pony knuckles.

"Hey, you ain't kidding? Got her in the pen, huh? I recollect that sow. She ain't purebred, but she's got a good way of raising pigs. How many pigs she got?"

"Ain't sure. Eight, nine, I guess."

He looked suspicious and drew back. "I thought you had them penned."

"Not the pigs, yet. Just the sow. Got her at daylight this morning."

He looked relieved. "Oh, well. The pigs'll come to her. Sally going to sell the pigs?"

"Of course not. Leastways, not till she fattens them out. I got corn knee high and water for it. We'll just rough them old pigs through until we got ear corn to feed them."

Dutchy's narrow eyes drew shrewd and his voice lowered. "I'll give you $3 apiece for them pigs. Plus $12 for the sow."

Well, I felt my heart leap. I'd heard many a trade start like this, and old Dutchy wasn't even being cute about it. I guess he figured me for a sucker.

"No, I guess not," I said. I walked to the counter and got out the bologna. "Them pigs are half grown already. Reckon we'll just keep them until they are worth $30 or so." I whacked off another slice of bologna and walked to the cracker barrel.

Nervous tension prickled the back of my neck and I hoped it wouldn't show. Dutchy followed me, which was exactly what I hoped he would do. I put four cents down on the counter, walked out the front door and sat down on the nail keg, Dutchy right behind me.

There was all sorts of activity in Salt River now. A pickup truck was parked at the filling station and a flivver limped in on a flat tire. Three teams and wagons moved toward town from the south road, bringing acres of dust with them. Chickens scratched in the shade by the blacksmith shop and at Dutchy's Butcher shop an old cow sent out a call for help.

"Sure is good bologna, Dutchy. You make it?"

"Nope. Comes from Fort Worth. I don't deliver nothing but fresh meat. Now about them pigs. I reckon I might go $5 each, sight unseen, mind you. That is, if Miss Sally'd sell them."

"Oh, she'd sell them, all right. If I told her to. I've got her power of attorney." I didn't know exactly what that meant, but I'd heard pa use it in an important tone, and I reckoned it fit the situation. "But I ain't about to sell."

Old Dutchy's mouth puckered up and he sat down, sighing. I figured I'd scared him off and I thought maybe I'd best soften him up some. I said, "I might make a trade."

He turned his head sideways and a hard, knowing light came into his eyes. He made a crooked grin and said, "Ain't you the sly one, though," he said. "Been playing cat and mouse with me." He let out a cackle. "Well, you want to trade, old Dutchy will trade. Let's get down to business. What do you want that I have?"

"I don't know if you have it," I said. "I want a saddle horse."

Dutchy pulled up a nail keg and sat facing me. "Son, you know better than that. A good saddle horse is worth $150. Your hogs, or Sally's hogs, ain't worth over $50 or $55. Of course, if you want to pay some boot..."

"Don't intend to give no boot," I said.

He laid a finger on his chin and looked at me steadily. "You know what a good mule is worth?" he ask.

"I reckon back home, about $250."

"Close enough. How would you like to trade for a top five-year-old mule?"

I reckon I'd like that. But if I can't trade for a $150 saddle horse, how can I trade for a $250 mule?"

"Easy," Dutchy said. "I've got the mule."

"But..."

He patted my knee and leaned over so his chin was almost touching my chest. The old biddies banged the screen door and came out, each clutching a few yards of cloth to her breast. Dutchy never missed a lick. "Listen, you bring me that sow and pigs and I'll let you have a top mule for $250. I'll trust you on credit for the first cows you bring me. I'll allow you $50 for each cow that dresses out over 400 pounds of meat. Then you take your mule over to old Ollie and he'll trade you a good saddle horse and likely you can draw some boot. Now, how does that strike you?"

I had to chase that around in my mind some, he'd given it to me so fast. But it sounded all right from the outside. I didn't care much for going into debt, but it wasn't debt so much as it was a trade. After all, Dutchy had made the proposition.

"Where's the mule?"

"Over in my pens. Come on."

We kicked through the dusty street, being filled now with farmers and ranchers, some headed for the blacksmith shop with pieces of broken cultivators or broken mowing machines, and the ranchers to the saddle shop with saddles that'd had horns ripped out or the girths busted.

Dutchy's butcher shop was a square frame building that didn't look too sturdy, and at the back he had pens covering a couple of acres. Gates open with a runway that ran the full length of pens, and a windlass with a cable on the drum was bolted to the back of the butcher shop.

"What the devil do you do with that windlass?" I asked.

"Oh, that? I stun my cattle out here in the alley, or else shoot them if they are too wild to get close to. Then I hook that cable on and drag them up to my meat hooks." He pointed overhead to a track that had the hooks hanging from it. "I hoist them up and take them inside to skin and cut up the meat. But never mind that. You want to see that prime mule, or talk?"

We went down the alley, past the cow that looked through the plank fence and had bawled so long and hard she was hoarse, and came to the last pen.

A bay mule stood at the hay manger, chomping and looking sleepy. I went in and walked around him, watching sharp for him to kick, but he only lifted one ear and opened an eye. I patted his neck and he didn't object when I peeled back his lips and looked at his big yellow teeth. Truth is, I didn't have any idea how to tell a mule or a horse's age by his teeth, but I'd seen pa do it, and then look wise and distrustful and so I tried to do the same.

"What else is wrong with him?" I said.

"What else? What do you mean, what else?"

"That mule was born at least 20 years ago," I said. "And he ain't overburdened with fat."

"He ain't a day over eight," Dutchy said, spitting and avoiding my eyes. "Get too much fat on him and he'll get lazy."

"Give you the sow, six pigs and bring you two cows before the week's up," I said.

"I guess you would," Dutchy said. "Three cows and all the pigs."

"Three cows and seven pigs," I agreed. "Providing you throw in an old set of harness."

"Done," Dutchy grinned, reaching out and shaking my hand. "You are a right good trader." Well, my heart leaped. Here it was, not even noon yet, and I'd got myself a piece of mule-flesh. Now all I had to do was trade my mule for a good saddle horse and draw some boot. I didn't figure on Dutchy being so easy to beat in a trade.

19

A Mule Called Houdini

Now I had something else in mind, and so I excused myself and hurried back to the store. A big old touring car had pulled up in front of the store, and the loafers had gathered; a black man was kept in perpetual glees by the jokes of a man with an Abe Lincoln face and body, another fellow was there, with hog-jowls for jaws and a horseshoe of white hair about his ears, and a fourth who must have been the town idiot because he smiled at everything and talked to the chickens that scratched for bugs beside the porch. I felt pretty important and strutted a little going up the steps, said "Howdy, men," and went into the store.

You could have knocked me down with a gnat's eyelash.

Who was standing there but little Alice Pigtails, a red all-day sucker in her mouth and a bag of cookies in her hand.

"Hi," she said, pert as a possum in a grapevine.

I tried to say "Hi" too, but my voice caught in my throat, like it hadn't done for nearly a year now, and all I got out was a squeak. I couldn't force my legs to take me beyond her.

"I saw you at church," she said.

I nodded and managed, "Yeah."

"You sure looked funny with your legs wrapped around Toby, hitting him. I was scared, though. Were you?"

"Uh, no, reckon not."

"I was. You know what was funny? When you dragged old Moosehead out from under the wagon and he started to bite you. Didn't you think that was funny?"

"Not exactly."

"I don't mean funny ha-ha. I mean funny-odd. Sort of scary. Here, want a cookie?"

She held out the sack, but I shook my head and talked my legs into going again. I don't know what was wrong with me. I'd sure enough wanted to talk to her. Now here she was, and I was plumb breathless and weak as if I had pneumonia fever. I got the soda pop cooler between us and felt lots better, and said, "'Cuse me," and turned and walked quick as I could to the back of the store where I saw Mr. Overalls figuring up with Mr. Keeper. Alice Pigtails followed me and I felt the back of my neck hot as a flat iron on ma's cook stove.

I said to Mr. Overalls, that wasn't his real name, his real name was Founder, but I'd always had the habit of giving everything names that seemed to fit them. I said, "Excuse me. Can I talk to you a minute?"

But before he could answer, the feed room door flew open and Ollie Oliver stomped through, a cigar belching smoke like a freight train engine. His black cowboy hat topped him off and below his fleshy face his thick neck threatened to pop the button off this shirt. His belly swung out over his blue jeans and then he began to taper down into his shiny, high-heeled boots.

"Balls of fire," he said. "If it ain't the Missouri kid, catcher of the wild bulls and cows. Why ain't you helping Sally this morning? Ain't got all them wild critters caught and tamed have you, Kid?"

He grinned at his jokes, which I didn't think had too much humor. "I ain't had time to catch cows yet," I said. "Been busy fixing fence and planting corn."

"You don't say so, fixing fence? And planting corn? Expect to raise a big crop, do you?"

"Middling, I expect. Enough to feed out a few pigs for winter meat and to keep a few cows going for Miss Sally."

Mr. Overalls grabbed me by the galluses and said, "Young feller, what you want of me? I got to get back to the country."

"Excuse me, Mr. Oliver," I said. "I got to talk to Mr. Founder."

"That's right, Founder. Merle E. Founder. Thankyee for loading my feed. What you want?"

I said, "That team of your's. I noticed you've got one Percheron work horse, and one saddle horse. How would you like to swap that saddle horse for a mule. I don't care if she has got the fistula. I can cure that, once I get her out of the work collar."

Mr. Oliver said, "There's a trade for you, Merle E. See what the boy's got."

Merle E. Founder pulled his head down like a terrapin going into a shell and I knew that was his trading stance. "You got a mule?" he said, cautiously.

That's right," I said, beginning to feel confident and nearly forgetting about Alice Pigtails standing right behind me. "I've got a big bay mule with a blazed face, 15 hands high and not a day over five."

I thought Merle E. Founder's face was going to disappear behind the bib of his overalls and he licked his lips liked I'd said ham and gravy. "How long you owned this mule, young feller?"

"About 10 minutes," I said. "Swapped Dutchy out of him."

Merle E. Founder's face came up out of his overalls and his scrawny neck followed and he lost his hungry look. He looked at Ollie Oliver and grinned. Mr. Oliver puffed furiously on his cigar, took it out of his mouth and rumbled, "Why, Merle E., that boy's the sharpest trader ever I saw. He's done swapped Dutchy out of Houdini."

"Houdini?" I said, getting a sinking sensation. "You mean that's the name of my mule?"

"That's right. You know why folks in Salt River calls him Houdini? Because he won't stay tied, that's why."

He stuck the cigar back into his mouth, his eyes glistening, and then Merle E. Founder let out a whoop and yelled, "If that's the way they trade in Missouri, I'm going there and get'n rich."

I felt like a black cloud was hanging over me, raining, and I turned around to see if Alice Pigtails had heard all this. She was right there, her face stone-cold sober and her eyes big as butterfly wings. Mr. Keeper peered at me over his glasses and showed his false teeth and said, "I swear, son. Did you let Dutchy pan Houdini off on you?"

"Well, he is a strong mule and ain't a day over five," I said. "I didn't see him tied up so I didn't know he wouldn't stand tied."

Ollie bit on the cigar and said, "Well, son, if you catch wild bulls like you trade mules, I don't reckon there's much chance you collecting my $100 bill. Sorry about that. But tell you what I'm gonna do. If you can break Houdini to stand tied, bring him over to my ranch. I'll trade you a good cow pony and give you some boot. How does that strike you?"

Well, he at least offered me a chance to keep from looking so foolish. "Would you sign a paper to that effect?" I said. He held his cigar away from him and made Merle E. Founder sneeze with it. "Why certainly," he said.

"Mr. Keeper, would you write out a contract?" Mr. Keeper grinned and pulled a cigar box out from under the counter, got out a tablet and said, "What do you want me to say?"

"Just say Mr. Oliver, that if I can break Houdini to stand tied, I can have the pick of his saddle stock."

"Hold on, Missouri Kid. I didn't say the pick."

Merle E. Founder, sneezing, said, "Heck, Ollie, you might's well have. People been trying to break Houdini to stand tied for 12 years. Or is it 15?"

Cigar smoke fogged out. "Yeah, yeah, you're right, Merle E. All right, Keeper, write it that way, I'm a sport. Write that. I'll give the Missouri Kid here his pick of my saddle stock, providing he makes Houdini stand tied to a hitch rail with a binder twine."

"Don't forget the boot," I said.

"Not if you get the pick."

"What kind of traders are you Texans? You trying to back out?"

His eyes got black and the veins stood out on his neck and he bit the cigar. "All right, Keeper. Make it $25 boot. Come on, Olivia, let's go home," He started for the door, making the floor shake with his long steps. Then he stopped and said, "Olivia, the Missouri Kid here wanted to meet you at church last Sunday. But before he got around to it, seems somebody hissed Moosehead onto his dog and he got real busy. Time it was over, he'd plumb forgot about you, I reckon. Missouri Kid, this here's my gal, Olivia. Olivia, meet the Missouri Kid, a mule-trading fool." He let that bull beller out of his belly again.

"Hi," she said again.

"Hi," I said.

"What's your real name?"

Frank McLin Farmer," I said. "Just call me Rowdy."

"Howdy, Rowdy." She giggled, with her hand over her mouth. She held out the cookie sack. "Want a cookie?"

"What kind are they?"

"Chocolate with marshmallow inside."

I took one, and she insisted I take another, and then she and her pa left, ripping up a tornado of dust as they left town by the south road. I went over to Dutchy's and made a deal to take Houdini back to the ranch and agreed to bring the sow and pigs in next day. I bought 100 pounds of shorts and 100 pounds of corn, promised Mr. Keeper I'd pay for it when we caught some cows or butchered the fat hogs, or else bring in some cured hams, and then headed for Miss Sally's. I carried a chunk of bologna and a bunch of crackers to keep my insides company, and a bottle of strawberry soda pop to wash it down.

I put Houdini next to Lady Midnight and tied Jackrabbit to the tailgate. Houdini didn't flicker a hair when I put him in the traces and he seemed glad enough to get out of the pen that he let out a derisive "Hee-haw, hee-haw," just as we left town.

And that's what he did when we drove up to Miss Sally's and it brought Miss Sally and JJ running up from the corn field, which was the only green thing in the country that I had seen so far. Everything else was brown or yellow with the summer heat, and I began to wonder if it ever rained here.

I climbed out of the wagon, unloaded the feed at the shed and was feeding the old sow some shelled corn by the time JJ panted up.

"What'cha got, Rowdy?" His face shined and he fairly danced as he ran around Houdini.

"Oh, I done a little swapping, I reckon," I said.

"Rowdy, where'd you get the mule?" Miss Sally asked, sharp as nails.

My heart hammered at her tone, for I'd heard ma use it, and I said, "I want you to look at that old sow go for that corn."

"Rowdy," she demanded.

"Yes, ma'am?"

"Answer my question."

"Oh, where did I get the mule? Why, I swapped Dutchy out of him. Why?"

"That's old Houdini."

"Yes ma'am. That's what they called him, all right."

"Why?" JJ said.

"Why? Why?" Miss Sally shouted. "That's old Houdini, that's why. He's spoiled. He ain't worth powder it'd take to blow his brains out."

"He's not?" I asked. "Why, he seemed like a right fair critter to me, for a mule. He kept his side of the doubletrees ahead of Lady Midnight's all the way home, and besides that, he was downright friendly to her. I don't see nothing wrong with Houdini."

I held out the palm of my hand with a few grains of corn in it and Houdini put his velvet lips against my hand. It tickled when he picked up the corn and he nudged me for more.

"Rowdy, you didn't buy Houdini, did you?"

"Well yes, and no."

"Yes and no what?"

"I didn't exactly buy him. I swapped for him."

"What did you swap?" Her tone was the same she'd used to make Toby and Polecat slink away form the church social.

"Well, the sow, for one thing."

"What else?"

"Seven pigs?"

"Is that all?"

"And two cows."

She sank down on a sack of feed and put her chin in her hands. "Well, if it's done, it's done."

JJ quit scratching Houdini's ears and said, "What's wrong, Miss Sally?"

"I'm afraid Rowdy didn't get a good trade," she said. "Houdini is the worst hated critter around here. He won't stand tied, that is what."

"What's wrong with that?"

I answered for her. "What's wrong is, a horse or mule that won't stand tied is worthless. You can't go off and leave them hitched to a wagon or they'll run away and wreck it. You can't ride them and leave them while you fix fence or milk a cow, because they will break the reins and leave you a-foot. That's what's wrong."

"Heck, I'd fix that," JJ said.

"How?" Miss Sally asked.

"Tie him with a chain to the barn. He couldn't pull the barn down."

"Ain't that simple, honey pot," Sally said. "Critter that won't stand tied will fight a rope until he breaks his neck and if he can't do that, he'll start kicking and kick anything that comes near to the next county. I'm sorry, but it looks like Rowdy's been took. And after such a glorious start for the day. Oh, well, it could be worse. At lease we'll have two or three pigs left over."

I tell you, I wanted to dig a hole, crawl in and pull it in behind me. But the sun was still in the sky, the trees hadn't withered and I was still Rowdy Farmer. I hadn't never run up against anything I couldn't lick, and I wasn't about to stop now. "I don't see anything to be so down in the mouth about," I said.

"You don't?" Miss Sally said, a little hope in her voice.

"Heck, no. I've seen my pa break lots of mules to stand tied."

"How? I ain't never seen it done."

"That's reasonable. Texas ain't mule country. Didn't you ever hear of the Missouri mule?"

"Of course. So's everybody else."

"Well, we know all there is to know about mules, and then some. You wait. I'll have old Houdini standing tied in no time. But I didn't tell you all of the deal. I ran into Mr. Oliver and he signed a contract with me that when I get Houdini broke, he'd give me the pick of his saddle stock for him, and some boot. Plus, he signed an agreement…" and then I shut up. I just remembered Miss Sally have given me what for about that black bull.

"Plus what, Rowdy? Don't you hold out on me."

"Plus a saddle and bridle," I lied. I sure didn't want to get into it with her over the bull, but I sure intended to try and collect that $100.

Well, JJ and I spent the rest of the afternoon fixing a top on Miss Sally's wagon so we could haul in the sow and pigs to Dutchy. JJ fussed and worried all afternoon because there wasn't any sign of the pigs, but it didn't bother me none. I heard the old sow grunt softly every once in a while and she stood all afternoon with her ears lifted and looking down toward the creek. I knew she could either hear or smell her babies, and as soon as dark came and we got out of sight, she would grunt them out of the brush and when they found the board I'd kicked loose and entered the pens she would stretch out on the warm earth and the pigs would line up at the dinner table and they'd all be happy again. The pigs wouldn't leave the sow and I could mend the pen again, come morning.

And that's exactly as it happened. By 6 a.m. the next morning, I'd loaded the sow and seven pigs in the wagon and was headed for Salt River. There had been nine pigs in all, so I left two behind, squealing and calling for their ma. She was upset too, but after rooting and shoving, she saw she couldn't get out of the wagon and laid down and let the pigs nurse. They were more scared than hungry, though, and nursing made them feel safer. The two pigs I'd left behind were plenty big to wean, and I had feed to help make them forget ma's milk. I also had a hammer and some nails so I could mend the wagon bed if the sow tore it up too bad.

All the way into Salt River, I thought hard as I could how I could break Houdini. He worked fine in the harness, and I didn't have a minute's trouble with him. I hadn't tried to tie him up, though, for I was afraid to. I'd figured how I would do when I got to Dutchy's. I'd just back the wagon into the alley of the pen, let down the tail gate and be gone without ever having to tie up Houdini.

Salt River was as deserted this morning as it was yesterday, but I figured there would be as much going on later as there was yesterday. A grease monkey at the filling station on the north side of town rolled out from under a car on his little cart, sat up and waved. I saw his teeth as he grinned and he yelled, "Hey, Missouri Kid. How you and old Houdini getting along?"

I acted like I didn't hear him, just drove on to Dutchy's and got down to open the gate. I sawed the reins until Lady and Houdini backed the wagon where I wanted it, then shut the gate so Houdini didn't have a chance to run away, and I didn't have to tie him. I pounded on Dutchy's back door, tried the latch but it was locked. I figured he wasn't up yet. I heard the screen door at Mr. Keeper's store slam and out came Mr. Keeper in his apron, sweeping up a storm.

I got the hammer and nails out of the wagon and went over. "Morning, Mr. Keeper," I said.

He looked down over his glasses. "Humpf," he said.

I'd got used to his grumpiness by now, figuring he hated to have to get up so early and sweep the store out. "Mind if I do something for you?"

He didn't pause. "What?" he said.

I sat down beside the loose board on the porch. "Figured while I waited for Dutchy I'd nail down your store porch boards. Somebody's apt to get hurt."

He puckered his lips. "What you up to?" All the time trying to do something for me."

"Well, no harm, is there?"

"Go on. Only don't blame me if you bust your finger."

So I nailed down the boards that were loose and got me a chunk of minced ham and some cheese and a bottle of root beer and went back to the store porch to wait for Dutchy. Mr. Keeper finally came out and sat down a minute and tried to be friendly in his funny way.

"Where's your partner? He scared to come to town?"

"Nope. He's busy."

"You the lazy one? Make him do all the work?"

That nettled me some, but I didn't let on. "Do I act lazy?" Come here before anybody except you is up of mornings. And fixing your screen door and porch."

He grunted. "Figured you'd throw that up to me. Well, I guess you ain't lazy, leastways. How you and Houdini getting alone? Busted any check reins yet?"

"He's a good work mule. Ain't tied him up any, yet."

"Well, then. Don't."

Like yesterday, Salt River came alive sleepy like, like an old hen clucking on the roost, when you went out with a lantern to see if any possums were trying to eat them or suck eggs.

First the saddler walked down the middle of the street and opened up, then the blacksmith. Out in the back of several houses, I could see several women hoeing their gardens or carrying water to soak their dry earth.

"I can break Houdini to stand tied," I said. "Got me an idea."

"Humpf," said Mr. Keeper, getting up abruptly and going into the store.

20

Booger Joe

I sipped my root beer slowly, making it last as long as possible and wished Dutchy would hurry and get to work. My eye caught a speck of a thing moving way out on the road leading to town from the west, the direction of the canyon. When I left town, it was by the north road and then turned back west after a couple of miles. I watched this speck grow bigger until it got to be two horses and one rider. Something about the slow, steady pace made me keep my eye on the rider. Maybe it was the deliberate, steady pace, maybe it was the outline of the man, but by the time he hit the west end of town it was plain to see he was a real cowboy. An old man cowboy.

He wore a grease-stained hat pulled low over his eyes and his face was wrinkled and gray with a beard. He had on a shirt once red, a leather vest and on his legs were scarred leather chaps. His boots were plain but run over, and spurs with sharp rowels jingled as the horses trotted up and stopped in front of the store. The old man's eyes swept around him, deep set under his shaggy gray brows. They were blue eyes, maybe not as blue as they seemed because his skin was the color of old saddle leather and set his eyes off like blue lights. He swung down from the saddle, wrapped the bridle reins around the hitch rack and stepped up on the porch.

He had bowed legs and walked humped over. He wasn't any part of a young man, but it was plain to see he was the first real cowboy I'd seen in Texas. Toby and Polecat were counterfeits, just playing at cowboying, as far as I was concerned.

The screen door popped and Mr. Keeper stepped out, peering over his glasses. "Well, by gum. Booger Joe. Figured you was dead or stove up. You're a month late. What you been living on?"

Booger Joe, accompanied by the jingle of his spurs, didn't seem to hear Mr. Keeper. He walked into the store and I got up and pressed my nose against the screen door so I could watch him. He went to the glass case where Mr. Keeper kept tobacco, got out two plugs of Star Chewing Tobacco, shoved one in his vest pocket and unwrapped the other. He pulled out a knife, whittled off a plug and fitted it into his right jaw. It made a lump like a toothache.

He moseyed back to the porch and I followed from a distance. Wherever he went, he left a smell of saddle leather and horse sweat, with maybe a little dung thrown in. But it wasn't a bad smell, just the smell of a man whose life was spent around horses and cows.

"Talkative as ever," said Mr. Keeper, lifting his shoulders and letting them drop. "Well, when you get your chewing and sitting done, yell out. I'll get your next six months supplies boxed up."

Mr. Keeper went back into the store and I sat on the bench at the end of the porch. I wanted to talk to Booger Joe, but I was afraid to. He just sat, chewed and spit.

After about 15 or 20 minutes, I saw Dutchy round the corner at the east edge of town and walk toward his shop. I edged off the porch and figured I'd go unload the sow and pigs and be on my way home, but Booger Joe's scratchy voice stopped me. "Who are you, boy?"

He stopped and saw his deep-set eyes studying me. "I'm Rowdy, who are you?"

I just sat there but didn't say anything more so I got nervous and went down the steps.

"Hey, Boy."

I turned and looked at him.

"You born in a barn?"

"What do you mean?"

"Ain't got no manners, have you, boy?"

"I still don't know what you mean."

"Always in a hurry, ain't you?"

"Not so's you can tell it."

"Yes you are. You young ones, always in a hurry. No manners."

I figured he must want to talk, so I went back to the nail keg. He never budged, just sat there hunched over and looking at nothing in front of him and chewing and spitting. I wanted to talk to him but he never said anything else. I said, "Hot, ain't it."

No answer.

"Ol' Dutchy's opening his butcher shop."

No answer.

"Are you a real cowboy?"

No answer.

"Where do you live? You rode in from the canyon country, didn't you?"

"Nosey ain't you boy?"

I sure was stumped as to how to get on with Booger Joe. He fascinated me but if I wanted to talk, he wouldn't, and if I walked away he stopped me. But I was anxious to get on with my work and head back to Miss Sally's.

"Well," I said, "I've got to go. Got some hogs to unload at Dutchy's and then I got to get back to the ranch."

This time Booger Joe didn't stop me and I walked to the butcher shop, having to wait for an old Chevrolet truck with a crate full of chickens in the back to pass me by. The floor of the butcher shop was covered with sawdust. Behind a low counter was Dutchy's butcher block, a big chunk of cottonwood tree log, about three feet high and three feet across. Behind it were two doors, one on the left an ice room with a sign that said, "Anybody Caught Messing Inside the Ice House Today Will Be Found There Tomorrow."

The one on the right I figured was the slaughter room. I found Dutchy whetting his butcher knife, his rubber boots and rubber apron were on.

"Howdy, Dutchy."

"Howdy, Rowdy. Get my hogs unloaded. I need the alley clear. How you and your mule getting along?"

I ignored his question. "Hey, Dutchy, an ol' cowboy just rode into town a little while ago. He don't look like he has ever been curried below the knees, he's so wild. Who is he?"

Dutch stuck the butcher knife in his belt and opened the back door, motioning to me. "Hurry up Rowdy. I got to butcher two steers this morning. Can you lend me a hand?"

"No," I said. "Who is that old cowboy?"

"I saw his spotted pony and his pack horse tied up to the hitching post. That's ol' Booger Joe. Don't anybody know his name, except Miss Sally, where he used to shack up.

"She knows everybody. Some say he and ol' Sally are hitched, but nobody knows for sure.

"He looks to be 60 but may be half that age for all anybody knows. Used to be wagon boss on one of the old time ranches around these parts until he just showed up running cows and calves deep in the canyon west of here.

"But if nobody knows much about him, he knows everything about everybody. He's what you call a genuine old-timer."

Dutchy climbed up on the wagon wheel and looked at the hogs. "That is a good old sow and fine pigs. I'm much obliged."

It wasn't any trick to unload the hogs. I hated to leave them behind since I had gotten attached to the old gal, even if she did cause me a lot of trouble. But heck, I didn't hold it against her. She didn't know any better. She was just trying to make a living for her family.

I had to grit my teeth to keep from thinking about Dutchy putting a bullet to her brain and cutting her throat to let her bleed out and then sloshing her up and down in boiling water to loosen the hair so she could be butchered and the parts cut into pieces for curing. Then the fat would be rendered and the meat ground up into sausage which would be flavored with sage and stuffed into muslin stockings for keeping. It just made my mouth water to think about it, and it took away some of the hurt inside me. So I stopped thinkin' about it and told Dutchy to hurry up and open the gate so I could get out of there.

I drove past the store, saw Booger Joe still sitting on the nail keg, his weathered old face lookin sharp as an eagle's but he didn't act like he even saw me.

I was just clear of the crossroad when a pickup truck without any cab dusted in from the south and wheeled around the corner past the bank and hauled up in front of the store. It was Toby and Polecat and that old mongrel, Moosehead. He stood with his hind feet in the back of the truck and forelegs resting on either side of Polecat's shoulders, his tongue lapping out like he was looking for bears to chase.

They threw up a shower of dust when they skidded to a halt in front of the store and got out, screeching like a couple of stuck hogs. Old Moosehead, the one that had whipped Moochie at the church social, jumped out and ran around and around the truck like he was chasing his tail, yelping happy-like.

"Dang me, Polecat," Toby yelled, "if it ain't the handsomest cowpoke in Salt River County. Hey, Booger, had your once-a-year bath yet?"

"Whoa Toby, hold on. We're still upwind of him. Don't go downwind until he answers. You'll die if he ain't took his once-a-year bath yet."

"Hey, Polecat, ask if he's ever got him a woman yet. Have you, Booger Joe?"

The two loudmouths stood at the foot of the stairs, holding onto each other and pointing their fingers at Booger Joe. It was plain to see there was going to be trouble. I leaned back on the reins and wheeled the wagon around and headed back to the store just as Toby walked up on the porch. He bent over and lifted up Booger Joe's hat with his thumb and forefingers and peered down on Booger Joe's thin grey hair.

"Hey, Polecat, Lookie here. Cooties. A whole family of 'em. Ain't they cute? There's Pa Cootie and Ma Cootie and all the little Cooties. Two of 'em chasing a bug out of their territory."

By gum, I got hot under the collar. I slapped Midnight and Houdini into a run and hauled up on the boys hazing him. I didn't reckon him to be a coward, but I couldn't see him taking those insults without doing something about it.

I jumped out of the wagon and ran up the steps. "Hey, you skinks. Leave him alone. He ain't hurt you none."

I took the two boys by surprise, but not for long. "Well, if it ain't the Missouri Kid," Polecat drawled, his lean jaw skewing sideways. He was narrow between the eyes and a hank of red hair hung down from under his greasy hat. To me, he didn't look much cleaner than Booger Joe, so I didn't figure he had any right to be poking fun at anybody.

"Well, if it ain't the mule trader himself," Toby said. "Hey, Missouri Kid, did you come to town to make some more sharp trades like you did on Houdini?"

"How about that Missouri Kid?" Polecat said. "First off, he's going to catch wild bulls and cows. Then he changes that to a poor old sow and pigs. A hog, phew-eeey."

I spread my feet apart and put up my fists. "All right, which one wants to get it first? I've tackled you old boys before and I ain't afraid to do it again."

Well, they looked at one another and grinned. They started for me from each side. I figured to get whipped if both of them jumped on me at once, but I also figured to get in some good licks first.

I drew back my right fist to let Polecat have it right on the spot when Booger Joe's voice cut in like a knife.

"Don't move a hair. Don't even twitch," he said.

In the quick silence that followed, there was a sharp click, like the hammer of a gun being cocked.

I looked down and at first didn't see it. Then I saw it plain as anything, sticking out from under his left arm, the muzzle of an old hog-leg .45 Colt.

The mild blue had gone from Booger Joe's eyes. They had turned into blue steel. Toby and Polecat didn't even take a deep breath and for a few seconds the air got pretty thin. I couldn't hardly breathe, expecting to see that gun muzzle spout fire and smoke and noise.

"You ninnyhammers," Booger Joe said. "Get back on your tin horse. See if you can't find some other place you'd rather be. I done put up with enough snot out of you two. Move easy, now. I ain't shot a man for nigh onto 10 years now and I'm thinking I'd like the feel again."

Toby and Polecat could have walked on eggs and not cracked a one, leaving that porch. Toby got under the wheel and Polecat on the other side.

"Take that cur with you, 'less you want his brains blowed out," Booger Joe said.

Toby snapped his fingers and tried to whistle to the dog, but his mouth was too dry. The engine cackled and Toby shoved it into gear and eased out careful as a kitten sneaking up on a ball of yarn. But when he figured he was clear of Booger Joe, he shoved down the gas and disappeared in a cloud of dust.

I realized I was standing stiff as a board, just like I had been standing when Booger Joe went on the prod.

"Well, boy. You gonna fight old Booger Joe? Put down your dukes. Fun's over."

I put down my fists and began to shake all over. Sweat poured down my face and all over my body. I looked for the gun muzzle and didn't see it and wondered if I had ever seen it. I realized he must have had that hog leg hidden in his chaps, belt with the vest pulled down over it.

"Sit a spell, boy?"

I'd like to have, but I had a sudden urge to be like Toby and Polecat, away from there. "Sorry," I said. "I got to get to the ranch."

"What ranch?"

"Miss Sally's."

"Old Salt River Sally's?"

"Yeah."

Booger Joe's eyes crinkled and his mouth split in a grin that showed tobacco-stained teeth. A trickle of brown tobacco juice followed the creases from the corner of his mouth and ended up under his chin.

"Old Sally's, huh? She's a good old gal."

"I'll be seeing you, Mr. Booger Joe." I climbed into the wagon and picked up the reins.

"Hey, boy. You ever get down into the canyon?"

"Not yet. Figure to, one of these days."

"Come see me."

My heart leaped into my throat. "All right. 'cept, I don't know how to get there."

"Ride up the river until you get there. Anybody ought to know that."

"All right," I said, slapping the reins against the team's rumps. "So long."

"So long, boy. Don't forget. Come see old Booger Joe, now."

21

Up the Creek and Canyon

I drove back to Miss Sally's so shook up by Booger Joe and the way he'd pulled the gun on Toby and Polecat I forgot about Houdini until I stopped at the shed, pulled down the hitch rein and tied him up.

The minute I tied the knot, Houdini, who had been so willing to let me scratch his ears and feed him corn out of my hand, pulled back his lips and opened his mouth. He came at me with front feet flying and teeth snapping like steel traps. I stumbled backwards and fell through the shed door. I saw Houdini lean back against the hitch rein, heard a snap and he ran a hundred yards away. He whirled around, threw up his head and went, "Hee-haw, hee-haw," about a dozen times, I reckon.

"Why, you old, you confounded counterfeit, you," I yelled.

Jackrabbit heard him too, and came charging out of the brush and ran up and looked Houdini in the eye. "Hee-haw-hee-haw," Jackrabbit snorted. They stood there in the middle of the clearing a couple of minutes, hee-hawing back and forth, then they kicked up their heels, nipped each other on the necks and ran into the brush.

I knew there wasn't any use in chasing them. I'd tried chasing horses and mules before when they'd got out and after they'd tasted freedom, being caught again was just something they couldn't stand for a while.

I knew these things all right. But I didn't always do what I knew. There was just one thought in my head, and that was I was about to lose Houdini. I'd already been made laughing stock by just trading for Houdini. Now, if I let him get away, I'd be considered the biggest fool ever seen in Salt River County.

Thinking only of this, I took out after Houdini and Jackrabbit as they dodged through the brush, hee-hawing and kicking up their heels with good feeling. I ran through the mesquite, dodging under limbs and leaping prickly pear until the sweat popped out on me. I could get just so close, maybe a hundred feet, and they they'd run off again. They were just playing games with me. Finally, they circled around and crossed the river and struck off upstream. I followed, jogging sometimes, walking sometimes, and gradually Houdini and Jackrabbit got their run out. They started walking and I got within fifty feet of them.

But if I ran after them, they ran. When I walked, they walked. The sun was straight overhead now, and I must have been five or six miles or more from Miss Sally's. Once, when I stopped to catch my breath, with Houdini and Jackrabbit stopping too, but watching so they could run away if they saw me start after them, I looked around me.

I was on the banks of the river, but now I really couldn't make sure where the main channel was. The channel looked half a mile wide, and slender trickles were split by sandbars and ran slowly. Somewhere below me, the trickles all ran together and made the river which ran by Miss Sally's. Then it ran on south of Salt River town, and then on east to where JJ and I had first tried to cross it and almost drowned.

The ground was sandy, with a funny cedar-like tree Miss Sally had called juniper. A mile or so south of me, I saw the wall of the canyon. Along there, I knew, was where JJ and Miss Sally and me had driven that day I got so down in the mouth. The country had looked so big it scared me, so far below and stretched out. But down here, with the ground under my feet and trees all around me, I didn't feel that way. There was the river, running eastward, and I could easily find my way around.

I looked south of me and could just barely see its rim, all blue and misty with distance. West of me, I supposed, the canyon came together, had its beginning like Miss Sally said, and there were springs up there where the river headed. And also, somewhere up there, Booger Joe had his home.

By this time I had caught my breath and cooled off a bit. Houdini and Jackrabbit had calmed down and cooled off some and walked down to a pool of water, and waded out to get a drink. This was the best chance I would have.

I eased into the river while Houdini had his muzzle in the water, swigging hard but keeping one eye on me. He did not act like he cared if I caught him so I waded up to my waste, slow-like. "Whoa, boy, easy now, I won't hurt you," I said, softly. I was just about ready to reach down and grab the bridle when Jackrabbit decided he wanted me to scratch his ears.

He splashed between me and Houdini, startling the mule so bad he ran out of the water and back onto the bank. Where Jackrabbit had not wanted anything to do with me on the bank, he now wanted to play with me in the water. He nuzzled me and nudged into my pocket for something to eat.

"Doggone you, Jackrabbit, you got in my way." I slapped his nose and waded out and he came to stand beside me. He looked like he was through playing games so I put my arms around his neck and scratched his nose. Houdini twisted his head sideways, trying to figure out what game I was playing.

Then I thought of something I had done back home, something Pa taught me when trying to fool a horse into coming to the barn.

Putting on my softest and most soothing voice, I said, "Houdini, you worthless bag of bones, I would like to loosen your brains with a board, if I had one." Of course, I knew he did not understand words, but he pricked up his ears at my friendly tone. I turned and walked slowly away from him, as if I did not care if I ever saw him again. He nickered and turned his rump as if to say, "I don't like you, either." But then he turned and started following me like a big dog.

Now here came Jackrabbit, walking so close I had to hurry to keep him from stepping on my heels. So I stopped walking and turned and rubbed his velvety nose and scratched his ears and talked soothingly to him. "All right, boys, you've had your fun. Now it's time to go home."

Just when I thought I had it made, both Jackrabbit and Houdini stopped dead in their tracks, whirled around to look behind, and then I heard the fierce bellow of a bull.

I whirled around to see the biggest, meanest looking bull I ever saw in my life. He was coming on like the wind and only slowed when we stopped. He stopped, too, and pawed great clouds of dirt until his back was covered, all the while letting out deep bellows that made the earth shake.

And there I was, out in the open and no place to go except into the river – if I could reach it before he decided to charge and gore me to mush.

Jackrabbit and Houdini didn't waste any time. They dug in their heels and ran past me. I made a wild grab and caught Jackrabbit's mane. But when he brushed against a low limb at the river, I lost my grip.

Jackrabbit and Houdini splashed in the water and turned to see if the bull was behind. He was. And he quit pawing the ground, eyed me, and began a slow trot directly at me.

I had just enough time to turn, crash through underbrush and find myself peddling air and falling into a deep pool of water.

I splashed toward the opposite bank, saw a sycamore tree with a low-lying branch, and headed for it. I reached for that limb, got one leg over it, and pulled myself up in time to see the bull splash through the water and head for the tree.

I just had time to catch my breath when the bull climbed out of the water and came to stand right under me, shaking these huge horns and scratching the tree as if to knock it down. All I could do was to hug the tree limb hard and hope and pray the bull would soon get tired of his game and go back where he came from.

After what seemed like an hour but was really only five or ten minutes, the bull settled down and parked himself under the tree. How long would it be, I wondered, before he gave up and went back to his herd, wherever that was.

Finally, I began to get mad. Mad at myself. Mad at Houdini and Jackrabbit. Mad at the bull. I wanted something to throw at him, but nothing I could throw would hurt him anyhow. I had never been afraid of farm animals in my life. I knew they were dangerous because a Jersey bull once got Dad down at home and would have killed him if Grandpa had not been around with a pitchfork. He stuck the bull with the sharp fork until Dad could roll under a fence to safety. That was enough of a lesson for me. It kept me from harm's way from then on.

But now, this was different. I was treed. Treed like a possum.

Ice water replaced the blood in my veins. How would I ever get out of this mess? I began to shake, and to wonder why I ever left home, and how I wished Dad would suddenly show up and save me, and then I realized I had up and left home on my own hook, and had no one to blame but myself.

And I made up my mind, that if ever I got out of this mess alive I would just write a letter back home and tell Dad where I was and that if he wasn't too mad at me would he please come to Texas and get me and take me back home to Missouri.

I cried. I prayed. I yelled. Finally, I just gave up and cried a bunch more. I thought, "You sound just like JJ would if he was up in this tree and helpless."

Hating myself, I continued whimpering, just like a big baby.

Then, as I was about to give up and fall out of the tree from exhaustion, I heard horses hooves. Hoping against hope, I yelled. "Help. Help. Over here by this big tree..."

The bull jumped to his feet and let out a bellow. From upstream came a voice that sounded familiar. "Who is it?"

That voice could only come from one source – "Polecat!" That same ornery cowpoke who stole my stuff when he left the boxcar, who got in a fight with JJ and me at the church picnic, and tormented Booger Joe.

But at this moment, I didn't care if it belonged to the Devil himself. I was desperate for help.

"It's me, Rowdy," I yelled. "I'm up in a tree and that black bull treed me like a possum."

I heard the clatter of hooves and the popping of brush and Toby and Polecat burst into the opening. They reined up short.

"Uh-oh," Toby said. "Trouble."

"Get out of here," Polecat said.

They spurred their horses and I realized they had not heard me; and were leaving. "Wait. Save me. Please." My voice was weak.

Only the sound of fading hoof beats. The bellow of the black bull grew faint. I was free, saved. Toby and Polecat had saved me, even if they didn't know it.

I dropped out of the tree, limb by limb, like a monkey. When I got my legs limbered up I started running downstream toward Miss Sally's. I ran until my lungs burst, having no idea if I was a mile from her house of five miles. When my wind gave out, I dropped to the ground, listening to hear if the bull was still around. Then I heard a blast from his lungs, a bellow of fury. He had stopped chasing the two cowboys, and had returned to search out his prey – me. I looked for a tree, but there was not one in sight big enough to save me again.

I took a deep breath and started running.

22

Booger Joe to the Rescue

I heard the bull's bellow closer and closer. I ran blindly now, then I heard hoof beats and a man's voice yelling, "Hi-ya, hi-ya!"

A horse and rider appeared at my side. The horse skidded to a stop and a man's arm grabbed my collar and in a flash I was lying across the saddle horn.

"Booger Joe!"

"Boy," he said, "You just about met your maker. Hang tight now."

He hit his spotted pony with spurs. The bellows of the bull faded. Booger Joe pulled up on the reins and the pony whirled around in the direction we had come from. He slid me off the front of the saddle. "Crawl on behind quick-like, and we'll ride some more. Give me your hand and I'll swing you up."

As I landed behind the cantle, I looked back where we had come from and saw the bull pawing up dust. To my surprise, rather than riding away from the bull, Booger Joe reined the horse toward the bull. "What are you doing?" I shouted. "Let's get out of here before he kills."

But instead of slowing down and turning away, he stuck the spurs in the horse's flanks and rode straight toward the bull at full speed. The bull stopped pawing, threw up his head and watched us. As we got within a dozen feet of him, he turned, let out another bellow, and to my surprise, rather than charging, he whirled and ran away from us.

Booger Joe rode close to him, jerked off his wide-brimmed hat, leaned over and whooped the bull on the rump and yelled at the top of his voice. "Hi-yi! Hi-yi!" The bull veered to one side, Booger Joe hauled back on the reins and the horse skidded to a stop in a cloud of dust.

Old Mr. Bull departed in a sloping run and within minutes was a quarter mile away from us and slowed to a stop. He looked back, let out a bellow of rage, shook his head as if to say, "I'll take care of you guys later," then turned and trotted in the direction he had come from.

In front of him, at the edge of a patch of brush, I saw a half-dozen whiteface cows running to meet him. Booger Joe chuckled. "That old boy got a taste of what he was dishing out, didn't he? His cows heard all the commotion and came to see what it was all about. Bet that old bull will spend the next day bragging to his momma cows about how he chased the cowboys away from his territory."

It occurred to me I had just heard Booger Joe say more words at one time than I had heard him say when we met at the store.

He touched the reins and his pony seemed to sense his thoughts. We rode at easy-riding canter, headed down river toward Miss Sally's ranch. As we rode past the corn field, where the plants had come up thick and deep green, he nodded and said, "You plant that corn for ol' Sal?"

"Me and JJ, my buddy."

The pony splashed through the cool water and we rode on up to the house. Miss Sally and JJ heard us and ran out to greet us. "Rowdy, where the devil have you been? We thought you had plumb got lost somewhere."

And then she looked straight at Booger Joe and said, "Joe, you old rascal, I told you if you ever came loafing around me again, I'd chase you off with a shotgun."

Booger Joe just crossed his arms, leaned over the saddle horn and spit tobacco juice. "Got to hankerin' for a warm bed," he said grinning, "You still sore at me?"

"You good-for-nothin' cowboy," she said. "But I reckon I missed you anyhow. If it hadn't been for these Missouri boys, reckon I'd just about have died with lonesome fever."

He got out off the saddle, pulled me to the ground, and said, "Sal, this here boy has had himself a time. Got himself cornered by ol' Blacky-bull and might ought to of got killed. Best get him to the house, get him a warm belly-full, and put him to bed. Reckon he's apt to sleep the clock around."

Booger Joe had to carry me into the house, and JJ came along and helped and I sure was grateful. My legs refused to carry me. It didn't take Miss Sally more than a minute to get some hot potato soup in me. I drank it right out of the bowl, and then I started on a piece of left-over fried chicken. She shoved a piece of cherry pie at me, and I ate about three bites before I leaned my head on the table and conked out – went to sleep at the table, so they told me the next morning when I woke up – still in bed.

I remembered dreaming of not one, but a herd of black bulls chasing me. They almost caught me, but somehow I managed to stay just one step ahead.

Finally, in my dreams, I wore out and everything went in slow motion. The bulls came closer and closer and then turned into just one huge bull with white horns that curved around and pinned me against a tree. I screamed at the top of my lungs and woke myself up.

I had dreamed I saw Miss Sally far, far away; just a tiny speck. She was running toward me in slow motion, yelling "Rowdy, Rowdy, Rowdy."

I sat up, her face right next to mine, and realized it was her I heard calling me, and not a dream at all.

She hugged me tight just like my mother used to do, and I had a hankering to see Ma. I choked back a sniffle.

JJ stood next to her, and Booger Joe was sitting at the table, a cup of coffee in his hands. I sat up, a little dizzy, and feeling mighty foolish.

"You poor boy," she said, hugging me tight. "Dang that old bull. I'm going out with my shotgun and blow a hole in his head you could drive a horse and wagon through."

I was put out and didn't know what to say, and all of a sudden I felt like I was going to vomit. "Excuse me, gotta go outside." And I got up shaky-like, and rushed out the door. I sort of staggered as I walked and realized my legs were still tired and sore.

I went around the corner so I could take a leak and be by myself a while and let my headache ease up. I wanted to be alone a while, so I walked down to the pond where we had dammed up to catch the spring water. The old red rooter ran past me and caught a hen over by the pig pen, where the pigs were bedded down in cool mud. A speckled hen clucked up her brood of a dozen fluffy yellow chicks and scratched like crazy all the time telling her babies in a happy little chuckle, "Come here, dears, and get this fat little black bug. And there's a juicy worm, too."

The chicks peeped happy as could be and played with each other to see who could take away the bug and the worm.

Down by the creek, which rustled by with a quiet murmur, I heard Jack Rabbit braying to Houdini and he hee-hawed back. All of a sudden, I remembered that sorry pair was responsible for my bad adventure yesterday. I realized I had not been smart to chase them, for they would have come back home if I had left them alone. They just thought I was playing with them, and they were having a big time.

Sure enough, Houdini did not have a stitch of harness on him. I hoped to backtrack and discover where he had lost it. I turned away and kicked a rock onto the big pool of water and saw a seven-pound black bass come to the surface, flash his striped sides as he flipped his tale and splashed water, then dived back into the deep.

I caught my breath. I didn't realize there was a fish that big in the pond. I reminded myself to sometime come back and catch him with a big soft-shelled crawfish. Then I went on up to the spring, splashed cold water in my face, laid down on my stomach and swigged up a big drink of cold, cold spring water.

I sat down to think, hugging my knees and listening to the sounds of life. A blue quail chirped in the distance and its mate answered; "Bob-white, bob white." A wild turkey gobbled and its mate chirped in that "put-put-put" they made with their throats.

Across the river, I saw the corn waving in the breeze and could almost hear it growing, for the earth was warm and moist, and the sun was big as all out doors, and red as a ripe apple.

But somehow, this morning something seemed wrong. It welled up in the pit of my stomach and sort of made me sick-like. The thought of that black bull stuck in my throat as I thought how he had treed me like I was a fat coon and then I thought, with a lump in my throat that my last thought when I just knew he was going to kill me, that I was a long way from home, and my folks back home would never know what happened to me.

I saw pictures of Ma flashing through my mind and of Pa's big shaggy head and big rough hands.

I ducked my head between my knees and just let 'er go bawling like a baby and didn't care. Oh, how I wanted to see them right now. I wanted to hug Ma, feel her soft white hair on my face and smell the fresh clean smell of it, and shake Pa's hand and feel the strength of his body flow through me.

In that moment, I wished I had never run away from home. I wished I had just taken my licking from Pa. After all, I had earned it. I said out loud, "God, I ain't much to brag on, but I got a good ma and pa. I want you to bless and keep them for me. Please let ma forget about me soon. I don't want her to suffer none, worrin' about a no-good scamp like me. And please don't let JJ's ma and pa worry none, either. I guess I best send JJ back home. Thanks, God. Amen."

I just sat there, thinking for a spell. A grasshopper skittered through the air and fell into the pond. That ol' bass rose up quick as flash and swallowed him up and sank back in the pool. Then I saw a rock sail over my head and plunk into the water. I whirled around and there was ol' Booger Joe, Miss Sally and JJ. Miss Sally's hands twisted up her apron and dried a flood of tears. "Rowdy, honey…Rowdy. Come here and let's talk a spell."

My lower jaw quivered. I bit my lip. They had heard every word I said. Well, what the heck. I didn't care. I wasn't ashamed of a word. I got up, "I'm hungry." She put her arm around me and guided me to the house, leaving Booger Joe and JJ sitting on the hill. "Rowdy, don't you think you better go home? I know your ma misses you something fierce."

I wrestled away. "No, no," I said. "I'm going to be a cowboy. And some day, I'm going to be the biggest rancher in all Texas."

I turned and ran to the house and grabbed a plate and broke a couple of big flakey biscuits and shoveled sausage and gravy on them. JJ came in and stared at me and never said a word and the more I ate, the madder I got at my weakness. By the time I had stuffed my stomach, I had decided what I was going to do.

I was going to catch that black bull first. Then, I was going to take him to Oliver's ranch and get my reward.

But the first thing I was going to do was to catch worthless Houdini and teach him some new tricks.

But no sooner had I made up my mind to do all this, than Miss Sally and Booger Joe sat down beside me, one on either side. Sally put an arm around my shoulder and squeezed.

"Rowdy, poor boy. You're mixed up, ain't you?"

I tried to shake her arm loose, but she held me tighter. "Tell me the truth, Rowdy. What is your real name, and why did you leave home? You ain't fooled ol' Sally. I knew the minute I set eyes on you and JJ that day in Salt River town that you two had run away from home and you didn't know what to do except to put on a big front."

"You ain't the first boys to run away from home and come to Texas. Why, my lordy, Rowdy, the west was half settled by boys like you. They heard-tell of the wild west and ran away from home to be cowboys. Some lived through the hardships and made top hands on ranches. Others got killed by outlaws or horses – some got killed by mean bulls or buffalo. Some even got killed by women."

"Most just went broke, trying to live on a cowhand's wages next to nothing. And one or two really made it and made it big, but they were the exception. Take ol' Booger Joe, here, he can tell you all about it, because that's what he did, a good many years ago. When I first knew him, he was a cleaned-up handsome boy, green as a goose, but I liked him and we got ourselves hitched. We never had no kids, Lord knows I wished I had a dozen to keep me company, but no such luck."

"But if I had been that lucky, I sure enough would not have let them stay out here in the sticks. Tryin' to make a living when it don't rain, or seeing cows freeze to death when a blue northern comes when you least expect it."

"Rowdy, you and JJ are going back home. You've had your fun. You've nigh onto worried your folks to death. And I ain't gonna let you get away with ruining your lives. Lord knows, you two have done ol' Sal a lot of good. It has warmed my old cold heart, the way you did things for me. And much as I am in love with this old piece of dirt I call a ranch, I'd like to go back east myself. That' where I came from, Missouri, same as you."

I just sat there, paralyzed. I had never had anyone talk so straight to me, and this was one time my big mouth stayed shut. I knew down deep inside I had done the wrong thing in running away from home. Even if I could not stand my dad's so-called new family, it was better than what I was facing. But my pride wrestled hard, and I couldn't just up and drag my tail back to Missouri between my legs.

I didn't know what to say, and Miss Sally started up again. In a softer voice this time.

"Rowdy, if you don't know by now, ol' Sal knows every rooster that crows in Salt River township, and who is good and who is bad, who you can count on and who is a slimy crook."

"Salt River is not any place for two good but misguided boys like you and JJ. And if I know all of these things, what makes you think I don't know who you are, where you came from and why, and that your Pa has been notified that you are in good health and good care and that he will be coming to get you just as soon as he gets his wheat crop cut and his corn laid by."

I began to tremble from toes to ears that burned. I felt like I had been stripped of all my clothing and was standing naked and helpless with all of the world looking at me and laughing. I did not know what to do or what to say at this point. I just put my head on my knees and closed my eyes and tried to imagine I was in a dream.

And then Booger Joe, who had sat silently through all of this sermon of Miss Sally's, put his hand on my knee and said, "Buck up, boy. It ain't the end of the world. In fact, your world is just about to get a lot brighter."

I mumbled, "But I made a fool out of myself. I promised I would catch that old bull and deliver him to Oliver's Ranch, and here I let him run me out of the county. If it had not been for you, I would probably be lying out there dead and mashed to gravy by that bull's horns."

Booger Joe laughed in that little cackle he had. "You got guts enough to help me?" I nodded yes. He said, "Then you do as I say, together we'll catch that old bull and before we're done with him, we'll have a ring in his nose and he'll be leading like a dog, right up to Oliver's door step."

That got my attention. I lifted my head and looked at him. "You really mean that?"

"I do. You game?"

I nodded. "All right. But first, I've got another chore to do."

"What's that?"

"I got to break that hammer-headed mule to stand hitched."

"How you gonna do that?"

"My grandpa back home showed me how. He was a horse and mule man and he taught me everything I need to know. If you will help me with Houdini, I will help you with that old black bull. Ok?"

He stuck out his rough old hand and said, "Shake, partner. It's a deal. When do we start?"

"But first, got to find my Moochie dog. Where is he?" It suddenly dawned on me I had not seen Moochie since the fight with the bull. He had disappeared about the time the two cowboys rode away and left me to deal with the bull all alone. Suddenly, I got sick at my stomach. Was Moochie dead? Did the bull injure him? Leave him out on the prairie to die?

"But Moochie. Where is he? I've got to see him. Call him. Have you tied him up? HERE, MOOCHIE. COME HERE, BOY. COME TO ROWDY."

"Wait a minute, Rowdy." she said. "We'll find Moochie. First, I want to know your real name so I can know for sure who am I'm talking to."

I tried to wiggle free but she had an iron grip on my arm. "Rowdy, I said..."

I finally shouted, "Frank McLin Farmer. Let go my arm."

All of a sudden Booger Joe leaped up and came down in front of me. He shook all over. "Say that again," he said. "That's my name - McLin - my real name. How did you know it?"

I just kind of froze in my shoes. For a split minute, I thought I must be dreaming. I sort of mumbled, "I said Frank McLin Farmer. I didn't say it was your name. I said that is my full name. They just called me Rowdy because everybody said that was what I was when I ought to of been shut-mouthed and quiet."

"Oh, my God," he said, suddenly sinking to his knees in front of me. "If that is your real name, and you ain't puttin' me on, I am your name sake. You were given my name when you were born. I left home just after your mother gave birth and nobody has known where to write me or where abouts I was in all of these 16 years since."

Now it was my turn to sink to my knees. We just sort of sat there on the ground, staring at each other. Salt River Sally staggered a little and finally she sank to her knees, too. And there we sat, just staring first at one then the other, while all of this soaked in. Then Booger Joe reached over and hugged me so tight I thought I would die, and I put my arms around his shoulders and hugged him as tight as I could, and Miss Sally, she just bawled right out loud like a cow calling her calf and shouted, "Praise God. Praise the Lord. I can't hardly believe what I'm hearing."

I don't know how long we sat there. Seemed like time just froze in place. Finally, we got to our feet and here came JJ, running fit to kill from where ever and whatever he had been doing at the cow shed, and said, "What in the name of the Lord is going on? Rowdy, why you cryin'? Miss Sally, what's wrong?"

She put her free arm around him and said, Let's go to the house and sit down so we can figure all of this out. I never believed in miracles before, but here I am right in the middle of one."

While all of this was going on, there was a nagging thought in my mind that demanded attention, but that I could not hardly focus on, and that was Moochie. Where was my pal, Moochie? I just had to go find him. It made my blood run cold to think that my dog, who I had had since I was old enough to toddle, was lost, hurt or dead.

So when we all finally calmed down a little – and it sure was hard to stop our hearts from pumping so hard, I managed to bring the subject up again.

"Rowdy – or Frank Mac – when I came upon that bull about to run you down, I saw your dog, running hard as he could after those two no-account Oliver boys. They skedaddled as fast as they could to get away from that bull. I don't know for sure, but if I was a guess'n man, I'd guess they hauled up a mile or so out of sight and somehow caught your dog.

"But how could they catch him?" I asked. "Moochie has had all he wants to do with those worthless cowboys."

"That's easy for two cowboys working together," he said. "While one got your dog's attention, the other could come in behind with his lasso and catch him. Then, they could haul him up in the saddle and ride back to the Oliver spread and tie him up."

"But why would they want to do that?"

"That's easy, from what I know about that worthless pair. They figured you would guess where your dog is, and would come a'runnin, after him. And then they would have a little more fun with you, or make you pay to get back your dog. Or they might even torture him before your very eyes and when you try to stop them, they would beat the tarnation out of you."

I just wanted to throw up. I could only mumble, "What can I do? I just can't let them get away with it." Booger Joe sat down on a kitchen chair and crossed one leg over the other and put his elbows on his knees and pulled out a plug of chewin' and said, "Let me figure on that a spell." He fell silent and closed his eyes.

JJ tapped me on the shoulder and motioned me to come aside. We walked down to the pond and he was quiet a minute, then said, "Rowdy, I reckon you can blame me. I got so dad-blamed homesick I spilled my guts to Miss Sally. I told her your real name, and your dad's real name, and she wrote a letter to him and mailed it a week ago. Hope you don't hate me for it."

Added to the other surprises I had been getting, there wasn't much I could do but take this in stride, too. "That's ok, JJ. It looks like our big adventure and ideas are about over. Just as soon as I can find Moochie – if he is not dead, I reckon we better start figuring how to get out of this mess the easiest way."

We sat down and flipped pebbles into the water, seeing that big old bass rise to see what was going on. "JJ, are you homesick?"

"I'd sure be a liar if I said I wasn't."

"But you've got no folks back in Cave Spring. You never did know your folks."

"Aw, Rowdy, you just don't know black folks as well as you think you do. In a way, I've got more family than you.

"All the black folks in and round Cave Spring are my family and..."

"But you don't stay any one place. You just sleep around with first one and then the other."

"I do that because they want me. I don't want to burden anybody if I can help it. You live in a rich family. The poorest white folks in Cave Spring are richer than the most well-off blacks. We hang together and help each other. I hate to say it, but us blacks stick together better than you whites. That's what we've had to do, or die."

On top of all of this, I just got another blow to my feelings. I had never thought about my relationship with JJ in those terms. I supposed they had plenty to eat and wear and warm places to live like I did.

"JJ, that makes me feel plumb awful. Why didn't you tell me this a long time ago?"

"Warn't no use to, sarg. You don't know it, but all the blacks around our parts think a lot of you. You don't put on no airs and when we have baseball games between the blacks and whites, we always try to get you to play on our side. You ain't stuck up, even if you live in the biggest house in the community. Maybe you don't know how lucky you are."

That made me think again. I always liked to play with the black kids, mostly because of the triplet daughters of Charlie and Tilda Rollin. They were then same age as me, and lived next door to my grandma McLin – and we had played together since we were toddlers. Ruby and Tina and May were stronger than any white boys their age. Their mother was what was called a pygmy, and old Charlie was from huge, barrel-chested Negroes.

Then there was the Johnson clan, with Slim being nearly seven feet tall, and his brother Willis – who was mean sometimes – and Steve, who was good natured but liked to sip whisky.

"JJ, tell you what. We've got to do something very important right now. We've got to find Moochie, and old Booger Joe – I mean my Uncle Frank – thinks the two Oliver boys stole him. When he wakes up, he's got a plan." And so in about thirty minutes Miss Sally and Booger Joe came to us.

Booger Joe put his arm around me and stuck a wad of chewing tobacco in his jaw.

"Rowdy, I reckon the best thing we can do about your dog is this. We saddle our ponies in about an hour, then take our time in riding to the Oliver ranch. It's about ten miles to the south of here, and we want to arrive after their bedtime.

"After they hit the hay, by that time we ought to have heard or seen the dogs. If your Moochie is there, likely he will have already caught your scent. Likely, if he's there, he'll be tied.

"Then we will have to get him loose without any commotion so's to wake up the ranch house. If every thing goes all right, we'll ease out of there real quiet like, and come home."

"But what if they hear us and come after us," I asked.

He spit tobacco juice at a grasshopper that sailed by, and grinned. He reached around behind him, and pulled out his two big six-shooters. "That's when the fun starts," he said. "That's when we git even."

I gulped. "You mean we shoot to kill?"

"Aw, Rowdy, this here ain't no movie show. We don't try to kill nobody. Just scare them up a little bit so's they know we got our dog and pin them down until we can get a running start.

"They sure ain't going to chase us in the dark and besides, before they could get their ponies caught and saddled, we'll be halfway home. This is kid-like games we play around these parts. No body gets shot-up, but we better look out for something lively in the future.

"Now let's go see that little mare you stole before you go to Salt River, and get her saddled up and ready for the trip."

I felt heat come up in my neck. "What do you mean that mare I stole? I caught her fair and square when a bunch of wild horses showed up at a watering tank a few days back. Caught her and that jackass at the same time."

"Rowdy, son, you got a lot to learn. That there bunch of horses that came to the water belong to a band of mustangs gathered for shipment to a stockyards in Oklahoma City. I even helped the shipper round them up and throw them in a big pasture to hold until the buyer's order was filled for shipment."

I just wilted slowly and sank to the ground. My face burned like fire and my heard thumped out of my chest and I could hardly breathe.

Boy, oh boy, it was beginning to look like I had messed up in just about everything I did.

"You mean I'm a horse thief? That wasn't a bunch of wild horses like I thought?"

"That's what I mean, son."

"What can I do? Can I take her back where I found her?"

"Well, Rowdy, let's take one thing at a time. Let's try to locate your dog first. Then we'll see about taking care of your mistake. It so happens after you left town the other day, the sheriff came along. He's an old roundup buddy of mine, and I told him about you and the horse.

"I told him you was green as Missouri grass, and that you were no hoss thief, and that I knew where the mare was and that I would deliver her at the right time.

"As a matter of fact, that's where I was headed – to ol' Sals place, and give you the bad news. There's no hurry to get her back to the horse buyer, for his order ain't filled yet and we've got a month or so to do that.

"Right now, let's concentrate on the matter at hand finding and recovering your dog."

23

Saddle Up, Cowboy

I must have looked like a whipped pup because Booger Joe slapped me on the back and said, "Stand up, Rowdy. Let's see who's tallest. Sal, check us out." And he turned around and we stood back-to-back.

Miss Sally giggled happy-like and said, "Rowdy, you got him beat by a half inch. When you're full grown, you'll be an inch and a half taller than your uncle."

"Dad-blame it, Sal, it's all on account of your cookin'. If you was a better cook, I'd eat more."

"You old cowpoke, you eat like a mule as it is. That's why I kick you out of the house once in a while, so I won't go broke buying you vittles."

He nudged me in the ribs with an elbow. "I take it back Rowdy. Your ol' Aunt Sal is noted all over Salt River township as the top roundup cook.

"Now let's get down to business. First, them Big Smith brand overalls you wear ain't exactly wild west garb. You need blue jeans help up with a belt, and a tough blue denim shirt with pearl buttons. Always keep your sleeves rolled down – that ain't the law but it keeps your arms from getting scratched up when you ride through thick brush hunting cattle.

"Next, you must have a pair of leather chaps to wear over your jeans. That's not for looks like the movie cowboys think, but to keeps your jeans from getting torn up when you ride and to protect your legs. Riding through mesquite without them will teach that real quick. Also chaps take the sting out of cold weather. They even keep out the hot sun.

"And don't make the mistake of calling chaps like the word sounds. Chaps is just a nick-name because the real word is Spanish – chapparhoes. I've got several old pair out in the shed that will just fit you – along with some high-heeled boots that are too loose for me. The boots have high heels to keep your feet from sliding through the saddle stirrups. When that happens, if the horse bucks, you get hung up and a horse can drag you to death."

For the first time since I came to Texas, I felt like somebody really cared about me. I realized now what the word "Tenderfoot" meant. It really meant, "Boy, you are a long way from being a cowboy."

So with Miss Sally's help, we dug out all the clothing I needed to look like a sure-enough cowboy. When I got all dressed, JJ's eyes popped and he said, "Gosh-a-mighty, Rowdy, you look just like Booger Joe. In fact, you look enough like Booger Joe to be his twin, instead of just a hick from Missouri."

Booger Joe slapped me on the back and said, "Time to saddle up, cowboy."

He led the way to the night pen where his spotted pony and Lady Midnight waited, led them to the pond for a drink, then climbed into the saddle. Lady Midnight turned her head first to the left and sniffed my leather chaps, and then to the right and sniffed. She must have felt like I was real for she humped her back and crow-hopped as if to say, "Finally I've got a real cowboy in my saddle again."

We rode past the pond with the big bass, crossed the river, circled the corn field, and headed straight south just as the sun started to slide down in the west.

Booger Joe said, "Let's let our horses trot for a mile until they warm up. Then we'll have to ride through brush single file for a few miles until we hit the open prairie. After that, we can walk our horses side-by-side and rest them for a hard ride home.

The thicket of mesquite trees began to thin. "That's because we are headed down hill," Booger Joe said. "At the bottom of this grade, there's a feeder stream that eventually flows into the fabled Red River, but we're miles from there.

"Ollie Oliver's ranch lies five miles dead ahead. We'll let our horses drink and rest at the creek before we go on. Now, Rowdy, ride along side me for a spell. I want you to tell me all about the folks back home.

"I tell you true, you must have been sent to me by the Good Lord Above. I have tortured myself all these years, but never got up enough nerve to go back and make amends."

"To start with, how's Ma and my sister Winnie?" Is Ma still living?"

Cold shivers ran along my backbone. The impact of that question reached plumb to my bones. It made me wonder why the devil I had been so brave – and wrong – as to think I could solve my unhappiness by running away from home.

"You have no way of knowing it, but I don't call my grandmother 'Ma,' as you call her. I call her Ella-ma, just like I call my dad's mother Stella-ma, and her mother Big-ma.

"Your ma is still alive and as well as you might expect for a woman 75 years old. Your sister Winnie never married, mainly because Ella-ma said one of her kids had to take care of her in her old age, since your father – my grandfather – died ten years ago."

"And how about my sister Nell, your mother, Rowdy?"

It really brought a lump in my throat to think about my mother, but I choked back the tears and answered. "She's all right, but you will be surprised to know she and my father broke up a couple of years ago. Dad re-married to a woman with two kids, and that's the main reason I left home. I couldn't take sharing my life with someone that didn't belong in our home."

"Ah-ha. So now we are gettin' down to the meat. I understand what you did that for, it's like what made me take out. Like uncle, like nephew. Go on. How's my three brothers?"

"Railroad men, all of them. Guy's got three girls, Carl's got a son and three girls, Will's wife has had seven children, but two died. They all are buried in the cemetery at Cave Spring."

We came to the river crossing and let our horses drink. Two mallard ducks rose up and saluted us. A flock of wild turkeys flew into the top of an oak tree to roost. As we crossed the river a huge covey of blue quail burst out of the grass and made our horses jump nearly from under us. Whippoorwills called. They made me shiver with their sad song.

The sun slid out of sight and what had been bright and cheery became gloomy – as did my mood. All was peaceful with wild things. It was only in the world of humans this night that things were out of whack.

And that brought me back to the reason we were taking this night-time ride.

Just to find my beloved Moochie.

24

The Grand Rescue

There was only the sound of our horse's hooves in the soft earth and the air from the damp ground rose up in a sort of perfume tinged with dew. As we rode up out of the low river bottom, the sweet smell of the clean country air made me think of home and gave me a healthy dose of home sickness.

Now that I knew my big adventure was coming to an end, that my dad had learned where I was, I could hardly wait. But one thing for sure, I was not going any place without my dog Moochie, so I asked Booger Joe, "How much longer before we get to the ranch?"

"Half an hour Rowdy. By the way, I been thinking about home territory. Tell me, does that old spring water still gush out of the mouth of the cave that gave our home town its name? Do the women still take their butter and milk in pots and pans to keep them cool over night?"

His question gave me a mental picture of what he was talking about. That good old spring was the heart of our little country town. It was what gave our part of the world a special meaning and when folks moved away from there, like to Springfield to get a better job or so, they never failed to come back to their home town on special days like Christmas and Easter and July 4th when we had our big picnic, as well as August 4th, when the black folks held their own Independence Day celebration."

We white folks held our picnic downstream of the bridge that spanned the river, but the blacks held their celebration upstream. The black folks were not welcome at the white folk's picnic, but the whites were welcome at the picnic of the blacks.

"Best I know, things are just like they were when I was five years old and began to notice the world around me," I said. "I expect you would notice a big difference. I remember riding to church one winter morning in granddad's one-horse sleigh, but after that it was parked behind the chicken house and is still there.

"Asher Creek is still the community swimming hole, and also the best fishing hole on the creek.

"There used to be an old steam engine boiler in the creek just above the bridge. Fred Brooks tried to cross the creek when it was in flood stage one time. His wagon turned over and dunked the engine. He was so disgusted he just left it there, all this time. It sure is a good place for fish to hide out. I never failed to catch my stringer full with worms or crawdad tails as bait..."

Booger Joe stopped me. "Now get ready, Rowdy. I can see a twinkle of lights ahead of us once in a while. Ol' Ollie got himself a newfangled 'lectric light plant so's he can have lights in the barn and around the cow pens at night. I reckon by now you've got 'lectric lights at your farm?"

"Yep. But we sold the old Delco engine. The rural electric light company came to our territory in 1934. I was alone in the house with Papa when the lights came on. Stelma had expected it a long time and she had an electric cook stove installed. It sure did save me from having to split so much kindling wood. I remember the first month's light bill was four dollars. She like to of fainted."

"Hush now, Rowdy. We are getting close enough to hear and be heard. Don't say a word until I give you the signal."

Now the barnyard lights were clear of trees ahead and the outlines of the house and barns and corrals was in plain sight. A cow bawled to her calf somewhere out of sight, and a horse nickered.

"But I don't hear a dog," I whispered. "Wouldn't Moochie be able to hear or smell us and bark to let us know?"

"Maybe so, maybe no. Quiet now. Hold the reins of my pony while I do a little scouting on my own."

By now I was shivering with tension and excitement. Somehow, I had in mind that Moochie would hear us from a long way off and come running if he was free, or at least welcome us with a bark or two.

Booger Joe was, gone ten or fifteen minutes. The starlight showed me his shadow when he got up close. He pulled on my saddle horn and whispered, "Rowdy, you ain't gonna believe this. I found Moochie. He is in the house."

I quivered so hard I could hear my teeth chatter. "You did? Why didn't you bring him back? Why didn't he bark at us? Can't he smell us?"

Booger Joe chuckled low and said, "Rowdy, I got to tell you. This is a sho'nuf miracle. Remember Olivia's female Border Collie you saw at the church social when you first landed in Salt River? And the time you told me about when you saw Olivia again at the store?"

"Of course I remember her dog. She was marked almost like Moochie – a white ring around her neck, but white only on three legs rather than four as Moochie had. She called her dog Dolly. So?

Booger Joe laughed and said, "Son, your Moochie is in love. Dolly is in heat. Chances are she is going to have pups one month from now."

"You mean..."

"Yes, I mean. Looks like to me we made a mistake. Now I don't think Moochie was dog-napped at all. When I saw the boys riding away from the bull, and Moochie seeming to chase them, I'd say he got the scent of that female dog either on the air blowing toward him, or on the horses the boys rode, or from their saddles.

"You know the mating instinct of animals is so sensitive it carries on the air for miles and miles. That's something the animal kingdom has on humans. That's God's way of keeping Earth populated forever and ever."

"But, it doesn't work that way with people."

He butted in. "You just don't know it yet, Rowdy. It works the same way, only you just don't recognize it yet. Or maybe you do, but have not admitted it. I saw you looking at Olivia when you first met her at the store."

"Now, let's just ride in to the homestead like we are lookins' for cows. If I don't miss my guess, the whole family is in the house listening to the radio and some such program as Amos and Andy or Fibber and Molly or Jack Benny."

And so we put the spurs to our horses and galloped straight toward the house and Booger Joe let out a loud yell – "Hello the house. It's Ol' Joe and Rowdy. Can we light a spell."

Almost at once the light came on and Ollie Oliver stepped out on the porch, shading his eyes to see us. "Booger Joe? That you? What the devil you doing out this late at night? Are you lost? Come on into the yard."

We cantered our horses and in a couple of minutes we were at the front porch and Ollie Oliver shook hands with Booger Joe and looked at me and said, "Kid, ain't you out late? Get down and come in. We was just listening to that newfangled radio."

He yelled to the house, "Ma, Olivia, come out here. We got company. Put on a pot of coffee."

Mrs. Oliver stepped out on the porch, shading her eyes to make out our faces. "Joe is that really you? What brings you way out here this time of night?"

"Howdy, Miz Oliver. If it was anybody else, I'd tell them a big windy. But to a lady like you, I got to tell the truth.

"The truth is that this here boy of mine has lost a dog, and we thought he might have showed up here. Any chance?"

"Law's a mercy yes. We were just talking about that. He showed up on our doorstep day before yesterday. From what I have seen since then, he was looking for female company," she said.

She turned back to the door and said, "Olivia, there's somebody here to see you. Please come out on the porch."

Olivia peeked out the screen door and said, "Who is it, Ma?" She stepped onto the porch and saw us. "Oh, is it our Rowdy? I'm so glad you came. There's someone here that wants to see you." She opened the door and out came Moochie, and close on his heels came – you guessed it – her dog Dolly."

I stepped down from the saddle and Moochie ran to me and stood on his hind legs and licked my hands. Then he turned around in a couple of circles, dancing like, as if to say to Dolly, "See, I told you he would come after me."

I kneeled on both knees and hugged him tight as I could and he licked my face until I made him stop. Then he and Dolly ran around in little circles to show how happy they were.

I didn't want to cry, but my eyes got a little wet and I choked up. By this time Booger Joe had gone into the house and Olivia stood there watching the display of happiness and she just beamed at me.

"Daddy and I were going to bring him home tomorrow," she said. "We couldn't bring him any sooner 'cause daddy had to go to a cattleman's meeting."

"I sure was worried about him. Then Booger Joe figured out where he was – at least where we thought he could be. And that's why we came."

"But why did you wait until after dark to come?"

"You aren't going to believe this, but we really thought your brothers had stolen him for a mean trick on me."

"And you were going to ride in here after dark and teach my brothers a lesson, right?"

"Something like that. Booger Joe said it's kind of a sport in this country to play dirty tricks on each other. Just so nobody really gets hurt. We were going to do something like riding around the house at midnight and shooting Booger Joe's guns up in the air and then ride back home."

She giggled. "That sounds like a trick my brothers would pull."

"Right. Give them a dose of their own medicine."

By now, both dogs had settled down and were lying next to us and we didn't speak for a while. Then I just had to tell her what had happened since I last saw her.

"Olivia, I am going home. My buddy JJ told Miss Sally we had run away from home in Missouri. She made him tell who my father was, and she secretly sent a letter telling him we were all right, but that he should come and get us before something dreadful happened."

"And?"

"Dad wrote back saying he wasn't mad at us. And that he understood why I ran away. And we would fix it all up. He said he couldn't get away until after his wheat had been cut and shocked, and then he would drive down and take us home."

"Why did you run away in the first place?"

"I was mad at Pa, and he gave me a good lickin' and I just decided I'd show him I wasn't going to take that any more. It wasn't my fault I was unhappy. It wasn't me that married another woman and brought her kids into my life."

"And? Is anything going to be different when you get back home?"

"In some ways, yes. In other ways, no. One thing I haven't told you yet. Booger Joe ran away from home when he was young and came to Texas to hitch up with Salt River Sally. And that ain't all. Booger Joe has turned into my best friend. Not only that, Booger Joe's name is not Joe – he is my blood uncle and his real name is Frank Oscar McLin. Olivia, he is my uncle and my namesake."

She leaped to her feet trembling. She reached out and touched me, and tears filled her eyes. She put her arms around my neck and hugged me tight, and I put my arms around her. It was the first and only time in my life I ever got that close to a girl, let alone have one hug me tight. Then she did the worst thing ever. She pulled my head down and kissed me real, real hard.

Suddenly I got a feeling inside that I had never known before. I shook from my head to my toes and all of a sudden I knew what happened when somebody said they were in love.

I was in love with a nice pretty girl, five hundred miles from my home. And here I was, on the verge of having to give her up just after I had fallen in love with her.

We stood like that for I don't know how long, then she said, "We better go inside with the folks before something else happens that should not happen."

25

Love and Black Bulls

Olivia and I broke apart, but still held hands. Her hands were like silk gloves against my rough and dirty ones, but she didn't seem to mind.

"Can you keep a secret?" she asked.

I gulped. It never occurred to me that we had a secret. But, then, I realized we really did have, after all. And with that admission my whole life turned around, just like that. "Sure," I said, "but it ain't anything to be ashamed of, is it?"

"No, silly, but it is our very own business, isn't it?"

"I can go along with that, ok." And so we walked to the porch, where she stopped at the door and gave my hand a good squeeze and then, much to my surprise, she popped a big juicy kiss on my lips.

"I swear, Olivia, you make me plumb dizzy. Lead on before I go crazy."

And so we went into the house where they were hearing the Jack Benny show. Ollie turned off the radio and Mrs. Oliver asked if anyone wanted popcorn, and without waiting for answer, she disappeared in the kitchen and we heard pots and pans rattling.

Booger Joe said, "I could eat a bushel, if it's got real butter on it."

Ollie changed the subject. "Rowdy, I hear you got into a real storm the other day with that black bull. That belongs to your uncle. Heard he put you up a tree. That right?"

Right then, I knew his two boys had seen me all right, and the cowards had run off to save their own hides and didn't care what happened to me.

"That's right, and those boys like to devil me, and that is all right, I guess. But then they ran off and left me to die, that's a horse of a different color. I wish I was big enough to take them both on at the same time. They need a good lickin'."

Ollie let out a belly roll and said, "You got that right, Rowdy. I don't know what to do with them, but then I don't know what I'd do without them. They are good ranch hands when I can get them settled down."

I couldn't let that go. "I saw my uncle settle them down one day in Salt River town. They got to teasing him and he sat there like a wooden Indian for a while, then he whipped out that pair of six shooters he carries on his hip, and they got in their old car and left in such a hurry they got in front of themselves."

Ollie roared with laughter and slapped my uncle on the back. "I heard about that," he said. "Rowdy wasn't the only one saw it. In fact, somebody reported it to the sheriff, and he just tossed it off, because he knows my boys and knew they were just playing their game with Joe, and that he could put them in their place any time he wanted to."

Mrs. Oliver delivered two big bowls full of popcorn and it smelled so good I took a double helping. Ollie said, "Now Rowdy, are you still going to deliver that bull so you can get that $100 I promised you?"

"I hate to go back on my word, but I guess he got me scared away. I knew some mean Jersey bulls back home, but I never saw one before that put the fear of God in me."

Olivia came to my rescue. She said, "Oh, daddy, everybody knows Rowdy was just bluffing. Even you can't catch that old range bull. He's got the sharpest pointed horns ever and could gore you to death before you knew what was happening."

I took up on that, between hands full of popcorn. "I've got to confess he was meaner than anything I ever saw. I thought Jersey's were mean, but that black bull takes the blue ribbon."

I took another handful of popcorn and should have kept my mouth shut, but somehow, I didn't. "I know how he can be caught. But the best thing to do would be to shoot him with a high powered riffle. Maybe a buffalo gun, like the old time buffalo hunters used."

"Wouldn't you be better off to use a purebred Hereford or Angus bull instead of that cathammed bull? He doesn't have any depth of rib and his hind quarters where the good meat is as skinny as a rail."

My uncle butted in. "Rowdy, let me tell you about that bull's history. He is the last bull of the breed that came across the water with the Spaniards,

500 years ago. They ran loose on this continent for all those years, until the white man came along and started killing them off and doing just what you said – breeding more meat on their bones and making them something less than man-killers.

"The old timers began to call them Longhorns and finally considered them a natural part of life, and now they are just about extinct. What we would really like to do is to save that bull, drive him and a few cows into a canyon, like down on my ranch, and try to rebuild the old breed before they are extinct.

"I've been babying a bunch of cows for ten years, and somehow that bull found a way out of the canyon, and then forgot how to get back. All ranchers have a weak spot for that bull, even if we do cuss him every day.

"If we could somehow catch him, and carry him back to that canyon where his momma cows wait for him, it would be a blessing. We've get some more Longhorn calves and try to renew the breed before they are all gone. In money, that bull is worth ten bulls of any other breed. We could easy kill him, but that ain't the point. Understand?"

For the first time, I began to see what that bull was all about. He was sort of a bovine heirloom. Olivia scooted over next to me and locked her arm in my arm. "Sure you understand, don't you, Rowdy? Daddy was only spoofing you. He knew you could not possibly catch the bull, but they didn't realize you took him seriously."

"Well, that is all right. I can take a joke. But I am thinking of something that might just turn the joke on all of you old cowboys."

Ollie let out a whoop of laughter, "All right, boy. Let's hear the next biggest lie anybody's told tonight."

"Well, all year long my dad has been talking to veterinarians at the university about a new drug they are experimenting with that just puts cattle to sleep for a while. Then they give the animal another shot, and this wakes them up again after you have operated on them.

"They tried it on dad's cattle and it works. I saw it with my very own eyes."

Another laugh died in Ollie's throat. He leaned forward. Tell me more, Rowdy." To Booger Joe, he asked, "Is he serious?"

"I don't know," Joe said. "I never heard of anything like that."

"But how do you get close enough to a bull or cow and give them that shot?"

"Dad saw the vet take a blow gun, put the medicine in the tip of a dart and blow the dart into the neck or hips of the animal. I couldn't believe it myself, but that old bull just jumped a little and swished his tail like horse fly had bitten him, and then he got drowsy."

"Finally laid down and snored. The vet treated him and after a while, the bull woke up, staggered a little, then walked away to the pasture."

"Booger, has that boy gone nuts?"

"Can't say. Reckon we best hit the hay and we'll talk about it tomorrow."

Finally Ollie invited us to stay the night and go back home later, and we were supposed to sleep in the stable on bed rolls kept for the roundup crews.

Olivia helped get my bedroll unrolled and when Booger Joe started snoring, she slipped back to the stable and cuddled up beside me.

"Oh, Rowdy. I think I will marry you. Will tomorrow be all right?"

"Olivia, you are scaring me to death. I am only 16 years old, well, almost 17. We can't talk like that."

"Stop me," she said. "I dare you." She kissed me again, this time on my lips, then jumped up and ran out of the stable. I just got weak all over.

She stuck her head around the door again and blew me a kiss and said, "I love you," and blew me another kiss.

"Dream of me," and she disappeared.

I dreamed that I had dreamed that, but finally I fell to sleep. And she was there, too.

26

The Ride

I woke up in a hurry for I felt Olivia kissing me. When I sat up and got the sleep out of my eyes, I saw Olivia standing there all right, but it wasn't her kissing me.

It was my Moochie, just so glad to see me he could hardly stand it. I put my arms around him, and then Olivia's dog, Dolly, got in the act, and pretty soon they were rolling in the sweet-smelling cedar bedding I had slept on, and Olivia was pulling the cover off of me and saying, "Crawl out of bed, sleepy head. Papa is going to take you and your uncle home in his new car."

"I can't do that," I said. "I've got to ride my horse back to Miss Sally's. And there is my uncle's horse, too."

"Same thing, Daddy said one of his cowboys will take the horses home. He wants to show off his new 1938 Chrysler Imperial. He just bought it yesterday and is dying to show it off. He got it just especially so he could get used to driving it before the 4th of July picnic."

As I got up, she picked the cedar out of my hair and brushed it back and ran her fingers through it to untangle it. She just made me tingle all over, so I didn't act like I was in any hurry, but she grabbed my hands and practically dragged me to the house.

"Daddy and Booger Joe are just eating their first hotcakes and bacon," she said. "We'll let them finish and then she will feed us. She is a great cook, and I am going to be just like her. She says the way to a man's heart is through his stomach..."

Just then two barn cats ran across the yard and the big one caught the little one and crawled on its back while biting the little cat's neck. She giggled and turned my head away. "Naughty, naughty," she said.

For sure, she was a country girl, just what I liked. She knew about the birds and bees and dogs and cats, as my mother used to say.

We met Ollie and my uncle coming out of the house, talking about cows and horses so deep they didn't even notice us, and in the kitchen Mrs. Oliver – Maybell – heard us enter and without looking over her shoulder said, "Grab your plates and knives and forks, the first pancakes are in the skillet and syrup's on the table. Wash your hands."

And so after eating six or eight pancakes and drinking a cup of milk, I was ready for the day, and Olivia had it all planned for me.

"Daddy's ready to go, and when he gets ready to travel, everybody better be ready, too. Let's get in the car, because if we are not in it when he is we will be seeing the dust as he drives away."

We walked to one of the big barns at his ranch headquarters and inside we saw something covered with a white wagon sheet. We got there just in time to see Mr. Oliver jerk the wagon sheet off, and there it was, a brand new, cherry red, four-door Chrysler Imperial. I'd seen pictures of them in the Saturday Evening Post magazine, but this was even more beautiful than I dreamed.

I peeked inside and the interior was blue velvet, and it felt like the smoothness of, well, the smoothness of Olivia's hair when she had brushed against my face last night.

Ollie crawled in the driver's seat, and said "Everybody aboard. This bronco is buckin' and rearin' to go." He leaned on the horn, circled the house, and yelled, "Come on, Ma, time's a wastin'. The car jumped and jerked when it started moving, and he stomped on the gas and it smoothed out, but kicked up a lot of dust and gravel as he roared toward the house, where Mrs. Oliver was standing, sunbonnet on and her best chicken-feed gingham dress all might' stylish.

She got in the back seat where I was sitting and patted the seat on her right, but Olivia edged her out and plopped down beside me and squeezed my hand.

Mr. Oliver had a heavy foot on the gas and he dug up dust and ruts. It was a pretty rough ride. Sometimes a bounce would throw all of us up until our heads hit the top of the car, but Ollie just laughed, hit the gas harder and yelled, "Ride'm cowboy. Let'er buck."

I had just about all of the new car ride I wanted when he ran a rock through a tire and boom, she went flat and we came to a quick stop. We all piled out of the car and located a spare tire and tools in the trunk, and after a fashion, Ollie and my uncle managed to get the flat tire off and the new one on.

As we got into the car and started, Maybell reached over and pulled her man's ear. "Now see her, Mr. Cowboy, this is not a bronc you are riding. You drive like a sensible cowboy or this ranch cook is going to make you walk home while she drives."

He took the chewing-out pretty good, and so nothing more happened, except he got interested in what he was talking about and nearly ran us off in a ditch or two.

The main thing he wanted to talk about was the big picnic Salt River town had on the fourth of July, and he let us know about it.

"Ringling Brothers, Barnum and Bailey was supposed to be in Dallas this week, but somebody go their wires crossed. They had to lay over a week because of the goof, and because of that, they will play Salt River just to keep in shape for the big show."

By that time, we were in the town itself and could see the big circus wagons parked in a circle on the west side of town, and the cages with lions and tigers, even a couple of elephants, and lots of horses in bright harnesses, all cleaned and curried and tied by halters and eating bright green prairie hay.

I wanted to stop and look around, but Ollie said he had to get on back to the ranch as soon as possible, because he had a cow buyer coming at noon and couldn't afford to miss him. We bounced over the wagon road to Miss Sally's house and when we pulled into her yard, there she was, standin' at the door way, wipin' her hands on her apron and stretching her neck to see what on earth was headed her way.

The car came to a stop about a foot from her toes and she shouted, "You dern fool, look or I'll..."

And when she looked inside the car and saw who we were, she let out her war screech, jerked open the door, reached inside and pulled me out and kissed me on both cheeks.

"Rowdy, you contrary Missouri mule, I feared you had got killed by them no-good Oliver boys, and here you are in a brand new car with Ollie driving. And you, Maybell... it's been a coon's age since you been to my house. Get down and come in, get down and come in.

"And my little darlin' Olivia." She smacked her lips on Olivia's cheek and squeezed her so tight she gasped for breath.

First thing I did was look around. "Where's JJ?" I asked. "I don't see him anywhere."

27

Back at Sally's

Miss Sally swarmed around like an old mother hen, grabbing everybody and smacking a big wet kiss on their cheeks, up to and including Ollie, Maybell and when she got to Ollie again, she grabbed his head between his fat cheeks and laid a big smacker on both sides.

"There, take that, you ornery old cuss. Ain't seen you for a coon's age."

Ollie grabbed her around the waist and swung her around in a do-see-do like in square dancing and yelled, "Dance me to the kitchen, Sal. I smell blackberry pie hot out of the oven."

So the old folks headed for the house, and left Olivia and me standing there, forgotten for the moment. Of course, the first thing out of the car was Moochie and Dolly, and they were already on an inspection trip around the homestead. It seemed to me like that was the same thing I ought to be doing with Olivia, so I said, something not too original, "Would you like to look around?"

She grabbed my hand and the first thing I did was take her to the horse pasture, where Houdini and Jackrabbit were hanging their heads over the fence taking in all of the human excitement.

"So this is the Quarter Horse you stole one night. And that must be the jackass that JJ roped. Rowdy, you sure don't do things in a little way when you get into action, do you?"

I felt my face grow hot at the reminder that I thought I'd found a real, honest-to-god wild horse, only to be told later she was a broke horse that was scheduled for shipment to a sale barn. And that Jackrabbit was a gentle old plug that helped trading horses how to find grass and water on his regular range. If he had been a goat, he would have been called a Judas Goat, for that's what they called a goat that led sheep into a box car when it is being loaded. Most folks don't know that sheep follow the leader, and sometimes the leader betrays them, so the term, Judas Goat.

"Aw, Olivia, I guess I am just a dumb Missouri country boy that has a lot to learn about Texas and real ranches and cowboys. But I won't make such a mistake again."

"My uncle told me what I had done wrong, but I guess every body in his part of the world knew about it before I did. And were laughing about it behind my back."

She took my hand and squeezed it. "Don't think anything about it, Rowdy. If people around these parts took everything seriously, everybody would be in jail. That was just an honest mistake."

"What you have got to look out for around here is who can play the biggest joke on somebody and get away with it for the longest time. That's our recreation, sort of."

So that made me feel better, and I took her hand and led her to the big pond. "There's a big old largemouth bass in that pond. He just about drives me crazy when he rolls up out of the water and snatches a big grasshopper or water bug off the water and sinks back into his home.

"One of these days I'm going to rig me up a fishing pole and have him dangling on a stringer. I bet he weighs five or six pounds. Won't he make a good meal, fried in real butter?"

"Oh, Rowdy. You wouldn't want to kill a beautiful creature like that, would you? Think of how free and happy he is – or is it a she? Don't catch it. Let it live."

Well, that sure took me back a piece or two. I had no idea she thought a fish should be sacred, like say, a pet dog like her Dolly or my Moochie, or a pet cat or even a horse. I just didn't know what to do.

"But, Olivia, back home, the people would starve to death if they didn't have lots of fish to eat. Everybody is dirt poor. A fish is just plain old food to us."

"I don't care. This is different. Fish are scarce here, because we don't have much water. Our streams dry up in summer time, and the rest of the time they are so low fish can't come up from deeper water, because sometimes our rivers go underneath the ground in dry times."

Well, I didn't have the answer for that, for I had never heard of such a thing. If that was what rivers were like in Texas, I wasn't so sure I was going to like it. After all, I was used to clean, cold water the year around, where we could catch fish all year long, even fish through the ice on lakes and ponds, and ducks and geese migrated twice a year, and it was always exciting to see the first flocks wing in overhead, and hear them honk and cackle, and sometimes land in wheat and rye fields by the thousands. They could also eat all your grass and dad would go out with his shotgun and shoot it so they would fly away to someone else's fields.

And there were also mink and muskrats that thrived in our waters, and you could set traps and catch them in the winter time, and sell their hides for real cash money. It helped ma and pa pay for my school clothes with my trapping money, and what I got for my rabbits.

I was discovering that there was a lot of things about both of us where I was different, but, then, I got to thinking, maybe that was why we kind of hitchup and enjoyed being together. I wondered if that was what caused my mother and dad to get together in the first place, but then again, maybe that was what went wrong that made them split and get a divorce and make me so unhappy.

But all that thinking didn't make me feel any different from the way I had begun to feel about Olivia, and so I took her on a walk down to the corn field we had planted, which seemed to grow a foot every day and night, and then we saw JJ hoeing the weeds out between the rows, and he stopped and came over and said, "Howdy, Miss Olivia. Glad to meet you." He took off his straw hat and used a red neckerchief to wipe the sweat from his head and then went back to hoeing. JJ was always nervous around girls, especially white girls, and that was because back home, the white race and black races did not socialize together. They worked together, all right, but each race had its own private times, recreational times, and different churches.

"Come on, Olivia, I want to show you where we shot our big wild turkeys." And so we sauntered into the woods that bordered the river, and it felt cool and inviting as we walked, and her hands were warm in mine. Birds chirped in the tree tops, and occasionally a flock of crows would fly over and spy us and shy away with a great flapping of wings.

And then just when we got the quietest and were wanting to stop and maybe hold hands a little tighter, and just be alone in our thinking, a whole huge covey of Texas blue quail burst out of the grass all around us.

There just seemed to be no end to the beautiful blue and white and brown bodies that hurtled out of the grass and flew away through the brush and the tree limbs. Texas quail amazed me. They covey up by the hundreds.

Then we saw what had scared up the quail. Dolly and Moochie scurried around in the weeds, sniffing and smelling the birds, and when they saw us, the came running and put their front legs on us and looked up with their tongues laughing as if to say, "Look what we found. Isn't that exciting?"

The excitement and surprise that interrupted our silence made Olivia grab me around the neck and say, "Oh, Rowdy. They scared me to death. I have never seen so many quail at one time."

I made a monumental statement like, "Me neither," and since the spell was broken, we turned around and headed back to the house.

Just as we broke into the clearing by the pond, we heard the clip'clop of horses' hooves, and Mr. Oliver's cowboy broke into the clearing riding a white Quarter Horse and leading my Lady Midnight and Booger Joe's spotted cow pony.

They splashed into the river, the horses stopped to swig in a great mouth full of water each, then shook their heads and plunged out of the water and ran full speed up to the house where the old folks were watching and waiting.

28

Olivia Makes it Better

Booger Joe, or, my Uncle Frank, and Ollie Oliver sat in the shade of a big mesquite tree, leaning back in ease. Ollie whittled on sticks, like loafers had done since time began and knives were invented. What pleasure men got out of what was known as 'spitten 'n whittlin' I never had found out, but anyhow that's what old men did.

"What you young scamps been doin'?" Ollie said. "You ain't supposed to do spoonin' until after sundown."

He winked and nudged Booger Joe in the ribs and he grinned and just spit tobacco juice at a passing rooster.

Ollie's cowboy, after unsaddling the two horses, walked bow-legged-like and stretched out on the ground in the shade of a tree. He pulled his grease stained old hat over his eyes, and was snoring before his eyelids closed.

Olivia just hung on my arm and wouldn't let go, and I expected her pa to get after her, but he just grinned and winked at me. For want of something to break the silence, I said, "Do I smell ham frying? I could eat a slab as big as a bucket."

"Yep, reckon we'd better ease on up so we won't get yelled at."

He laughed and got up holding his back and saying, "Oh, changing that flat tire just about did me in, how about you, Joe? That's harder than shoe'n a kickin' horse."

And so just as we about got to the kitchen door, Miss Sally waddled to the door and yelled out, "Come and get it, you bow-legged, no-good cow punchers, 'fore I throw it out." She stretched her neck to look at the cowboy with his hat pulled over his eyes and said, "Just let him sleep, poor boy. I know he's dead beat after that late breakfast."

Maybell hugged Olivia and held her close while looking at me to see, I guess, if I had done anything with her that I ought not have done, and then everything was silent except the nonsense job of eating all we could eat as fast as we could. Then the men folk went to thanking the women folk and bragging a lot about how good the cooking was. Ollie said, "If you don't mind, I'd like to have another piece of that blackberry pie."

After that, there was less talk, and the two men went back out to the mesquite tree and sprawled out on the ground, with their hats over their heads, and pretty soon there was a trio of sleepy time music makers.

Miss Sally and Maybell pulled rocking chairs up on the front porch, rocked back and forth and laughed and talked a little while, then things got real quiet and first thing you knew, their heads dropped and they slept soundly, except for a little snore or two once in a while.

That left Olivia and me all alone, and we took advantage of it to just say silly things like how pretty the sky and clouds are, and how we wished we could fly like the birds, and I told her an airplane flew over our house in Cave Springs once.

"Tell me what life is like in your home town," she said. "Turn about's fair play. You have seen what my life is like."

And so I first began to tell her I lived in a big two-story white house my grandpa and grandma had built when they made a lot of money on a grand champion bull, and then times got hard and we had to start milking cows for a living, and then we got some sheep and hogs and started getting out of debt again.

Then I told her about my mother and father getting into a fuss they couldn't stop and how ma finally left home, got a job and then dad married another woman, with kids.

The more I talked, the lower I got and by the time I was finished, I could not stop the tears and a wave of home sickness like I had never known swept over me and I just had to quit talking and put my head down on my lap and big tears wet my face.

Olivia knew just what to do. She put her arms around me and didn't say a word, and held me tight and put her sweet-smelling hair across my face until I got myself under control. Finally she said in a soft voice, "You'll be going home in a few days, Rowdy. Don't cry. No. Do cry. That will make you feel better when you get the pain out of your system.

"And think of the bright side. Maybe your mother will come to get you with your father, and you can be together again, just like in a story book."

I felt a wave of love and tenderness sweep through me that I never knew existed. She had lifted me up and put me back together again, and she took her handkerchief and wiped my eyes and patted me on the cheek and brushed my hair out of my eyes. Then she tenderly took her hands and turned my face toward her and put her sweet, warm lips against mine and just held them there until I felt like we had become just one person, and that all the world suddenly stood still.

29

How to Break a Mule

"Oh, Rowdy, I just never want this moment to end. But I hear the old folks stirring. They are waking up, so we better go up to the house and see if and when we are going home. Can you go back with us and stay until your father comes after you?"

I hadn't had time to think about what my next move would be. I told her so, and she said, "What did you tell me once about your mule? You know the one you said that wouldn't stand tied.

"Why don't you do it now while daddy is here? He laughed when he told me about that, and said he sure would like to see how you go about it. He had never seen any one teach a hard-headed mule anything."

I grinned at the thought. I remembered back home that my dad had learned a trick from his grandfather, and he had won many a dollar bet by doing the trick for strangers – as well as neighbors.

I looked around and saw the old folks beginning to stir. Oliver's cowboy was just getting out from under his hat, and Miss Sally called him to come eat. Booger Joe and Ollie were trying to get their bones limbered out, so they could go back to the kitchen for yet another piece of pie.

"Tell you what, Olivia, this just might be the right time to do that. Let me get the halter on Houdini find a good stout piece of rope, and we'll have a little fun."

So she walked over to the ol' shed with me, and I found a strong piece of rope, and then went to the horse pasture where the mule and donkey and Lady Midnight were dozing with their heads drooped down and their tails occasionally brushing away the flies that buzzed around them.

My call woke them up and they just stood there. I picked up a bucket with some oats in it and shook it and said, "Come on boys, time for dinner." They walked slowly to me and I put some oats in my hand and held it out and each one tried to get it at once.

I slipped the noose around the mule's neck. He knew what was coming then, and he threw back his head and reared up a little, but I jerked him back down, opened the gate and led him out.

By then, the men were watching. "What you fixing to do?"

"I'm going to show Olivia my trick mule," I said. "That old rascal is going to learn a lesson about breaking ropes and halters. Bet you a dollar after I get through with him, he will never rear back and break another halter."

"Yeah, sure," Ollie said. "I've been waiting to see how you pull that trick."

The mule walked easily behind me, never suspecting that in a few minutes he was going to get the surprise of his life. He even did a little buck or two, just to show he was rested after his nap and was ready to go to work, or whatever it was I had in mind for him to do.

The spot I had in mind for my trick – or job, if you want to call it that, was on a slight slope at the top of the hill, with the deep pond about ten steps down hill from the top.

The mule didn't give any sign he new what was coming. I stopped leading him, reached back and scratched him behind the ears, patted his neck and ran my hand over his back.

Then, moving quickly, and seeing the women come down the hill, and with Olivia beside her father, I turned the mule around in a circle four times, whipped the end of the rope around the tree trunk, tied a knot and stepped back.

All of a sudden, the mule's head came up, he did a little dance with his front feet, and felt tension on the rope and his neck, let out a mighty "Hee-hah, He-haw," and reared up into the air, his hooves pawing, and jerked back on the rope.

The first jerk on the rope didn't do the job, so for the next jump, he went higher, leaned back with his hind feet dug in, and jerked with all his might.

"Wham." The rope broke just as he had the maximum height and weight going backward.

The momentum of his fall and the sudden release of the broken rope sent him tumbling head over heels backward and just as I planned it, right into the deepest water in the pond.

For a couple of minutes, he was completely out of sight in the pond water. Then, with a mighty splashing and waves of water, he broke through to the surface, pawed the water with his feet until he struck bottom, and, with only his nose and neck above water, set out for the shore.

Of course, by now the splashing water had wet down the ground, and when he put his feet on the ground, the slippery slope didn't hold him. He slid back into the water and after trying the same thing another time or two, he finally got enough traction to heave out of the pond, slip and slide up the hill, and stand quivering from head to toe, his head hanging low in surprise and fear, and he wouldn't move until I went to him, rubbed his nose, talked real nice to him, and then gently led him back to the pasture and removed the rope.

By this time, the surprise from the folks had turned to roaring laughter and slapping of sides. Ollie and Booger Joe came over and shook my hand, and Ollie hoisted me on his shoulder and pranced around, yelling, "Here he is, ladies and gentlemen. The champion mule skinner of all time, the Missouri Kid."

And although I didn't realize it at the time, he gave me a nickname that would stay with me a long time.

Olivia ran to me and hugged me and said, "Rowdy, that was the funniest thing I ever saw. You taught that old mule a good lesson that didn't hurt 'em. And he got a good bath as well."

Just then, Miss Sally waddled toward me, yelling at the top of her voice.

"Rowdy, Rowdy. Look back at the pond. Your big bass, he's jumping clean out of the water and he just jumped so high he's up on the bank flopping around."

Sure enough, there he was, apparently scared to death at the flurry of the water, and had decided to leave home. But there was no place to go, except the bank, and despite his flopping around, he couldn't get back into the water.

Olivia let out a scream and ran toward him, yelling, Rowdy, quick. He's dying, I mean he can't get back. Put him back into the water."

But I had a different thought. I had long planned to catch that old bass and make a meal out of him, so I didn't hurry.

She yelled, "Rowdy, if you let that a poor fish die, I will never, never speak to you again."

That got my attention. I ran to the flopping fish, grabbed him with both hands, hefted him to guess his weight, and yelled out, "Ten pounds unless I miss my guess. He is bigger even than I thought."

"Rowdy! You hurry or I'll never, I'll never-never kiss you again."

That was the magic word. I have that wonderful old bass a heave, he splashed water up on the bank, and then disappeared in the deep.

Behind me there were five people lying on the ground, rolling with laughter and trying to find handkerchiefs and aprons to wipe the tears from their eyes.

I couldn't laugh for grinning so big, but I had not only showed off my mule trick, but put on a big show doing it.

To cap it off, here came Moochie and Dollie running up from nowhere to see what was all the fun. They jumped up on me so hard I fell over backwards, never feeling better in my life.

The men finished their last piece of pie, emptied the coffee pot, and got up from the table. Ollie stretched, patted Miss Sally on the back, and said, "That shore was good, ma'am. Reckon you must come visit us next time you get a chance. Been a coon's age since you come to visit and gossip."

"Shucks, Ollie, if I ever get there again, it will be a miracle. Like as not you'd try to pay me to stay so your Maybell could get a bit of rest."

"Don't let that old fraud talk you into anything, Sally," said Maybell. "When he proposed to me, he promised to do all the heavy lifting and cooking, but precious little of either one I have seen. And especially now that he got himself a fancy new car, he won't be worth shooting."

"Now, ma, you know better than that. It was you talked me into spending the price of a good Hereford bull for that automobile. Now grab your things and let's get going. I'm anxious to see if them two worthless boys of ours have got back with the cows I bought over in Deaf Smith County."

"You and your cows. You'll break us yet, what with your new car on top of more cows. How many cows do you want, anyhow?"

30

Fittin' JJ In

Ollie cackled and slapped her on the behind and said, "How many is there, Maybell? I'll take all I can get, even if I have to drive them down in Booger's canyon to make room. In fact, Booger Joe and I just made a deal to go halvers on the canyon.

"He'll take the lower half for his Longhorns, and I'll take the north half for my Herefords. Just as soon as the boys get back with our new herd, we'll be driving them down."

That made me perk up my ears, I always dreamed of going on a roundup, or trail drive like the cowboys in the books Zane Grey and Luke Short wrote.

I piped up and said, "Hey, can I go with you on the cattle drive? That's the thing I most wanted to do when I ran away from home to Texas. That, plus catching wild horses."

He laughed deep in his belly, making it jump, and grabbed me by the shoulder. "Son, you bet you can go along. Anybody from Missouri that can teach an old cow hand like me how to break a mule sure can ride a cow horse down to the canyon and back out."

"When can we start?"

"Just as soon as them two whippersnapper boys of mine get back with the cows. That could be tomorrow or the next day. So rest up and get ready. I'll send word as soon as we are ready to start, but you won't have to come to my place. We'll be driving the cows along the river were that bull chased you up a tree.

"What I hope for is that the bull is still hanging around and when he sees a new herd of cows, he will forget all about chasing Missouri boys, or any boys, away. We'll just see. Booger Joe and I have agreed if your idea works, we will let the old bull live. If not, he's going to catch a 30-06 bullet square between the eyes. We've put up with him long enough."

And so he and Maybell started for the car, and Olivia hung back. She put her finger up to her lips and whispered, "Don't say anything. Maybe they will forget about me and I'll stay here with you."

The old folks got into the car and started up with a roar and skidding of gravel and then all of a sudden, circled around and returned. "Hey, you Olivia. Come get in this car. What you trying to do? Keep that poor Missouri kid from breaking any more mules?"

"Please, Daddy. Let me stay, Miss Sally said she'd teach me how to make blackberry pie."

Maybell piled out of the car, came around to Olivia, and grabbed her by the arm with a no-nonsense look.

"Young lady, you get into this car this minute. I've got other plans for you."

And so my heart slid back down where it belonged, and I watched her crawl into the back seat and turn around and wave at me as long as we could see each other and when I could see nothing but a trail of dust, I turned around and walked back to the pond to see if that old bass would jump and lift up my spirits.

All of a sudden, I heard something I had not heard for quite a while.

It was the sound of silence.

Ever so often in the out-of-doors, on a farm or ranch, you suddenly become aware that nothing is moving or stirring, not even a breeze to move the tree leaves or the grass, or the little creatures that live in nature.

It is strange, and when nature sometimes plays that trick, it makes me shiver and shake and want to shout as loud as I can, just to shake things loose. My mother used to say, "It sounds like a tomb." But I always thought if there is no sound, how can anything sound like a tomb? Took me a while to figure that out.

I wondered if it was not a trick my ears were playing on. I thought, it must be because we have had so much sound with so many people around the ranch, and the horses whinnying, it was just a matter of imagination.

I shook the thought away, and at that moment the wind stared blowing, the leaves rustling and the little creatures of the land woke up and began buzzing, croaking and moving about.

The world was awake again, and I had to get moving for help, because it was spooky, it being so deathly quiet.

When I moved, the horses and mules talked to me, the mother hen clucked to her babies and the door slammed as Miss Sally stepped out on the porch and said, "Rowdy, come here a minute please."

"Sure. What you want?"

"Have you seen JJ today?"

Come to think of it, I had not seen him since morning when Olivia and I bounced all around the place on our adventure. I cupped my hands and yelled, loud as I could, and when I got no answer, my heart skipped a beat or so.

"I'll run down to the melon patch to see if I can rouse him. You check all the out buildings. He may have laid down and gone to sleep."

"Oh," she moaned, "I was so busy with our company, I forgot all about him, poor boy."

I had not gone very far when she yelled out, "Never mind, Rowdy. I found him. Come back."

I ran back up the hill just in time to see him come out of the back room of the house. "JJ, where have you been? I have not seen you for hours. Are you sick? Did you go in the house to sleep? You scared the daylights out of me."

JJ sat down on a tree stump and just mumbled.

"Can't hear you, buddy. Is anything wrong?" I asked.

He nodded and then I made out that he said. "Homesick. That's all."

My heart came up in my throat and as quick as that, I figured what was wrong – he had been left out of all the fun and laughing and joking we had with our company.

I had hardly been with him for the last couple of days, and he had been depending on me to keep up his spirits and be his buddy.

"Aw, come on, buddy, shake it off. I just got so busy I couldn't get everything done. It's all right now. From now on, where I go, you go, too."

He shook his head. "No I won't, Rowdy. Things have changed."

"What do you mean?"

"Well, I saw you with Olivia. And it was pretty plain you two have a heavy crush on each other. And that leaves me out of the circle."

"No, it doesn't."

"And I heard you make plans to work cattle down into the canyon. Nobody asked me if I wanted to go."

"Well, I'm asking you, right now, and if you don't go, I won't either." I put my arm around him and said, "Come on into the kitchen and get some dinner. You'll feel better. Then we'll sit down and write my dad a letter and tell him we are sorry we ran away and caused so much trouble and ask him if he will come and get us and take us back home. We will tell him we are sorry, and that we know we did wrong, and will take our lickin'.

"Rowdy."

"I need a girl, too. When we get back home, will you help me find one that likes me as much as Olivia likes you?"

"I'll do better than that. How about those triplets that live next door to my grandma? Ruby, Tina and May."

JJ laughed and we walked back to the kitchen, buddies again.

31

Letters Home

After I got JJ out of the dumps and Miss Sally mixed up some pancake batter and put a hot stack on his plate, and drowned them in maple syrup for him, I asked for a pencil and paper.

"What are you going to do?" she asked.

"It's time I was writing my father and apologizing for causing him so much trouble. I want to explain to him that it was all my fault, and ask for forgiveness."

"My mother tried to explain to me why we must forgive our enemies and not hold grudges, or God will not forgive us. I guess I sort of forgot to do that because I was so unhappy."

She brought me a pencil and some paper and an envelope and stamp. And then bent down and gave me a big wet smacker on the cheek and said, "Rowdy, I surely wish I had had a good boy like you. But the Lord didn't see fit for that to happen. He did bring me your uncle, and he has been a blessing. And just think, He brought you to both of us out of the great blue sky. The Lord has seen our affliction, and He has helped us through our trial and tribulation."

I never expected the hear a sermon from Miss Sally, but it made a lot more sense than that fist pounding and yelling our preacher did at church.

> *"Dear Pa," I wrote, "I am fine. How is my grandmother and grandpa? I hope you are ok. How is my cow Betty and her little calf. I will be glad to get back home again and get them ready for the show at the fair.*

I am sorry I ran away from home. I hope you did not miss me too much. But I have had a lifetime of learning in just two short months. I am anxious to tell you about it.

I fell into some mighty fine people on my trip. It must have been a miracle, but I almost accidentally ran into my mother's brother, my uncle Frank. He is what I always wanted to be – a real cowboy, not one of those movie actor cowboys.

You ought to see him ride a horse. He put down a real mean bull that was trying to kill me.

Miss Sally told me she wrote you and told you of my whereabouts. I am glad she did, for I never would have had the nerve to owned up to my mistakes. I guess I would never have had any hopes of ever seeing you again, if it had not been for her.

But I really missed you. Something fierce. She told me she gave you the direction to the ranch, and the name of the town. When you come, will you please bring the stuff the veterinarian used to knock out our mean bull, and then doctor him and bring him back to life?

I want to show a neighbor named Oliver who has a big ranch and more cows than I knew existed, how to do that knockout-come-back-to-life trick. There is a real mean bull that almost killed me, but he is called the last of the true Longhorns and they value his calves. But he is really mean, with horns you would not believe.

I guess that is about all I have to say. But I have a lot to tell you when you come and get me.

P.S. Please tell JJ's friends he is ok, and that he is homesick, too. Hurry. I can't wait to see you. I am sorry I have been a bad son, I will make it up to you when I get home.

Love from your son,

Rowdy

After I got through with it, and JJ had his belly full of pancakes, he sat beside me while I read him the letter. When I got through, he was grinning ear to ear. He said, "I got a lot to tell all my folks back there. None of them ever had a big adventure like this. Rowdy… you are my best friend I ever had or ever will have. You are a real smart boy, for a white boy."

Miss Sally took the letter from me and read it, then gave me another smacker on the cheeks, and said, "Rowdy, your letter almost makes me want to go back to Missouri to meet your father. Maybe, I betcha, your uncle might want to go back some time, too. Are his mother and his sister still living?"

"They were when I left home, and my paternal grandmother as well. Would you go back with us? I think you would like our part of the country. We have a lot more rain than in Texas, and you can run two cows to the acre, instead of only one to about 20 acres in Texas. And it don't get as hot in summer either, and we have lots more rain than you do, and our rivers are a lot bigger and prettier, too, and you can go swimming, just like it was a bath that you wanted to take."

"I would think about it. But let's get you and JJ taken care of first. You still have several days before you leave. We have a trail drive to make, and the July fourth picnic, and the circus to go to in the next few days. Let's take care of the evening chores and we'll talk about it after the sun goes down and gets cooler."

I never felt better after our talk, and I went about our chores happily until I got a horrible thought.

When I left, I would never, ever, get to see my girl, Olivia, again.

My heart just went through the bottom of my shoes.

32

The Surprise

Just as I began to feel good about myself again, I heard the clip-clop of Booger Joe's horse. He rode to the corral, and I walked out to meet him at the gate.

"Well, nephew, what did you get done while I was riding the pastures?"

"A little bit, I guess. I wrote a letter to pa, telling him I was sorry. Now I've got to take it to the post office in the morning. Joe, I admit I will be glad to get back home, but I sure hate to leave you all."

"Yeah," he said, draping an arm around my shoulder. "You mostly hate to think about leaving little Olivia behind, don't you?"

I swallowed hard. "That's the worst part."

He sat down on the grinding rock where we sharpened tools. "Let me ask you some things about the old home folks. Do all the black folks still live there? Old Aunt Mary, still a'fishin' I bet? Aunt Tilda and Charlie Rollin, Laughin' Earl Pike – they still kick'n?"

"Aunt Mary died a long time ago, but the others are still there."

"And Joe Johnson and Minnie – and their brood?"

"Yep. "Their oldest daughter, Mary, works for my grandma six days a week and …"

"Stop right there, Rowdy. Tell me more about Mary. What does she look like? Quiet and pretty as ever? Still good natured? What kind of baby did she have – boy or girl?"

His question startled me. "Far as I know, Mary never was married. She doesn't have a child, not that I know of."

He got up and started toward the kitchen door, kind of quiet like.

"No child, huh? Something must of happened along the way. Well, well. She was sure enough bulging around the middle last time I saw her."

Something hit me like a mule kicking. My uncle had known her when she was a young girl? My uncle had run away from home when she was pregnant? Could it be…? Ah, no. I tried to put it out of my mind.

Abruptly, he said, "Let's go in and see if ol' Sal has us anything to eat."

Just as we got to the door, we heard in the distance the most gosh-awful bawling and wailing of a cow I ever heard in my life. It sounded like it was a long way off and coming closer at a run. But I had never known a cow that could run as fast as this one that kept getting closer and closer in split seconds.

We ran toward the trail that lead back to Salt River town, and in the distance there was a cloud of dust a mile high, and the cow seemed to be hidden in that billowing of dust, and getting closer by the second.

All of a sudden, a dusty automobile appeared just in front of the cloud of dust and it screeched to a halt at our feet.

We coughed and spit dust and when it settled, there was Ollie Oliver stepping out, coughing and slapping dust off his hat. "What you think of my new cow horn?" he asked. "Makes cows come a'runnin' when they hear it."

Right behind him was – guess who? My little sweetheart, Olivia. She held a handkerchief over her nose and gasped for air.

His new Chrysler Imperial had a bad dent in the left front fender, but other than seeming to be a different color, it was the same new car I had ridden in a day earlier.

I helped fan the dust off Olivia and she just fell against me, gasping. "Oh, Rowdy, I'll take a good pony any day, rather than ride in a car with the windows rolled down."

Ollie laughed and his big belly bounced. "Young'ens these days can't take a little hardship. Let's get a big drink of water and sit a spell. I got news for you."

And so we went to the windmill, which was whirling at a good clip because of the strong southwest wind, and drank our fill while Ollie and Olivia washed their layers of dust off. Then we went to the front porch and sat down with Miss Sally hovering around her company as always, and offering them something to eat.

"Don't have much time," Ollie said. Just wanted to tell you I have moved up the schedule for the cattle drive from next week to begin tomorrow. That's why I was in such a toot to get here.

"My two boys got in early with the new herd I bought, and we've got to start tomorrow moving out the mother cows at the home place and driving them down to the canyon pasture for the rest of the summer."

"I need some more riders, and I thought you, Joe, and JJ, would help us. How about it?"

My heart leaped at the chance. This was the one thing I most wanted to do, and it was what I thought I would miss when pa came to take JJ and me home.

"Don't know why not," Booger Joe said. "How about it, Rowdy?"

"Best news I had today," I said dancing a little jug and putting my arm around Olivia. "Can she ride too?"

"Don't know about that," Ollie said. "Some mighty rough territory we will be riding through, but Olivia and you can stay behind when we get to the roughest part of the canyon."

And so it was settled, and Miss Sally of course would not hear to them leaving without eating supper, and she butchered a fat chicken, fried it and made gravy and one of her famous blackberry pies.

When Ollie got through eating, he said, "Booger, you and Rowdy best get in my Imperial and go home with us. You won't need your horses, because I brought on a big remuda for the hands. You can take your pick. We will have to roll out before daylight, grab some grub and string out in the biggest pasture I have.

"We want to be in place to start to gather the herd before sunup, then trail them thirty miles to the canyon.

"So grab your boots and spurs and brush jackets and chaps, and let's get going."

Inside of thirty minutes, we said goodbye to Miss Sally, and crawled in the car – my uncle and JJ in front with Ollie, and Olivia and me in the back seat. It was a cozy and comfortable ride for the next hour, and we dropped off to sleep, our arms around each other and happy as two bedbugs in a rug.

33

The Trap

Olivia and I didn't talk much on the way back to the ranch. We were both sobered by the fact we could virtually count the days that I would still be in Texas, and wondering what we would do about it. We knew what the old folks were thinking – that it was just puppy love.

Well, so what if it was? Love is love, isn't it? Doesn't everyone go through those stages?

But our love was not what was on the minds of Booger Joe and Ollie Oliver. One minute they were talking cow and horse pedigrees, the next if it would ever rain again, and then the good times they had in the past at roundups.

By the time we pulled into the ranch yard, the sun had dipped below the horizon, leaving an orange glow over the mesquite that seemed to reflect a duplicate vision from the sky above, leaving the impression the world was encased in a gigantic, endless upside down cherry-red bowl.

"Come see momma," she said. "Then you can take a bed roll from the bunkhouse and sleep where you did the last time you were our guests."

"What about you? Can you…"

She clapped a soft hand over my mouth and whispered, "Not so loud. Wait until everyone is sound asleep and I just might slip through the dark and come to see you."

Booger Joe and JJ had gone on down to the bunkhouse beyond the home place, and the new electric lights gave a dim glow that was punctuated by the occasional laughter of the gathered cow hands. She left then, and I evidently fell asleep, although I thought I could stay awake until she came.

All of a sudden, I was awakened by a pitter-patter on the soft straw bed, and then some kind of an animal pounced right on top of me and brought me straight up. A warm and wet slobbery tongue wet my face and ears and whined, and I was stunned to see that it was my Moochie. I thought he had stayed behind at Miss Sally's, but he hadn't, and he had by instinct taken a shortcut across the land, come straight to me, and at the same time, found his only girlfriend, Dolly.

Dolly got into the act, too, and both seemed to be so glad to see each other, and to find me, that they scampered around like puppies, and finally settled down and curled up at the bottom of my bedroll.

Olivia did not come to be with me, as I expected, and sometime later I fell asleep and was awakened only when Booger Joe touched my side with the toe of his boot, and said, "Wake up, Rowdy. The ranch hands are beginning to stir and the cook is already getting breakfast." JJ stood beside him, grinning.

"Soon as we eat, we'll all drive a mile south to the pen where the remuda is waiting. The wagon boss will rope the horses for each cowboy, one by one, and they will saddle up. When everybody has his horse we will get the signal to ride. It will take about twenty minutes to ride to the two-thousand acre pasture where the drive will be made.

"Then, the lead cowboys will ride out ahead and about every 40 or 50 steps, one man will drop off and wait there until the last man is at the far end. That will be the wagon boss, and he will let out a signal – Wahhh… Whaaa!

"As the signal rolls down the line, each of us will move ahead in a long line, and all the cows and calves in front of us will strike out for the other end of the pasture. When they reach the end of the pasture, they will be confused and start milling around in a circle, and finally the circle will close and the cattle will be held until they settle down.

"When they get quiet, the wagon boss will start a few head in the direction of the canyon where we are taking them, and gradually they will string out in a long line that can be controlled. It is the final destination you must see. It is a deep cleft in the side of the canyon, about 500 feet deep and just wide enough at the top for a dozen or so cows to walk, and as it gets lower, there is only room for about two or three head to go down at a time.

"It will take at least an hour until they are all down. It is one of the most wonderful and beautiful sights in all of Texas, and makes you feel you are the most important man on the face of the earth.

"Now let's get on down to headquarters and load up our tin plates, eat all we can hold, and get ready for your first roundup and trail drive."

He led the way through the early morning glow that was already lifting high in the heavens and would soon be cleared of all clouds and fog.

At the cook shack, a dozen men were already filing past tubs of scrambled eggs and bacon, plus fried steak for anyone that asked for it. There was hardly a sound, for all attention was focused on the food, which would be the only thing in the stomachs for nearly twelve hours, Booger Joe said. And we waited until the end of the line to load our plates and get ready to mount up.

34

The Rules

Olivia came and joined me in line, looking as fresh as the morning sun. A tall, lanky cowboy, with gray hair curling around the edge of his great hat, dropped back to walk alongside us.

"Glad to see you again, Missy Olivia. Who is this handsome young feller with you? Haven't seen him around these parts before."

"Oh, hi, Mr. Fussel. This is my boyfriend. His name is Rowdy and he is Booger Joe's nephew. He has been staying with Miss Sally, and has never seen a real roundup before.

"Rowdy, this is Claud Fussel. He is my daddy's best friend and neighbor. They help each other on roundups, not because they have to, but because to them, all this hard work is fun."

He reached down and shook my hand, nearly crushing it, and then slapped me on the back. I had learned a handshake and a blow to the shoulders was the cowboy's welcome to Texas. But when I tried to match his grip, he just crushed my hand so hard I couldn't budge it.

"Glad to be here," I said, weakly. He let go my hand, but took a death grip on my shoulder as we neared the horse corral.

"Never seen a roundup? Well, you are in for a treat. Let me tell you how it works. Now, see that bunch of horses milling around in the corral? They are the best quarter horses on the ranch."

"That young feller with the lasso just now opening the corral gate and going in with the horses, he is the wagon boss. The oldest cowboy has first right to call out the name of the horse he wants to ride today. Listen, now…"

And sure enough, a skinny old cowboy they had called, "Boy" said, "Gimmee Rondo."

"Now watch the wagon boss – name's Wes, and he's the best roper on the ranch. See him bending down, so's to get the outline of the horse's head against the skyline? Now watch his rope hand. He'll give a little twitch and see – there it goes – settling over the head and neck of Rondo. Now he is leading Rondo to the end of the pen and turning him over to Boy."

The old-time cowboy took the rope from Wes, handed him another, and led Rondo out the gate and began putting on the bridle and blanket and saddle.

It took only about 30 minutes for Wes to catch the horses and then lead out one for himself and saddle up. The most amazing thing was that he never missed a throw, and he always caught the horse the cowboy wanted.

"How can he tell the horse's name when he can only see the outline of the horse against the sky?" I asked.

Fussel chuckled, "That's the reason he is the top hand."

35

The Descent

I was given a horse named Papoose to ride, and Olivia rode Heel Fly. JJ had taken up with another cowboy, Thomas, and stuck by his side, both cowboy and kid riding sorrel horses. Thoughout the great pasture known as the South Plains we rode, past hundreds of mesquite trees. Far, far below the cap rock gentled off into the Lower Plains and, an infinity away, the day began to break and light the world. The pink streamer of the approaching dawn yielded to a pinwheel of raucous reds, purples and yellows.

Ahead and behind cowboys rode in groups of twos and threes, their heads jogging up and down to the rhythm of the horses. Occasionally a sharp laugh floated across the great silent plains.

Gradually the east whitened and showed us the land. Mesquite hid the terrain in front of us, but all around the caprock reared its wrinkled face gray as death. Not a cow, not a calf was visible, but they were there, hidden by the mesquite and the rocks. Slowly, we formed a great line across the end of the pasture. Olivia and I found ourselves between Fussel, or Fuss as the men called him, and Boy, the old camper who had lived all of his life on the ranch.

Then came the signal, faint and far away. Papoose flipped his ears forward and danced on his front feet. Each cowboy took up the yell in turn and the echoing sound rolled down the line. "Whoo-whaaa!" bellowed Fuss.

I opened my lungs and sucked in the crisp air and passed on the yell, and Olivia did the same. Boy answered last, his old voice a crackle.

The drive was on.

Papoose had been on many drives before, and knew what to do. Now and then I saw Fuss, on my left, moving easily through the mesquite, and then Boy, missing nothing. Between Olivia and me, a jackrabbit eyed my approach from his home beneath a clump of yucca; a covey of top-knotted quail scurried in front, finally taking flight and roaring away. Then I saw a cow and calf moving among the mesquite.

The calf, a square-rumped, cherry-red ball of inquisitiveness, with bright white face, stood his ground momentarily. Then, with a frightened blat, he bounced stiff-legged to his mother.

Now other cows and calves hurried through the brush. The cries of the punchers drifted on the crisp air and I began to distinguish between them. I came to a deep gash in the red earth, with crumbling clay banks glinting dully as the sun peeped over the caprock and gave us full light. Walking Papoose along the edge, I searched for a way to cross.

Down in the gulch, a cow and calf were sneaking away. Papoose thrust his ears forward and decided the issue; he bolted down the embankment. We hit the flat of the canyon in a great bond. Like an arrow Papoose shot away and headed off the delinquent pair. No longer was Papoose a meek pony; he was a fiery cow horse. The cow and calf loped up the draw and with an effort, I pulled Papoose into a jog.

As we came out onto the prairie again, I saw a great line of cows and calves and burley bulls lumbering toward the gathering grounds – Hay Lake, a huge natural depression. Already some of the punchers were holding the herd, shaping it up. I pushed my little bunch of cattle into the main wedge and looked around. Like water rushing down ravines in flood time, red and white cattle poured into the surrounding slopes and joined the herd. The sun, now a ball of fire, showed hard-riding men as fleeting shapes. The color of the scene made me catch my breath – the gold of the sky, the pale green of the mesquite, the cherry-red and white of the cattle. The prairie seethed with movement and sound.

I sat back and rested in my saddle for a signal from Fuss, and Olivia reined Heel Fly over to me.

"Oh, Rowdy. Did you ever see anything on earth so wonderful? So beautiful? I could stay right here, doing this, forever, couldn't you?"

"Yes, Olivia. Just as long as we are together."

We instinctively leaned over and kissed. That surely was the happiest moment of my entire life. How wonderful to be young, together, doing what you would rather do than anything else in the entire world.

The cowboys began slowly to circle around the milling herd, and as cow after cow located her calf, the deafening sound drifted away, and the dust soon followed.

When the herd was quiet, Wes, Boy and Fuss, the three top hands of the drive, began to slip a few cows and calves on the west side of the dry lake bed, and in majestic step, timed for the calves to stay with their mothers, the last phase of the cattle drive began.

When the herd was stretched out in a line about a mile in length, I felt the land begin to tilt downward slightly. Soon, the herd stopped moving forward, and Fuss came back to us, and motioned for us to follow him.

At the front of the herd, the tilt of the land increased, and almost before I knew it, I came to the edge of that great plateau.

Looking downward, I became dizzy at the depth of the canyon, and at the bottom, looking like miniature cows and calves, the herd was already spreading out in their new home, nipping at the shoots of grass and leaves.

It took another hour for the last cow and calf to make their way to the floor of the canyon. By now, the front of the herd was but specks of red and white mingled with the deep green of the vegetation, and we lined up behind, and silently looked at the more awesome sight of nature I had ever seen.

"Well, kids, what you think of that?" Fuss asked.

Olivia and I were so awed with the experience we could only shake our heads. We had seen something very few people had seen, or ever would see and my first thought was, "Will we ever see it again?"

And she said, "Rowdy, if I have my way, you and I will someday be married, and we will always come back to see this canyon – and remember the first time we saw it – together."

36

Pieces of the Past

To my surprise, Fuss did not ride in the direction we came from with the herd. He continued to follow the canyon in a northwesterly direction.

"Why are we riding in the opposite direction?" I asked, "Is this a shortcut or something?"

He laughed and flipped his bridle reins to make his horse walk faster, "Glad you asked. Most folks get their directions mixed up in this big country, but you noticed. Just be patient. I want you to see and know something that millions of people would like to know or to see, but probably never will."

He lifted his horse into a slightly faster pace as we started up an incline and it was plain to see we were riding on higher ground. Then at the top of a large plateau, he abruptly reined his horse to the left and I suddenly saw we were on the very edge of the canyon, hundreds of feet below us.

I involuntarily backed my pony up to a safer distance from the edge of the canyon, jumped out of the saddle and tied the reins to a sapling. Olivia, pale as a ghost, did the same and we walked carefully back to Fuss, who had also dismounted.

"Awesome sight, right? Notice the many layers of different colored sediment that form the walls of the canyon.

"Each layer tells the story of a period of time – maybe millions of years each – that it took to hollow out this great gash in the earth we now call the Palo Duro Canyon.

"Now come closer – careful, so you won't get dizzy and fall of this bluff – and look at that little ribbon of water at the very bottom.

Looks like it is all of two or three feet wide, doesn't it? Truth is, when it is running full, it is forty or fifty feet wide.

"Now let's rest in the shade a while and I will tell you and amazing story. And tell you some history in a painless way."

Olivia and I sat side by side on an outcropping of sandstone. She squeezed my arm and shivered slightly as if afraid the canyon walls might crumble and send us sailing to the bottom to our death.

"You kids probably have heard and read about the days of the wild, wild, west, and all of the stories about the pioneers and ranchers. And about the Indians and the way they lived and were finally driven to virtual extinction. And how it frustrated the U.S. troops and settlers that they could never locate the wintering grounds and the places the Indians hid after committing raids and ambushes, trying to drive the white man out of their lands.

"And about how the Indians were driven into their last hiding place after the buffalo were finally killed. The buffalo was their food supply, and their clothing material, and it furnished hides for their teepees."

"And how it was nearly impossible for the soldiers to locate them so they could be captured and either killed or relocated on reservations. What you probably don't know is that the hiding place is right beneath us – this magnificent canyon below us, the Palo Duro."

"What you are seeing is the location of the last fight the Indians made. Their last fight for freedom. The Comanche Indians were finished as a nation."

I felt Olivia shiver. She clung tighter to me, her fingers digging into my arm. I took advantage of the opportunity to draw her closer and she responded by lying her head on my shoulder. I felt love cascade throughout my heart.

"You mean," I said, "that at some time in the past, some Indian boy and some Indian girl were sitting on this very rock, getting to know and love each other. And falling in love like… like Olivia and me."

I could hardly finish, and choked up at the thought. For a few seconds, I felt the actual love I had expressed and felt Olivia's heart beat faster against my arm. "And then maybe some soldier came along and saw them and …" I could go on no longer. I don't know how long we just sat there and thought our thoughts.

How cruel life must have been in those days. For centuries, their ancestors had lived and died on this land, in the normal cycles of life, and one day white men and soldiers came along and slaughtered their buffalo and burned their homes and raped and pillaged and murdered and drove the last ones into virtual slavery.

Olivia murmured, “Maybe they were just like us, Rowdy… dreaming their dreams and thinking of raising babies and…”

“That’s right, kids,” Fuss said quietly. “They had feelings and homes and dreams and knew happiness just like us. Maybe more so, because they were so free of many things that control us and prevent our full life as God intended. Why do you think I chose to remain a cowboy, a rancher, a free man, or as free as it is possible to be today?”

“You see, I am a quarter-blood Comanche. My great-great grandmother and grandfather lived in this canyon. This was their home, their buffalo hide teepee was their shelter in storms. The sun their mother, the air their father.”

“The record of their lives, and of their ancestors was kept on a tanned deer hide. I inherited it. It is my most precious possession. It keeps me in touch with everything they do in their home today. They are alive as they ever were, just in a different form, in a different place. But I feel them all of the time, and they surely feel me as well.”

We sat quietly, not daring to break the spell that had been cast over us. But all of a sudden, a flash of thought came from me and I sat up quickly. Olivia cried out, “Rowdy, what’s wrong?”

“Nothing is wrong, Olivia. I just thought of something. I might be a distant cousin to Fuss. My great-great mother was a full blood Cherokee, born back in the early days when Cave Springs had not white or black settlers. But like the Comanches, they were driven out of their homes and captured and slaughtered sometimes, and forced to move west to the Indian Territory in Oklahoma.

“I have always known these things, but never thought much about them, until now.”

Fuss stretched out his long arm, grasped my hand and said, “Shake, brother. We may be more alike than you know. Why are you here in Texas? In my company? In the one-time home of my own people?”

“My grandmother used to tell me Indians were once just one people, one person broken up in pieces and that when we died, the pieces all went back together again.”

“And when all of the pieces get back together, the Great Spirit is happy and we stay together for all the time there is, forever.”

He stood up, breaking the majestic spell, and walked to the edge of the canyon, and looked a long, long time, just looked, while Olivia and I watched silently, feeling the all-together feeling he had just described.

Fuss said slowly in his deep voice, “One day in 1860 a scout for the army stumbled on to this canyon, so well hidden in the wilderness. He walked to its edge, looked down upon hundreds of lodges, hundreds of campfires, thousands of laughing Indians.

"They had been free and safe for hundreds, perhaps thousands of years. The Great Spirit had been their father and their mother and all was well.

"But the white man's medicine was greater.

"The scout reported his discovery to the general. The general sent troops down the trail where we drove the cows into the canyon. They caught the Indians without guards, with their horses downriver in pasture, the women at work, children at play. The braves had few weapons when the soldiers began shooting.

"Hundreds were killed, but they staved off the soldiers while their women and children ran down the canyon to freedom. When the Indians fled, they had to leave their horses behind. The soldiers burned all the food and clothing, all the tee-pees, and drove 1,500 horses to the top of the canyon and shot them.

"For many years the rotting and bleaching bones of the horses could be found at this very place we are today. Their bones rotted and vanished, but occasionally the wind will uncover a bleached bone. We could find some today, if we only had time. But it is best to let them lay where they are, for others to discover and wonder how they got there."

"What happened to the Indians that escaped?" I asked.

"The Indian wars were over. The remaining ones made their pitiful ways to the reservations. Many died before they got there. Some killed themselves rather than yield to slavery. A few became a half-civilized tribe and today they live in various placed around the nation – forgotten, except by their own kind.

"One of them was a half-breed named Quanah Parker. He was the son of a white girl captured as a three year old and raised as an Indian. She gave birth at age 15, and was found by whites and rescued. But she was raised an Indian and escaped to go back to her tribe. Her son grew up to be a great leader of Indians and was famous even to white people. He may have been the greatest Indian that ever lived. And his footsteps were on this ground we walked on today."

"He was my great-great grandfather."

We got into the saddle and rode slowly toward the home camp. Not a word was spoken to destroy the mood. I felt like I had lived a hundred years in just a few hours. Olivia rode beside me and we held hands the entire ride back.

I knew this day had changed my life – our lives – forever.

37

The Magazine Men

By the time we rode into sight of the ranch headquarters, the sun was well to our backs and sinking fast.

It seemed we had had a very, very long day, one full of excitement and action and sights I never thought I would see.

And besides that, my tail bone was sore and Olivia's head was drooping on my shoulder and I had to sort of hold her to keep her from falling out of the saddle.

There seemed to be a lot of activity around the house and main barn, and then I saw a couple of familiar faces – Booger Joe and Miss Sally. And tied up to the hitch rack was Lady Midnight and Jackrabbit. Our dogs, Moochie and Dolly, swarmed all over us, whining and licking us all over and barking and running in circles. It was a grand welcome for an exciting day.

Miss Sally came running – waddling would be more like it – up to me, took Olivia out of my arms and cuddled her in her arms. "This poor child," she said. "You men have just about done her in. She's sound asleep in my arms."

Fuss grinned and said, "She is some little cow-gal. Don't worry about it. She is all right."

As for myself, I could only mumble, "What are you doing here?" and I slid from the saddle, groaning as my feet hit the ground and the blood began to circulate again.

"I got worried about my boy so JJ harnessed the team and drove me here. It's been years since I've used the old shortcut and I almost got lost."

Mrs. Maybell came to the front porch and banged on a tin pan. "Grub's on. Come and get it."

And JJ came running from the cow shed with a bucket of fresh foaming milk in his hand. He grinned ear to ear and slapped me on the back. "Boy, is it good to see you. I felt real important, driving with the cowboys through the prairie."

"Where's my uncle?" I said. "I don't see him any place."

"He rode off with the cowboys. Said they had to take the remuda to another part of the ranch to be ready to bring in the herd the boys are driving. "Hey, Rowdy, I feel like a real cowboy now. Do I look the part? Miss Sally dug out some of Booger Joe's old things."

For the first time, I noticed he had on some old cowboy boots, a set of well-worn chaps, and a checked shirt. His hat was an old hand-me-down felt with a feather stuck in the band. I wondered if I looked like him.

"JJ, you make a real handsome cowboy. Wait until I get you on the back of a wild mustang, and I bet you can ride him all day long."

Mrs. Maybell came out on the porch banging on her pan again, and Miss Sally said, "Let's get it before she throws it out." We sat in the shade of a Chinese elm and drank gallons of iced tea. Olivia even woke up and had her share and asked for a second glass of tea and then cracked the ice with her teeth. "Never tasted anything so cold and good," she said, leaning against my shoulder and grabbing my hand.

"Oh, mom, we had the most glorious time ever. We drove the cows and calves down into the canyon – which I had never seen before.

"And then, to top it off, Fuss made us ride another five miles to show us the part of the canyon where the Indians were trapped and killed and driven out into the Great Plains.

"Oh, it was so marvelous, but so sad, too. To think we now own a part of that historic place."

"But, Olivia, dear," said Maybell, "You must keep that your secret. If the government – or writers and photographers – ever learn about it, the public will crash in here and we will be swamped with people and maybe have to give up the canyon section of the ranch.

"Ollie thinks we ought to turn it over to the state as a historic site, but we have not decided that as yet."

Now we heard the roar of a car with no exhaust, and a cloud of dust coming from the distance and it turned out to be – you guessed it – Ollie Oliver in his new Chrysler Imperial, now sounding like the muffler had been knocked off, and with one fender bent out of shape.

But when he roared into the yard and stopped, all you could see was his big grin. He jumped out of the car, grinning ear to ear, and yelled, "Hey, you lazybones, come and see what I've got."

He walked to the back of the car, opened the trunk, and lifted out a watermelon that weighed at least 75 pounds, and that was dripping ice water. There were four or five more just like it.

"We got a bonanza on those cows and calves the boys brought home, and they'll be here first thing in the morning. Now let's try out one of these melons and then pack the others in ice and straw until tomorrow, and we will have a big celebration.

So we sliced that melon and ate and spit seeds for the next hour until we could hardly move.

When my eyes finally would stay open no longer, I got up and headed to the barn and my sleeping bag. I was followed by Olivia. And Olivia was followed by her mother. And we were all followed by Moochie and Dolly. Maybell marched Olivia back to the house, but the dogs stayed with me, and I didn't know anything until the sun shined in my eyes the next morning, and I heard the clatter and bawling of cows and calves.

I sat up and what did I see, but those wild hair Oliver boys and what looked like a million cows and calves headed my way.

I grabbed my bed roll and got out of the way just in time.

Although there were only 150 whiteface cows and three bulls in the herd the Oliver boys drove in, they were not easily penned. A blowing leaf or weed, a mouse running across their path was enough to spook them and start them milling around in a circle.

Finally, however, the gates were slammed shut and the boys waved at me as the cowboys headed for the bunkhouse for some rest and, later, hot coffee and breakfast.

I didn't know whether to double up my fists and get ready for a fight, or just stand still and see why they were walking toward me in their bow-legged gait.

"Hey there, Missouri kid. Hold on a minute. We've got an apology for you."

That got my attention, so I relaxed.

"Listen, kid, we've got to have some grub, and after that, let's have a little friendly talk for a change. All right?"

"Sure. What about?"

Polecat grinned and slapped me on the back sort of friendly-like, and said, "There's no problem. Just rest easy." And they walked toward the cook shack just as Claud Fussel stopped a couple of minutes to talk to them, and gesture toward the cows, then walk in his bowlegged gait to me.

"We've got to drive these cattle down into another arm of the canyon later this morning," he said. "It's a different part of the canyon than you saw yesterday, and it's sure worth your time.

"This time, instead of seeing the canyon from the top, we will drive all the way to the bottom on another trail. You will see a sight as old as the world – and …well, just take my word for it. It will take your breath away.

"But let the cattle rest and drink a few hours before we go. Meanwhile, we've got another little matter to take care of."

"What matter? Have I done something wrong. I know Olivia and I were pretty close yesterday. Did she…"

"Ah no Rowdy, nothing like that. This matter is a couple of guys that drove up just before daylight. They are in the boss's office right now hashing out something."

"Hashing out what?"

"Well, it seems a couple of months ago while Ollie was away to a stock show in Amarillo, I got a call from some guy from your home state - Missouri – who said he was a writer for a big magazine in the east, and wanted to do a story about cowboys and ranches. He said his editor wanted to find out what was going on in the west these days. If cowboys still herded cattle, branded and trailed them to market like they did in the old days.

"I told him it was all right with me, that the boss was away, and that he had always welcomed writers and photographers to visit the ranch. So I told them to come on, I was sure the boss would not care.

"But I forgot to tell Ollie about it, and so when they showed up, got him out of bed and told them they were here to do a story, it riled Ollie quite a bit."

He told them to get lost so he could go back to sleep, but one of them, the older one who acted pretty cocky, told Ollie they by'god, were not going to leave until they got their story.

"I thought Ollie was going to clean his plow, but the young guy, who said he is the writer, calmed Ollie down, and said there had been some misunderstanding. And then I remembered talking to him and told Ollie so. He calmed down and invited the guys in for breakfast, and they are still talking.

"Let's go eat some hotcakes and bacon and then we'll see what's up. Probably the boss will let them take a few pictures and they will be on their way.

So after stuffing down a half dozen hot cakes, and nearly choking on bunkhouse coffee, we meandered back to Ollie's house and went into his office at a side door.

"Fuss," he said, "these here boys work for a really big magazine back in New York. In fact, it so happens the boss man of that magazine is an ol' Texas boy, and we were roommates at A and M. I was just fixin' to give him a ring and check them out for sure, and if they check out, I want you to take them around the ranch and give them a big time. Take Rowdy, too, if you like."

Then he turned to me and said, "Rowdy, my boy, when I got in Salt River town yesterday, I checked with the post office and they gave me a letter for you." His eyes crinkled and I caught my breath. Could it be…?

And when he handed it to me, I recognized the writing as that of my father, and my hands trembled so bad I could hardly open it.

> It started out, *"Dear Rowdy. I love you more than you can ever know, and my heart just about broke when I got up and discovered you were gone from home. If only you would have told me you were so unhappy. If only I had of been more forgiving of you…*
>
> *"But after I settled down, and did some investigating, I discovered JJ was also gone, it didn't take me long to guess what had happened. I read the books you have been reading, and realized you were a Texas cowboy and horse nut, and that sooner or later you would get ready to come home and we would somehow hear from you.*
>
> *"I also remembered that your uncle Frank had done much the same thing and that you probably would call or write some time and want to come home.*
>
> *"But just as I was about to give up hope, here came a letter from you and one from your friend, Salt River Sally… and you know the rest.*
>
> *"A lot has happened here at home since you left. I know you will be surprised and very, very happy. According to your letter I received just today, you are ready and willing to come home. And I am just as anxious as you are.*
>
> *"You are a man now. It is always hard for a father to accept that his son must grow up, too, just like your father had to do. So just as soon as I get the wheat harvest finished – we had a bumper crop – I will be down to bring you home.*
>
> *"I have the biggest surprise in your whole life for you. And I think you will agree, when you find out what it is."*

I was so glad I was alone when I finished reading that letter. I could not prevent the tears from rolling down my cheeks, and my hands trembled something fierce. I was glad Olivia was not here to see me cry, and that Ollie and Fuss and the magazine men were not here.

It took about a half hour to get under control, and during that time, I had to think of Olivia. How could I ever tell her I was going home?

Once again, the happiest moment of my life was also one of the most sad moments of my life.

I longed to be with Olivia just as much as I ever longed to be with my family.

I didn't feel like a man at all. I felt like a piece of mush.

Was I born to be free and easy, like my dog Moochie, or my horse Lady Midnight? Or, for that matter, my best friend, JJ, just an orphan boy who had no family and whose best friend was now a hopeless emotional wreck?

38

Family

But there was no time to feel sorry for myself this day.

No sooner had I digested the letter from home, than the two Oliver boys came out the bunkhouse door and headed for me.

"Hey, Missouri kid. I guess it's better to start calling you by your real name, instead of Missouri kid," Polecat said.

"Yeah," Toby chimed in, "if our sis says you are all right, then that's good enough for us. Anyhow, we found out a long time ago – like when you jumped into that boxcar back in Missouri, that you were made out of the right stuff. Our pranks were just to try you out. Now, kid – mean Rowdy – sis says to lay off the rough stuff and get serious…"

"Yeah, because she is serious about you. If sis goes for you, then we do too. Us Oliver folks stick together."

I could hardly believe my ears, but here they were, the two guys that had bedevilled me ever since we met.

"You guys can't be serious," I said.

"Try us, buddy. You treat our sis right, we treat you right. You serious about Olivia?"

I hesitated. How was I to tell her brothers I was in love with her and would marry her on the spot if I was a year or so older. So my face just turned red and hot as fire and I couldn't say a word, which for me was unthinkable. I could only nod my head.

And with that they grabbed my arms, one on each side, and escorted me toward the office where the writer was attempting to interview Ollie.

They were absorbed in looking at the pictures of cows and bulls and horses that Ollie had framed in his office, but turned to greet us.

"Hey, city clickers, I'm Ollie Junior, but they call me Polecat. "This is my little brother, Toby. Our ol' man says we are to escort you around the ranch today and as long as you want to stay."

He stuck out his hand and tried to break the bones in it and grinned, knowing the photographer had lily-white hands.

"Toby, here," said the younger brother. "He's the brawn. I'm the brain." And he dodged a make-believe fist from his brother. "What's your deal?"

"I'm Jerry Maness," said the younger one. "I write the story. My partner there, with the necklace of cameras is Fred Covello. We have never worked together before, but you have surely seen his photographs if you take any of the big slick magazines such as "Life" or "Colliers."

"So…?" said Polecat.

"Just go about your business and let us tag along."

"Don't do anything different than you do in your work every day. Don't pose for us. For God's sake, don't pose. We want action in the pictures, just like you do every day.

"And, don't let us see any rattlesnakes. I am violently afraid of them."

Boy, I thought, he should never have said that, for I caught a twinkle in Polecat's eyes, even though his voice was ever so sweet and polite. "Oh, sir, we never see a snake of any kind, much less a rattler. You can be sure we don't have any snakes on our ranch."

"So, why don't we get started. Just lead on and we will follow," said Maness. "We've got a rented Jeep and can follow you any place."

Toby snorted. "Not unless you have wings, you can't. And that is exactly where we are going today, and we've got to get started. The kid here, and our sister will ride with you and Polecat and I will ride horses, along with a couple of cowhands, you stay behind us at all times, and if you get in front of our cattle and stampede them, well, say your prayers and drive like hell to get away from us."

And so began one of the more adventurous days of my life.

I whispered to Toby, "I sure would like to see Olivia before we head out. Okay?"

He nodded and said, "follow me," and he opened a door that lead into the main part of the house, waked down a hallway toward the smell of bacon frying, and there was Maybell and Olivia, the former dishing up hotcakes to her sleepy-eyed daughter. Olivia brightened her sleepy eyes and came to hug me. To Toby, she said, "Did you tell him what I told you to tell him?" "Sure did, sis. He's one of us now – unless he does you dirty."

So help me, Olivia stretched to her tip toes and gave me a good morning kiss and Maybell lifted and eyebrow, but said nothing except, "Sit down at the table Rowdy," and she dropped three hotcakes on a platter, handed it to me and said, "Sit down before you fall down, Rowdy. You look as tired as you did last night."

"Rowdy, when you and Olivia finish breakfast, hurry down to the stables. We'll be ready to ride in thirty minutes," said Toby.

39

The Monument

I finished off the pancakes Maybell gave me, thanked her and Olivia and I headed out the door.

Outside, Toby wheeled an old Army surplus Jeep out of the machine shed and roared up to where Fuss and the old cowboy, Boy, waited patiently for their two guests.

Already the photographer had unlimbered his cameras, shooting first with one, then another. I asked his writer companion, "Why does he have so many cameras? Won't one do?"

He laughed. "It depends on several things. Whether he takes a picture of a horse standing still, or running, or a close up shot or one long distance.

"But that's all I can tell you about him, for he is very snappish and can tell you off in a heartbeat. Best leave him be when he's working, I've found out. He's got a quick, hot temper and a long tongue."

Covello shot pictures of Fuss and Boy and I made the mistake of telling Fuss to push his hat back off his forehead, and quick as flash, Covello chewed me out, but loud and strong. "Get away from him," he shouted. "I want him to look natural, not like some city jackass posing for a glamour shot."

Covello told Fuss to call the riders, then he said to tell them to run their horses, then to haul up on the reins and make the horses rear up, and so on. Finally, Fuss put a stop to that by saying, "Say, mister, I'm riding the horse and you are running off at the mouth. I was ordered by the boss to take you down deep into the canyon to see what is an unknown national monument, unknown to scientists and almost anybody else.

"Now you follow me at my pace and we'll get along just fine. Any more of your mouth and driving around like a maniac, and I will find a place to leave you out in this brush until your bones rot."

Maness smacked the steering wheel with glee and Covello growled under his breath and said, "Let's do what he said. The dumb SOB don't know what I could do to him. I could report him to the police."

At that, Olivia laughed as loud as she could. "Mister," she said, "do you know who the closest police are to you? That's my father. He's a deputy sheriff in this county and he wouldn't even blink an eye if you fell to the bottom of this canyon. Shape up, or we will turn around this minute and escort you off this ranch."

Covello turned and stared at her, his eyes wide and mouth open, speechless. Then began a slow grin and he said, "I think you really mean it."

"Just try me, buster," Olivia said.

Boy, oh boy, was I ever surprised. My gentle little Olivia, full of fire. I felt extreme pride and a rush of love for her that exceeded all others.

So after a rocky start, things settled down. Fuss and Boy trotted their horses, and the land before us kept falling away and winding in corkscrews until we came to a windmill where Fuss and Boy let their horses drink while they got out of the saddle, drew grease guns out of their saddle bags and began servicing the bearings.

Covello got out of the jeep, kept his mouth shut, and snapped shot after shot. Then the cowboys warned that from here on down to the bottom, "Better put 'er in low gear, it is not straight up and down to the bottom, but you will see the horses slide on their rear ends and it will test the brakes on your jeep. Understand?"

Maness nodded, shoved the stick in compound, and the descent began. In perhaps 15 minutes of twisting and turning on hairpin curves, Olivia and I hugged each other as, at times, the trail narrowed to a drop off on either side. A slight carelessness and the jeep would roll over and over forty or fifty feet to the bottom.

Finally, we leveled off and all of us gave a sigh of relief. Covello had lost his cocky look, Maness's hands were white from gripping the steering wheel – and the two horses trembled, their muscles exhausted by the strain of holding back their own weight and that of their riders.

We climbed out of the jeep to rest our shaky legs and relax. For the first time, we saw what we had been taken to see – a petrified forest.

What at first had seemed to be only the trunks and limbs of dead trees became an entirely different thing. It was like stepping back into time, like seeing the earth in its very beginning. No, that is not right. Like seeing the earth at its death, and then seeing the years or the decades of the centuries roll by until time had ceased to matter.

For long minutes, we looked in awe. Then, gradually, reverently, cautiously, we began to move, to reach out and gently touch these legends of time upon time, feel their frozen records of immortality.

If anyone spoke, it was a whisper, but gradually our shock lifted and we began to speak in hushed but reverent tones. Even the click of Covello's camera seemed to echo off the time-frozen monsters around us.

"May I carry off just one little piece of this… this national monument?" he asked Olivia.

She turned and walked a few steps. Then she said, "Yes, but only for proof. And swear you will not be the one who releases this information. That will be the privilege of my father. Okay?"

This tough guy, who had been around the world with his camera, nodded. "Yes," he said. "You've got a deal."

She turned to Fuss and Boy, both of whom were now in the saddle. "How do we get out of here? It looks as if we may be trapped on foot, unless you can produce a miracle."

"Don't worry, missy. I've been in and out of here many times in my lifetime. I promise it won't be as exciting as getting down here, but it will take longer. If you are ready, follow us."

To the driver he said, "Just go slow, follow the path of cattle and wildlife, and in an hour we will be headed for the caprock."

40

Time Standing Still

As four of us piled into the Jeep, with Maness again at the wheel and Covello quiet from shock and awe at the fantastic handiwork of nature we had just discovered, I missed something.

That something was the presence of Toby and Polecat. They were nowhere in sight.

"Hey, Fuss, where are Toby and Polecat? They are nowhere to be seen."

Fuss reined his horse around and waved his arm upwards. "They stayed on top the caprock," he said. "I sent them back eastward along the top the break in the caprock where we will climb out of the canyon. There is also a heavy fence at that location to keep the buffalo from getting out."

He spurred his horse around and caught up with Boy, the old cowboy who seldom spoke a word, and the jeep started rolling in gear, dodging bits and pieces of petrified rock. "I sure would like to have a couple of pieces of that rock," I said to Olivia. "Would your dad care?"

"Of course not, Rowdy. Jump out and get some." To Maness, she said, "Stop here while Rowdy gets some souvenirs."

I quickly grabbed four chunks of rock, weighing about 10 or 15 pounds each, and tossed them in the jeep, and then we were off again.

The ground we traveled on was level as a baseball field for at least five miles in diameter. At the eastern edge, we began a steep climb from this huge bowl of petrified forest, and here the ground turned from a lava base to a fine powder mixed with rock. We obviously had been in what at some ancient time was a crater, perhaps caused by a giant meteorite, and then filled with a burst of lava as the earth exploded underneath.

We continued to climb steeply and as we climbed, the vegetation turned into short shrubs and, finally, a rich grassland stretching for miles.

Clear water seeping from under slabs of rock created streams where the buffalo could drink.

Covello had unlimbered his cameras again and was shooting pictures. Maness kept pace with the two cowboys ahead.

Then Fuss and Boy stopped, waved us down, and said, "Look carefully straight ahead and you will see animals of the past. Buffalo."

I quivered all over as my eyes picked out the brown forms of the ancient past.

"Think of it, Rowdy," Olivia said. "This is almost like being taken back into history in a time machine. The lava and petrified wood came first, maybe a million or a hundred million years before. And then, something happened and the ground rose from underneath and kept on rising, but left the lakebed of lava.

"Then erosion of the caprock began, and gradually was ground into dust – but by what? The wind? Water later disappeared. And then came the first animals, and the buffalo developed.

"And, as my daddy has told me, these buffalo are the offspring of the very first buffalo that were created, or were born, or whatever it was that God made them for."

She hugged me tightly as we grew closer and closer to the gigantic animals who seemed to have no fear of this strange caravan.

Fuss held up his hand for us to stop, and the horses seemed as astounded to see the buffalo grazing alone, occasionally looking up at us but showing no attempt to run or to fear us.

As if to read my thoughts, Fuss said, "They have never been hunted or shot, so they have no reason to be afraid. As far as we know, they were here when the Spanish explorers were here. Their ancestors may have been here even before the first animal-like men crossed the Bearing Straight when there was a land bridge between what is now Asia and North America.

"There are people who would give a fortune to see these buffalo and to own them. Or to capture them and put them in a zoo. Now wouldn't that be grand to capture these animals and enclose them in a high fence so people could look at them?

"There are people who would give as much for those buffalo and this ancient valley as a whole great city is worth."

Maness, the writer, had a pad and pencil at work, scribbling rapidly. After being virtually frozen in place, Covello once again had his cameras clicking furiously until, at last, he cursed and said, "I have used up all of the film I had with me. But I have a fortune in pictures in my cameras. Let's go back to the real world again."

Fuss and Boy gently reined their horses to the north, and we began the slow trek out of the canyon to the eventual trail up and out to the caprock. We left the buffalo grazing peacefully, their heads lifting occasionally to view our retreat.

"What do you suppose they are thinking," mused Olivia. I did not answer. I was to stunned to find words.

In a few minutes, the path rose above us so steeply the Jeep growled and tires spun out ruts, but we managed to get to the top, and waiting patiently, were Toby and Polecat, their horses grazing peacefully.

We stopped in the jeep and got out to stretch and look south and downward where we could see only the black dots that marked the herd of buffalo we had seen.

Covello walked close to the edge of the overhang and cursed again because he had run out of film.

All of a sudden, he let out a scream that would have awakened the dead. He leaped into the air, ran a few steps to grab Fuss by the arm, his face white with fear.

He screamed, "It almost bit me."

I ran to his side, to see there, some fifteen to twenty feet away, its long, thick mottled tail wrapped around itself and its tail sticking up six inches and the rattles singing a song – sure enough, a real, honest-to-gosh Texas rattlesnake.

Without thinking, acting just as automatically as I had may times back home, I reached down, picked up a flat piece of shale rock, drew back my pitchin' arm, and let fly that rock.

Would you believe that rock sailed straight as a knife and cut the head off of that rattlesnake as clean as if it had been a butcher knife.

There was total silence by the group of us as we saw the coils uncoil and the six fool long carcass of this once deadly snake twist and turn in its death – and finally lay still?

After a few minutes recovering from shock, Covello walked carefully to the snake, picked up a stick, and unrolled each coil. But the coils just as quickly unrolled and the creature lay still.

Covello finally said, "Poor thing." He looked daggers at me and said, "Why did you have to kill it?"

I just threw up my hands in disgust, turned and walked back to the Jeep where Olivia waited, her face drawn tightly in suspense.

"You city jerk," she screamed. "You better get back in this Jeep and let us take you back to town. You'd never make a cowboy – or a rock thrower like my Rowdy."

And in another hour, we were in sight of the ranch headquarters.

"How big is your father's ranch?" I asked, looking back at the enormous distance of land and sky we had traveled that day.

"I don't really know," she said. "Let's ask when we get there."

41

The Party

When we were about five miles from headquarters the sun was near the horizon in the west. The last rays of the sun cast a bright glow on a huge thunderhead that appeared to enclose all of the world. The faint smell of rain drifted to us.

Our driver, the writer, and his buddy, the photographer, had finally stopped their bickering through fatigue I suppose, and were obviously eager to get back in sight of civilization again.

It even looked good to me to realize we were where we could get some rest, some ice cold water and something to eat. Even so, the haunting memories of the day were burned into my brain and I could hardly think of anything else.

The memory of my home, the adventure JJ and I had experienced in a little over two months almost seemed like a lifetime away, in the past. Two things fought each other for attention – how much I missed my family in Missouri and how much I had come to love Texas and the down-home, anything goes folks I had met.

There was something about these Texans that was the same as the folks back home, but there was also something very, very different.

The Texans seemed to be looking for a good time all the time, with a new adventure every day, while folks back in Missouri always seemed to be worrying about disaster tomorrow. They were both honest, but a joke and laughter and big ideas won over Texas, and things folks feared and dreaded in Missouri kept them expecting the devil to appear on their door step every minute.

The Missourians treasured every penny while the Texans bet their farm on the toss of a penny.

When our jeep got on smooth ground, we picked up speed and soon were well ahead of Fuss, Boy, Toby and Polecat. Looking ahead it appeared there was some kind of unusual activity around ranch headquarters and when we got to within a quarter mile, it was plain to see there were a lot of people milling around.

As we pulled into the big open lot between the house and barns, I counted five stock trucks, 10 cars and another approaching from Salt River town's direction, and people coming and going from the main house.

I nudged Olivia to wake up, since her head was drooping, and she sat up and rubbed her eyes.

"Good heavens," she said. "I wonder if something has gone wrong. There's enough people around the place for a funeral."

My heart leaped and my breathing became short. But Olivia soon put me at ease. "Look, Rowdy. There is smoke coming from daddy's barbeque pit and tables being set. They must be planning to have a barbeque, Texas style. There are bales of hay and straw placed in a circle and there are mother's friends coming and going with bowls of food in their arms. There's a big tarp covering something by the porch – I bet that's some more of those big watermelons daddy's been buying."

Manes leaned on the Jeep's horn as arms, hats and aprons waved us to a screeching halt.

First one out of the pack was Ollie, his big ten-gallon hat pushed back and revealing his big jolly grin. Come to think about it, I don't think I had ever seen him when he was not grinning, laughing or teasing something or somebody. He rushed out to greet us, took Olivia in his big arms and held her like a baby.

"Puddin, you're plum' tuckered out," and gave her a gentle kiss. He reached out a hand and took me by the arm with his other hand and virtually hoisted me out of the Jeep, and held us, a big roar of happiness rolling out for all to see – and to hear.

To myself I thought, "What a guy. Nothing bothers him or worries him, it's just as if life was one great big party and he wanted to enjoy it for himself and his friends."

"What's going on, Daddy," Olivia asked. "I didn't know we were going to have a barbeque."

"Well, it is on short order, I admit. But something very, very important is going to happen tonight, maybe just any minute – I hope."

She was puzzled. "But what, Daddy? Give us a clue."

His belly shook with laughter and he said, "Just be patient, sugarplum. You too, Rowdy."

Just then JJ came rushing from out of the barn. His grin stretched the corners of his mouth. "Rowdy, Rowdy. Wait until you hear who's…"

Quick as lightning Ollie dropped me and grabbed JJ. “Hush your mouth, boy. You aimin’ to spoil my surprise party.” He clapped his hand over JJ’s mouth and grinned.

JJ’s eyes grew big and he looked scared for a minute. Then he couldn’t hold it in, and began giggling. Then I saw Miss Sally and my uncle, Booger Joe, coming out of the barn. He was leading two ponies, one his spotted pony and the other a big gray quarter horse he used for roping. Miss Sally waddled up and hugged me tight and grinned.

“What’s everybody so dang happy and all giggles about?” I asked. “Whose birthday is it?”

“Boy, you just hold your horses. We’re gonna have a whing-ding tonight you never saw the likes of. Okay?”

What else could I do except nod my head and say, “Okay. If you say so. Could I have a big cold drink?” I asked.

Then Ollie announced, “Now everybody is here ‘cept some special guests that will be along sooner or later, and better sooner than later.

“Everybody join up in a great big circle and hold hands. Maybell, hustle out here and grab my hand. Stir up the fire under that barbeque and let’s give thanks to our Maker.”

Maybell barely got there in time before he began praying. I grabbed Olivia’s hands, her mother gave her a quick smacker and held her hand, she grabbed Ollie’s big arm and in the distance, there was the sound of galloping hooves.

“Hold everything, folks. Here comes Fuss and ol’ Boy, my two best cowhands.”

And when the circle was completed, I counted 40 people before I lost count and just as Ollie started to shout, “Hey, God, thanks for the great state of Texas on this great day, for all of us, your worthy cowboys and cowgirls, for this young black boy you brought to us, for Rowdy and for his ma and pa, who are just apt to show up for this party at any minute.”

It took a while for his words to soak through my head, and when they did, my closed eyes opened, I forgot we were supposed to be praying, and my heart began to beat so hard I thought it would break through my chest.

I stopped breathing for a minute and barely heard him say, “Amen,” and I felt Olivia’s arms go around my neck and she kissed me on the lips and hugged me and then she did the most strange thing.

She busted out crying and held onto me so tight I could hardly breathe. JJ came around behind me patted me on the back, jumped up and down, and said, “Hey, Rowdy. Look down at the barn.”

I did so and my blurry eyes saw somebody walking toward us, with Booger Joe holding one arm and Miss Sally on the other and…

"Pa! Is it really you?"

He walked up to me, trembling and sweating and crying at the same time. He put his big arms around my shoulders, I could feel his whiskers against my cheeks and feel the hot tears rolling down. I got so weak somebody – I don't know who – held me up.

I barely heard the sound of lots of people blowing their noses, of tough cowboys clearing their throats and turning away to wipe their eyes, and from somewhere came my Moochie dog and his girlfriend Dolly, and finally all the tears began to dry. Someone brought me a chair to sit on and my pa got one and we held hands, and every time we looked at each other we began to cry all over again.

Finally, pa said, "There's somebody else wants to see you, Rowdy. Are you ready?"

I nodded – at least I think I nodded. Surely he didn't bring "Her" to get me, too. After all, "She" was the main reason I had run away from home. Was this all I had to look forward to, this going back home to the same old misery?

But I couldn't let my pa down. I realized now, what I had never realized before. My pa came before anyone else in the world except, of course, my ma – my real mother.

And so I nodded and said, "Yes," in a quiet voice.

Raising his voice and looking in the direction of the barn Pa yelled, "You can come on now. He wants to see you."

And everybody, including me, looked in the direction of the barn.

And there, stepping out and walking gracefully toward our circle was… I did not know her.

That was not anyone I ever knew.

But there was something familiar about her walk.

It was her clothing that puzzled me. Mom had never worn a uniform at all. Just a house dress or maybe a dress up dress for Sunday.

But the person in the khaki uniform of the U.S. Army walked just like…

It hit me like a bomb!

"Mom," I shouted at the top of my voice. "Is it really you?"

The crowd opened to form a path as my mother broke into a run to get to me and I ran to get to her and we cried happy tears by the gallons and Ollie and Maybell, and Booger Joe and Miss Sally and JJ all tried to get to us and touch us and cry with us.

Once I even got a glimpse of the writer and the photographer milling around, taking pictures and notes and maybe sniffling a little bit.

I knew there could never be a better day in all of the rest of time.

But there was JJ. What about him? Where was my pal, JJ?

Then I saw him edge through the crowd and there was someone holding his hand, and I knew her.

It was Mary, the woman who was my grandmother's helper, Mary Johnson.

"Mary," I said, "What are you doing here?"

42

The Release

I had heard it said many times that in a person's lifetime things could happen and your whole life would flash before you in a matter of seconds.

This was what was happening to me. It seemed that time was standing still. I knew where I was, I saw my tall, handsome father and my beautiful mother with her coal black shiny hair looking so dignified and beautiful in her Armed Services uniform standing right before me. I knew Olivia was beside me, knew Ollie and Maybell were here, Toby and Polecat at my back, Booger Joe and Miss Sally squeezed in around me and a host of Texas ranchers and farmers crowding around.

For a while my brain stopped processing the present and that deep, mysterious inner record of memory went by in a flash, so fast it could not be spoken, but as real and emotional as if it was appearing in the years of my life.

There was the flash of childhood, of being surrounded by doting parents and grandparents, the sense of nudging at the breast for nourishment, of learning to walk and of the floor rushing up to meet me as I fell until I could learn to stand upright and walk alone.

There was the sense of learning the warmth of sunshine, a roaring fire in the fireplace, of the smell and sound of cattle grazing, of the joy of sunsets and feel of rain on a warm summer day.

Of the strength of growing up, running so freely as the wind flew past my face, of bare feet in the mud, of being stuck by briers, of church with other children my age, eating ice cream made in a five gallon freezer turned by the church elders, and the angel food cake of my mother's as we began to eat.

Of becoming the fastest runner in my age class, of learning to hit a baseball farther and run faster than any of the other boys, of diving into the cold waters of spring-fed Asher Creek.

And then in a flash of memory I could not stop even though I did not want to, of when I saw the arrival of the new preacher and his wife and two children who suddenly arrived in this now dark-clouded retrieval of life.

I lost my warm hearted, lust for life, I began to pout, to be hateful, to use my speed to chase down and beat up on other boys, to tease the girls until they cried. They began to hate me, and I began to hate everything and all about my life around me.

I went through the sense of being in the third grade, of not knowing about my lessons or caring about them. I relived the day I left the classroom thinking it was noon, of walking downtown in Willard to get my noontime ice cream cone from Huck's store, of suddenly remembering it was not noontime at all, but only recess and the school bell rang and that I would be late for class and that I would be held in for being late.

I dreaded to go home at night. I started getting off the bus and stopping at the home of my grandmother rather than my real home where my mother and father had lived, but where my stepmother and her two children now lived. I begged dad to let me live in my grandmother's house on the excuse that she needed help with my grandfather, who suffered severe headaches, and I relived the day he died and a lot of me died with him and of hearing the singing of "Out of the Ivory Palaces into a world of tears, only his Great Eternal life made my Savior go."

And then, worst of all, "she" became my fourth grade teacher. That whole school year became a blank. Even to this day, I cannot not remember a single thing about it.

Mercifully, God wiped my memory free.

This real-life vision flashed through me in a fraction of seconds and I realized why I had come to be disliked by my age mates, become impossible for my father to govern, brought tears of love and worry from my grandmothers, and my father to become so angry at me he punished me for the slightest infractions.

Finally, it all built up in me so deeply I conceived the idea of running away from home, more to spite my father for destroying my wonderful life by quarreling with my mother and sending her away, and at her for not taking me with her.

For as much as I loved my life on the farm and all of its joy and never-ending changing of the seasons, the rabbits, the quail, the ducks, the wild berries and apples and cherries and blackberries in season, the perfect life for any boy, I needed my mother for love and guidance.

My grandmothers were wonderful beyond reason, and understood why I had become the "mean little kid," for there never was and never will be, a substitute for the womb from which a child emerges.

It is without a doubt the most sacred relationship of any mammal on earth – and too often the most abused. Gradually my real life of the moment returned and I was again of the moment, with my mother's arm around me, and my father's arm holding me close, and I felt anger and hate draining out of me like a healing and cleansing flush.

I heard myself saying, as if in a daze, "Mom, you are not going to believe this. But your long-lost brother is not lost."

She looked at me – I was as tall as she was now – and her eyes widened in astonishment.

"My what?"

"Your brother - my uncle Frank."

I felt her body quiver and she could not say a word for a while. I said, "Booger Joe, come here."

For a moment, he did not move. Miss Sally started sobbing and wailing but everybody else in the group became perfectly silent. You could only hear the passing of a flock of geese, the hooting of an owl and the reply of its mate in the distance. Booger Joe seemed to stagger as he broke through the group of ranchers and eased through to stand in front of me and stare directly into my mother's eyes.

"Nellie, is that really you. Or am I in a dream?"

I felt mother sag and my dad grabbed her arms and held her up. Her face turned chalky white and I thought she would faint.

But gradually, she recovered her composure, but I could hear her heart beating a million miles an hour. She opened her mouth to speak but no words could come out. Then she reached out and touched him, and he stepped forward and put his arms around her.

"Yes, Nellie. It is me. Just try to look through the whiskers. How's Ma? And Winnie? And my three brothers? I am ashamed of myself. I don't deserve to even live, for what I did to you and my family.

That was more than she could take. She went totally limp and collapsed in my father's arms. Booger Joe and Ollie shoved a couple of bales of straw under her and they carefully placed her on the improvised bed and began fanning her with a big cowboy hat Ollie handed him.

43

JJ's Big Surprise

I realized that everybody had crowded around us in a circle that got tighter and tighter as my family gathering developed.

Ollie took charge - you could not keep him from being in charge any time he was around, he was that kind of a guy – and he said in no uncertain terms, "Here, here folks, back off and give these good folks some air. They have just had some real shockers hit them. Wonderful shockers, to be sure, but what I have heard is enough to shock anybody's pants off.

"Maybell, bring a pitcher of ice water over here, and Olivia, honey, run into the kitchen and bring out some face towels and a couple of fans. We don't want Miss Nellie to faint away on us. Now, all you cowboys and cowgals back up a little. Soon as her head stops spinning, she's going to be the happiest gal alive, is my bet."

My mother reached out a hand for Ollie and she smiled up at him. "Thank you, my friend. But I will be alright in a moment. You are so right. I have indeed had the shock of my life, with so much coming all at once, that I just became a bit too emotional. This is indeed one of the most important moments of my life, as you can imagine. Now, all of you good folks just go on about enjoying this wonderful barbeque. If someone would be so kind as to fetch me a big glass of iced tea, I would be grateful."

No sooner had she said that than two or three hands stretched outward and handed her the ice tea and there she sat with tea in both hands and drank her fill and, a little shaky but smiling greatly, she got to her feet, my dad on one arm and me steadying her on the other.

"Now why don't you good people get in line and go on with your barbeque and I will join you in just a moment. Thank you, thank you from heart and soul. And you, Olivia, come to me and let me give you a great big hug. You are a beautiful child."

And so the crowd drifted away and formed the lines at the table and there was buzzing laughter and talk as they filled their plates.

But now, JJ suddenly appeared in front of me and said, "Rowdy, Rowdy, can you take some more good news?"

He was just fairly dancing, he was so excited, and all of a sudden I realized he was looking down at me instead of up, and I thought to myself how he had grown this summer. I said, "I think I have had about all of the good news I can stand for one day. What is it?"

"Mary is my mother. Can you believe it? My very own flesh and blood. And guess what else, Rowdy. You remember the other day when I was down in the mouth and told you I wanted a girlfriend just like you had?"

"Why, JJ – yeah, I remember."

"Well, just you wait right here, and see." He started toward the bunk house and then turned and said, "Now stand still. I won't be a minute. Now keep your eyes closed. Miss Nellie, you don't have to close your eyes. You already know something."

My mother laughed and said, "All right. Yes, I know your surprise. Go on."

JJ ran to the barn, went inside and a minute later stuck his head around the door and yelled, "Ready? Now close your eyes and turn around. I don't want you to ruin my surprise. Ready now? Here I come."

And so, somewhat bewildered, I did as he said, and muttered, "What the dickens has JJ got in his mind." And mother said, laughing lightly, "Just do as he asks, Rowdy. He wants to surprise you. And believe you me, you will be surprised."

I heard JJ giggling as he came closer and closer to me and then he said, "Now don't move a muscle until I tell you to, Rowdy, and don't open your eyes."

And then I felt a soft, warm hand touch my right hand and clasp it tightly. My heart skipped a beat. And then, I felt a soft warm hand grasp me left hand and my heart skipped another beat.

And then I felt two more warm hands close over my eyes and JJ yelled, "Okay. Now open your eyes."

And in a flash, I knew JJ's surprise. I whirled around, opened my eyes and shouted… "Ruby! Tina! May! How the dickens did you get here?"

Now it was my turn to find the bale of straw and sit down to recover my senses. Vaguely it occurred to me that not only had my mother and father come to Texas to get me, but JJ's family and friends had also made the trip.

The girls, who usually only spoke when spoken to just hid their giggles behind their hands and backed away. JJ danced a little jig - I had never seen him so happy – and he said, "They rode in the back seat of your car."

And though the thought struck me, how were we all to get back home in one car, but it quickly passed away in the celebration that followed. JJ and the triplets joined hands and danced a little jig and a ring-around-the-rosy while all the guests brought their plates of food and laughed and shouted until they were hoarse.

"Best dad-blamed celebration I ever saw on this old homestead," shouted Ollie.

And finally we all went to the chow line, filled our plates, ate until we nearly busted, and then Ollie and Maybell and Miss Sally and Booger Joe sliced big juicy, red watermelons and one big party went on until midnight.

Some guests drove away into the night, others unrolled bedrolls and bedded down in the horse barn, some on the front porch and my family and I, well, we huddled up in a circle and sat and talked until the morning star rose, then we unrolled a canvas, pulled up blankets and snoozed until the sun came up.

When the sun hit me in the eyes, I sat up and looked around. What did I see but Olivia sleeping next to my mother, their arms thrown around each other, and peace on their faces.

My life was full again, and I was at peace inside, for the first time in years.

44

Getting Acquainted

I thought I had been the first one on the ranch to wake up, but found out differently, as a huge dinner bell down by the bunkhouse, where the cow hands bunked, began clanging fit to kill.

That was followed by the cook yelling at the top of his voice, "Chuck'll be ready in 30 minutes. Be ready or I'll throw it out."

All my folks sat up in a hurry, started rubbing their eyes and looking around to get their bearings. Olivia and my mother looked at each other, then broke out laughing. Mother grabbed her and hugged her and said, "Honey, we must have fallen asleep without knowing it. Someone was kind enough to throw a cover over us, weren't they?"

Olivia rubbed the sleep out of her eyes and said, "Never slept so hard in my life. Come with me and we will go into the house to freshen up."

And Pa, well, he must have gotten up earlier, because there was only a clump of bedding where he had been. It was not at all unusual for my family to go on fishing trips and sleep out in the open, and dad never went anywhere without his camping gear.

So now all I had to do was throw off my covers and look around to find a private place where I could relieve myself. Meanwhile, I heard the distant sound of hoof beats and then Ollie's voice came booming out, "Everybody up and at'm. Sun's comin' up and you can't sleep all day."

I looked out and riding alongside Ollie were my dad and Booger Joe. Dad dismounted, grinned at me and said, "Rowdy, I may be just an old farm hand, but I can wake up just as early as your Texas friend. Get a move on, for I can tell we are already in for a busy day. He's got it all planned, and he is not easy to stop when he gets started."

I laughed, "I found that out the hard way, dad. When I first met him, I thought he was just a big bag of wind. Well, he may be that, too. But where he blows, the wind comes along later."

Ollie came over and said, "Women folks sleep all right? They could have stayed with Maybell in the house, you know."

"No problem," dad said. "We are used to going on camping trips and sleeping on the ground, if nothing else is available. But that early morning ride put me in a mood for a big platter of hotcakes and bacon."

Booger Joe grinned, "You going to talk or eat?" And he put his horse in a stall, along with the other horses, and led the way to the bunkhouse where Fuss, Boy, and four other cowboys were already lining up to eat.

"Good gosh, Ollie," dad said, "I had no idea you ran a major ranch outfit. How many acres do you have anyway?"

I remembered this was a question Olivia and I had planned to put to Ollie, but had been too busy the day before to get out the question.

Ollie said, "Now, Mr. Farmer, you know it ain't polite to ask a man his bank account. But I don't hold it against you for asking, and all I can tell you, it is a far piece from one end to the other.

"Truth is, I don't really know how big it is, because there is no record – accurate, at least – that we know of. I guess we will get all the claims and deeds straightened out one day, but what with the canyon land and prairie land, well along with old time homestead claims and corruption of all kinds few really know how much land they have and how much may belong to somebody else."

"So you just operate whatever you are big enough to keep?"

"Sort of like that," Ollie laughed. "The theory is the bigger you are, the harder you are to push around. But I can't ride from one end of the place to the other in one day's time."

"How many head of cows can you run?"

Ollie's voice boomed out again. "Would you tell me how much money you have in your bank account? Of course not, asking a man how many cows he has is about the same thing. If I told you, first thing you know the tax collector would come along and want a lot of money I don't want him to have. Some things just have to kind of be guessed at."

We lined up for hotcakes with real butter on them, a hunk of fried steak, black coffee which I never could handle, and I listened to cow, horse and land talk until I was dizzy. I could tell dad and Ollie really liked each other, and Ollie asked as many questions about life in Missouri as dad did about Texas.

"I have a mind there might someday be an opportunity to ship calves and yearlings to someplace like Missouri or Kansas to finish them. Nowadays, we just sell the calves when they are weaned from the cow, so somebody else puts the market finish on them after we go to the work of raising them. Seems there ought to be some good cheap grazing land in Missouri where this could be done."

"I have thought about the same thing," dad said. "But I think it would also be a good place for the entire operation – mother cows to bring the calves, and good grass to finish them for market. We can run a cow to four acres. How many acres does it take in Texas for a cow?"

"Some places 20 acres to the cow, farther west it may take thirty or forty."

And so the talk went until breakfast was over and around that time, in came the magazine writer and photographer, rubbing sleep filled eyes. "Doesn't anybody around here sleep or rest?" Covello asked, picking out a tin plate and begging a couple of hotcakes. Maness was too sleepy to talk, but did offer a grin and nod.

Ollie led us over to the house, where he entered his office, and showed us pictures of his prize bulls and cows and quarter horses, then sat down and looked at me. "Rowdy, here, he has turned into quite a famous character in these parts. Sort of livened up the summer for us, some of the stunts he has pulled. Take that wild horse thing. Guess Booger Joe got that straightened out. Of course there might be a little fine or something to get it all tided over, but that won't amount to anything.

"I sort of liked the spirit he shows. Took a lot of guts for him and that black boy to leave home with nothing but the shirts on their backs, and try to make there way alone in the wild, wild west.

"That's a whole lot like my old granddaddy and daddy did, back in the other century. They, and others like them, took all kinds of risks that did not make any sense at the time. But look at where it got us. "I had the rough broken off the land for me, so it was just a matter of picking up where they left off. It was easy for me. That's the same spirit Rowdy showed when he blew here – all innocence and determination. We maybe made it a bit hard for him at the first, but he proved he could take it like a sport. When it happened that his uncle turned out to be Booger Joe, well, that did it. We figured your boy was to tie to.

"We'd like to keep him, but I know he belongs back in Missouri, with his family. That is, at least until he is a full grown man and old enough to sign for himself and to vote. Then, if he wants to come to Texas and become a rancher, all right. I would be glad to help him. What you say to that?"

Dad did not stutter. "I think you hit the nail on the head. He is quite a man for a boy his age, and I respect him – perhaps more than he realizes. He is so head strong he has been a handful, but so is many a spirited horse that is the best you have.

"Rowdy tells me he is ready to come home, and his mother and I could not be happier. In fact, it is our fault that Rowdy became so discontented he left home in the first place. And as the preacher says, the Lord works his wonders in strange fashion sometimes. I guess this is just one of those times, right?"

Ollie grinned that great big grin, boomed out and said, "Right, brother. Shake on it."

And then he said, "Want to show you around the ranch today, if you are not in a hurry to leave. We'll take you into the canyon – Rowdy has already been there – and show you my horses and cattle. Agreed?"

"Wouldn't leave without it," said dad. "And I also understand there is a wager, something about a mean bull, that Rowdy has committed himself to catch."

Ollie busted out laughing and my face got red and hot.

"Ah, he don't have to go through that to prove himself. He has already done that. Let the bull go. Booger Joe and I and some cowboys will take care of that later."

But dad put a stop to that. "No sir. If Rowdy said he would do it, I know him enough to know he'll try it. He's got a plan and doggone if I don't think it might work. Especially if he's got somebody to help pull it off – somebody like Booger Joe. It's my understanding Booger Joe is somewhat of a character of his own when it comes to riding fast horses and had handling mean cattle."

And so Booger Joe, who had done a lot more listening this morning than talking, just grinned, whipped out his plug of Star chewing tobacco and stuck it in his jaw.

"When do we start?" he said.

"First things first," said Ollie. "Today, it's the tour of the ranch and canyon. Tomorrow, why not the bull?"

45

God Bless Texas

"So that settles it," said Ollie. "We've beat around the mesquite tree all summer long about that ol' bull and Rowdy's big plan – all a kind of good natured joke.

"But I guess now it has become more than a joke. If we aim to control the breeding of those old time Longhorns – to say nothing about keeping our blooded stock from getting run down – we might as well get on with it.

"Booger Joe, step outside the door and ring that big ol' bell five times. That's the signal for all the cowboys within hearing to come to the office. I want to get ol' Fuss in here to talk to our friend from Missouri. Fuss is the best story teller we've got. And besides, his pedigree in this part of the world goes back as far as the first Indians, I reckon. He's part Indian, part Mexican, part Texan, and proud of every drop of his blood."

As Booger Joe stepped out and started ringing the bell, Ollie turned to my dad and said, "Way I calculate, that car of yours carried seven passengers down here. How you going to carry them all back, along with your son?"

Dad grinned and shrugged his shoulders. "I'm sort of tired of milking cows and growing wheat for a living. I thought it just might be possible to begin switching over to some good stock cattle. Say, like Herefords. It strikes me your range-bred and reared cattle might do well up in our part of the world. We need some hardy cattle instead of pen raised ones that have to be fed corn and oats and alfalfa hay."

"That figures," Ollie said. "If I remember my trail driving history, the first big trail drive from Texas to the east went right through

Missouri, and on through to New York. That was the longest trail drive in history. "Two gutsy men named Tom Ponting and Washington Malone paid gold for six hundred head of Longhorns and headed for Illinois in 1852. They crossed Red River and pastured their herd in Indian Territory while they scouted for more cattle, and bought 80 big steers, and started east again.

"They drove to Springfield, cut northeast at St. Louis, and finally found a rail head in Muncey, Indiana.

"They loaded 150 of their best steers on rail cars, hauled them to New York City and sold them for $89 a head.

"Just think of that. Two years to get to market and make a profit. But it did more than that, because it made starving Tex cattlemen realize they could make a fortune on their cheap cattle if they could get them to the market.

"The Civil War slowed things down, but when it ended, a stock buyer named Joseph McCoy realized the best way to get cattle east was by rail. With his pushing and prodding, a rail line was established at Abilene, Kansas. That's when trailing cattle from Texas opened up for one of the most exciting chapters in history of the cattle business – of the great American West as well."

Ollie leaned back and was silent for a few minutes, apparently thinking back in time and place. Then he said, "Whew, Lord, them was the days. If only I had lived then, but heck, if I had, I wouldn't be here today, would I?" And he bellowed out laughter and slapped my father on the shoulder.

By this time, Fuss and Booger Joe were back at the office, and Ollie said, "Fuss, you old windbag you, I started to tell this Missourian about the history of the old black bull, and the Longhorns we're playing nurse maid to. You know that history better than any of the rest of us. How about it?"

Claud Fussel, tall, broad shouldered, ruddy of face and with hands big as hams, smiled, sat down, rested his ten gallon hat on his knee and leaned back.

"Glad to oblige, Ollie. Someday reckon I ought to strike out this story on paper, but guess I never will. But somebody ought to.

"It all started in the year 1561 when the Spanish explorer Cortez carried six heifers and a bull calf of Andalusian stock on his ship to Mexico.

"Somehow – whether by design or accident – the heifers were bred and calved and the history of the Longhorn cattle in the Americas began.

"Twenty years later the explorer Coronado drove 500 head for food supplies during his futile search for gold. He lost his life, failed in his search for gold, but left the beginnings of the tens of thousands of Longhorns running wild on the greatest grass pasture in the world – the southern plains of the central United States.

"As the years passed, the buffalo were nearly extinguished, and the Longhorns flourished to unbelievable numbers. They were to be had for the taking – a long rope and a good horse was all that was necessary for a man to get rich – if he could get the cattle to market.

"Many failed, but others prospered. And none was more successful than a man named Charles Goodnight.

"At the age of eleven, he rode a horse bare back from his home in Illinois to Texas and was soon running a herd of his own cattle in Texas. As the years went on, he was the most successful trail driver of them all, but he capped it off when he was lead to the Palo Duro Canyon, which is in our backyard.

"It is said there was only one natural entrance to the canyon – an entrance where the cattle had to be driven in single file to the great grass plains at the bottom. There were ten million buffalo grazing in the canyon, and Goodnight had to drive them out before he could take cattle in.

"In partnership with an Irish rich man, he established the famous J A Ranch. In later years, he established his own ranch, had the town of Goodnight named after him, and lived to the age of 93. He died in 1929."

"Wonderful, Fuss. Great story. But you have not told why we are so bent on saving our old mean black bull."

"So I haven't," said Fuss. "But if you have heard my story, you should have already guessed why. Cattlemen preserved, as far as we can tell, a select herd of Longhorns that had lived in straight-line generations with the original stock found in the canyon, along with the buffalo. They were driven to side canyons, sealed off from other stock, and are treasured as a direct link to the arrival of the Andalusian cattle brought over by Cortez.

"Our black bull is without a doubt the finest of the fine sires ever born, and he is believed to be the son of the legendary Red River Roan, dead these long years but to be forever remembered by all Texas cattlemen."

There was a long and respectful silence when Fuss stopped speaking. I felt ripples throughout as the meaning of his story soaked through my brain. In his few words, I felt I had lived five hundred years in side a matter of minutes.

Dad broke the silence with a soft, "Fantastic, What a story, I must write that down word for word before I leave."

For once, Ollie's booming voice was soft and reverent. "So you know now part of why us good ol' Texas boys are so confounded conceited and proud of Texas and our way of life. Long live the Alamo. Long live the great Lone Star Texas. God bless Sam Houston. And I'll throw in Charles Goodnight for good measure."

Nobody else said a word until the door leading into the house opened. Olivia poked her pretty little head around and said, "I thought you all must be sick. Every thing got so quiet all of a sudden."

Ollie said in a soft, loving voice, "Come here, my little chicky-babe. Your ol' daddy needs a great big hug."

And it was forthcoming, and then she came over and sat down by me, and squeezed my hand.

"What's next?" she asked.

46

The Plan

When Ollie set his mind on something, he didn't beat around the bush. He got right down to the point.

"Booger Joe, you and Fuss are my eyes and ears on the range. What is your best guess as to where the bull and his cows are holed up this time of year?"

Joe didn't hesitate. "I haven't seen him since that episode with Rowdy. He hung around the lower north leg of the main canyon, then disappeared. But you can bet if he is still alive, and I believe he is, then he somehow found a way to get back to his herd.

"That means he had to enter one of the north branches. There's water in them all, so he could be in any one. Best way to find out is to send riders into each branch, make a wide circle and look for a sign.

"How long would that take?"

Booger Joe opened the door and spit tobacco juice. "Take half a day for each branch. Two men ought to go together. That means four riders if we do it today."

"Where's Toby and Polecat?" Ollie asked.

"They rode out an hour ago to carry salt to your yearling heifers. They should be back by now."

"Good. Take plenty of drinking water and something to eat. You ought to be back by mid-afternoon. Each of you take a 30-06 rifle in case that bull hides in a patch of brush and comes to say hello, you hear?"

Booger Joe grinned. "I can smell him a mile away."

"Yeah. Sure. And that bull can smell you two miles away. Get a move on."

"Done. Let's go, Fuss."

Ollie settled back in his chair and propped his boots on the desk. "Now, Mr. Farmer, tell us about that major equipment Rowdy said you were going to bring. That stuff to put the bull to sleep and bring him awake again. Sounds like a lot of hocus-pocus, to me."

Dad grasped his legs and leaned back, a big grin splitting his face.

"Sounds pretty weird, I admit. But so help me, it works. Slickest thing I ever saw. And the only way I could ever take the horns off of a mature jersey bull."

"And so what's in this needle or whatever it is?"

"You will have to ask somebody smarter than me. All I can tell you is, it works."

"And after the animal goes down, how long do you have to treat it?"

"Ten, maybe fifteen minutes. There is also a shot you give to bring them awake. If you don't do that, they could die."

Ollie shook his head, grinned and said, "You wouldn't fool an old fooler would you?"

"I asked the vet the same question. He just said to show him the bull he was to treat. Only difference I see in your deal is my bull was in a pen and we could reach over it to stick in the needle to put him down. He just got sleepy, staggered a few steps, and slowly went down and went to sleep,"

Ollie shook his head in disbelief. "What'll they think of next? Well, I'm game to try it."

Dad cautioned, "Got to remember we are dealing with a man-killer, the way you talk, your bull is not going to just be pawing dirt and bellowing. He's going to be on the prod, and like as not in a dead run, either after your rider or ahead of him."

"Mister, you ain't never seen a Texas cowboy ride a horse after wild cattle. I guarantee you, when Fuss or Booger Joe – or even my own boys – get after that bull on a top cow pony, you are going to see a circus. Whoever gets the needle in his hand will stick it in the rump of that bull."

Ollie turned to me and said, "Rowdy, I have an idea you would like to spend most of this day showing your folks around my place and Salt River Sally's. Seems to me you've got a lot of catchin' up to do on all sides, and you need some time alone. About noon, we'll eat a bite and I'll take you on a quick tour of my little ol' place.

"But meanwhile, just remember one thing, you are our guests, and we will do anything we can to help you or to make you and Rowdy happy. We have come to think a lot of that boy, and it looks like he thinks a lot of us. Now, you just make yourselves at home while I talk to those tenderfoot journalists and bring them up to snuff on what we aim to do tomorrow."

With that, he jammed on his hat, stormed out the door and yelled, "Hey you dad-blamed boys of mine, where you been hidin' out? Go get your orders from Fuss and Booger Joe. And be ready for some excitement tomorrow.

"And you picture-takin' dude and story teller, what are you going to do today to earn your keep? I hear-tell you love them little ol' rattler snakes. That so?" And that big laugh of his rumbled out his belly.

Olivia, who had taken all of this in with a quiet smile, took my hand and dad's and led us through the office door and down a long hallway to the kitchen. We could hear the laughter of JJ and his mother, Mary, and the triplet girls.

When we entered the spacious kitchen, JJ leaped up, shook hands with dad, and jumped up and down in his happiness. Maybell laughed and said, "I declare, I never in my life saw such happy folks. They all want to talk at the same time, except May. She's the quiet one of the three. And Mary – why JJ just keeps her laughing all the time. She has just told me that for private reasons, she kept the birth of JJ from anybody except her mother and father, didn't even tell JJ until just today. He almost leaped through the ceiling with excitement."

Well, I knew there was a lot more things I would learn, but right now, I was anxious to be alone with my parents.

As politely as possible, I explained that to Maybell, and she said, "I understand perfectly, Rowdy. Let me take you into our private living room, and you make yourself at home. Anything you want, you just yell out.

"Meanwhile, I'll take my other guests out to my garden. I just planted some flowers I want them to see." And so for the first time in two years, my father and mother and I sat down alone. It was awkward, at first, until mother broke the silence and said, "Rowdy, the first thing you need to know is that your father and mother are not perfect. We made mistakes, and you are the one that suffered the most.

"But your father and I suffered, too, and we have paid an awful price. We ask you to forgive us, and accept our apology. It will never happen again. Just as you have done a lot of growing up, so have we. It was you that made us realize that. We love you more than anything or anyone else on earth. But it took your pain and mistake to make us realize what is most important. That is – you, and our family life together.

"So we have done our best to undo the damage and mistakes that have been made. And let us put it all behind us, love each other again. Let it be a lesson for all of us."

"And my step-mother?" I asked.

"She is gone, son. She never wanted to be our family, really. She took her boys and went out East, I guess. We divorced. Then I called your mother to tell her about you, and she came home…" My father's voice got misty as he looked at my mother.

"We were so worried for you, it brought us together. And I realized quickly that I, a newly divorced man, was wanting to try to salvage the one marriage I truly lost," he ended.

My mother cried, I cried, and my father cried, healing, cleansing tears.

47

The Tour

Dad opened the door for mother, she followed and I motioned to Olivia. "You are part of the family. Let's go."

"Really? Oh, I wanted to go. But I didn't know if I would be welcome or not."

I never was one for sweet talk, but this time I said, "Sugarplum, you will always be welcome to go where I go."

She gave me a little pinch on the cheek and we followed the folks to the wagon, piled in and started off. But we saw Ollie frantically waving his arms, so dad whirled around and drove over to him.

"Hate to hold you up, but I wanted to tell you to try to be back by noon or so. We've got a long day ahead of us, and if I am going to have time to show you the canyon and be back before dark, we'll have to keep moving."

He looked in the back seat at Olivia, started to say something, but said to me, "Rowdy, take care of my baby, okay?"

"Oh, daddy. Baby my foot. I've got to take care of Rowdy."

My folks laughed, a bit uneasy, I thought, but then we were off in a cloud of dust. "Show me the way, Rowdy," dad said, "and tell me when to slow down for the bumps. This ranch road is better suited for horses than motor cars."

It took about ten minutes to get off the ranch road and on the road to Salt River. The unusually sleepy little trading center was just waking up and I looked around for my old friend, Dutchy, and Mr. Keeper, the operator of the general store. No one else was in sight, other than a few of the towns people dusting off porches or sprinkling some flowers.

I noticed the circus had picked up and left and I hated that for I had hoped Olivia and I would have a chance to go on some of the wild rides. But we had plenty of wild rides of another kind, as dad turned back west on Miss Sally's road. There wasn't much conversation, for the road was full of bumps, and the car windows had to be rolled up because of the dust, and down because of the need for air.

But we finally reached the left turn to the ranch road to Miss Sally's place. The road was up hill and in a few minutes we began to look down upon the great prairie to the south, and caught a glimpse now and then of the river.

We burst out of the thicket of mesquite and brush and there was Miss Sally, standing on the porch as if she was expecting us. We stopped with dust swirling around us, got out and were greeted with the usual round of hugs and kisses and "Law's a'mercy, it's shore good to see you again. Get down and let's get a cup of coffee. And I got bacon frying in the pan."

And while mother and Olivia went into the house I took dad around the place to show him what we had done. First, we went to the pond where I hoped the big bass would surface, but he didn't, and I told him how I had broken the mule from breaking his halters when he was tied. Then we toured the corn field, and I told him about catching the sow and pigs, and we walked down the lane where I shot the turkeys and where Olivia and I had flushed that big covey of quail.

The last thing on the tour was the horse pasture. The three, with Lady Midnight in the lead, came racing up to the fence to see us, reaching out with their tongues hoping for some oats or sugar or something to eat.

Lady Midnight really showed off for dad, with a high head and a kick or two.

"That is really a fine mare, son," dad said. "Tell me again how you caught her." And he laughed until tears ran down his cheeks. "Bet you could not do that again in a million years," he said.

I told him again about how foolish I felt when I rode her into Salt River before all of the people and reared her up on her hind legs and the girth of the saddle broke and I slid off.

And I also told him what Booger Joe had told me – that I had not caught wild stock, but stock that was about to be shipped to a buyer.

"Uncle Joe said he would take care of it," I said. "Is there any way we could buy her?"

"That is possible," he said. "But how would we get her home? That would be a 500 mile ride if we took her on foot."

We went back to the house, where we ate another breakfast, then told Miss Sally we had to go if we were to get back in time for our tour of the canyon.

As we got into the car for the trip back to the ranch, mother said, "Rowdy, why don't you sit up front with father, so you can talk about cows and the ranch?

"Olivia and I want to ride in the back seat so we can get better acquainted, don't we Olivia?"

Olivia's face brightened and a pretty smile made her blue eyes sparkle. She hugged mother and said, "I would like that. I've got a million things to tell you about how Rowdy and I met..."

Dad chuckled, I crawled in the front seat and we bounced back toward Salt River town which was basking in heat and dust and without anyone in sight. They had gone inside to get out of the noonday sun, and I knew they would not stir much until it began to cool late in the afternoon.

And we did not talk much either, one reason being I wanted to hear what mother and Olivia were talking about as much as anything.

It seemed they were getting along well together, with mother asking dozens of questions about life on a big Texas ranch, with cowboys always hanging around, and if they flirted with her and if they were good, honest, clean-talking men.

"Daddy has a rule that any cowboys heard talking dirty or taking the Lord's name in vain had better clear the gate before he gets hold of them.

"The truth is the cowboys are not at all like the impression most folks have. Mother said that from the first day cattle men arrived in Texas, they brought the Bible with them, and that respect for God and women were the first rules.

"The second rule was, for anyone who didn't like Texas, they should head for the border before Texans learned about it."

Mother laughed at the quick and blunt answer. "You certainly do talk straight, Olivia. I appreciate that about you. And I suppose you would not want to live any place except Texas?"

"Oh, of course not. But then... well, there might be certain circumstances where I might have to think about that some more before I answered that question."

"And why would that be?"

I glanced over my shoulder and saw her blush while mother had a quizzical smile on her face.

"Well, you see, Rowdy and I ..."

"Yes, go on, honey."

"Well, Rowdy is the only boy I ever knew that I really liked. Mother always told me that you would know when you met the right boy. I've been around boys... well, cowboys, and they were mostly men... since I was a baby. They were always nice to me, and were what are called gentlemen.

"But I never had any reason to think of them any other way except as, well, as cowboys who rode horses and worked with cows and calves and were always worried because it didn't rain enough, and if it rained, they worried because it would wash out crops or ditches and roads.

"When they were around women, and especially young girls, they always tipped their hats politely and never looked directly into their eyes, but were quiet and careful with their language. Of course, sometimes when the horses got bulky or a cow kicked them, and they were out of sight of the house, they said things that made me put my hands over my ears."

Mother laughed ad hugged her. "I have often seen and heard that kind of behavior myself. It seems that is the habit of men wherever they are found."

"Can I tell you about the time I first saw Rowdy?"

"Oh, please do. I want to hear everything."

I felt my face get hot and I kept my eyes peeled on the road ahead, but strained my ears to hear every word.

"Well, it was a nice, cool day in early summer, and a Saturday. Everybody around Salt River was in town shopping for supplies to carry them through the week. And also to gossip. That is the main entertainment in Salt River.

And somebody at the store said to look down the road in the east, at what looked like two boys in farm clothing were headed our way.

When they got closer, we saw a burro, what some call a jackass, with a gangling black boy riding him. His legs were so long they almost dragged the ground. I remember somebody said, "Well, if that don't look like Jesus Christ, riding into Bethlehem. Except it can't be, because he is the wrong color."

"And then we looked at the beautiful little mare ridden by a white boy who was dressed in farm clothing and sat in a saddle that looked like it was falling apart."

"Just as they got to the store, with everybody looking and not knowing whether to laugh or cry, the boy on the mare pulled hard on the reins. The mare reared up, stood on her hind legs and just then the saddle girth broke. The saddle and boy slid off the rump of the mare and landed in the dirt road. The boy got up, red in the face and pretty puzzled about what to do next."

"Everybody expected to see him get up and hit the mare or something like that. But instead, he got up, dusted himself off and shouted –"

"Just call me Rowdy, I'm from Missouri, and I came to Texas to be a rancher. Anybody got ranches they want to sell?"

"The people were so startled and surprised at that bold announcement they didn't say anything. Actually, they expected the boy to fly into a fit and kick or slap the mare and blame her. But he just took it in stride. Then a fight started."

"Then the best thing I can think of happened to that boy who said he was Rowdy, from Missouri. Salt River Sally went to his rescue, dusted him off, and told everybody to get on about their business and she would take care of that poor lost boy that wanted to be a cowboy but obviously was a long way from being one."

"And as you may have already guessed by now, Salt River Sally can be a holy terror, or soft as an angel. She took Rowdy and his partner in her custody, and now you know the rest of the story."

"The first thing I knew, Rowdy was drinking a bottle of ice cold strawberry soda pop and looking at me as if he could not see anybody else. I fell in love with him, right then and there. And I am still in love with him. And I am going to marry him someday, whether he knows it or not."

Boy, did I ever get my ears full by my eaves dropping. Dad had heard, too, and he burst out laughing, glanced over his shoulder and said, "Olivia, that is a great story. I will remember it until the day I kick the bucket."

I glanced over my shoulder, looked at mother, and she was gasping for breath, laughing so hard she had to wipe tears out of her eyes.

Olivia didn't laugh, but her eyes were big as saucers and then she realized the humor she had created with her story of how she first saw me she began to laugh, too.

Mother pulled her over, hugged her tight, and they sat that way until we pulled into the lane to the ranch.

Ollie standing by his office door and he came running to greet us, that big friendly grin providing a welcome home.

"Get down and come in," he said. "Get down and come in. Chuck's on the table and gettin' cold."

48

A New Family

Ollie didn't do things half way, for sure. He hustled – or herded – us into the house where Maybell had the table set and roast beef, biscuits and gravy ready to take out of the oven. I spied two pies cooling on the window sill.

Even before Maybell had everything on the table or had time to sit down, he was passing the biscuits, gravy and beef around and saying, "Hurry up, Ma, time's wastin' and we got lots to do this afternoon.

"I want to take you good folks out to see my band of quarter horses, and show off my new stallion and new foals. Then, we will take a quick buzz around the edge of the canyon, maybe even catch a glimpse of the buffalo from a distance, and then breeze right back here. By that time, Fuss and Boy ought to be back with Toby and Polecat and news of their scout for the Longhorns."

"Then we'll sit down and make our plans for the big bull chase tomorrow. You all ready, Rowdy? By the way, where is your little mare? Is she here, or is she still at Sally's place?"

No one had a chance to answer or say anything, and wouldn't have if Ollie hadn't talked so fast while he was chewing and got choked.

Finally he got to eating and that gave the rest of us a chance to catch up with him. "No, Lady Midnight is still at Miss Sally's place. You said we could leave her there, because we had to go that direction on our bull hunt."

And my mother said, "I'm sorry, but there has been so much going on that I am bushed. If you don't mind, I would rather freshen up with a shower and take a little snooze for a few hours. But I am sure my husband and Rowdy will want to go with you. Perhaps I can catch up with the scenery later."

Of course Olivia had to tune up, too. "Where are you going, Rowdy? Where you go, that's where I'm going."

Ollie looked up sharply and said, "Now, young lady, you best stay with your ma and help with the dishes. You've been running around like a chicken with its head cut off the last few days. And if you expect to tag along on the bull chase, you got another think coming."

He finally got busy with his biscuits and gravy and fell to eating, and when he finished, he said, "I've got to find those magazine fellers and see what they are up to. I sure enough don't want them with us tomorrow on the bull business."

And he hustled out the door, always in motion and wanting to keep everybody up to date and in a good mood.

After we finished eating, mother helped clean off the table and while they were washing and drying, that gave Olivia and I a chance to slip out the door and be alone for a little while.

While I was thinking of all we had done and what we were planning next, I happened to hear a familiar sound.

"Moochie! Where is that dog?" I had forgotten all about him, what with being in such a hurry and so many things happening so fast.

"Oh. I haven't seen him for a while, either," Olivia said. "But don't worry about him. This is a big place, with lots of buildings and things for dog to do. But it is sort of curious, not seeing them for a while. Both were with us all of the time a few days ago.

"Let's take a walk down to the stock barn and look around. They always liked to dig for mice and rats, maybe even an armadillo."

So we headed for the barn, where about every tool or piece of junk found around a farm or ranch always seems to end up, holding hands and not saying much.

Finally, Olivia broke the silence. "Rowdy, I've been thinking."

"What have you been thinking? The same thing I have?"

We stopped and looked at each other and suddenly her lower lip began quivering and tears appeared in her eyes. She nodded? "Your folks are here. They will be going home soon. And they came to get you – to take you back home with them. And I... I am going to be all alone. And I don't want to be alone without you. Never, never, never again. Oh, Rowdy. What did I ever do without you? How can I ever live without you?"

She put her arms around me and I held her tightly and choked back a few tears of my own.

It was a few minutes before I could speak and finally I whispered, "I know. I've been thinking the same thing."

We made our way to the barn, holding tightly to each other, and our legs got weak and we found a place to sit down inside the building. We just held tightly to each other and sat silently, thinking, thinking. What could we do? Just kids, too young to get married. Too old to live without each other again. Feeling that at last our heart's desires had been fulfilled.

Finally, Olivia sobbing, dried her tears on the hem of her dress, and took a deep breath.

"Could I go home with you, Rowdy? Could I live with you and your parents until I become of age and we could marry? My mother would understand, I am sure. She was married when she was 15. Daddy was 21."

She turned to me with a new glow in her eyes. "That's it, Rowdy. Let's ask them. They will understand, won't they?"

My heart took a giant leap as her words hit my mind. That's it, I thought. But would they buy it? After all, my mother and father had just been through a terrible crisis that about killed all of us. And here they were just trying to put their lives together again, and they have us to worry about, as well.

I did not dare tell her at this moment it would be impossible. I just said, meekly, "I don't see how it is possible. But, let's think about it."

She kissed me, long and tenderly, brushed my hair with her trembling hands, and pressed her tear-stained cheeks against mine.

We just sat there dreamlike, wishing time would never end, when all of a sudden I was aware of a wagging tail and whimpering dog at my feet.

"Moochie," I said. "There you are."

At my voice, he placed his forepaws on my knees, licked my hands and furiously wagged his tail. He whimpered, time and time again and bounced away, then came back to me.

Olivia sat up and held out her hands. Moochie came to her, licked her hands, then turned and darted off a few steps and whined. He came back to her, licked her hands again, and repeated his retreat.

"Look," she said. "He is trying to tell us something."

It was as if Moochie knew her language. He barked sharply, turned and ran a few steps away, then ran a few steps back, and barked again.

"He is trying to tell us something," she said. "Let's follow him."

She tugged my hand and we followed and Moochie showed his gratitude by running ahead, looking back and barking again, and then ran out of sight behind a pile of hay.

We rounded the hay and there, bedded down in deep, yellow straw, was the object Moochie was trying to tell us about. There lay Dolly and a full litter of new-born puppies.

Moochie leaped and tried his best to talk. Short, happy little yelps that seemed to say, "Look what we have done. Now I have a family too."

Dolly rolled and Olivia bent down and counted "one, two, three, four – and three more – she has seven puppies," she cried.

She stood up, pulled me beside her, looked up with sparkling eyes and said, "Look what our doggies have done for us, Rowdy. "They are telling us something. Seven puppies."

"Does that mean anything to you, Rowdy? Seven puppies our doggies gave us? Will God give us seven babies, too? Seven is a large number. Oh, Rowdy, I love you so."

She put her arms around me and I hugged her and complete peace and happiness filled my soul.

There was never any doubt from that moment on.

Olivia and I had been born for each other. It was a strange, long path we had to travel to find each other.

But find each other, we had. Now it was just a matter of being patient and waiting for the rest of our lifetimes to roll out before us like a magic carpet.

49

The Scouts Return

I realized that everything had become very quiet. It was as if the whole world had decided to rest and let all of her creatures go within themselves.

Olivia had snuggled up against me, three puppies cuddled up on her lap, Dolly had come to sleep at her feet and Moochie lay by me, his head resting on my feet, his eyes closed. I leaned back against the bales of straw and closed my eyes.

It came to me like a dream that this was the first time since I left home that I had really settled down, relaxed, felt warm and happy inside, at peace with the world and having a hazy thought that my world had been put back together again.

My thoughts were so deep, so contented that I thought I heard muffled voices, that someone was standing near me, that one of the voices sounded like my mother's, and that she was talking to someone named Maybell.

Then I heard her say "Oh, Maybell. Did you ever see a picture so peaceful and beautiful? Our two children, they are indeed very much in love."

And in my dreams, I heard Olivia's mother say, "I do declare, Nellie, all of this has happened right under my eyes. I thought it was just puppy love."

And mother said, "Puppy love is right. Just look at those little darlings on Olivia's lap. And more in the nest."

"Shhh... Let's don't wake them. They would be mortified to know we found them like this..."

And I struggled through my sleepy haze and realized I was not hearing them in my dream, but that mother and Maybell were actually standing near us, talking to each other.

It gradually dawned on me that Olivia and I had been going on nervous energy for days now, and when we finally got settled down to rest, at one very special and happy moment, we fell asleep.

Olivia still had not awakened, and I hardly knew what to say but struggled to make an excuse. "Uh, we came out to see about Dolly and Moochie," I stammered, "and look what we found."

"Well! I should say you found a handful, or perhaps a lap full would be more like it. How many puppies did she have?"

By now, Olivia began to stir and she rubbed her eyes and looked around. "Oh," she said. "Oh, where are we?" Her voice and movement aroused the puppies, and they began to squeal softly and climb around her lap with closed eyes, searching for their milk.

Now Olivia came wide awake. "How did you get here, mom, and Rowdy's mother? Look what Rowdy and I found," and she held out a puppy which promptly squirmed off her lap and fell in the straw at her feet."

Our mothers came over to us, stooped and each took a puppy in their hands and caressed it and Dolly whined and put her paws on their legs as if to say, "Now you have seen my babies. Put them back."

And within minutes all of the little Dollies were on her stomach, licking and nudging at the nipples full with milk. Moochie lay beside her and looked up at us and barked a time or two, wiggled his tale and placed his face down between his paws, but kept a watchful eye on the proceedings.

"We should go now and leave them alone," said Maybell.

And so Olivia and I got up, brushed the straw off our clothing, and followed our mothers out into the sunshine and warm breeze.

I heard Maybell say, "Thank the Lord for little favors. At least we found them asleep in love – not making love."

The sunlight grew dimmer and the shadows longer and outside, looking to the west, I saw a cloud of dust.

"That looks like my man, always in a hurry," said Maybell. "At least he didn't drive the car into the canyon.

"And look toward the northwest," mother said. "Isn't that four horses I see kicking up dust? That must be the cowboys coming back from their search for the bull and his herd."

Within minutes, Ollie and my father, along with the magazine men, hauled up at our feet and we choked on the dust.

Ollie bawled out, "Boy, have we got an earful for you."

Maybell coughed and flapped her apron to blow away the dust. "Oliver, I'm going to take your car away from you if you don't slow down."

"Come on to the shade, folks. Let's have a little something cold to drink and something hot to eat. Then we are going to have a bull session. A real bull session."

He looked at the four horsemen still a couple of miles out. "Bet they are hot and ready for some ice water. Hope they have good news."

By the time the riders – Fuss, Booger Joe and Toby and Polecat rode into the yard, their horses foaming with sweat and fighting the bits in their hurry to get water, Ollie's long picnic table had been shoved into place under a huge elm tree.

"Get down and come in," he shouted, "get down and come in. How did you make out in your bull hunt?"

They all dismounted except Polecat, and he gathered the reins. "Give 'em water slow," Fuss said, "then give 'em a good rubdown and a big feed of oats. They had a mighty hard day."

He slapped dust from his big hat, shook hands with a little bow to the ladies and said, "we had an almighty interesting day, Ollie. I've lots to tell you. But we have not had any water and nothing to eat and I would appreciate it if we could start out sort of slow like."

Already Maybell was pouring huge glasses of iced tea and cutting huge slices from watermelons. Fuss accepted the chair Ollie shoved to him, while Booger Joe, quiet grin on his face, and Toby plopped down on the ground under the elm tree, slapped the dust off their hats and leaned back with exclamations of relief.

But success was written on all of their faces.

While they were catching their breath, a half dozen of the regular cowhands drifted up from the bunkhouse, plopped down straddle legged under the tree and waited quietly.

The magazine boys stood up, with one jotting down notes on a pad, the other shooting pictures. I heard Maness in a stage whisper to Cavello, "Boy, did we ever strike paydirt on this assignment. This will not only make a great magazine story, but I bet I will get a book out of it. How about let's also plan a documentary film?"

Finally, my mother and Olivia came out of the house and along with my dad and sat on the table benches. Everyone's eyes were fixed on Claud Fussel.

He looked at Ollie. "We were on high ground looking toward the south, and about five miles from your little trip. We could see things you obviously could not see. And as you were driving along the rim of the canyon, we picked up movement of a little bunch of cattle ahead of you, and drifting more to the north.

"As we watched, we occasionally saw the cattle as they would come out of patches of cedar and cross a clearing, all the while heading northwesterly. Finally, Booger Joe, with his Indian-sharp eyes, said he believed he knew where they were going and were headed for a hideout to get away from your vehicle. Right, Booger?"

"Right, and I knew exactly where they were headed. I had seen a cow path in that direction because it was only a quarter mile from my cabin in the bottom of the canyon. But I had never tracked them down. We watched them until they were nearly out of sight, and then rode hard to come in from behind."

Fuss took over again. "And we cut across country until we came in behind their path, followed it, and came to high ground where we could see. And you will never guess what. We saw where a great sandstone overhang had broken off from its own weight – I would say in the last year or so – and gave them an opening to a thousand acres virgin canyon, with lots of grass and an ever-lasting spring."

"A wild cow paradise, I'd say," chimed in Booger Joe.

Ollie sat transfixed, his mouth dropped open in surprise and awe and interest. Sweat dripped from his forehead and for once he was silent and let the others do the talking.

It was Fuss's time again. "We didn't dare track them all the way, because we couldn't tell for sure where they would end up. But my hunch is that there is a second, and bigger canyon, a mile or so north of where they entered. And that second canyon could be either one of several things.

"It would lead to an opening onto the great grassy plains that would in turn lead out of the canyon and onto the greater caprock. Or it would lead to a blind wall, that man's eyes has never seen."

"So that's your story," Ollie said finally. And here I thought we had a pretty good day. And we did, too. We got to see our band of brood mares and stallions, counted a great group of foals, and on top of that, we climbed up on a high point, over-looking the buffalo canyon, and found ourselves right over a grassy plain.

"And as luck would have it, a big shaggy old buffalo cow picked that moment to deliver a calf. We watched the whole thing, for an hour or more, until the calf go up on its wobbly legs and the cow licked it dry and it was suckling.

"The picture guy like to of went nuts. He kept cussing himself because he had not brought along a movie camera. But he says he got some wonderful pictures."

Heads turned to Cavello. He just grinned and showed his white teeth.

The whole bunch of us under that old elm tree, with the sun in the west just about to drop out of sight by a peaceful sky, didn't make a sound. They just let that magic moment soak in. I felt myself quivering with excitement. It was all so real, the way it was told by those two old cowboys, that it could not have been much more real if I had been with them, riding along.

Finally, Ollie broke the spell.

"Well, what do we do next? That knocks our black bull hunt in the head, I reckon. What do, Fuss?"

Fuss picked up his big hat, ran his fingers around the brim and was silent for a time.

Finally, he said, "That is not the end of my story, Ollie. The rest of the story is going to sound like we took a trip back in time."

All heads shook and Maybell grasped. "Oh, nothing terrible, is it?"

Fuss smiled quietly at her and said, "No, Missie Maybell. The rest of the story is wonderful to hear. And when I tell it to you, you will swear I am lying. But as I sit here before you, remember that my great-great-grandfather was a full blood Indian. And know that his stories have been passed down over the generations, and over a full century.

"The story I am going to tell you has never been told to white man until now. I am going to tell it to you."

"It is the story of a black bull in another time, no doubt the ancestor of the bull we have with us today."

"And of a Longhorn calf sired by the back bull and that was given the name, in white man's language, of Red River Roan."

50

Pigan's Miracle

I found myself quivering with excitement as Fuss paused, took a deep breath, and appeared to be searching his memory. Olivia squeezed me tight, and I saw my mother and father stiffen as the old cowboy took a deep breath and begin his ancient story.

"You see, our so-called black bull, the one that has caused us so much trouble, is a direct descendent of a famous bull brought to the New World by the Spaniards. By some strange quirk of genetics, the first black bull sired several sons, but many were roan in color – meaning their bodies were speckled with splotches of red, white and brown or black – roan, it is called.

"The one my ancestors first knew was named the Red River Roan – he was to become famed for his strength, feared for his hatred of men, yet worshiped for his pursuit of freedom. I think we all agree our present bull possesses those qualities.

"And not known by most of us, was the fact that every other offspring of the first black bull was a roan. And as of today, I know this pattern continues – for I spotted a roan bull calf in his little herd."

Fuss let that sink in, took a deep breath, and settled back in his chair. "Let's go back to the original red roan bull. Legend has it that no man ever laid hands on him and bullets and arrows were absorbed in his tough hide. His herd numbered 30 or 40 of the wiry offspring of the Spanish Longhorns.

"Yet, the roan never should have lived, for he was a freak of birth. I will now tell his story in the exact words of my ancestors, whose story has been handed down to my brothers for over 100 years.

"The time came for Pigan, the cow, to give birth. She felt the movement deep inside, sensed the stirring of muscle and membrane, the spasms that moved the calf from the birth canal. Around her in the panhandle grazed others of her kind - Longhorns of rainbow colors, save for one, the bull Crosesus. Many of the cows had already dropped their calves, some so new the naval cords hung red and wet, others old enough they strayed from their mothers, after sucking foaming warm milk, and now galloped across the buffalo grassed plains in love of life.

"This was virgin country, as far as Pigan and her kind were concerned. Seldom had man strayed onto this hostile land, only passing through as fast as possible for one less harsh. Here the vegetation has claws. The sand holes were home to poisonous snakes and lizards and spiders. The summers were brutal, the wind a knife of death in winter.

"Buffalo passed here twice yearly, headed southward in the fall, northward in spring. Buffalo had already passed this spring, leaving the grass soiled with dung. But this was home to Pigan and her kind and while they went off their feed a few days, showers freshened the grass and wild flowers bloomed, they soon grazed again in the shadows of the caprock which led to the high plains.

"Pigan was a five-year-old this spring, in her prime, and was already shedding winter hair. Her horns thrust our from her skull a foot either side, they flared upward another foot. They were tipped in red, as if dipped in blood. Her hide was pure white except for the blood-red roan splotches against the white background. Her belly now stood deep and round, her udder strutted with rich colostrum, the first milk she had prepared for her calf.

Instinct told her to seek her bedding ground. Without being obvious, she changed her pattern of grazing so that an hour's movement took her to the edge of the herd, to a swale where swamp grass grew high enough to touch her withers. Here there was water to soothe her fever, and assist in dropping her afterbirth. Here, there was privacy.

"Now a great spasm struck her, a moan escaped her lips. She whirled and sniffed the ground at the discharge as instinct told her to destroy the evidence of birth from wolves.

"The spasm came again, and she lay on her side, grunting and straining. Gradually the calf moved, but finally it stalled. Rather than the normal delivery, with head cradled on the forehooves, the rear legs protruded, leaving the head to exit last – if that could ever be accomplished.

"Now, Pigan sensed what was wrong. Instinct told her to conserve her strength for a last mighty effort.

"The sun eased behind the caprock, casting the canyon in gloom; from the opposite side of the canyon a pale moon arosė. And still, Pigan lay, resisting the urge to strain again, allowing her strength to build.

"Finally she could resist no longer. The calf must be born or she would burst. She stretched flat on the ground, braced her lower rear hoof in the ground and heaved mightily. An inch, two inches. Slowly, the calf moved. A set of white legs appeared. At the hocks, they were mottled with red roan splotches. The thick haunches, slick with fluid that had protected the calf, oozed out. The tail appeared. But the hips could not come. They were locked in the pelvis.

"Pigan moaned, feeling strength ebbing. Again, she rested, again she heaved, feeling life weakening. She knew her calf would die. And she with it.

"But now the calf came to a decision, born not of thought but of instinct, by virtue of accident of its birth. The naval cord, which had fed it from the time of conception, had been stretched to the breaking point by the movement of the womb.

"The cord broke, serving the calf from the ties with its mother. Some special vitality of this calf resisted the fact it would smother, drown in the birth fluids. Now was the last time to try.

"Pigan sensed the determination within her. She lifted her head, bellowed mightily and gave her remaining energy in a mighty effort.

"Perhaps the struggles of the calf had loosened the hold of the pelvic muscles, the hip bones. But the calf slid rapidly from its birth prison to lie gasping and wet on the grass, retching for air, trying to maneuver its body.

"Pigan's breath came in great heaves. She sighed from relief of pain, but the film of death was in her eyes. She barely heard the bellow of new life from her calf as it rolled to its feet. Quivering, it rested, then tried again. It found its legs in a headlong dive that sent it into a heap. Another dive brought it to its mother's head and while she thrust out her tongue to lick it, she had not the strength to move her head.

"A third try brought it to its feet and there it took its first notice of the new world, a world of wind sighing through the grass, a cow bellowing in the distance and Crosesus bellowing his challenge to the moonlight."

"A stalk of grass brushed the calf's face and it thrust out its tongue, but the result was disappointing. Then a warm odor reached its nostrils and it felt for the source. The tongue touched the teat, the mouth opened, and the warm life-giving milk poured into its stomach.

"Life for the Red Roan was assured."

Fuss stopped for breath and looked around the semi-circle. Not a sound could be heard except the soft blessing of the wind. No one spoke a word, so great was the enchantment of the moment. Fuss had virtually hypnotized us and no one dared break the magic of the moment.

I knew I had heard the best story of my life.

But Fuss was not yet finished.

51

Wrapping It Up

The silence was broken when mother arose from her chair and made her way over to Claud Fussel. She kneeled at his feet, reached for his hand and held it as she said, "That is without a doubt the most captivating emotional story I have ever heard.

"Thank you. Thank you from the bottom of my heart. Thank you for my son, who has learned so much from you and all the others gathered here tonight. Thank you for my husband, who has learned how wonderful all of you Texans have been to our son and his companion who ran away from home, and in so doing found themselves part of a greater world with great people."

"What could have been a total disaster has turned out to be a gift from God that reunited our family and brought our son a greater appreciation for the trials and tribulations of life than he could ever have gotten from any other source."

Dad went over and shook the cowboy's hand. "I have been a farmer all of my life. But I have also been a writer for magazines. But I never wrote as touching and real a story as you have delivered to us. I suggest you talk to these professional journalists who are with us tonight. But don't just give them your story. Sell it to them."

That brought Ollie up from his chair, where he had remained hypnotized by the story of the Longhorns. He got to his feet with a roar of approval and said, "Everybody give Fuss a rousing cheer. That was great, Fuss, just great. I have cowboyed with you since I was a kid, and you never related that to me. I thank you."

After the round of applause, mother said, "My guess is that there is much more to your story. I bet you didn't finish. What happened to the roan calf after he got his first meal, even though his dam had died? Where did he get his milk after that? Obviously he could not have survived on grass and water..." Fuss smiled warmly, clasped both of her hands in his big rough ones and said, "Thank you for knowing that. You are so right. But I did not want to prolong my story to your boredom. Should I continue?"

There was an instant clapping of hands and then the cowboys began to yell, "Bravo, Fuss. Finish the story. You are the greatest cowboy in the Panhandle. No, in all Texas."

Fuss picked his battered hat off the ground, ran his hand around the brim, and said, "All right, if you insist. But stop me when you are weary."

Before he could go on, the writer, Maness, spoke from the back row of hay bales where he had been sitting, taking notes. "I want to know something about yourself. You told us a wonderful story. But you did not speak in cowboy lingo. You spoke perfect English. How can I reconcile your evident education with an uneducated Texas cowboy?"

Fuss smiled and nodded. "That is easy. I am not an unlettered cowboy, as you suggest. I was born on this ranch to a mother and father who never went to school a day in their lives.

"But the owner of this great ranch, the father of Ollie Oliver, took charge of me when I was a boy. They took me into their home. They saw to it I had a tutor. And when I was old enough, they sent me to school in the Midwest, and all the way through college. They wanted me to continue my education further, but my heart and my soul were in Texas, on this ranch where my ancestors had lived and died.

"I came back to start a small ranch on my own, with the help of Ollie and Maybell, and I helped them in every way I could help, whenever they needed it. Unfortunately, I never found a girl who wanted to marry me, and I have remained a bachelor all these years. But my heart is with the Olivers – and all of their friends.

"Now, may I continue the request for the rest of my story?"

"You may. With my congratulations."

Looking down at my mother, who was seated at his knees and holding his grizzled hand, Fuss said, "Of course the roan calf could not live without nursing a cow. But with his mother dead, it seemed he had no chance. And he would not have, had it not been for the cooperation of his sire.

"You see, the wily old bull knew full well one of his cows had hid out to calve. After an unusual wait for her to return to the herd, he went to investigate. He found her, of course, lying in the tall grass. When she did not move as he nudged her, when he sniffed her cold body, he pawed the earth in anger, turned to walk away.

"But as he passed by the calf, now sleeping with a full stomach, the calf awakened, leaped to his feet and started following as if he was following his dam. When the bull stopped to graze, the calf wanted to nurse but the bull had no patience with that. He tossed the calf into a heap nearby, and went on his way back to his herd.

"But this calf was not to be denied. He ran after the bull on strong legs, kept up with him until he reached the main herd and blindly bumped into a cow that was standing, nursing her own calf. It did not take long for our orphan calf to catch the odor of warm milk, to hear the soft, slurping noise of the other calf nursing, and he found a teat for himself.

"And this is how he lived, how he was to live for the next eight or ten months. He learned to rob milk from every cow in the herd and if one kicked him off, there was always another. He would suckle with them standing still, or with them running, and eventually he became bigger and stronger than any other calf in the herd.

"But always, because the first scent of his life had been the old bull, his sire, who was given the name of Crosesus by man, became the roan calf's leader, his hero, you might say.

"My ancestors, of course, kept track of the herd of buffalo, followed them as they migrated, because the herd was their bread and butter, their meat, and when one died, its hide became one of their homes. So they were well versed on the life and times of the buffalo.

"They saw him live in the deep snow, they watched him turn his back to the storms and sleet and rain and hail, hover close to the bull in these times, and the bull accepted him not as a nuisance, but as a companion, a special member of the herd.

"It was as if the old bull had selected the young bull as his protégé, the one selected and dedicated to become his successor.

"And when the time came, as it inevitably would, the old bull had to yield leadership of the herd to the young bull. It said they fought for leadership from one full departure of the moon until the next until youth won over age. From that time on, it was the massive, full grown roan who led the herd."

"But he never outlawed the old bull, never drove him away from the herd, but only reversed their relationship. The old bull accepted the inevitable."

"And when it finally came time for the first offspring of the young bull – Red River Roan – to breed, it was remarkable that all of his male offspring were black – black as the master sire. And when those calves became sires, the reverse was true. Their male offspring was always roan.

"Most strange, but true. And so apparently it is holding true even to this day. The young bull I saw this day is carrying on the pattern. One day, the black bull we have come to know so well as the killer of our Hereford bulls and the stealer of our Hereford cows will be the victim of his own son.

"It is written not in the stars, not in mythology, but in the genetics, the cross-prepotency we can only accept as nature. It was ordained by the law of God, the Father of us all and of all creatures on His earth.

"He is the Master. We are but the players."

Silence, dead silence for long, long minutes. No applause. No shouts of congratulations. Just respect from one man's peers to the Master Story Teller.

Even Ollie was subdued, for the first time I ever saw that happen. He got up, went to Fuss, shook his hand, gave him a bear hug, and then went around the circle to do the same for every one of his guests, saving his last hug for Olivia.

"Fellers, set your alarms for 4 a.m. We'll have breakfast at the bunkhouse and by that time, I'll lay out my plans for a very, very important day. Shall we kill the black bull that has tormented us so long? Or can we find a better way to solve our problem?"

And he went around the circle shaking hands again, hugging just about everybody. No one really wanted to break up the gang. It seemed a new brother and sister-hood had been formed.

I stole a kiss from Olivia as we said good night, mother kissed her, too, and dad patted her on her head, but she stood on tip-toes for her smack. "Good night. I love you all."

It must have been midnight or later before I relaxed enough to go to sleep, and when I did, my dreams were all mixed up.

Part of the time I was reliving my escape from the horns of the black bull, part of the time I was running after Olivia and the rest of the time I was telling my mother I wanted her to go home with us and never, never leave her again.

Finally, the black bull broke apart all of the vivid dreams and somehow Olivia got into the dreams and together we were running away from the bull that finally stopped after cornering us behind a tree.

I woke up, shouting hoarsely some sort of gibberish and sat upright in my bedroll on fresh straw in the horse barn. I swallowed my gibberish, looked around in the dim light provided by day breaking in the east, and clammed up, grateful no one had been awakened by my bad dream.

I saw lights on in the bunkhouse kitchen down the lane to the house, and the smell of bacon frying brought me to my feet. I dressed quickly, rolled up the bedroll and saw two shadows headed in my direction.

"That you, Rowdy?"

I recognized Polecat's voice. "Don't take long to spend the night around here does it, Rowdy?" said Toby. They nudged my arm and gave me a friendly shove. "You ready to go for the big bull today?" he asked.

I shivered. "Tell the truth about it," I said, "I am more than a little sick of hearing about that bull. Back home, if we had a bull we couldn't manage, why, dad took him to the stockyards. Next thing you knew, you were seeing him in a baloney sandwich."

Their laughter woke up a pair of bucket calves as we walked past their pens, and we hurried on to the bunkhouse, aided by the smell of coffee along with the bacon.

Half a dozen cowboys were already in the bunkhouse, quiet as they were sleeping on the church house steps. The cowboys, their faces in the shadow of their big greasy, battered hats, waited for the hot coffee to operate their vocal cords.

The cook – "Coosey" they called him, had both hands in a huge bowl of biscuit dough. "Morn'n fellers," he said. "One of you roust out Ollie and ask him how many of you bums I've got to feed this morning."

Toby lit out for the house and I sat down on a bunk, feeling out of place and lost, for I had not met these men. They didn't pay any attention to me, nor to each other, but kept emptying the coffee pot and heaving long sighs.

"Might as well get over it," said Coosey. "Ol' Ollie has fooled around with this black bull for two or three years, and maybe today he'll get it out of his system."

"A well placed 30-30 bullet between the eyes is the best medicine to cure that headache," grumbled one.

He looked at me. "Are you the kid he chased down a while back?"

I nodded and cold chills made me shiver as the memory of that day flooded back.

"What you think about it, then?"

"I reckon if it was my bull, I'd..." then I stopped. I didn't figure it was my business to make a decision like that. I began again. "Mr. Oliver and Fuss think the bull is a tie with the past and that he is valuable for history, more than for siring calves."

At that moment, Ollie stepped through the door, and he picked up on the conversation fast.

"Hey, Venus, ol' Rowdy here is the first cowhand I ever knew that took on the bull out in the open, on foot, and lived to tell it. But you asked him a good question, and I reckon he has a right to speak his piece."

"How about it, Rowdy – am I crazy to want to hunt that bull down to preserve his blood for history? Or should we shoot him and skin his hide off to hang on the wall of a museum?"

"If I had not heard the history of the Longhorns from Claud Fussel just a few hours before, I think the answer would have been easy. I remember the fear I had when the bull caught me on foot, out in the open, with nothing to save my life but my feet, a tree to climb, and the accidental fact that Booger Joe had come along just in time to save my life. The answer would have been easy – kill the bull any way possible, and let him rot."

But now, I was not sure what to say. I looked up at Ollie. He had a sober, but kind look in his eyes. "Everything being equal," I said, "if the bull can be caught without anyone getting hurt or killed, he deserves the right to live and to die a natural life."

Ollie gave a whoop and a holler, grabbed me and hugged me and said, "See there, cowboy, there's your answer. We save the bull if we can. But if we can't, well, so be it."

By this time, a dozen cowboys and some visitors I had never seen before were crowding into the bunkhouse. "This is sort of like a free-wheeling circus," yelled Ollie. "Coosey, feed these hungry men so we can get a move on. I intend to be saddled up and on the move by sunup."

And so in his bulldozing manner, Ollie had again solved a problem, made a decision, had his way, and got things moving.

One of the new-comers was a tall, thin dignified-looking man with a friendly smile, dressed in neat cowboy boots and a red bandanna tied around his neck. It set off his deep blue shirt with the pearl buttons.

Ollie pulled me to one side after I had filled my plate twice and dumped it in the wreck pan. He had the tall, dignified man in tow. "Rowdy, this man wants to meet you. He is Mr. Bill Word, head of the cattleman's association. It seems he has heard talk around Salt River town about somebody missing a fine bay mare and a jackass a few weeks ago. Would you happen to know anything about it?"

The firm grip in the tall man's hand and his flint eyes made my heart jump into my throat. My face burned.

I heard my voice come from a long way off and I felt unsteady on my feet.

"Yes sir. I caught them. But I did not know somebody owned them. I believed they were wild horses and who ever caught wild horses had the right to keep them."

I saw my father standing behind him. My teeth chattered and my head got dizzy. After all this time, just as things were getting the best ever, was I going to be arrested and charged with horse theft?

It came to me in a flash what happened to horse thieves in stories in Ace Western Magazine. Horse thieves were hanged by the neck until dead.

Things went black before my eyes and the last thing I could remember, someone yelled, "Catch him. He's falling."

52

The Beginning

I didn't pass out. I just suddenly got weak all over and started to fall, but strong arms on both sides caught me and sort of half-carried, half-guided me to a chair.

My mouth got dry as dust and I tried to tell them I was all right. But the words just stuck in my throat.

Ollie came up with a wet towel and wiped my face and somebody handed him a glass of water and he held it to my lips. "Give him a little room," Ollie was saying. "He's all right. Just tired, I imagine. He's been burning the candle at both ends for too many days, I reckon."

By this time, I got my voice back. I took a few swigs of the cold water, and Ollie dashed some on his hands and rubbed the back of my neck. I started to stand up, but he gently held me down. "Easy, boy. Give yourself a couple minutes before you try to get up."

My dad stood behind me, his jaw set, and his eyes told me he wondered what the heck was going on. I reached out and grabbed his hand and he squeezed it tight, and I recovered my voice.

"I'm ok. I guess I just had too big a day yesterday, and didn't get much sleep. All of a sudden, I got weak all over when Mr. Word mentioned Lady Midnight. I thought he was going to arrest me and everything just got woozy in my head."

I looked up at the brand inspector. "You weren't going to arrest me, were you? I thought the horse deal was taken care of. I'm sorry I was so dumb. But I really did think those horses were just wild horses. And my uncle..."

Mr. Word said, "I didn't intend to either arrest or scare you. I thought I would have a little fun at your expense. But let me assure you that the horse deal is all settled. Your Uncle Joe did explain the situation, and I just supposed he had told you about it."

"He did tell me, and so that settled me in my mind. I am just sorry I am so dumb. Do I have to return the mare?"

"No, son. The mare is your very own, complements of your uncle. And I want to say that you have yourself a fine piece of horse flesh. She had the makin's of a fine roping horse for the rodeo circuit, but she got injured and had to be pensioned off. She was gentle and served as a blind to help keep the horses together for local horse traders."

"And then, it is all right if I ride her today? When we go wild bull hunting?"

"No, son," he said. "I'm afraid not."

"But why not? If she is mine..."

He chuckled and placed a hand on my shoulder. "You mean you haven't noticed?"

"Noticed what?"

"Son, she is going to have a foal. She is about nine or ten months pregnant."

My mouth dropped open. I had to swallow hard as I digested that information. "You mean she's going to have a colt?"

He laughed again. "I don't know if it will be a colt or not. It may be a filly."

I frowned. "I don't know what you mean. A baby horse is a colt, isn't it?"

"Well, yes, if it is a male. But if it is a female, then it is properly called filly. Understand? It's like cattle. A calf is a calf is a calf. But it is properly a heifer calf if it is a female. If it is a male, it is properly a bull calf. Understand the difference?"

I nodded my head. My face flushed hot. "I guess I don't know as much as I thought I did. They didn't say anything about that in Ace Western Magazine."

That brought a round of laughter from all the men standing around. Mr. Word grabbed me, lifted me up off the bale of hay, stood me beside him and hugged me tightly. "You'll do, Rowdy. You are all right.

Ollie scraped his plate and dropped it in the wreck pan, cleared his throat and said, "Sun's up, boys. Time to move."

He stepped out the door and grabbed the rope attached to the old-fashioned dinner bell and pulled. The bell broke the morning air and when it had clanged 20 times, he stopped.

"Saddle up, boys. Fuss and Booger Joe and my sons have the horses in the corral. Hustle down and call your horses for today. Saddle your best ones. It may be a fast and furious day.

"Rowdy, you'll ride Papoose today, same as you did moving the herd the other day. How about your dad? Is he a good rider?"

"He learn't me..." I started to say, but quickly corrected my English "He taught me how to ride when I was five, and I guess he can ride better than me."

Ollie grinned. To one of his cowboys he said, "Put a saddle on Rondo for Mr. Farmer. "He's slow until the action starts, then grabs a lot of leather."

Dad grinned. "Hey, as long as I can grab leather, I'll be all right. But first, I have not showed you how to use the needle and chemical to put that bull to sleep - that is, if he don't put us to sleep first."

Ollie pushed his hat back and scratched his head. "By gosh, I was in such a hurry to get started I plumb forgot the details. You ought to know, of course, I've used a needle gun to give shots to thousands of calves.

"It's just that I have never used this particular kind of medicine before. Never heard of it, in fact, until Rowdy told me about it. You must have an up-to-snuff vet in Missouri."

"That we do, but fact is, this stuff is only in the experimental stage. Hasn't been released for general use yet. You know how it is with the government. They got to have everything tested a long time ahead of general use. But it works. I guarantee it."

Dad reached into his jacket pocket, pulled out two little bottles. One bottle was red, the other white.

"The red bottle is the knockout drops," he said. "The white bottle is what brings them awake. I can't tell you the fancy scientific name, but the red medicine is the tranquilizer. It will last about ten or twelve minutes.

"By that time, the dope starts to wear off, but it might take an hour or so before the critter can get up on its own. That white stuff makes them come around a lot quicker, so they don't suffer from the knockout dope."

"And the needle gun?"

Dad showed him the syringes – one red, one white. "Sharp but strong enough to easily penetrate a bull's tough hide. Just like any other needle-gun you've used for vaccination. The trick is to hold it in your palm, slap it straight down into the muscle of the hip. The force of your palm against the gun automatically ejects the serum, so jerk out the needle and pull your horse away to the side.

"How long does it take to have an effect?"

"Hard to say with a tough old bull like you are talking about. But I'd keep my horse running away for a good three to five minutes. Then you will see the animal slow down, take a couple of steps, then stop and start wobbling. Usually, they just sort of quiver and settle to the ground like they are going to sleep.

"That's when you ride back, get your dehorning or operating over with, in, say, ten minutes at the most. Then stand back and watch the critter come awake. You don't have to rush off, for it will take five or ten minutes to get him to his feet. They are pretty sleepy when they get up, but you've got plenty of time to get out of the way. Best not to try to move them. Just walk away and let nature take its way."

Ollie rolled the two bottles around in his hand, thinking. "Who's my best riders," he said, sort of to himself. "Fuss, I'd say. Except he's getting on in years. Hate to see a horse stumble and get him hurt. Killed, maybe. Booger Joe... yeah, Booger Joe is the best rider in the outfit. Yeah, Booger Joe and both my boys, by dang. Toby and Polecat are hell to handle sometimes, but one thing they can do, that's ride. And they love to take chances. That's just excitement to them."

He let out a yell that shook the bushes. "Toby, Polecat, you and Booger Joe, get out here."

A muffled voice came back from the direction of the horse corral.

"Hold on, Pa, we are dang near ready. Give us four or five minutes."

Ollie started walking toward the house, saying as he went, "You fellers hang tight. When the boys get here with your horses, hold on to ol' Tinker Tee for me. I'll see the women folks and tell them we are about to take off, and not to look for us until they see us coming.

"You boys ought to scrape up some canteens with fresh water. There's plenty of water where we are going, but it is pretty poor. Won't hurt you if you can stand it, but it'll sure enough clean out your pipes."

One of the cowboys went into the bunkhouse and I heard him rattling around, and pretty soon he came out with a half dozen water bottles, and then here came the two Oliver boys, Fuss and Booger Joe, each on horseback and each leading saddled horses for the rest of us to ride.

Leather creaked as we all climbed into the saddle, without much snorting and jumping around by the horses, and one special horse, a black that looked lean as a race horse, was held for Ollie.

Ollie took the lead, with my dad on one side and me on the other, and the rest of the crew riding in twos and threes behind us - twelve riders in all. Just as we rounded the corner of the corral grounds, he saw a cloud of dust riding from the direction of Salt River town, and Ollie held up his hand and yelled, "Hold your horses a minute, boys. That ol' flivver looks like Reverend Dwiggins coming to visit - and get a belly full of free grub.

"You boys ride on. I'll see what he wants, and then I'll catch up with you."

With that, Fuss pulled along side of Dad, and Booger Joe alongside of me, and we rode out in a line, headed north by northwest. The sun was at our backs and promised a hot day, but right at the moment, it was warm with a cool breeze in our faces. I guess I never in my whole life felt more secure, more important, more grown up. I guess I felt a little too important.

Just look what all had happened to me because I decided to run away to Texas. Somehow, my whole life felt like it was coming back together again.

I put my mind to the moment, began thinking what I would do if we came across the black bull and he took in after me again. I got the shivers.

I heard hoofbeats behind, looked around to see Ollie headed our way in a gallop. Fuss and Booger Joe pulled back and let Ollie squeeze beside us again.

He laughed, "Can up beat this. Ol' Reverend Dwiggins drove in to see what was going on. He wanted me to saddle him a horse so he could go, too. I told him he better guard the watermelons and keep the women folks calm. He decided that was a better idea.

"And then, just as I was getting him settled down, I saw another cloud of dust rolling toward the ranch. It was them two tenderfoots with the magazine. They had pulled out, driven into Salt River, and got themselves real cowboy outfits.

"The said they were going to go with us. Is said, tarnation, no, you can't go. I got enough problems taking care of this crew without having a couple of city dudes to look after.

"They didn't like it, but I put my foot down, and ..."

I heard a strange sound about then. I looked around and there, of all things, the two city dudes drove along side of us in their car, waving their new cowboy hats.

Ollie pulled his horse to a stop. When he saw it was the magazine guys, he muttered a mouthful of bad words, pulled his hat down, clamped his teeth together, turned back and put his horse in a fast gallop, his face was red and I think it was the only time I'd ever seen him angry.

We kept up the fast pace for a few miles, then Ollie pulled up his horse, wheeled around and held up his hands and stopped our crew. He got off his horse and handed my dad the reins and walked back to the journalists. His face was still red, his arms slung hard at his side, but he didn't make a fool out of himself.

"Feller," he said, "I didn't invite you to my ranch, but I was kind to you. I didn't invite you to come with us this day, but here you are.

"Now we are going on a dangerous mission that may end up with some body hurt bad, or even killed. I got other things to do than nursemaid you two boys. But now you are here, and by the gods, you are just going to have to take whatever comes today like real men, not two city dudes playing cowboys, which you are not.

"No you let up on the gas. Keep your iron horse at the back of our line and keep it there. When I want you someplace I will let you know. Understand?"

Red in the face, obviously flustered, they nodded. As we moved our horses along, they sat still. When we were well ahead, they followed slowly, eating dust, which made Ollie laugh.

"They are really pretty good boys," he said. "Dumb as hell. But I kind of admire their spirit. Come on, we've got two more hours of this before we even get where Fuss and Booger Joe think that bull and his cows are hanging out. "

"Besides, I want the dad blamed pictures just for the heck of it."

53

The Bull's Down

Ollie took the lead at a fast pace that made us all ride hard to follow. But when he cooled off after his lecture to the journalists, he slowed his horse to a trot and then gradually to a walk.

Then we began a steady climb and Ollie told my father, "We are now beginning to ride out of the rough edge of the canyon and in a half mile or so, we will be on the lower edge of the caprock. That's where the prairie begins.

"What I am going to do is try to guess where Fuss and the boys saw the Longhorns enter the canyon, which will be well below us. If we are lucky, it will save us a hard, slow journey down in the canyon itself."

After we climbed upward for about ten minutes, the land began to level off, and soon we saw the caprock begin to shimmer in the distance as the sun rose higher in the eastern sky.

Ollie turned in the saddle and said to Fuss, "Have we come far enough?"

Fuss pulled his horse so he could look southward, and the bunch of us did the same thing, then stopped.

By now, the sun was rising and slowly, but clearly, as it inched higher, you could see it striking the rugged canyon floor. At this height, I could look further out into the canyon than ever before. The cedars, the mesquite, the cactus, all looked from this distance as a grouping of flowers in miniature. Dark sides of the landscape were gradually turned into shimmering colors of all shades of the rainbow. A pair of coyotes, pups trailing their mother, trotted along, stopping now and then to dig for mice and rats. A herd of whitetail deer trooped along leisurely, stopping to nip leaves and grass, and overhead twittered flocks of birds as they sought berries and safe places to land in trees.

Never had I seen such an awesome display of natural beauty.

Ollie swept out his hand and waved it from east to west. "Boys, look at that grand sight. You are looking at a huge slice of God's green earth, but you are seeing just a fraction of one of the great wonders on earth.

"You are seeing a small part of the second longest and deepest canyon in the United States. It's a long way from being as big as the Grand Canyon. But it's a pretty big ditch, just the same.

"It is about 150 miles east to west, and ranges from 300 feet deep at the west end to about 1,300 feet deep at the east end. The far west end has been turned over to the State of Texas for a park, and there is talk of building a scenic road from west to east on the south side of the canyon.

"This is the canyon tamed in 1870 by a remarkable man named Charles Goodnight, and at one time his herd branded JA numbered more than 10,000 mother cows. Since then, the canyons have been divided up into many ranches, and I have a small slice of it myself. But it is, and always will be, one of the most wonderful and interesting pieces of real estate on the North American continent."

"There was an estimated 10,000 buffalo grazing in the canyon when Colonel Goodnight first saw it and gained control. He had to drive the Buffalo off and sometimes even had to chase the Indians away, with help of the Army. The Indians had to leave a half century ago, but some of the original buffalo are still here, as you've seen. As far as I am concerned, I hope they are always here, but my guess is that the day will come - may it be a long time - when they will be driven out as well."

He stopped talking and just sat there, leaning on his saddle horn, deep in thought, as if he had just spoken a prayer to God. I even whispered a little prayer to God himself, asking him to please let this wonderful land exist forever - and to let the buffalo stay until the end of time.

Finally, Ollie said, "All right boys, let's get on with our job. I have talked a long time about the day that would come when we have to clean this range up, get rid of the Longhorns and so on. I guess I am getting soft in my old age. Looking out over this wonderful land, I feel like it would be an insult to God to remove all of His creatures from their home. Let's see if we can't handle this situation better than going after our Longhorn bull and his cows and calves with guns blazing."

He set a slow pace, letting the horses breath easier, as he continued to talk. Waving his hands toward the canyon, he said, "Notice how the deep canyon runs roughly from northwest to southeast? It started with the Prairie Dog Fork of the Red River. Along the way, it is bisected with a dozen or more pretty good-sized rivers.

"As rains came, the water rushed downhill and over the centuries, erosion from the rushing water carved out little canyons of their own. What we are looking for now is one of these smaller canyons - which are not small, by any means. In one of these canyons is where Fuss and the boys spotted the Longhorns yesterday. Now keep your eyes peeled. The cattle will be grazing for another hours or so, but when the sun gets overhead, they will hide in the brush and will be hard to spot."

So saying, he kicked his horse into a brisk trot, and we continued to climb higher until we were walking along a perfectly level plain. Suddenly, Booger Joe reined his horse to the left, pulled to a halt, and said, "Look straight south, boys. There's the herd we are looking for."

I looked but could see nothing. Nothing, that is, except space and undulating grass and trees and rolling hills. Then, following the direction Booger Joe was pointing, I saw a light movement. Gradually, it turned into the form of a cow, and then another, and then a red and white calf ran across an open field, followed by another, and I could make out that they were running and playing, just like the calves in our pastures back home.

A thrill like I had never known before ran all the way through me and back and I just sat there in the saddle hoping I could remember this vision as long as I lived.

Ollie broke my reverie. "Well, Fuss, what do we do now? We have located them. We know where they are. But how are we going to get to them?"

"Ollie, you are asking me something I cannot tell you right off. But at least we found the herd, in a place we never before would have looked for them. If we can find a smaller canyon somewhere along the north rim, perhaps we can work our way down, single file. If we cannot, we would have to go back at least halfway to headquarters, and turn back west again. But that would take all day. Let's first look for a way down."

Ollie waved his hand. "All right, boys. Spread out, couple together, and see if you can find an erosion ditch or a wash on one of the little canyons where it runs off the prairie. If we can't find a place within five miles of here, we will have to go back and ride down into the canyon. And that would take another full day. Scat."

"Toby, you take three riders down the hogback on the east side of the canyon. Ride south until you can see the main canyon. If you find your way down, send one rider back to notify us, and you and your team go down. If you find the black bull and his cows, don't move a muscle. Just stay back, observe them, but don't get them on the prod, what ever you do."

"Polecat, you reckless devil you, you do the same on the west side ridge. Do just what I told Toby. You hear? Mess up, and I'll tan the seat of your britches."

"The rest of us - Rowdy and his dad, and Fuss, Boy Blackwell and Booger Joe, we'll rest our saddles until we hear back from you. Now, scat."

That said, Ollie slid from his saddle, motioned for the rest of us to dismount, and loosened the saddle girth. His horse let out a heavy breath of wind and shook his body to shed some of the sweat he had worked up.

The rest of the men did the same and I tried to act like I had planned to do it all the time, but watched out of the corner of my eyes to make sure I did it right. My horse, Papoose, reached down and nibbled a few bites of grass.

"Don't let your horse eat right now," Rowdy. "If he gets a gut full of grass, and we get into a chase with the cattle, the fill will slow him down. That might make the difference between life and death."

The old-time cowboys took advantage of the chance to rest by promptly lying down on their backs, pulling their hats over their head, crossing their arms across their chests, and falling asleep at once. The newspaper men even snoozed in their car.

Ollie saw me watching and laughed. "That's the way you do it, Rowdy. Rest every time you get a chance, for you never know when you get in a hustle and may not rest for all day and all night. That's this here cattle business for you. Sure you want to get in it?"

"More than anything in the world," I said, then, feeling sort of silly, added, "This is as close to heaven as I'll ever get."

"Good boy, Rowdy. You are going to make one real, honest to God cowboy." He stretched out on his back, pulled his big hat down over his eyes, and within a couple of minutes, was snoring.

My dad laughed. "Rowdy, that's me too." And before I knew it, I was napping, too.

I don't guess we rested more than thirty minutes when I heard hoof beats right beside my head and Toby was yelling at my ear.

"Wake up, you sleepy-headed galoots. We hit paydirt." Ollie leaped up from a dead sleep, pulling his hat on in one motion, and roaring, "Roll out, boys. Hit the saddle. Now then, Toby, tell me what you found."

"Just a dang minute, dad. I'm plumb out of breath, and my horse is, too. We found a good path down the hogback leading right into the center of the little canyon - which ain't so little, at that. It must be a mile and a half side to side, and tapers off into the main canyon for a good ten miles before leveling out.

'Good water. Grass running out our ears. Cattle signs everywhere. These cattle must have been here all summer long. We got a bare glimpse of a big herd, but pulled away so we wouldn't spook them.

"The other boys are resting their saddles, waiting for everybody else. Now one of you sleepy heads climb on board your horse and ride after Polecat and his gang. I'll take a little snooze while you guys mosey on down to meet the other bunch."

So saying, he tied his horse to a small cedar tree, pulled off the saddle, used the blanket for a cushion, pulled his hat over his head and was snoring within seconds.

Ollie broke out a big grin, slapped my father on the back, and said, "How's that for timing, Mr. Farmer? "Great luck, no?"

Within ten minutes our horses were saddled again and we were in the saddle with Ollie in the lead.

"We don't need to be in any hurry," he said. "We don't want to get down into the canyon until everybody is here. Once we do, I want half of us to ride on south toward the mouth of the canyon, then spread out in a row to head off a stampede. If the herd takes a notion to escape, we want to head them north, trap them at the upper end so the only way out would be to sprout wings and fly."

It took something like an hour for the rest of the crew to backtrack north, reach the head of the canyon, and head south again. Looking back, we finally spotted them and Ollie pulled up in the shade of huge mesquite tree, got down and loosened the girth of his saddle. A wave of his hand told us he wanted to rest our horses a while before entering the canyon.

Polecat grinned when he dismounted, saying, "Well, pa, we gonna do it?"

"No sweat, son. That bull is the same as our own. That is, providing that magic potion works like it is supposed to. And provided Booger Joe can ride alongside the bull and needle him in the right place. And providing his horse don't step in a prairie dog hole. And providing light'n don't strike. Ah, no, nothin' to it."

After we had all rested our saddles Ollie said, "Ok, boys. This is it. Toby, you and Polecat lead on. Take us down the trail. Slow. Don't take any chances. Don't make any noise. Keep your traps shut and speak in whispers. Those native cattle are wild animals, you know. They can hear and see things beyond our range."

He looked to the newspaper men. "This, my friends, is where we leave you." Covello looked disgusted but Maness couldn't hide his relief. His clean new cowboy garb couldn't change the fact he was scared of heading down the steep canyon wall to chase a man-killing bull.

So without further ado, Cavello threw the car in reverse and sailed backwards, ranchwards. "Good riddance," Ollie muttered.

Ollie led the way down the narrow, steep washout on the side of the canyon. "One at a time," he said. "Toby start down. That trail is something like a quarter mile long and so steep at places your horse will skid on his rump."

He indicated for me to follow next, and was I ever glad I had a strong horse like Papoose under me. I held onto the saddle horn for dear life, closed my eyes then I saw the steep slope at the bottom coming and felt the speed of the descent increase, and before I knew it, Papoose was level again. I opened my eyes and found myself alongside Ollie. He slapped me on the back and said, "Good boy, Rowdy, good boy. You'll do."

One by one, the rest of the team slide and skidded down, and when the last one was down, It looked like the path was a mile deeper.

"Lead on, boys," said Ollie. "Take us to the rest of our crew."

The others were waiting for us about a mile down the canyon. They, too, had taken advantage of the chance to rest, and when we were all saddled and standing in a circle around Ollie, he motioned for Fuss and Booger Joe to go to the middle. "All right, boys, what's our game?"

Nobody spoke. Finally, Fuss said, "That's for you to tell us, boss."

"Okay, men. We have to play our cards after we see them. Joe, you and Fuss scout ahead, right down the middle of this canyon. The rest of us will stay a quarter mile back. If and when you spot something, turn around, come back to the main gang, and give us a report. Got it?"

Without replying, Fuss and Booger Joe headed north, walking slowly, hunched well down in the saddle, and riding about a hundred yards apart. When they were ahead of us a quarter mile, Ollie said, "All right, boys, spread out some but don't get out of sight. Watch me. When I raise my arm, stop. If I raise both arms, it will be to warn that Booger Joe and Fuss are reporting back to me."

We were strung out across the canyon floor about a half mile with my father and I in the middle a few yards behind Ollie, and other riders forming a semi-circle. We walked our horses slowly, and I cast my eyes right and left.

I was getting so nervous my teeth chattered and I clamped my jaws together, trying to get my nerves calmed down. My dad caught my attention and gave me the "Thumbs up" signal, and I waved back.

Ollie was in plain sight just ahead, his hat bobbing side to side as he made sure not to miss any movement around him. Now, both Fuss and Booger Joe began to descend as the canyon floor ahead started dripping into a bowl, or huge sinkhole. In just a few steps their horses were out of sight, and soon their hats disappeared.

However, Ollie, who was a hundred yards in front of us, suddenly shot up both hands – the signal for us to stop. In a couple of minutes, we saw both Fuss and Booger Joe's horses come in sight, and then the riders themselves, and they headed in a brisk gallop straight for Ollie. Ollie motioned for the rest of us to ride toward him. It didn't take but a couple of minutes until were standing in a semi-circle, crowding as close as possible to Ollie while Fuss and Booger Joe arrived, big grins on their faces.

"Well, men," Fuss said, "We've got the herd ahead, less than a half mile. They have finished grazing for the morning, and are lying down, chewing their cud. The calves have nursed and are resting while their mothers are digesting their forage."

Ollie's voice almost quivered as he asked, "Well what about the bull? Did you see him?"

"That we did, boss. The old bull himself is snoozing, dead to the world. It's in your lap now. What do we do next?"

Quick as a flash, Ollie turned to Booger Joe. "Well, Joe speak up. You're the bull master from a long ways back."

Booger Joe took out a hunk of Bees Wax chewing tobacco, worked it well into his jaw, and spit before he answered.

"Reckon as how the herd is resting. We go in full blast and wake them up fast, they are going to stampede and raise all sorts of hell. We got to move in quiet as little field mice, spread well out in a circle plumb surrounding them, and never stir a tree leaf until we got them surrounded. We do, they will jump up running headlong and couldn't be caught until they get to Amarillo.

"We want them to wake up nice and easy-like, let their calves suckle and get full. That way, the old cows will not get spooked and start running. They will just take us for some stray horses and let it go at that – until we start to move in on them. When we do make a move, it's got to be a slow walk – just Fuss and me – while you boys stand still as statues.

"My hunch is that even the bull won't rouse up until we finally begin to close in on him. Then, we will – Fuss and me – will walk up slow as possible to him, coming in opposite directions. It won't dawn on him that we are after him until it's too late. When he finally realizes it, he won't go on the prod, but will try to run away from us.

"That's when Fuss and me close in on him, from opposite sides. He will have to run straight ahead – and that's when I pull out my little needle gun, right up against him, lean out of the saddle – and pop the sleepy-time stuff in his rump."

He shifted the tobacco, spit a long brown stream, and grinned. "Simple, ain't it?"

"Joe, you old cuss, I think you've got it down right. Okay, boys, you heard him, start making a great big circle from west to east. Don't move a hair toward the herd if the cows wake up and see you. Just stop once in a while, and let your horses graze a bit. Watch for Fuss and Joe and take your signals from them. If the herd starts to run, don't try to stop them. Your attention is on the bull. Once we get him on the knock-out drops, the herd will run a spell, but stop for their calves, so long as we don't try to control them. This time, it's brain work, not bull dogging."

I felt like a quivering mass of flesh and bones, wondering if we could pull it off as quick and smooth as Booger Joe said. But we were already in the process of beginning our move, and Ollie signaled for my dad and me to ride alongside him. "Just so's I can keep you close enough to save you if we get into a storm."

I saw the other riders gradually make their circle, moving closer and closer to the big swale where the cow herd was bedded down. And when we got close enough to the rim we could just see over it, and look down into the bottom, I saw one of the most peaceful and beautiful sights I had ever seen.

The entire herd – I guessed 35 or 40 cows, was lying either stretched out head to tail, sleeping with their heads turned around and touching their sides. The calves were sleeping in little bunches of threes and fours, and one of the first to catch my eye was a roan calf, red, white and black splotches making him stand out among all of the others, that were less colorful.

I gasped and motioned to dad and silently mouthed the words – "Dad, look. There's the roan calf Fuss said black bulls always sire."

Dad nodded and grinned. I read his lips. "Some adventure, no?"

Ollie held up his hand, motioning for us to stop. The other riders on the side were in place, and Toby and Polecat, who had the furtherest to go to close the circle of riders, were a few yards away. Finally, they too halted their horses, turned them toward us, and the circle was complete.

Then, from opposite sides of the circle, Fuss and Booger Joe began a slow, cautious advance, stopping now and then to let their horses nip a few blades of grass. The horses, hungry and wanting something to eat, occasionally lifted their heads, looked curiously toward the sleeping herd of Longhorns, then resumed grazing.

From all accounts, the herd up to this point had nothing to disturb it. The old bull, sleeping in the shade of a scrub cedar, lifted his head and looked at the horses, but although intent, showed no sign of alarm.

But with each step of the horses, his head got a little higher, and finally, he rose on his rear legs, lifted his front legs, and stretched the full length of his body. Still no sign of alarm.

The advancing riders stopped every few feet until they were approximately 30 yards away from the bull. Now, a few cows began to sense something was going on. They rose to their feet, immediately awakening several calves, who ran quickly to their mothers and began nursing.

Still no panic.

Then I saw Booger Joe reach inside his brush jumper, pull the loaded syringe from his pocket, place it between his teeth, and lift the reins. His horse picked up his pace slightly, walking as if to get around behind the bull.

From the other side of the bull, Fuss lifted his horse into a controlled walk and the bull by now began to switch his tail and move from side to side, as if to know danger was near, but he did not know from which side.

If he turned to the left, Fuss moved up while Booger Joe stopped. Then, the reverse was made and finally, the bull selected his worst enemy – Fuss. He took tentative steps and Booger Joe began to close in. Suddenly the bull realized he was in a trap and started to trot. That's when Booger Joe and Fuss, without any outcry or noise, kicked their horses into a run. The chase was on.

I held my breath and every nerve in my body trembled. I realized I was watching two great riders and great cattlemen at work – men who loved what they were doing, but loved cattle as much or more than life.

The two horses closed the gap immediately. On three strides, Fuss and Joe were alongside the bull, running now, but could not outrun the horses, and the horses actually brushed both sides of the bull, forcing him to run straight away.

Just a few steps away from running into the bulk of the watching cows, Booger Joe leaned nearly out of his saddle, took the needle gun from his teeth, slammed it into the meaty portion of the bull's rump with his right hand, and just as fast pulled his horse to the left, ran through the edge of the cows, now beginning to run along with their calves.

On the other side of the bull, Fuss pulled to the right and away from the bull.

The race was over. The job was done. The outlying riders began to circle and enclose the entire herd. As one cow and calf would try to break away, they were turned back upon themselves. And inside of two or three minutes, the herd was milling around, trapped upon themselves. Little calves bawled relentlessly, seeking their mothers.

I turned my attention to the bull. He was standing stock still, wobbling slightly. He took a tentative step, staggered another step. His front knees buckled. He slowly collapsed to the ground, his mighty head went down as in sleep, and finally, he stretched on his side.

Ollie rode to Joe and Fuss, who were already out of the saddle and standing over the bull. Booger Joe ran his hands over the sleek, shimmering black sides of the bull. "Oh, dear God, Joe. The most magnificent animal I ever saw. And it was so easy. What a monster. Better than a ton, at the least."

"For gosh sakes, Boss," Joe said as Ollie leaped out of the saddle. "What's the span of those horns?"

Ollie reached into his saddle bag and pulled out a short saw. "They will never be as long again as they are right here," he said. "Those horns have gutted their last horse and killed their last bull."

"I thought you wanted to kill him?" Fuss teased, digging an elbow into Joe's side. "How many times have you said you would like to get him in your sights."

"I know, Fuss. But I was mad enough at times to do that. But the older I get, the more I admire any man or creature that can defend himself or itself and survive. I want to take this bull, his cows and their calves back to the ranch.

"I want to put them in a special place in the canyon where they can never starve, never be threatened by man, and can continue to live as long as this canyon is in Texas."

The saw bit into the horns so that about twelve inches were cut off one, leaving the ends blunt and harmless as far as fighting, killing other bulls or killing horses or men. He stuffed the tips into his saddle bag and said, "Boys, this has been one of the greatest days of my life. How about the rest of you?"

My dad got off, walked around the bull, marveling at his size and strength. "In my wildest dreams, I never thought I would see a sight like this – or participate in it."

He put his arm around my shoulder. "Thanks to you, Rowdy."

Ollie didn't waste any more time. "Joe, give the bull his wake-up shot. Fuss, you get the rest of the crew lined out. Put the herd together and start it on a drive to the lower end of the canyon. Take them all the way to my ranch. We are going to have a sight that will one day draw thousands of people. The Longhorns of the Great American West."

54

The Deal

The chase and the dehorning had taken the fight out of the bull. Puzzled at the loss of part of his horns, he kept shaking his head. This helped us get a tighter circle around the herd and when we got them to stop milling around in a circle, they calmed down.

Ollie signaled for the riders to back off a few yards, then rode around the outside of the circle and gave each rider his orders.

Fuss, the veteran cowboy, was to lead the herd and Toby and Polecat were to drop back on either side of Fuss and keep the herd from running around him. Four of the other cowboys, two on either side, were to keep the herd from splitting away, and my dad and I were to bring up the "drag," they called it, with Ollie in the middle of that triangle to direct my father and me and help if any cows or calves tried to break away.

"Start them out slow, boys," Ollie said. "Make them know they are under control, but don't let them stop for at least one hour. By then, they will be over their scare, and will begin to get tired and thirsty. Don't let them stop at the first water hole, but keep them thirsty until they want to take on a really big fill.

"That way, with their bellies full of water, they couldn't stampede if they wanted to. It's probably ten or fifteen miles until we hit a part of my range. We can't stop there. If they bed down and get rested, they would get up early tomorrow morning and scatter back toward their home range. We've got to push them on until we get to ranch headquarters, where we can feed and water them, and get them so tired they won't want to start walking until morning.

"By that time, they will be hungry and we'll give them some cottonseed pellets, some salt blocks and plenty of water.

"Even the old bull will think he has been living in hell but woke up in Longhorn heaven."

Within an hour, the Longhorns had adapted to the steady pace. Any cows that tried to break away were soon turned by the cow ponies, who did not have to be guided in their work, for they enjoyed it probably more than the cowboys.

After we had driven the herd for what I guessed was three or four miles, I finally felt the nervous tension begin to ease and then I was able to bring thoughts of Olivia back in my mind.

My first thought was how I wished she had been with us to see it all happen. And the next one was how proud she would be to see how successful we had been.

And I also thought about the magazine guys, and what they had missed. And my mother! How strange it seemed – almost like a dream –that just a few days ago I had no idea she was back with my father, or that she would show up and give me the surprise of a lifetime.

Could it be that this was just a dream? But deep down, I knew it was for real, that we were family once more. A stray thought also hit me – were they married again? If so, when and where?

But some little calves started getting tired and I had to ride Papoose up and use the end of my lasso to drive them back with their mothers.

The cow, too, began to slow down and once in a while one would turn back and bawl for her calf, and the calf would break through the group to find its mother, bawling back to let its mother know it was trying to find its way back to the dinner table.

As the morning wore on, as the sun got overhead and bore down on us, I took off my jacket and draped it behind the cantle of the saddle and looked around.

The canyon walls were deeper here than at any place we had ridden through so far, and I wondered if we were riding through what had been the home of the Indians so many years and centuries ago. I guessed we might have been halfway between the head of the canyon and its end, where it merged into more open country – or prairie – that would be cotton or wheat country, or dozens of kinds of grass for cattle to graze.

After another hour or so, I began to nod my head now and then, I got so sleepy, and once I woke up with a startle and realized I had dozed off.

Ollie rode up, told me to not dare fall asleep again. "If the herd should break and run, like as not you could be killed. I know you are near dead for sleep, Rowdy, but this ain't no picnic for kids. It is real life, and a good one, but it can be deadly, too."

He rode over to check on my dad, and soon he was back in the middle of the "drag" as he called it.

Finally, after what seemed to have been all day, we came to a clear stream of water running out of the side of the canyon, and the cows stopped to drink. Ollie said to let them drink and rest for two hours, and we could take turns resting while the others guarded the herd, and then we would reverse riders.

I flopped down on my stomach – first making sure there were no rattlesnakes around – washed my face in the clear, cold water, and drank until my stomach ached.

At the end of a two hour rest, which the calves utilized in finding their mothers and getting their bellies full of sweet, warm, life-giving milk, we rode around the herd, got it in line again, and began the drive.

I must admit that as the day went on, as the sun began to fall lower and lower in the horizon, that I had had about all of the trail driving I wanted. It was not only tiresome to sit in the saddle that long a period of time, but it was hard on the tailbone, too. I began to wonder why anybody thought it was fun to ride a horse, when it was actually real work instead.

At long last, the canyon walls began to be farther and farther apart, and lower and lower, and we found a well worn trail.

Ollie drifted over again and said, "It won't be long now, Rowdy. Hang on. In another half hour, we will be back on the prairie and the cows can spread out and we will let them graze. But we won't let them stop, for they will be thirsty and want to turn back to the water hole. We've got to push them along until we come to ranch pastures where we can fence them in and ride to the ranch for a bit of food and some well-deserved rest.

"Rowdy, this has been a day I will never forget. And you, you little tenderfoot Missouri kid, have been mostly the cause of it. I want to thank you for it." And he reached out his hand and near broke my fingers, and turned his horse to check things out with my father.

By now, I was wide awake, and while my stomach growled for some food again, I felt real warm and good inside.

My greatest longing right now was to find a big soft pillow to rest my rear end on. And next, to see Olivia and give her a great big hug.

First thing I knew, I was staring into the eyes of that old black bull, with dried blood on his horns. He stared at me and I got tense and figured he was about to charge and we would have another race for life, but he didn't even snort. He just switched his tail to knock off a few flies, turned and shoved his way back into the middle of the herd and laid down to rest. Just like his cows and calves and a dozen tired cowboys were fixin' to do.

I wanted to get out of the saddle and stretch my legs, but didn't dare until Ollie – who had proved this day that while he was an easy-going, great fun guy, could be plenty tough when he had to be – said so.

I watched him give hand signals to stop and the cowboys passed the signals along so that by the time Fuss gave the hand signals to me, I knew what to do.

These signals meant, "Hold your horses and don't move a muscle as long as the herd is quiet." Then he began a slow walk, circling the herd, stopping to say a few words to every one of the drovers, and then got around to me.

"How you holdin' up, son?" he asked.

"I'm so tired my tail bone can't even feel it," I said. "But I'm still game. What do I do next?"

"Rowdy, me-boy, you've earned the respect of all of us. I can tell the way you sit in the saddle you are about bushed. I want you to come along with me to ranch headquarters."

"I want to see if there are a couple of hands hanging around. If there is, I'll send them out to replace your dad, Fuss and Booger Joe. We'll rotate so that everybody will get some rest. If the herd doesn't take a notion to stampede, we'll be all right. But I think they are too tired, and unless a coyote runs through the herd, or a thunderstorm comes up, I don't think they will move a hair until tomorrow morning."

He neck-reined his horse, and Papoose didn't need to be told what to do. He cantered right along beside Ollie's horse and we headed for ranch headquarters that lay a couple of miles away.

The folks at headquarters had obviously seen the herd as we came in, and there was quite a crowd waiting. They started running to meet us, and the first one in the lead was Olivia, running so hard her hair blew behind her, and next in line was that long-legged, energetic preacher, Reverend Dwiggins. Far behind were the two magazine boys and the others just stood waiting for us to arrive. In front were my mother, Maybell and Salt River Sally.

The sight of that wonderful bunch of family and friends quickly made me forget my aches and pains.

Then I heard a roar of an engine and the spinning of wheels, and here came the two magazine guys, passing all of the others and pulling up at Ollie's feet so fast and noisy that Ollie's horse reared up and nearly jerked the reins out of his hands.

Ollie's face turned red and he cussed under his breath, but his lips gave away his words.

He reached into the cab, jerked the keys out of the ignition, and stuck them in his pocket.

"You dang city dudes, this is the last straw. Get out of the vehicle and walk back to headquarters. I'll deal with you later. He opened the door and helped the photographer out pretty roughly, and the reporter, his face scarlet, got out with apologies on his lips.

"I warned him not to do this," he said, "I …"

"Hush up, boy. Don't get me riled. Now, git, git."

By now, the Reverend Dwiggins has arrived, panting and fanning himself with his hat. "Ollie, you got to stop these people from sleeping together. It's against God's law."

Still red of face, Ollie said, "What in God's name are you talking about?"

"These Missouri people, that's who. Rowdy's mother and dad. I found out they are divorced. Yes, the misses admitted to me today that when she went back to her husband a few days ago, that they began sleeping together, just as if nothing had ever happened. I ask her if they got married again before they did this highly immoral act that is against God's law, and she said, "No, but…"

Now Ollie's face got even redder, and he took off his Stetson and threw it on the ground.

"For Good Godalmighty's sake, Preacher Dwiggings, is that man's greatest sin? What do you want me to do about it? That's their business, ain't it?"

"Yes, but the Bible specifically warns about adultery. It's …" Ollie muttered something I couldn't hear, and bent over, picked up his hat, dusted it off and put it on Reverend Dwiggins head, patted it down, brushed it off, then pulled it down over his ears.

"Reverend Dwiggings. I'm sure the Lord is apt to strike the very ground we are standing on. I suggest you go get into your flivver, run into Salt River town, go to the court house, arrange for a marriage license to be made out, and rush back here as fast as you can."

"Tomorrow, we will call for an hour of atonement and hold a big wedding, which you will perform-that is, if the two culprits that have sinned agree, and then we will slice a big watermelon, have a picnic, pray for their sinful souls, and ask for a couple of inches of rain to boot. Now, don't you feel better?"

And he left the good reverend struggling to get the cowboy hat up over his ears, and walked at a fast clip to where mother, Maybell and Miss Sally were waiting, trying to hold back their laughter.

As for Olivia, I jumped down to give her a tight hug and kiss, lifted her into the saddle, took the reins and walked over to the folks and went through another round of hugs and kisses.

The two magazine guys were already well on their way back to headquarters, on foot. If they had been dogs, their tails would have been dragging between their legs.

Now Ollie got down to business, quickly telling how we surprised the Longhorn, caught the black bull and dehorned him safely, and drove the herd all day long and finally had bedded them down on the home ranch.

"Now, tell me how many cowboys are at headquarters. I want them to relieve the men holding the herd on the bed grounds so we can all get some rest. It's been a long day. But it is one of the best days I ever had."

He turned to my mother. "Mrs. Farmer, I suppose you heard the good reverend's hysteria over your sinful ways. Just for curiosity, was he telling the truth? You and your – uh, husband, er, Rowdy's father. Is it… is that true?"

Mother, always cool under any circumstances, said, "Yes, it is true. But we haven't felt the Devil's fire yet. I'm sure that would greatly disappoint the good reverend. And if he wishes to perform a ceremony, I am sure Rowdy's father would have no objection."

She took Olivia's hand in her own and said, I'm sure Olivia would be glad to serve as a bridesmaid, and Rowdy would make a handsome best man. Right?

Olivia let out a little squeal of delight, put both arms around mother, and said, "Oh, Mammsie. I think that is a delightful idea. When can we do it?"

Mother gave her a quick peck on her cheeks. "What's wrong with tomorrow?"

I could hardly believe my ears, about what all that had happened in such a flash. But if I had digested everything right, I thought it would be just dandy.

Ollie climbed into the saddle, saying, "I've got to get hold of the boys at headquarters and send them out to relieve the men holding the Longhorns. Nobody goes to the herd, understand? They are bedded down and I don't want to take any chances of them getting spooked."

He lightly spurred his horse and rode away at a gallop, leaving the rest of us to walk back, arm in arm, and chattering like blue jays in a treetop.

Maybell herded us to the shade of the big old elm tree in her front yard and settled us down in easy chairs. I was so tired I could hardly stay awake but they wouldn't let me rest.

"Now everybody hush up," Olivia said, linking her arm around mine and pulling her chair as close as possible. "I want him to tell us everything that happened from the time he and daddy and the others left this morning."

And so I did the best I could, and as I talked it kind of woke me up so that after while I was talking up pretty lively-like.

"First off, we hadn't much more than got started until Ollie had to go back and get Reverend Dwiggins headed in the right direction. Then, just as he got back to where we were waiting on our horses, here came the magazine guys, and he had to put them in their places as well."

"Everything went all right except it was hard on the seat of my britches to ride so long without rest, but when we finally got to the highest point on the caprock, as Ollie calls it, we had to wait for Toby and Polecat to scout for a place to get down into the side canyons.

"Once they scouted the floor of the canyon, and discovered the Longhorns bedded down, they rode back to get us and we all went down together.

"We surrounded the cattle before they knew what was happening and from that point on, things happened so fast I couldn't hardly keep up with it…"

I stopped there, trying to think back just exactly what did happen. There were so many men doing so many things it all sort of blended into one big storm in my head.

"First thing I knew, Booger Joe and Fuss were riding side by side and came up behind the black bull before he knew it. Next thing, the bull was running for his life. Joe was leaning out of his saddle and plunging his needle-gun into the bull's rump, then both Booger Joe and Fuss rode away, stopped their horses, and then I saw the bull getting wobbly on his feet."

"He just went down easy-like, as if going to bed. Then they cut off the tips of his horns so he couldn't kill anybody, we got around the herd and rode, seemed like forever."

"And here we are. And the herd is in the pasture south of here a mile or so. That's about all there is to it. "Except my tail-bone feels mighty raw and sore."

By this time, Ollie was riding back with three cowboys. He motioned for them to head for the bed grounds and I heard him tell them, "You boys ride mighty slow and quiet-like as you approach the herd. If you scare the cattle while they are resting, they will all jump up in one motion and be back in the canyon before they stop running."

He rode over to where we were sitting. "Maybell, honey, why don't you and Sally whomp up some vittles for Rowdy and me, and for the three riders that will be coming back hungry as bears when they are relieved."

"I see the magazine guys down by the bunkhouse. I was pretty hard on them today. Reckon I'll go down and sort of apologize, and see if they want to eat with us."

And again, he was off and running, pulling up at the tie rail in front of the bunkhouse and tying up at the hitchrack.

Mother said, “Mercy, Maybell, is he always wound up like a clock?”

“Just about. I don’t think I ever saw him still a minute, except in his sleep. And then, he snores so loud he wakes himself up sometimes.” She laughed, took my mother by one arm and Salt River Sally by the other and they walked off toward the house arm in arm, like real pals.

That left Olivia and me alone, except for Reverend Dwiggins, who had leaned back in his chair and was snoring like a freight train. I stretched out on my back on the grass and Olivia laid down beside me and I didn’t even remember hitting the ground before I was dead asleep.

Later, they told me I was so sound asleep that when Toby and Polecat picked me up and carried me to the bunkhouse and put me to bed I didn’t even know it, until I woke up the next morning and wondered where the dickens I was and how I got there.

It didn’t take long for me to pull on my jeans and shirt and to make my way to the bunkhouse chow line, for the smell of bacon and coffee made me hurry.

I bumped into my father and Ollie just as they were coming out, with Ollie talking a mile a minute as he did most of the time.

“Howdy, Rowdy,” he yelled, slapping me on the back and near knocking me down.

“Thought you were going to sleep the clock around. But you deserve it. You put in a hard day yesterday and you deserve to sleep late. Soon as you get your belly full, hustle to my office. Your dad and I are hatching up a great idea I think you will like.”

So I filled up on hotcakes drowned in sorghum syrup, skipped the coffee and found a glass of milk in the ice box, and headed to the office eating a piece of left-over apple pie.

I eased through the door in time to hear dad say, “There is a section of land not too far from our home place in southwest Missouri that is for sale. It might be rented for pasture, and if our deal works out, we could take an option to buy after a year or two.”

“That sounds good to me,” Ollie said. “But a little ol’ section of land – 640 acres – sounds like a handkerchief to a Texan.

“How can you justify buying that little bit of land for cattle?”

“Very simple,” dad said. “Part of Missouri gets forty to forty-five inches of rainfall a year. We can keep a cow for a year on two to four acres of pasture, and still have grass leftover at the end of the year, barring a drought, which is rare. We can run two to three little steers or heifers to the acre.”

Ollie scratched his head and figured on a scrap of paper.

"Can you do that all over the state?" If you can, are there any large tracts of land available – say three or four sections – enough for a major ranch?"

"Nobody thinks in terms that big," he said. "But yes, there are huge tracks of land, but mostly in timber, that can be bought for as little as $5 an acre or even less. There's a joke in Missouri that if you buy a piece of land, you better watch out, for they will throw in an extra forty or fifty acres."

"Then you would be willing to go partners with me for a year or so? If I would furnish, let's say, a cattle-car load of weaned heifers or steers, you will keep an eye on them, buy whatever supplement and salt they need, and we split the profits at the end of the year?"

"Sure. But if the deal works out as I think it will, I want first option to buy you out at the end of the year. If you don't agree, we will split the net profit and see if we want to try it again."

But I warn you. Missouri is the darkhorse of cattle states. The time will come when there are more mother cows raising calves in Missouri than any other state, save Texas."

Ollie grinned. "Aw, come on, man. L'ol' Missouri? Against Wyoming and Montana with four or five times as much land? Or California, which stretches from Mexico nearly to Canada?"

"You got it," dad said. "Give it a few years – say thirty of forty – and you will see Missouri rise to become a major cow-calf state."

Ollie tapped his fingers on his desk for a few minutes, gazed out the window at his huge stretch of land, and suddenly stood up, thrust out his hand, and said, "You got a deal. First thing we got to do is to have the railroad agent spot a couple of cattle cars at the Salt River siding. Let's get moving."

He grabbed the telephone on his desk, picked up the receiver and clicked it a couple of times. "Mollie, get me the railroad station agent, please. I want to have a couple of stock cars on the siding in a few days."

My heart like to of pounded out of my chest. I had a sudden inspiration. While Ollie was waiting for the phone connection, I whispered to dad, "Can we take Lady Midnight and Jackrabbit home with us?" Couldn't we make room in a cattle car for them, too?"

Dad's first thought was to shake his head and whisper, "No."

My hopes plunged. But all at once a smile lit up his face and he said, "Let me think about it a minute. I think you might have a bright idea. If the cattle thing works out, we could use a good cow pony or two on our ranch. The cattle would be used to horses and not men on foot. They would be easier to handle."

The grin on his face got wider and he squeezed my hand.

When Ollie got through talking to the railroad agent and hung up, dad said, "Ollie, Rowdy just came up with a bright idea. We will need a couple of good cow ponies along with the cattle. Could we fix up a couple of stalls in the cattle cars for Lady Midnight, and would you swap us another gentle horse – and take Jackrabbit for part payment?"

The idea lighted Ollie's face. "By gum, your boy has come up with another good idea. I don't know what I am going to do without that boy, come time for him to go home."

But enough talk was enough for Ollie, and he barged out of his chair and said, "Let's get to work. I want to see how our herd of Longhorns survived the night. And in less time that it takes to tell about it, he had three horses saddled and we were on our way to check on the cattle and relieve the riders who were waiting so they could get something to eat at the bunk house.

55

Longhorns and Licenses

The weather was cool this morning and the horses were ready to run. But Ollie told us to hold them to a fast trot and whatever we did, not let them get out of control when we were in sight of the herd.

"We've got the sneak up on them," he said. "If we come running up to them, they will spook and start running. They would get away from us and we might never round them up again.

"And as soon as we get in sight of them, hold your horse with a tight rein. We won't ride directly toward them, but begin a wide circle like we did when we started to get around them yesterday. We'll close in a little bit, but we don't want to get too close. Just want them to not feel crowded. Let them stay on the bed ground if they will."

"Your horses have an easy gait," dad mentioned as we rode. "And another thing, I noticed your horses are the same color. Dun, a dark to light shade of brown, with black mane and tail."

"You are right. That line of horses was started late in the last century when they were developed on the JA Ranch – that's the one Col. Goodnight started northwest of here. At that time – in the 1880s, the JA covered more than a million acres and ran 100,000 head. The widow of the founding partner, Mrs. Cornelia Adair Ritchie, wanted nothing but dun horses, and so hundreds, if not thousands, of this breed are still working on ranches all over Texas even to this day."

By this time we were in sight of the cattle. Most were still on the bed grounds, but a few calves were up and nursing their mothers, and it wouldn't be long before they were all awake, and then the cows would slowly graze heading in the direction of a large pond, or tank, as Texans called it, to drink.

We spotted Toby and Polecat ahead and soon we held up our horses and let them ride to us.

"Pa, they sure enough behaved themselves last night. I am sure glad to see you coming to relieve us. Can we go on now?"

"Not yet, son. I just came out to make sure all was going well. Your relief will be here in a few minutes. They were just saddling up as we left."

Now I saw the old black bull get up from his bed ground. He stretched, head to tail, shook his head a little as if he still had a little pain because the tips of his horns were gone, but he did not appear to be in any hurry to move.

Ollie notice it, too. "Sawing off the tips of his horns sort of took the fight out of him, didn't it," Ollie said. "What you think about that Rowdy? Would you want to tempt him again today, like you did a few months ago?"

Just the memory of that day when I thought sure I was going to die brought a shudder. I involuntarily pulled back on the reins and my horse backed up. "No thanks, boss. Once in a lifetime is more than enough for me."

I looked at my father and he had a proud, but quizzical look on his face. He didn't say anything. Just shook his head as if to say, "Rowdy, you do beat all I ever saw. And am I ever proud of you."

Ollie touched his horse's flank lightly and said, "Let's ride on around the herd and head for the house. We've got a full day's work ahead. I want a couple of riders to round up a pasture full of lightweight heifers I weaned off of some old cows. That's the ones we will ship to Missouri. We'll need a few days for them to be confined in a small pasture and start eating cottonseed cake and prairie hay. That will take the loose manure out of them, and they will ship better after we load them on the boxcar."

And so as we circled around the herd and headed toward headquarters, all was peaceful – until Ollie suddenly burst out – "Holy-molly, what the devil is that coming toward us? We got to head it off."

He kicked his horse in the flanks and rode at race-horse speed directly toward the approaching rattletrap car. I recognized it as belonging to Reverend Dwiggins. And he was at the wheel.

The reverend skidded to a screeching halt as Ollie pulled up hard on his reins.

"Preacher what the h… I mean what the devil you doin' driving out here in a toot like this? Don't you know if you had driven any farther you would have spooked that herd of Longhorns? Like as not they would have stampeded and run over the canyon walls and killed every last one of them. Great God almighty – I mean, excuse me, Lord, but preacher you should have known better."

Reverend Dwiggins acted as if he had not heard his scolding; he was so frustrated as he jumped out of the car. "Ollie, you know that wedding was scheduled for today, and I got a bum deal at the recorder's office. You know you told me to hurry into Salt River and go to the recorder's office."

"Well, I did just that, but it was too late when I got there and he had gone home. So I couldn't get the marriage license, like you said to do."

"So I thought, well, I will just wait until morning and get up early and be the first one at the office and I can get the license and that will be plenty of time. But would you believe the recorder would not give me the license. He said, "Why, Reverend I didn't know you were going to get hitched. Who you 'bout to hitch up with?"

"And I told him I wasn't going to hitch up with anybody, but I had a nice man and woman I was going to hitch up if he would make out the license and give it to me.

"And I told him it was for Mr. and Mrs. Farmer, and he said, well, if they are already Mr. and Mrs., why do they need to be hitched up again. And I said..."

"Whoa, reverend," Ollie said. "You don't mean you took me for earnest yesterday when we had that little set-to as I rode in from the pasture?

"Why I was just joshing. I was all worked up around getting the Longhorns caught and driven up to a pasture where they could be controlled, and there was so much else to do, I just was aggravated because you bothered me at that particular time.

"So I just pulled your hat down over your ears as sort of a little prank, and went on about my business."

"But, but, but... Mrs. Farmer was standing right there, and she heard every word and she chimed in and said, "Rowdy and Olivia were going to be the whatever it is you call it that the little kids do at a wedding. And so I tore off for Salt River in earnest for I just knew we were going to get these good folks hitched up legal like so they would not disobey the scripture and God's warnin' that thou shalt not commit adultery..."

I looked at dad and his jaw was actually sagging in disbelief. It suddenly dawned on me that in all of the excitement of yesterday, plus all the stress and tired people, that I guessed all of us had gotten our wires crossed. Dad finally said, "Whoa, hoss. Will somebody please tell me what the Hell is going on here?"

Ollie jerked around, and like me he suddenly got a sheepish look on his face. He climbed out of the saddle, knelt down and plucked a few blades of grass, stuck them in the corner of his mouth, and then looked up at my father.

"Mr. Farmer, I guess I owe you a heap of apology. You see, it was like this. The good reverend thought you and your wife-uh, sort of thought it would be a sin for you to do, you know, without the proper credentials, and I sort of... you know, in the spirit of fun and good times, didn't make myself clear. And, uh..."

My dad busted out laughing and nearly fell out of the saddle. When he caught his breath, he said, "Rowdy, did you have anything to do with this?"

"Well, yes, well, sort of I guess. But... I didn't see anything wrong with it. It just seemed like a good thing to do."

"Is that what you want us to do, Rowdy?"

I gulped, swallowed hard, looked down at the ground, then into his eyes, and said, "Yes, sir. Exactly."

"Then it shall be done. This very day. Ollie, I will get Nellie and we will go to Salt River, get the marriage license, and come back here. We will get hitched proper like and after that, you better haul out a big watermelon or two, for we are going to have a wing-ding."

Whew! I was never so glad of anything in my whole life.

I could see Ollie was getting a little out of sorts with Rev. Dwiggins, but he shoved back his hat and said, "Well, then it's settled. If that's the way it is, then that's the way it is. Let's get on with it.

"Preacher Dwiggins, I'll take charge of this little problem. You just go back up to headquarters, pour a lot of black coffee, and leave the rest to me. The wedding will go forward as planned, or I'll eat slop with the hogs.

"Let's get back to headquarters. Rowdy, you tell your mom and Maybell to put on their traveling clothes. We might as well kill two or three stones with one bird, or something like that. We will just bypass that bureaucrat that runs the local branch of the recorder's office and drive on to the county seat and talk to the elected recorder.

"That way, I will get to show you some new country and we'll pass by a few of the big ranches in this part of the country.

"Then, if there is time left, we'll come back by Salt River and see if the railroad crew has spotted our cattle car, and if so, I'll get a crew of carpenters to build the stalls and partition one end of one of the cars for Rowdy's mare and donkey – as well as a place for a couple of cowboys to tend to the cattle.

"How does that grab you all?"

Dad said, “Sounds all right with me. But I can’t help wondering if it wouldn’t be a good idea for Rowdy and me to ride in the boxcar to make sure the calves and horses are doing all right. After all, that mare is getting pretty close to foaling, and I’d hate to see anything go wrong and us not be there to help the birth.”

“Right now, let’s ride. We’ve got a lot of travel to do before time for the wedding.” And he lifted his horse into a fast clip and within thirty minutes we were at headquarters and unsaddling our horses. The Rev. Dwiggins was right behind us.

Ollie burst through the door of his office shouting for Maybell. “Ma, grab your purse, you and Mrs. Farmer, and come running. We got to do a little fast travel.” He turned to go out the door, but changed his mind abruptly, and said to me, “Rowdy, would you like to ride along with us? It would give you a good chance to see a stretch of cow country and some other ranches before you leave Texas for your ol’ Missouri home.”

The idea struck me so suddenly, I had to stop and think a minute. Of course I would, I thought. But on the heels of that, I had a sinking sensation. My time with Olivia was growing shorter each passing moment. “I’d like to except... you know, I thought maybe I would stay here and be with Olivia. It won’t be many days, you know, that we won’t be together for, well, maybe a long time.” I choked on my last words and tears welled up in my eyes.” I realized I really had a crush on Olivia, and I didn’t even want to think about not being with her, all of the time.

Ollie saw my condition at once. His eyes softened and he came to me and hugged me tight. “Rowdy, ol’ kid, you’ve just about become another one of my kids. I know how you feel. I felt the same about Maybell a long time ago. I’ll never forget it.

“Tell you what let’s do. Instead of your folks and Maybell and me going along, let’s just pack you and Olivia in the car too. We’ll have a big time traveling together, seeing the sights, and taking care of our business as well. How does that sound?”

He bear-hugged me and I felt the strength and compassion of him, and my anxiety turned into relief.

“That’s a great idea. Let’s get started.”

And so, inside of ten minutes we were in Ollie’s big Chrysler and kicking up dust behind us.

As usual, Ollie held the foot feed down to the floor board, and as usual, Maybell was telling him, “If you don’t stop driving like a wild man, just stop and let me out right now,” and Ollie hugged her with one arm saying, “Ah, ma, just take it easy. You know ol' Ollie can ride any bucking horse ever was." And she said, "Yes, but this isn't a buckin' horse. This is a car being spurred by a maniac." And Ollie saying, "Hey, that's a pretty good one, Ma." And he just plowed ahead as if she hadn't said anything.

And Olivia and I sat in the back seat, with mother, watching the miles roll by and oblivious of anything except each other and trying to swallow the fact that our days together were drawing shorter with each turn of the wheels. It made us hug each other all the tighter.

As Ollie drove along, he pointed out the location of various ranches and the only thing that would slow him down was if he passed by a bunch of cows and calves grazing along the pastures, or if he saw a windmill spinning in the wind and pumping water into a tank, or if a cowboy or two were riding and then he would slow down and exchange howdy's as he drove along, and then explain to dad who they were and what ranch they rode for.

"We are headed east by southeast," he said. "That is taking us farther and farther downhill from the canyon. We are getting into big ranch country, some of the oldest ranches in Texas. Right now we are passing by the Pitchfork Ranch, one of the best run outfits in Texas and a Missouri man, believe it or not, owns half interest in it."

"Pretty soon, we'd turn back north and come to Hall County, and the town of Memphis. That's where we'll get the marriage license. This is getting to be more and more farming country, and they are starting to grow lots of cotton here."

It was noon by now, and Ollie wheeled into a cafe and stopped. We got out and stretched, used the rest room facilities, and sat down for a little rest and a big order of burgers, pie, and ice cream. It was quite a relief to me to be back into a city that pretty much resembled my home town in Missouri, and it gave me a little flash of homesickness, and I told this to Olivia.

"Oh, Rowdy, I do so much want to see your home. And your towns. And your school. You will be a senior when school starts, won't you?"

I nodded, with a lump in my throat. "Yes. And it will be a year before I am old enough to get married." It was quite a while before Olivia could say anything, and she could hardly keep from crying.

We ate, Ollie paid the bill, left a ten dollar bill for a tip, and we all went to the car and piled in. Ollie turned on the key, pressed the starter and nothing happened. He kept on trying to start it, and finally the battery ran down and we were just left sitting there, not knowing what to do.

Ollie got out, jerked the hood latch and looked at the engine. He called to dad.

"Do you know anything about a car engine," he said. "The only thing I know about them is how to start it and turn the wheel and hit the brakes. This dad-burn piece of junk won't run."

The upshot of it was that Ollie spotted a car agency across the street, went over and brought back a man in coveralls and another man in a dress suit. The man in coveralls opened the hood, took a quick look, and said, "you don't have any oil pressure. Looks to me like you have hit a rock or something and knocked a hole in the oil pan."

"Meaning?" Ollie asked.

"Meaning the engine is shot and you'll have to overhaul it or buy a new engine."

Ollie's face blazed red but he managed to hold his temper. "That's the trouble with these dad blamed horseless carriages. My old horses at the ranch wouldn't let me down."

He looked around sort of helplessly, trying to figure out what to do. Then his eyes brightened when the man in the blue suit said, "I can fix your problem real easy."

"How's that?"

"I can have you in a brand new Buick in about five minutes."

Ollie's face brightened. "Where is it?"

"Follow me."

And within five minutes, Ollie motioned for us to get out and cross the street, and he was shouting loud enough for the town to hear, "Get over here right now. I've bought a new Buick."

And the salesman was saying, "Don't worry about the papers right now," he said. "I'll fill them out and mail them to you later. The check of Ollie Oliver is good anywhere in the panhandle."

We were no sooner in the car and settled down than Ollie, laughing like a kid, said, "Folks, roll up the windows. This here iron horse has got air conditioning."

He drove to the center of town, where the county courthouse stood solid as granite, got out and went into the office of the recorder of deeds.

Dad and mother, acting sort of nervous and kid-like, went up to the counter, told the clerk they wanted a license to get married, and signed their names, giggling and acting as two kittens with a ball of yarn.

I just felt warm and happy inside, and Olivia and I held hands the whole time, and she whispered, "I wish that was us, Rowdy," and I made a brilliant reply, "Me too."

Ollie and Maybell were waiting outside in the new Buick, with the windows rolled up and the air condition running, big smiles on their faces.

"Well, folks, back to Salt River we go. By the time we inspect our cattle cars and get back to the ranch, the Rev. Dwiggins will be hopping up and down on one leg, worrying about saving our souls."

An hour later we topped a hill where JJ and I had first spotted the lively little Texas cow town of Salt River. It brought back a lot of memories and I nudged Olivia and whispered, "Take a look ahead. This is what I saw the first day we met. And this is where I got down and tightened the girth on the saddle, got back on and told JJ, 'Here I go.' That's the Texas cow town where I made up my mind I was going to ride into and show off what a great rider I was.

She looked out the window and started giggling. Mother and Maybell looked around. "What's so funny?"

Olivia said, "This is where Rowdy began his great ride into Salt River. Just a quarter mile away, right in the middle of the business district. That's where Lady Midnight reared up in the air, Rowdy waved his hat, and then it happened. The saddle girth broke and he went sliding to the ground."

She giggled and hugged me. "I didn't know then I was going to meet the boy of my dreams. But I'm glad I did."

Ollie boomed with laughter. "I remember that, too. But I had to admire the kid. He took it like a man. Got up and brushed of the seat of his britches and didn't blame the mare for his predicament.

"Now you all just sit tight. I'm going to stop at Keeper's store and buy a few little things I need."

And he brought the new Buick to a sliding halt in front of the store steps where I had first talked to Booger Joe, jumped out and was gone in the store about ten minutes. When he came out, he was carrying a big box, which he stashed in the car trunk, then got back behind the wheel and roared away.

But instead of turning south, toward his ranch, he turned north and I pretty soon saw the reason why. The two cattle cars he had ordered loomed dead ahead.

We all got out to stretch our legs and look inside the cars and walk around them. I don't know what we expected to see, because they looked just like the cattle cars we had seen many a time back home in Missouri. But Ollie was looking for things the rest of us didn't see. "Got to make certain there isn't a flat place on any of the big steel wheels," he said. "If there is, a worn place could cause the box car to jump up and down every time it turned over. Enough of that and the calves would get sore legs or maybe get down and be trampled on.

"Also, I will have my carpenter divide the car in partitions so only a fourth of the calves will be in each section. That way, there is less chance of the calves milling around and getting down and injured.

"And if you plan to ride in the car, which I would advise against, you must have a partition across one end. You will need sleeping quarters, for the trip will take at least three days. And you will have to have a special stall for your mare, Rowdy."

That done, we headed back toward the ranch and when the buildings showed up in the distance, it was a welcomed sight. I felt almost as good as if I had been seeing our home back in Missouri looming up ahead.

Dad said, "Do you worry about what can go wrong while you are gone? I do."

Ollie laughed. "You too? Boy, I do. The minute I turn my back on the old place, I start to worry about what can go wrong. One time a herd of calves got out and were almost in Salt River town when I missed them. I had a dickens of a time getting them turned around and headed back home.

"Another time, a mare got down and couldn't give birth without help, and I don't know what else. Seems like sometimes cows and horses just try to commit suicide. You've got to be there looking out for them all the time."

We pulled up in front of the house, got out, stretched, and dad and Ollie headed for the barns where a couple of men were unsaddling.

"How's the Longhorns, boys?"

"Slick as ice," said one. "They have settled down and spread out to gaze. Nary a head tried to go back to their old range. I suspect it is because you had us set out those fifty-pound molasses blocks that helped. They just stand around after they lick them, go eat some grass, and then bed down and chew their cud."

Ollie had one of the cowboys ride out to the herd to get Toby and Polecat and when the boys rode up, Ollie said, "You boys harness a team of work horses and hitch onto the pair of the wagons we take out at roundup time. I want you to pull them up half way between the house and the horse stables.

"Park them facing each other but about six feet apart. Then unhitch the teams and put them back to pasture and return and lift the wagon tongues and cross them against each other.

"When you get that done, hitch onto a regular hay wagon, take it down to the cedar brakes and cut a big load of cedar branches and bring them back here."

Polecat pushed back his hat and said, "Good gosh, Pa, what the devil you want all that cedar for?"

"Well, son, we are going to have a grand occasion here about sundown. We are going to have a wedding party, and I want the cedar to be leaned up against the wagon tongues so it can be a little stage for Preacher Dwiggins and the man and woman that's going to be married, and for the best man and best woman."

Toby spit a stream of tobacco juice on the ground. Ollie said, "I thought I told you to leave off that nasty stuff." But Toby said, "Pa, ain't this a lot of trouble for two people that don't need anything but to be hitched up by the preacher? This is more trouble than herding cattle."

Ollie turned away, saying, "Get with it, boys. This is a special deal. You'll see. And when you get done with that, go down to the big water tank at the barn. Skim off the dirt and straw and anything else and pump fresh, cold water."

"Oh, pa, what for?"

"You'll see. Just do it."

He then went to the bunkhouse, and we followed with dad and me wondering what else he was up to. Then he told the cook, "Put on a big feed for tonight. Reckon time we are through there will be fifty or sixty to feed. I left word in Salt River we were going to throw a big party."

To us, he said, "You boys better get some shut-eye. I got some more things to check out before the big whing-ding. And by the way, I wonder where the Rev. Dwiggins is? His old car is still parked down by the sheds. Reckon I'd better look him up. Would be just like him to get soused up so he couldn't perform the wedding."

Dad and I crossed our fingers and did as Ollie said. It was nice to be alone a while, Olivia and mother having disappeared in the house with Maybell.

Every one seemed to be accounted for except the preacher and Miss Sally. "Where do you suppose she is?" I asked.

"Rowdy, I smell cookin' and see smoke coming from the kitchen window. If I know ol' Sal, there is a dozen or so pies fixin' to come out of the oven. Now you two boys just settle down and get some rest."

And so we did. And it didn't take long to find the shade of the front porch, stretch out and start snoring.

56

Preparing

I was dead to the world when dad shook me. "Wake up, Rowdy. Company's coming."

I sat up, rubbed the sleep out of my eyes and saw Rev. Dwiggins bringing his old flivver to a stop right in front of us. He got out, slapping the dust out of his britches, and then I saw he had two passengers – the magazine guys.

And what a difference there was in them from the time they showed up on the ranch a couple of weeks before, all dressed up in city clothes and wrinkling their noses around the cattle.

Now, I swear they almost looked like real cowboys.

"Well," dad said, "I believe you two city dudes kind of like the wild and woolly west. How about it? And where you three guys been anyway?"

They grinned and sat down on the porch steps. They were friendly now, and you could tell they had really fallen for the life of cowboys and cattle.

"Reckon you got that right pard," Covello said in his effort to talk like a cowboy. "If we had a few million bucks to spare, we'd just buy this spread from Ollie and spend the rest of our lives here."

I couldn't help but blurt out, "What's got into you guys? Two weeks ago you were green as grass and looked like you hated Texas, cows, and cowboys and you were just doing this because you had to do it."

Covello said, kind of sheepish-like, "Rowdy, we were born and raised in a big city. To survive, you had to become suspicious, hard eyed, tough, and fight like cur dogs just to survive, let alone get ahead.

"But out here, either you people are putting on a good show, or this is for real. And we kind of believe now it is real. We'll never make real cowboys, but we decided to make the most of it as long as we are on this assignment. And who knows? Maybe our pictures and story will start a new trend on movies that only show singing cowboys shooting pistols with blanks to make the noise. The movies are phony."

Rev. Dwiggins elbowed his way up the steps, sat down and fanned his face and wiped the sweat off his balding head. "When did you get back from your trip? Where are the lovers I'm supposed to hitch so's they can live together without sin and the Lord's fire and brimstone?"

"Well," dad said, "Let's just go down to the stables and bunkhouse and see if we can find out."

We rounded the corner of the house and saw Ollie was thinking the same thing about us. "Hey, you hoodlums, where you city buckaroos been hanging out?"

Covello and Maness glanced to each other and looked sheepish. "Well, tell the truth we wanted to see the Longhorns, and the good reverend said to hop in his flivver and he would take us to see them, and that's where we have been and ..."

Ollie bellowed like a mad bull. "What? You mean the three of you dared violate the orders I had given? Nobody was to approach that herd on foot or in a car? All right, give me the rest of your story Preacher, did you stampede the Longhorns?"

Rev. Dwiggins shook his head so hard he had to put his false teeth back in place as he stuttered, "Oh, no, Ollie. Everything is just like it was when we drove out to the pasture so..."

Covello broke in. "We didn't get any closer to the cattle than half a mile," he said. "I just wanted to get some good pictures."

"Well, how the devil can you get good pictures from a mile away?"

"Telephoto lens," he said hurriedly. "You can bring them up right into your face with these new cameras. Here, let me show you."

And he took one of the cameras from around his neck, handed it to Ollie and said, "Look for your self." And Ollie fumbled around until he got focused on a horse standing a half mile away in the pasture.

"My gosh, you are right. Why, I can see his brand. And his teeth when he takes a bite of grass."

He handed the camera back and said, "Well, we will talk about that later. You can show me where to get a camera like that, and how to use it.

"Right now, Reverend, it's about time to get your vocal cords warmed up. Let's get this wedding thing wrapped up so we can get on with the rest of the show. I've got a few surprises in store for these good Missouri folks, as well as for the rest of you."

Dad grinned. "Ollie, if you are thinking what I think you are thinking about after the ceremony it..."

Ollie clapped a hand over his mouth and gave it his best sober face, but there was also a distinct twinkle in his eyes.

He said, "Come on boys, let's get this carnival going. Maybell said for me to hustle, pronto – and if you look behind you, you'll see the reason. Company's a comin' from Salt River and ranches all around us."

And sure enough, the dust was fogging up the ranch road as what looked like a regular caravan drove in sight.

57 Gettin' Hitched

But I didn't have long to think about it, for people began piling out of cars and trucks and first thing I knew I was surrounded and everybody was talking at once.

Some swarmed around me and told me their names and the ladies hugged me and ruffled my hair and that was better than those that wanted to hug me and lay a big smacking kiss on my cheeks.

The main thing they said was, "So you are that run away boy from Missouri that near got killed by the black bull," or "So you're the Missouri kid we've been hearing about all summer," and "Somebody told me Booger Joe is your real uncle. Is that a fact?"

I answered best I could and finally Ollie saved me by pulling me alongside him and yelling, "Hey, folks, give us a break. I want you to meet Rowdy and his dad, from Missouri. They are our guests of honor for tonight. Rowdy's ma and pa, well they are the star attraction tonight, and Rowdy's mother will be out directly. I 'spect she is in the house with Maybell right now, and pretty soon the bride-to-be is going to come out and there's going to be a wedding."

Some guy at the back of the mob yelled out, "You mean they had the boy 16 or 17 years ago, and they ain't never been hitched?"

"Now don't go cooking up some crazy scheme," Ollie yelled back. "Shore, he was born legal, same as me, only I ain't certain about you. This is a wedding just for good measure, sort of a way to celebrate the blessing of this here young man.

"And soon as the hitching is over, we're going to dig into the barbecue and have us some fun, just for the heck of it. But also, this is a farewell party for these Missouri folks that have livened up our summer in these parts. I intend that we give them a rousing farewell and show them some good old Texas hospitality."

And so the cheers rang out and everybody in the crowd came up and shook hands with dad and me and made us feel that we really were good friends of everybody.

When the handshaking and hugging were over, the folks began to spread out. The women went looking for Maybell, Sally and my mom, and the men crowded up around the two chuck wagons, which by now were decorated with a thick cover of cedar branches. It always made me wonder why God made cedar smell so good, but did not make it taste good.

To my surprise, I saw the chuck boxes on both of the wagons were piled high with steaming pots and pans of barbecue, gravy, sweet potatoes and just about every other good thing to eat and it was all Ollie could do to hold the crowd back.

"Hey, folks, now just take good deep breath of the vittles, but no fair starting to eat yet. Let's get the main business over with, then we'll wade in and eat and drink and dance until morning."

A great cheer went up and just at that minute, all eyes turned toward the front porch, for there, standing in the light of the setting sun, looking like an angel, stood my mother. I almost didn't recognize her. She was dressed in a full length wedding dress which Maybell surely had loaned her, and her deepest black hair flowing down her shoulders. Her sweet perfect face was warmed by her perpetual smile, and she waved at the guests – waved a branch cut from Maybell's bed of mums.

I heard the women whispering about her beauty, her smile, her poise and grace as she stepped off the porch and made her way through the throng, getting a hug here, and light peck on the cheek there. The good ol' boys just pulled off their hats and nodded politely to her, and stepped back, and mother made her way to where my dad and Ollie were standing.

"Well," she said, "I never dreamed I would be the center of interest to so many wonderful people. My heartfelt love goes out to all of you – especially those who had something to do with looking after my son this summer. And to the sister-in-law I never knew I had," and here she stopped to give Salt River Sally a hug and kiss, and the guests sent up a roar of laughter and clapped – "to say nothing of having found my long-lost brother.

"I knew him as Frank Joseph McLin. You know him, I believe, Booger Joe, the hard ridin', hard shootin' man Sally tries to keep in line."

The crowd at first gasped and then gradually the reality of what she said soaked in and a great round of clapping and yelling began.

It took something like five or ten minutes for the guests to settle down and then somebody had located Booger Joe and were shoving him through and he bashfully went up to my mom and hugged her and gave her a peck on the cheek – but only after he had taken off his hat – and then turned around and waved to the people he had known for years, but who had never really known him.

Booger Joe tried to get out of the crowd, but he couldn't. Everybody tried to get to him and my mother at once, and in a flash, they gathered around them so tight they could hardly breathe. I was squeezed so hard I had to get down on my hands and knees and crawl out to where I could stand up and get my breath.

Ollie, hidden somewhere deep in the people, was both laughing and yelling at the same time.

"Hold on, there, friends and neighbors. Ease up. You are going to mash us folks in the middle."

Only then did they begin to back off, but just enough for mother and uncle to breathe, and some men lifted Booger Joe on their shoulders, and the cheers and clapping began again.

JJ had been laying low since being re-introduced to his mother. It was almost like they were afraid to leave each other's side. But now JJ came up to me and shook my hand, just like a man, and congratulated me.

"It's just like you always hoped, Rowdy. That nasty old step-mom's gone and your mother is back. My mother is here, too. We sure are lucky Son-of-a-guns, huh?"

"We sure are, JJ," I grinned back at him.

Little by little, the knot of people broke up, and there was Ollie standing beside my mother and father, trying to push his way through.

"All right, folks, let's get this thing underway. Where's Preacher Dwiggins? Anybody seen the good reverend?"

This brought order to the chaos, and everybody looked around. "Hey, preacher, where are you?" Ollie yelled at the top of his voice, but the preacher didn't answer. Then everybody quieted down and began looking at each other, and then they looked behind them, but no preacher.

Ollie yelled again still no answer. He said a few naughty words but that didn't help, either.

Finally, Ollie said, "Folks, we can't have a wedding without the preacher. He must have crawled back in his car to take a nap, or maybe he went down to the bunkhouse to grab a snooze like the rest of us, and he just ain't woke up yet.

"Somebody check out the bunkhouse. Hey, you, Toby and Polecat, get a move on."

And so the crowd broke up into little knots and they fell to talking about the price of cattle and the weather and would it ever rain again, and Ollie pushed his way through and went off in the direction of the bunkhouse and corrals. I tagged along with him, thinking surely the reverend would turn up, when I heard Polecat yell, "Hey, pop, he's down here – in the cow pen below the bunkhouse. Sounds like his voice is coming from the outhouse."

Ollie broke into a run, and I followed and by the time I located Polecat, he and Toby were doubled up, they were laughing so hard.

"Paw, you ain't gonna believe this. Preacher Dwiggins is trapped in the outhouse. Looky there."

And we looked, and then we heard the muffled voice of Rev. Dwiggins coming from the outhouse.

"Help, help. Get me out of here. That danged old cow thought I was going to hurt her calf when I just went out to pet it. The only way I could get away from her was to get in the outhouse. And when she hit the door with her horns, it knocked the latch shut, and I can't get out."

Sure enough, the cow was standing at the door of the outhouse, her calf bawling for ma at the top of its voice. And the old cow just stood tight, raking her horn against the door of the outhouse where the preacher was imprisoned, and butting the little building with her head, and running around and around, trying to get at the person she thought was trying to harm her calf.

Ollie busted out laughing, but broke it off pretty quick. "Toby, climb into that pen and see if you can get the cow's attention, then run like the dickens. Polecat, get behind him, when the cow chases Toby, open the latch and get the preacher out quick-like."

And so within a couple of minutes, the cow was chasing Toby to the back of the lot, and Polecat was hustling the Rev. Dwiggins to safety.

"Preacher," Ollie said, "sorry I have to laugh but this is pretty funny. Do you need to change your pants?" And he busted out laughing again. I had to giggle a little bit myself.

But the Reverend Dwiggins didn't think there was anything funny about it. For a minute, I thought he was going to forget the scripture and say a few bad words, but he finally got himself under control, and said, "I hold nothing against that mother cow. She was just doing what God told her – protect her baby. I assure you the good Lord above gave me that experience for a reason. That will make a good sermon."

And so he held his head up and walked so fast to get back to the house, I had to run to keep up with him. He stopped long enough to say, "Rowdy, do not mention this to anyone. It is sort of against my dignity as a representative of the Lord above and it might not be good for my image."

Thinking that this was the man who was going to marry my father and mother, I could see what he meant. And so when he walked up to the crowd, I dropped back and told Ollie what he had said. And after Ollie got through having another laughing fit, he agreed, and said he would tell his boys the same thing. But once in a while as we walked, Ollie had to catch his breath and pinch himself to stop laughing.

But the Reverend Dwiggins had no more than arrived back to where the wedding was to be held then he forgot about what he had asked me to do – he began his sermon on the message the Lord had just given him.

He stepped up on one of the bales of hay Ollie had placed around the yard for seats, and said, "The Lord has saved me again. He just showed me the love of a cow for her calf by imprisoning me at her mercy.

"That is a sign for certain. I am the guardian of my herd – or my flock, that is. And I am here tonight to relay that message of salvation to all of his children around me. I..."

Ollie caught up with him. He pulled the Reverend's head down and said in sort of a loud whisper, "Reverend, this is not the time or place for your sermon. That will be next Sunday at church."

The good Reverend appeared shocked for a moment, but quickly recovered.

"And yes, my children, I was so excited about the great lesson the Lord gave me that I for a short time forgot that there is another service I am to perform tonight. That is the marriage vows of two pilgrims who had forgotten their way, and I am privileged to help them wash away their sins and recover their Christian values. I..."

Ollie tapped him on the shoulder again and whispered, "The wedding, Reverend. The wedding."

"Ah, yes, the wedding. I am so enlightened by the revelation given to me by God this very night, that I forget the matter at hand. I am supposed to unite the parents of this wayward child of God so they can have their sins washed away and resume their lives in cooperation with the Trinity.

"Now will the sinful couple please step forward."

Ollie again whispered, "Just a minute, Reverend, I had figured to have a little musical introduction by our harmonica-playing cowboy. You know. Claud Fussel, your old friend and cowboy in Jesus."

"Ah, yes, yes indeed. I had not forgotten. I just got a little ahead of myself in my enthusiasm. Where is the good Shepherd, Reverend Fussel."

"Not Rev. Fussel. Just plain ol' Claud, the cowboy."

"Oh, yes, cowboys are to be welcomed in Heaven, also. But not if they are addicted to hard liquor and wild, wild women."

Ollie took his elbows and helped him step down from the bale of hay. To the smiling but polite visitors who, obviously were acquainted with the Rev. Dwiggins occasional lapse of memory, they politely applauded and looked somewhat impatiently for Ollie to get things rolling. After all, I was thinking, the barbeque might get cold if the main event of the night wasn't taken care of right soon.

So Ollie waved his hand like it was a magic wand, "you cowhands, take your seats to the left and you women, go to the right and leave an alley in between for the newly-weds-to-be.

"I know this ain't very fancy. But we are just plain country folks and don't put on aires. Brother Farmer, you come on down and take your seat on the bale of hay to the left of me, and you, Rowdy, you being the best man, or boy, in this case. You come right along side of him.

"Not Miss Nellie – you're gonna be Mrs. Nellie again right shortly, you stay at the back while my little chickadee Olivia comes down the aisle with your basket of alfalfa leaves... that's it, honey you can start coming down right now, slow-like.

"All right, Fuss, you ol' cowboy, you can start the wedding march on your french harp."

And so help me, it all began just like so. There wasn't a whisper of any kind, except I overheard a sniffle or two and saw a few ladies dabbing at their eyes with their handkerchiefs, and Olivia was walking softly toward the front, and behind her, escorted on either side by Maybell and Miss Sally was my mom. My real mother!

I wanted to shout and cry happy tears at the same time, but all I could do was hold my breath and hope that I wasn't dreaming and what was happening was real.

But when I saw mother look directly at me, and wink, then as she passed me, lean over and kiss me, I knew it was for real.

She stopped in front of Rev. Dwiggins, and he said, "The gentleman will take his place beside the bride to be," and dad did so, and fumbled in his pocket and pulled out a – I could hardly believe it – a horse shoe nail bent in the shape of a ring. That had long been a joke between my mother and father. He had told her he didn't have the money for a real diamond ring, but he could afford a homemade one, and that was what he had given her when they were first married.

Mother somehow kept from laughing, but held her face straight, as the Rev. Dwiggins cut through his jabbering and said, "Do you, Paul Clifford Farmer, take this woman for your lawfully wedded wife," and he said, "You're darn right I do," and he said to mother, "Do you Eleanor McLin Farmer, take this man for your legally wedded husband?" And she said, "In the name of the Lord God above never to part again until the good Lord sends us to our eternal rest in Heaven."

"I do."

"I therefore pronounce you husband and wife and mother of your son, Rowdy."

All of a sudden, there were cowboy hats flying in the air, and women rushing to touch my mother's hand and pat her on the cheeks and telling her how beautiful she was and that she had better stay in Texas, and asking if they could come visit her in her Missouri home sometime, and telling her to be sure and sample the wedding cake they brought.

All of a sudden four of five of the good ol' Texas boys pulled out their six shooters that had been gathering dust for years and started shooting in the air. Then, Toby and Polecat carted out a box, opened it and pulled out firecrackers and sky rockets and I don't know what else and I knew than what the box contained that Ollie brought back to the car when we had stopped in Salt River.

After the shouting had died down, and the fire works had stopped, Ollie and Booger Joe walked up to dad, one on either side of him, and grasped his arm.

"You know what a country shivaree is I reckon?"

Dad groaned. "I reckon I do."

"Have you ever participated in one?"

"I reckon I have."

"And what was the favorite thing that your best buddies did to you to make you wonder if marrin' was the right thing to do?"

Dad groaned and tugged to get his arms free. But no luck. "All right, you win. I reckon the worst thing I ever did was to dunk the lucky man in the water tank to bring him to his senses."

"Then you agree that this is guaranteed to work?"

"I guarantee."

"All right, boys, let's escort this gentleman to the waterin' hole and initiate him in the sacred baptism of marriage."

And so the march to the water tank began, and I remembered Ollie's instructions to a cowboy to flush the tank and fill it with clean water, but I really dreaded to see dad undergo that humiliation.

But with Ollie's strong hands on one arm, and Booger Joe's on the other, I knew dad didn't have a chance of doing anything but undergoing the humiliation.

Just as they got to the tank, however, something happened and happened so quickly I could scarce believe my eyes.

As Ollie and Booger Joe stiffened their arms to pitch dad in the tank, he suddenly tensed up, pulled back as if to get away, and then lunged forward and threw Ollie and Booger Joe off balance. Then, Dad hurled all his body weight forward, pulling the two men with him – and the result was that all three of them splashed in the water. They came up blubbering and gasping for air.

Dad was the first to stand up and wipe the water from his eyes, and Ollie and Booger Joe came up spitting, coughing and wiping their eyes.

The air turned blue for four or five minutes, and all the men around the tank were doubled up laughing and I didn't know what the heck to think. Would they kill dad for his trick?

But to my surprise, they splashed water on each other just like three grown boys, and climbed out of the tank, dripping wet and laughing so hard they had to roll on the ground to get over it.

I didn't know grown men could act so silly.

But I had to believe it, because it all happened right before my eyes.

What a day it had been. The feast began, camp fires lighted the sky, cowboys played french harps with every known cowboy song and Fussel told stories until after midnight. I fell asleep on bales of hay, with Olivia beside me, and neither one of us knew what the grown up "kids" did except have a wild good time until the sun came up and they crawled out of their pallets and off the bales of hay, groaning and just as quiet as they had been loud a few hours earlier – except for groans and rubbing out headaches.

The odor of coffee, bacon and frying steak were heavy on the air and a glance in the direction of the bunkhouse where the cowboys ate told us there was a crew of overnight company down there eating.

I suggested to Olivia that she go into the kitchen at the "Big House," as she called her home, and that I would meet her as soon as I could eat a bite and find out the schedule for the day.

Something seemed to weigh heavily on my mind, for I had a sober, somber feeling in my brain. It took me a while to sort it out and as I walked toward the smell of ham and coffee it struck me like a blow to the stomach.

It was time for my family to head back home in Missouri. And that meant I had to go, in fact wanted to go. I longed to see our big old southern style two-story house and my grandfather's championship bull, Repeater the Seventh's Model, "Built" for us after he was grand champion at the American Royal in Kansas City. Built because his calves were so much in demand. But even stronger than that urge was the urge for the girl of my dreams – Olivia.

I thought how wonderful it would be if we were a couple of years older, or even just one year older. I would be out of school after one more year, and I was certain my parents would agree to us getting married – and that Ollie and Maybell would also give in.

After all, early marriage of young lovers was not only the normal thing to do, but often the wise thing to do. Farm and ranch folks had to work hard to cultivate the land and plant and harvest crops, and there was always valuable work for the children to do. And learning to work at an early age, and to accept responsibility, was believed to be getting a start in life. After all, the average length of life was quite low, sixty-five to sixty-eight years were about the limit. Seldom did the "old folks" make it into the 70s, virtually never into the 80s.

I set my mind to trying to think of a way to approach my parents and just tell them I wanted to either stay in Texas for another year, so Olivia and I could tie the knot, or perhaps persuade Ollie and Maybell to let Olivia go home with us and live with our family for another year and attend school with me.

JJ stopped me on the way to the Big House. "Me, mom and the triplets are catching the train home today, Rowdy."

I winced at the thought of my original partner-in-crime already heading back, putting me that much closer to my own ride home.

"Your ma thought it would be a more comfortable ride," he added.

I thought to myself how my mom probably hoped to have time for just her newly reunited family.

"I understand, JJ. You've been my best partner on this journey. And we'll always remember our great adventure."

"I've said my good-byes," he sniffled.

Mary and the twins came up behind them.

"We'll be off to Missouri by noon."

"And I'll see you there not long after," I said, tears in my eyes at what that really meant, leaving my beloved Olivia.

My thoughts were interrupted as a car pulled up and stopped in front of the bunkhouse. The two magazine guys got out, waved at me and I stopped to see what they wanted.

I noticed they no longer wore their cowboy outfits, but were dressed in city clothes, were shaved and gave off a strong odor of shaving lotion.

"You guys are all dolled up," I said. "Going somewhere?"

"Back where we came from, Rowdy. Our assignment is over and we've got to fly back to New York. Just stopped by on the way to Amarillo to catch a plane and wanted to say so-long to everybody."

"I hate to see you go," I said. "I learned a lot from you guys. You came here looking for a bunch of dumb hicks and we couldn't stand your city ways. But I guess we all got to understand each other and even like each other a little bit."

They slapped me on the back as we opened the bunkhouse door and stepped inside where a dozen sleepy visitors and cowboys were already eating breakfast.

We loaded our plates and ate in silence – there was little talk around the ranch until everybody had eaten I had discovered. Finally the cowboys came around and got the message, and they shook hands with the city guys, wished them well, asked if they would send some pictures when they got them developed, and walked out the door toward the stables to saddle and ride out to tend the herds.

After we finished eating, we walked to the house office where we figured Ollie and my father were talking ranch and cow talk.

Ollie greeted them like long-lost relatives. "What you boys doing out so early," he asked.

"We're done, Ollie. Want to thank you for putting up with us. Hope we didn't aggravate you too bad with our stupidity, but we sure have a better idea about where our food comes from, and the kind of people who make it possible."

"Well, I got irritated a lot of times at you," Ollie said. "But we were glad to have you and want you to come back, anytime. Spread the word in your magazines that food don't grow in grocery stores and somebody's got to work hard so you can have it. You need us to provide it – and we need you to eat it so you can buy some more. What difference would it make if we raised all kinds of food if we didn't have somebody that needed it?"

We shook hands all around and they walked out the door and out of our lives, so far as we knew. There were goodbyes being said across the board. But no time to dwell.

Dad looked me straight in the eye and said, "Rowdy, we've got our work cut out for today and tomorrow. We've got to help Ollie's carpenters finish modifying the box cars, cut out the calves we want and drive them to the rail siding so we can head for home. You game?"

I nodded, numb to the core. I just had to say it. "Dad, can I stay with Ollie and Maybell and Olivia another year? We want to be married."

My ears rang and I felt dizzy. I didn't know I had enough courage to say it. But I did.

Dad sat down and took a long breath. He looked at Ollie, who also sat down. It was a long minute before either one answered.

"It is pretty plain you and Olivia are deeply in love, Rowdy," dad said. "Don't you think you two should have a little time to be apart so you can be sure you want to tie the knot?"

I thought on that a long time. "Well, yes. And no, but we have become so attached to each other I think we would die if we were apart – even for a month. Or a week even. Even a day. Dad, you don't understand..."

In a very quiet and gentle voice, Ollie said, "Rowdy, my boy. That's just it. We do know. We have been in love, too. That's God's will. We have been talking. You and Olivia may not realize it, but what is happening to you and Olivia – what is happening – happened to your mother and dad. And it happened to Maybell and me. That's natural. That's God's work.

"And we are happy about it. You are the right stuff, and so are your folks. Maybell and I have seen this coming on. So it is no surprise. And what your mother and father have done – in forgiving each other for mistakes and forgetting bad words they may have said in the past is all gone. It's just as if they had never happened."

"Here's what I believe. Maybell and I will give consent for our daughter to marry you – if that is what she wants, also. And she has already told us several times this is what she wants. Let's say it will be done. But let's let Mother Nature take her time. And when both you and Olivia say, it is time, then it will be done. Okay?"

Suddenly, I felt as if I had grown a foot, and my insides felt better, but my head was buzzing. Had I really heard what I thought I had heard?

And then I heard myself saying, "Okay. Yes. Bless you."

Ollie stood up and squeezed me so hard I thought he would crack my ribs. Dad stood up and said, "Let's get your mother and Maybell and Olivia in here and see if we are all of the same mind."

Mother and Maybell were sober and long-faced while Ollie broke the news, and Olivia sat beside me, holding my hand; I could hear her heart beating fast.

And Miss Sally sat in as well, and she was the only one who cried tears when the meeting was over, and the first to come and hug us, and then she left the room, saying, "I just prayed it would happen this way."

I guess Olivia and I took things more calmly than anyone, except, of course, my mother. She seemed to have steel nerves, and she and my father held each other tightly and exchanged a warm kiss. Maybell just held Ollie's hand and kept a big smile on her face.

Finally, Ollie said, "Well, let's break it up, folks. There's work to be done, and lots of it. Rowdy, come with your father and me to check out the ranch and make sure the hands are doing what I want them to do. Olivia, sugarplum, stay with the women folk and keep them busy."

And so we got in Ollie's pickup truck and spun around to check up on the ranch.

First thing we did was head for the Longhorn's pasture, found them settled down, not even looking up from their grazing as we drove around them. "The boys have opened up a bigger pasture," he said. "They will keep feeding them protein pellets while they are getting used to their new home."

Next, we entered the pasture where Ollie had cut out the heifer calves he and dad had agreed on, counted them, marked a couple of underage heifers to cut out, and then headed for the railroad siding to see how work was progressing on the stalls in the box car.

A strong set of corrals had been built at the siding, and a ramp had been built level with the boxcars. That way, the calves could walk right into the cars and be penned.

A loft had been built overhead and a crew of men were busy stacking the loft with bales of sweet bluestem hay.

"The law says the calves will have to be unloaded at least every 12 hours so they can drink, rest and eat hay. That means it will take another 12 hours-plus longer to get them to Missouri than if they were shipped straight on through. But this way, they won't lose weight or get sick as easy."

"When you get home, you will have to give each calf a shot for a disease called shipping fever. Nobody knows what causes it, but it makes them get a high fever, and if it isn't treated early, the calves will die. There's a new medicine called penicillin you inject with a needle that has proved very effective in both preventing and curing the disease. And you may have to treat them two or three times over a period of days. But I would also warn you to not be disappointed if you lose one or two calves. That's just part of this crazy thing called the cattle business," Ollie informed us.

Back then to Salt River for a quick stop at the store, where we were greeted by some of the folks who had been at the wedding, and there was a lot of back-slapping and laughing over the good dunking at the shivaree.

"Just you wait until I get the chance," Ollie bristled. "I'll teach this ol' Missouri hillbilly a thing or two."

As we walked out to the car, a truck pulled up and stopped. A man in a snap brim hat, wearing corduroy pants and a plaid shirt, got out and said, "Any you guys know how to get to the Double O Ranch?"

"Reckon as how I might be able to help you," said Ollie. "So?"

"You know the boss man? Guy named Ollie Oliver."

"I've heard of him. What of it?"

"I'm in the oil drilling business. Want to talk to him."

"Well, sir, I reckon you are just about as close to that old cuss as you will ever get. The Ollie Oliver I know of is a cowboy. And he wouldn't let no oil driller on his ranch if you dangled a million dollars in front of him."

"Oh, so how do you know so much about him?"

"Because I am Ollie Oliver. What's left of him."

The man opened the door of his truck and got out. He stood eyeball to eyeball to Ollie. "You say he wouldn't let a man with a million dollars on his ranch if he wanted to drill for oil?"

"You heard it right."

The man cut off a slice of chewing tobacco from a plug and put it in his mouth. He rolled it around a few times, then spit and looked squarely at Ollie. "How about two million?"

For once, I saw Ollie stammer. But he didn't let up. "How about four million?"

The man grinned. "Let's go talk."

"You sum-bitch," Ollie said. "Show me your credentials. And see if you can keep up with my dust to headquarters."

We piled into Ollie's car and headed for the home place, 80 miles an hour. The only words we heard Ollie say between Salt River town and ranch headquarters was when Ollie growled, "I must be a weak-kneed SOB. I always said I'd shoot the first oil man ever set foot on my place. Now that shows what a lyin' hypocrite I really am."

58

Negotiating

I caught dad's eye and he had a quizzical look on his face. I could see he was having a bit of trouble figuring just how Ollie was thinking. He seemed half glad the oil driller was with us, and half mad.

But by the time we arrived at ranch headquarters, Ollie was his same old jolly, joking self again. About the only thing we had heard out of the oil driller was his name – Buster Dempsey, and that he was an independent driller and prospector.

Dad asked Ollie to let him out at the ranch headquarters, telling him, "I better tell my new bride to start packing if we are going to head back home tomorrow as soon as our heifers are loaded and the train pulls out."

I got out, too, but Ollie said, "Rowdy, unless your dad wants you to stay with him, I'd like you to go with me. I want a witness to what ol' Mr. Oil Driller here tells me."

The driller grinned and winked at me, and dad told me to go with Ollie, and we zoomed toward the bunkhouse and stopped at the stone corral where Fuss and Booger Joe and a couple of cowboys were branding a set of orphan calves.

"Fuss, as soon as you and Joe get finished there, you better hustle down to the rail siding. I plumb forgot about Rowdy's mare he wants to take home. Plus, Papoose as a gift to Rowdy."

I was overwhelmed at the gift, and also glad Ollie had thought of the horses at all. I was learning every day Ollie was a lot more than a happy-go-lucky cowboy, but had a brain and a memory that kept him on top of things all the way.

And with that, he zoomed across the pastures, headed southeast, and, after about ten minutes, he stopped the car, got out and looked at the rolling prairie stretching as far as the eye could see to the southeast. He waved a hand and said, "There is the best part of my ranch. Is there any oil under it?"

The oil man found a stick and began drawing lines in the dust. "I'd like a contract to drill a dozen holes, five miles apart, in a semi-circle. If there is any oil under your dirt, we can find out in a couple of weeks."

"And what if there is no oil?"

"Well, we'll just cap the holes in the ground and move on."

"And if there is oil?"

"We'll have to pick out the most promising sites and drill as deep as necessary to be able to estimate the size of the field and the pressure. That could take a month or so."

"What's your deal?"

"I'll take two thirds, you take a third."

"Get back in the car," Ollie said tartly. "I wasn't born yesterday."

"Wait. I take a fourth."

"One-fifth. Plus…"

"Plus what?"

"You got a bulldozer?"

"Of course."

"I want you to throw in the building of a dozen water tanks on my land. I want them at least fifteen feet deep and as wide as the gullies where we dig them."

"Show me the sites."

"And that ain't all. Everywhere you drill a hole that shows no oil, I want the holes cased with six-gage, one inch pipe dropped down the depth of the holes, and windmills set. I'll pay for the casing, pipe and windmills. You do the work."

The man did a bit of figuring on a note pad, looked off into the shimmering distance, kicked at the dirt and said, "You are a hard-nosed ol' SOB – that's Sweet Old Boy – but you've got a deal."

Ollie shook his hand and we got back in the car. As we drove along, Ollie said to me, "Son, Rowdy, that is. You are going to be a member of my family not too long in the future. You've got a better head on your shoulders than my own sons. The difference in you and my sons is that you stay hitched to something until it is done. Until my boys learn to do that, they will never be ranch managers.

"You have just received your first lesson in ranch and estate management."

And he pushed on the gas and in no time we were back at headquarters, and my mind was whirling so fast I hardly knew what to think next.

But Ollie settled that for me, too.

"Son, how do you figure on going back home. Do you want to ride in the cattle cars with the heifers and help tend to them? Or would you prefer to ride with your parents?"

That's the first I had thought about that. It made me flash back to the train ride JJ and I had made, it seemed like an eternity ago. The rumble of the steel wheels on the track, the whistle of the engine at the crossings, the smoke and grit we sometimes choked on came back in a flash.

While I gave it little thought at the time, I realized now I was in misery after misery. Did I really want to undergo that experience again?

And then it flashed across my mind that I was about to be torn away from the one thing I most wanted to not be torn away from, and that was Olivia. I just about choked and had to hold back tears at the thought.

"I say, Rowdy, did you hear me?"

I was slow in getting out the words, but I said, "Truth is, I had not thought about it. Could you understand if I said part of me does want to go back home, and the other part of me wants to stay here all of the rest of my life – with you and Maybell and the boys – and especially Olivia."

He laid a hand on my shoulder and said softly – or at least as softly as Ollie could say anything – "I know what you are thinking. I had an occasion in my young years when I was at that same crossroad."

"What did you do?"

He laughed and a smile crinkled his sunburned face. "I let my heart guide me."

"And what did your heart tell you?"

"Same as your's is telling you right now. I stayed with Maybelle."

I felt a deep affection for him at that moment. But it still didn't seem right, my mother and father finally settling their problems and tying the knot again, this time I believed for good. They needed each other, just as bad as I needed Olivia and she needed me.

But was there anyway to make one decision that would cover both problems? I tried this one on Ollie, but without any hope it would work.

"How about sending Booger Joe and Fuss with the heifers. After all, that's a lot of the responsibility for something I have never done. There's a lot of money involved, and if I was placed in charge of the calves, and something happened, I might make the wrong decision and make some of the calves die."

"Good thinkin'. But what about yourself? Does this mean you are going to ride home in the car with your parents?"

My heart nearly stopped, for that would mean riding in the back seat alone, thinking of nothing except that I did not want to do that. In fact, that was out.

"I'm going to stay here. With you and Maybell and Olivia. I can work for you as a chore boy until I catch on to things, and I can sleep and live in the bunkhouse with the cowboys, and …"

Ollie stopped the car and turned off the key. He looked me square in the eyes as he said, "Rowdy, I would do that in a minute – except for one thing. Your parents. They have gone through hell and high water to get to this point in their lives. I know you are the glue that can hold them together. You are the reason they got back together."

We sat there watching a pair of crows fly over, circle and go on their way. I felt pressured as never before. Gradually, a thought came to me that might work.

"Could you – and Maybell – go back home with us? I mean, it is your cattle that are being shipped, and dad and you and Maybell and Olivia could stay in my grandmother's big two-story house for a few days – or weeks – and that would give you a chance to look over the country to see if there is any land you might want to buy and start another ranch. Would that work?"

A slow smile softened his sunburned face. "Son, you may have hit on it. Tell me more."

"Well, for one thing, if Booger Joe goes along, and Fuss, that means Booger Joe will get to see his mother and sister again. Grandma could pass away any day, at her age. I have a feeling Booger Joe would like to make it up to her for running away and never letting them know where he was. That was a pretty cold-hearted thing, when you stop to think about it. I believe he would like for her to forgive him.

"And then, there is Miss Sally to think about, too. I bet she would like to see some of the rest of the world, too. So she could go. Maybell and you could take your car, and she could ride with you. And Olivia and I could ride with my mother and father. And we would be all set."

He rumpled my hair and gave me a hug. "I am thinking more of you all the time. Let me try that on the rest of the old folks."

He started the car, laughing, and said, "Let's circle around the Longhorns and see how that old bull and his girls are doing before we go in."

59

Heading Out

It was only a fifteen minute drive to the pasture where we had penned the Longhorns. The cows were all lying down, chewing their cuds, and the calves were nestled up beside them, their heads curled around and eyes closed.

Only the old bull was standing, and he was so lazy he was chewing his cud standing up.

The bull showed no distress from his few minutes of being "knocked out" or of having a substantial section of his horns sawed off. The blood had disappeared and the end of the horns had healed.

In fact, it seemed his bad temper had disappeared with the horn operation. "Ollie," I asked, "could it be that the weight of the horns was uncomfortable and that made him angry all of the time? Is that why we saw him so many times pawing the ground or butting a tree – trying to relieve himself of that horrible weight."

Ollie chuckled. "Could be, Rowdy. I sure wouldn't want to carry a set of horns ten feet long around on the top of my head all the time, would you?"

We drove around the herd, headed back to the ranch headquarters and stopped at the corrals where Toby and Polecat were breaking some new quarter horses to ride. Ollie motioned them to ride over to us.

"Boys, I want you to send Fuss and Booger Joe to me in the office as soon as they ride in. Your mother and I, and Olivia, are leaving in the morning for Missouri. Just as soon as Fuss and Joe drive the heifers to the rail siding and load them out, we will be on our way. Fuss and Joe are going to ride with the cattle."

"You two are going to be in charge while we are in Missouri. It may be a week, it may be more. You can get in touch with me by calling Rowdy's folks at their home. I'm going to scout for some land. We may start a ranch up there. They say there is lots of good land, cheap."

"I'll send Fuss back on the train, but like as not Booger Joe may stay a while, for Sally is going along with us. I'll leave directions on how to reach me, and you be sure and call me every day, at high noon. You hear?"

And we were off again, this time stopping at the house where my folks were already packing the trunk of the car with their bags.

"Rowdy, what do you have you want to take back home?" dad asked.

That was the first I had thought about my so-called belongings. Fact was, I didn't hardly have any belongings, except what I had worn all summer long. Oh, Miss Sally had patched my jeans, and she had dug out some of Booger Joe's old jeans and shirts for both JJ and me. And Joe had given me a pair of his old boots and a jumper.

"What little I have to pack back home is at Miss Sally's," I said. "We'll have to drive by her place on the way out."

Olivia came out of the house and said, "Supper's ready when you are. What are you gossiping about?"

"About going to Missouri," Ollie said. "Better get your things packed early so we can be ready to roll in the morning. Is there anything in particular you want to take?"

"Of course, I want to take my puppies and their mother. I couldn't live without my seven babies for a single day."

And so the day ended with a big meal, lots of happy, light-hearted talk, but with the least hint of tension at the idea of just what might lie ahead of us.

Booger Joe in particular was subdued, a little nervous as opposed to his usual wise-cracking mood. The bags were packed with everything we would need, except for the things we would pick up in the morning at Miss Sally's place.

I longed to be alone with Olivia for a little while and she got permission from her mother to go out and sit on the porch swing, "But don't stay out past 10 p.m.," she said. "You know what a sleepy head you are."

And so the lights went out, all except for that big fat one in the sky, and Olivia and I just sat there, looking at it, and thinking and planning. We were both thinking the same thing.

It would be great being together for another week, possibly more. But what then?

"I'm not coming back without you, Rowdy."

"I won't let you," I said, as she snuggled down deep into my arms.

And that's how Maybell found us when she got out of bed and found the moon sinking into the western sky and she more or less walked two sleepy heads to bed.

While Maybell hustled Olivia off to get dressed, Ollie came by and said, "Hustle up, Rowdy. This is going to be the busiest day of your life. Let's grab a quick bite at the bunkhouse and be on our way."

"On our way where?"

"You and I have to hook onto the horse trailer and go to Miss Sally's and load your mare and Papoose. We are to meet the boys at the ranch. They are getting ready to drive the whiteface calves to the siding. We want to be loaded no later than 9 a.m. because if we don't, we will have to wait another 24 hours to ship out the cattle."

The camp cook had ham sandwiches and hot coffee, which we took to the car, and we were spinning down the lane to the road almost before my eyes were open. But before we left, we had to stop.

Salt River Sally was in the front yard, with a stranger sitting in a kitchen chair. She was welding a pair of scissors and trimming a stranger's hair.

"What the…?" Ollie exclaimed. He got out of the car and walked over to her and then turned around laughing and said, "Hey, Rowdy. Come see who's getting a haircut and shave."

I walked over and was flabbergasted. The "stranger" in the chair, with a towel around his neck and shoulders and long hair covering on the ground around him was none other than my uncle – Booger Joe.

"Well, I couldn't let my man go out in civilization looking like an animal. Joe hasn't trimmed his beard or shaved his face in a coon's age."

Joe just wrinkled his nose and scratched it. "Didn't think I ought to scare Ma when I get back to Missouri," he said. "Doubt she will know me anyhow."

We got a good laugh, if not a somber one, then we were off.

Ollie drove with one hand while he stuffed a huge ham sandwich in his mouth. I took my time on mine, for in the first place, I ate slowly, and in the second place, it tasted so good I wanted it to last.

It didn't take over thirty minutes, the way he was driving, for us to pull up in Miss Sally's yard, pile out and head to the horse pen.

"Will she come to you, Rowdy?"

"I doubt it, but I can catch her in the pasture all right. Just wait on me. She might spook if you go after her."

Sure enough, Lady Midnight had not forgotten me, and although I had forgotten to get a handful of oats for her, she trusted me and I slipped a halter on her and then led her to the oat bin.

She took the oats from my hand, I patted her on the neck and rubbed her nose and she nickered as if to say, "Thanks a lot, buddy. And by the way, where have you been the last week or so?"

Ollie let down the tailgate of the trailer, she walked up the ramp, and we closed it and were on our way. "Another thirty minutes and we'll be at the rail siding. I hope the boys didn't forget to build the partition to keep the calves and the mare separate. I swear, she is apt to have her baby any hour now."

"I wonder what she is bred to," I mused. "I hope it is not some clod-hopper work horse. Or something just as bad."

"I wouldn't worry about that," said Ollie. "The only horses she had been running with are just good ol' cow ponies. There's no work horses left in this part of Texas."

We arrived at the rail siding just as the sun peeked over the horizon, got out and unloaded the mare and led her to the boxcar. The ramp was down, but Ollie had me hold her by the halter strap until he shoved the roller doors back and examined the inside of the boxcar.

"The boys did a good job," he said. "She has a nice spacious stall, with a watering cup and feed box in place. See if she will let you lead her up the ramp and into the car."

She balked just a bit, but after I petted her, walked the length of the halter strap and showed her I could walk up the ramp, she nickered and nodded her head and came clattering up the ramp and inspected her new quarters.

The minute we closed the gate into her stall, she started eating prairie hay, nickering at us as if to say, "Thanks a bunch, fellows. This sure is a nice new home."

And so it was back to the ranch to see how the drive to the rail siding was progressing. We got there just as the 200 short-yearling whiteface heifers were being driven out of the pasture, headed for the railroad.

Fuss led the way on his white gelding, with Booger Joe in the drag, Polecat and Toby on the west side and two other cowboys on the right side.

The calves wanted to graze at first, but the cowboys kept them in close until they began to hold into a bunch and travel.

After the initial start, when the calves wanted to run, they quieted down into a close bunch, and in an hour's time, they were being driven into the pen at the stockyards.

Booger Joe slammed the gate shut. The calves circled the pen, looking for a way out, but settled down. Inside the pen, the six cowboys began to press the calves toward the loading ramp, taking their time, until finally the calves in the lead begin to nibble at the bedding, and then the horses pushed the calves and they flowed into the boxcars as if they welcomed the clean straw bedding with the prairie hay strung along the sides of the box car.

The gates slammed shut on the first car, then on the second car, and Ollie yelled, "Well done, men. And just in time, for here comes the locomotive."

The train whistled four or five miles to the east of us, and let out its long, mournful cry and we could see the smoke from the locomotive, and within ten minutes it was chuffing to a halt. The brakeman jerked loose the coupling at the middle of the train, the engineer tooted its movement signal, and pulled ahead. The brakeman broke the coupling in the rails, the engineer backed up the train until pulled to the siding, backed up and with a loud "clang" and a jerking of the cars, closed the coupling and began to pull forward. Once on the track, the brakeman closed the coupling, the train backed up with another loud "clang" that signified the coupling was complete.

Fuss and Booger Joe threw their war bags on to the train, next to Lady Midnight's stall while Ollie cornered the brakeman. "You've got your orders and destination?"

"Right, we go through Tulsa, into Missouri at Clinton, then south toward Springfield, Missouri."

"Right, but you drop the two cars at Pearl, Missouri. That's twenty miles north of Springfield."

"Gotcha. So long." He waved at the engineer, leaning out of the engine in front, and he signaled with two short "Toot-toots" and the train moved slowly forward.

As it began to pick up speed, the first car carrying Fuss and Booger Joe passed by. They had Lady Midnight where she could look out at us, and they waved their hats and finally disappeared miles ahead, black smoke a silent signal of Missouri bound travelers.

Ollie put his arm around my shoulders as we walked back to his car. "Son, this is a far cry from the first day you hit in Salt River, isn't it? Who would have dreamed it could begin so innocently, and end up so great?"

I couldn't answer because there was a lump in my throat.

What a crazy thing I had done. Run away from home with my pal, JJ, and have a summer-long adventure that ended with changes in my life that far exceeded anything I had ever read in Ace Western Magazine.

I said that to Ollie.

He let out that deep bellowing laugh. "And this is the real thing, ain't it, Rowdy? Everything except the barrooms, whisky and wild, wild women."

Now we had to hustle back to the ranch, gather up our families for the trip back to Missouri – and try to envision what would happen next.

When we pulled up in front of the house, my mother and dad came to the porch and asked me to come and help with their baggage, Olivia waved at me and asked me to help with her suitcase and in less time than it takes to tell it, the cars were packed, and we were ready to get in the car.

But Olivia let out a yell. "Oh, my gosh. I nearly forgot. My doggies."

"Oh, come on, sis," Ollie said. "You don't want to take your pups on the trip. Leave them be."

But nothing would do but that we had to go to the barn, get a bushel basket to put the puppies in and carry them back to the car. Moochie and Dolly wagged along, anxious to see what we were going to do with the puppies, and we put them in the back seat. Olivia sat on one side of the basket, I was on the other side, and Dolly and Moochie were on the floor board.

Sally piled in the back seat of the other car with Ollie at the wheel, and Maybell yelled at him, "Now you just slow down and drive careful and no looking at the cows and horses in the pastures while you are supposed to be driving."

And our little caravan was off in a rush in a cloud of dust, headed for Missouri.

And my home, sweet home. Olivia reached out and squeezed my hand and gave me a peck on the cheek and both of us felt the excitement of the moment. What things lay ahead of us? We had no idea. Except we knew they were going to be good things.

We buzzed through Salt River, gave a salute to the few people up and working at that hour, and headed for the major highway to the north about fifty miles – Route 66, the main road leading from St. Louis, Missouri through Oklahoma and into Texas, and as far as I knew, all the way to California.

But I didn't care what lay to the west. What I was anxious to see, and as soon as possible, was good old Missouri – my home state.

We made remarkable time, there not being many cars on the road at that hour, and before long Olivia and I fell asleep. When we woke up, my mother was driving while dad slept, and she said, "We will take turns driving and stop only for gasoline, restroom stops and sandwiches. I think we are all anxious to get home as soon as possible."

And so it was into Oklahoma, through the amazing cities of Oklahoma City and Tulsa. I could not believe the amount of business buildings and skyscrapers, but they did not appeal to me. I was plenty satisfied just to pass on by, and I liked the looks of the ranch land a lot better.

By the time we hit the Missouri border, we were all about to go to sleep so we stopped – it was nearly dusk by now – and got out to stretch and eat our first real meal of the trip.

"But it was soon time to roll again, this time with dad driving and the rest of us snoozing in our seats and plenty ready to end the trip as soon as possible. It must have been midnight when I suddenly had the sensation that we were slowing down and getting ready to stop.

Dad said, "Hey, sleepy heads, wake up. We're home. Home at last, thank God Almighty."

Sure enough. I looked up to see the lights blazing at my grandmother's big two-story colonial house. She was standing on the porch, waiting for us.

"Land-a-mercy," she cried. She ran down the steps, gave each one of us a hug and kiss, and guided us to the long front porch and under the electric lights. To Olivia, she said, "So you are the main attraction that took care of my baby boy while he was in Texas." She gave Olivia a bear hug and kiss, and took her hand and lead her into the living room, as the rest of us followed.

But dead tired from the trip, we all begged for relief. She guided us upstairs to the bedrooms, where the covers were all laid back and ready.

"Let's all go to bed. There will be plenty of time for talking after the sun comes up. Olivia, you come with me. I have a special bedroom ready just for you."

And so ended my homecoming. Little fanfare. But lots of love.

"Good night, all." And we were all at peace, but keenly aware that a lot lay ahead of us, still.

The calves and Lady Midnight, Booger Joe and Fuss, would they be in tomorrow?

And the larger matter. How would my other grandmother react when she once again saw her long lost son Frank, whom she had given up for dead?

60

The Reunion

My grandmother Farmer-Stellama was accustomed to feeding crews at harvest time.

So it was no trick at all for her to have steaming sausage, eggs and hotcakes for her family and guests the following morning. The mood was light, as we were all happy to be in Missouri.

The first subject of the day was how to approach my other grandmother, Ellama, about her long-lost son, Joe.

Mother brought up the subject. "If we don't do it carefully, at her age she could have a heart attack and die right before our very eyes.

"Rowdy, my son, I think you should go with me to help."

Booger Joe and Fuss were to be in on the morning train, so it was decided Ollie and Pa would tend to the calves' transport. Ma and I would pick up Booger Joe, and we three would head to Cave Spring.

And so the laughing and joking and banter went on until the sound of a steam engine whistle broke up the party.

"Oh, Lord, how time flies when you're having fun," dad said. "The train is early this morning. We've got about thirty minutes before she stops at Pearl, cuts loose our two cars of calves and the mare. Let's be on the way. You girls want to tag along?"

"Of course," Olivia said, her eyes shining.

So in a jiffy, the kitchen was empty and we all piled into two cars and drove the two miles to the Pearl station of the Frisco Railroad.

We stood by the siding, watching the sun clear the timber and show off the barns and houses in the countryside, but anxious to see the engine come in sight around the long bend from the little village of Walnut Grove, an even smaller stop than Pearl.

Finally, we could see the smoke lifting above the tree tops and the Frisco engine left the trees and came directly toward us at only a three mile distance.

What a thrill stirred through me as I saw it coming. Within minutes I knew I would see my very own cowpony, one I had ridden on a Texas ranch with real cowboys, and my heart was just about to burst.

And then the train chuffed even with us, slowing down, but passing us. I could see the white faces of the heifer calves peering out to see where they were. They bawled lustily, as if saying they were glad to see us, begging to be free.

The engine backed up to put the two cattle cars on the siding, the clang-clang of the cars slipping on past the engine pulling ahead to clear the siding rails, and then backing up to lock on to the rest of the train.

And then with two "toot-toots" of the departure, the engine and train were headed toward Willard, and we were all rushing across the tracks to peer through the slats in the cars and see the calves.

"Suddenly, the heavy door on the last car slid open, and there, leaning over the heavy plank railing and waving their big Texas hats, were Claud Fussell and Joe.

They lowered the rail and I was the first to get to them.

"How's my lady Midnight?"

Fuss thrust out his work-hardened hand and grabbed me, and in one pull had me standing inside the cars. "See for yourself," he shouted, over the calves.

I took two steps in the direction he pointed, and there was Lady Midnight, her delicate head with the white star between the eyes and the Little pin-like ears thrusting forward. She knew me. Then Papoose came to me nickering.

"Baby," I cried. "You are home. Home at last." I hugged her and rubbed her neck and she nuzzled my face and a soft, almost inaudible nicker came from her. She nibbled my ear as if to say, "Bless you, Rowdy."

But then Fuss came to stand by. "Look over in yon corner of the boxcar, Rowdy. See anything?"

I peered around my mare and there, cuddled up in a corner, on a nest of bright yellow straw was my prize…

Lady Midnight's foal snoozed soundly in her nest. At last, my dreams had come true. I began with none, and great fortune left me with three fine horses.

We unloaded the calves and drove them to the pasture where they were to graze until moving them to a corral for special care.

I picked up the foal and put her into the bed of a pickup truck, and tied Lady Midnight to the side of the truck so she could look after her baby as we drove slowly back to the farm.

We placed them in my grandmother's front yard where she could be in the shade of the ancient sugar maples, and we could watch them from the broad front porch.

Booger Joe was collected, and me, my mother and my uncle were off the Cave Spring.

My grandmother and my aunt, Winnie, lived in a three-room frame house at the end of an alley a quarter mile from the Mt. Zion church, "the first Presbyterian church west of the Mississippi," as my folks were fond of saying.

Somehow, as we drove up and parked in front of the little house, I had expected to see it look differently. Larger, perhaps.

But nothing had changed just because of my absence. The same huge oak tree stood guard at the front gate, and the gate still squeaked because it needed oil, and the lawn had been mowed to perfection by my aunt pushing her lawnmower. Out back, her milk cow bawled to her calf, than galloped to her and began nursing. The old two-hole privy was still intact behind the hen house and the hens were out scratching for worms and clucking to their little ones. The big mulberry tree I used to climb showed signs of having produced a bumper crop this year.

Next door was the unpainted little home of Charlie and Tillda Rollin, and the triplets, Ruby, Tina and May. I was anxious to see them, and check in on JJ and Mary. But first things first.

I walked beside mother as she stepped on the concrete porch, freshly swept as usual, and mother opened the front door, stuck her head inside, and said, "Yoo-hoo. Anybody home?"

I could hear my aunt's footsteps coming to the door and as mother stepped inside, she made her customary gesture of throwing up her hands and saying, "Law's a-mercy. Nellie."

And I stepped around mother and said, "Hi, Winnie." Mother actually had to grasp her arm and steady her to prevent her from falling backward.

"He's home, sis," mother said. "We are all home. Everything is back to normal – and then some. How's ma?"

My aunt was always in control, and it didn't take long for her to size up the situation. She stepped out on the porch, gave me a bear hug and a kiss, scolded me for being a bad boy, but that God said to forgive, and she had forgiven me.

She looked out in the car and said, "Who is your company?"

Mother took her arm and said, "Maybe we had better sit down while I tell you something. Our dear brother is alive and well, and has been all these years. Rowdy found him. It's a long story, but he is well – and he is the passenger in my car." This really gave my aunt the shakes. She grabbed my arm and mother's and we kept her from falling. She trembled all over, but she did not panic. She said, "God tells us to have the faith of angels, and angels would be sent to us."

Mother said, "Rowdy, go tell Joe to get out and come in. All is well."

And so I did. And my uncle Joe – Booger Joe – came walking slowly but steadily toward his two sisters, a huge grin on his face. He grabbed Winnie and hugged her tight and she just wouldn't let go, and it was the first time in my life I ever saw tears in her eyes.

She said, "My prayers have been answered. This will ease the pain Ma has carried with her ever since you disappeared."

Mother left them sitting on the front porch, while she went in to prepare Ellama for the surprise of her life. And when Winnie came to the door and said, "It is alright." I told her, "She doesn't believe it. So break the news slow and easy. She cannot see well. She will want to feel your face and your eyes and when she is satisfied, I know she will smother you with kisses."

I had to choke back tears myself, and I followed them into the house where Ellama was sitting, as usual, in her old wicker rocking chair she had inherited from her half-Cherokee mother. It was a controlled reunion, and the air was thick with love and happiness, and she and Uncle Joe sat side by side, just holding on to each other, not talking, but letting the sorrow and pain wash away and become replaced once more with flesh and blood contact.

I used this interlude to slip out and go next door to see if the triplets were home, and they were, helping their bent, old and frail mother pour boiling water into a kettle in which she washed her clothes.

The girls all gave hugs, shouting, "Now we can play baseball with you again," and "Does JJ know you are home? When did you get back?"

I told them I didn't have time just then to talk more, but to run and tell JJ I was back home, too, now, and to come and see me. Then I went back to be with my family.

Things had loosened up by now. Ellama was cracking jokes as usual and shaking her cane at Uncle Joe now and then and threatened to turn him over her knee like she used to do, if he ever ran away from home again.

And Uncle Joe was telling her not to worry, he would never run away again – but he would still try get out of the reach of her hickory stick.

We stayed a couple of hours until mother suggested we get back to the Farmer home but Uncle Joe said he would stay, visit, maybe look around the place some, but mostly, "Just sit and talk to ma and make up for lost time."

Mother and I walked out to our car, turned around to drive back home when we saw what appeared to be half the population of Cave Spring walking and running toward us.

"Gosh sakes, mom, look who is coming to see us. JJ, the triplet girls, and all the store porch loafers in town."

I started running toward JJ fast as I could, and he ran toward me. We cuffed each other on the shoulder, backed off and started laughing.

"You son-of-a-gun," he said. "You made it back home, didn't you?

I half thought I'd never see you again, I thought you'd stay in Texas forever."

By that time, of course, Ruby, Tina and May were crowding up to talk, and then the store porch gang arrived, and it took fifteen or twenty minutes to get the folks settled down.

I had figured I would be treated like some kind of bum, for having run away from home and worried my family near to death, but here I was being treated like a hero. I tried to change the subject by letting on that I had really gone on a trip to try and find my uncle – and while that was the truth in a way, I really never expected to find him. So that made it all right.

Nothing would do the town folks but that we stop in at the store and let them buy us a couple of bottles of soda pop, and visit with other folks that happened to stop at the store, and then we got into mother's car, waved so-long, and headed back to our farm.

As we crossed the bridge over Asher Creek, I glanced down to see what the water looked like. It was crystal clear, as usual, and I thought I could see a big bunch of minnows swimming around. I just couldn't wait to wet a line again.

We drove back home to see Olivia, Miss Sally and Maybell rocking and swinging on the front porch and enjoying the cool breeze. Dad and Ollie were headed for the gate and dad said, "Just going to show Ollie our milk cows, then I'll take him around the country and see if he likes what he sees."

So that left Olivia and me to tend to our dogs and puppies, and then I took her in grandmother's big house and showed her all the rooms, and the pictures of our ancestors on the walls, and finally we walked down a cow path to the timber a quarter mile away.

We were pretty quiet by this time, as we began to realize there was a lot of things ahead of us, but we really didn't know just what to do.

Finally, Olivia said, "Rowdy, do you really want me?"

"Olivia, there is no doubt about it. You are the girl of my dreams, although I never really dreamed about a girl. But this summer has made me grow up. Just a few months ago, I was just a spoiled kid, angry at my dad, my mother, and just about all the world. I wanted to hurt them as they had hurt me, and I did."

"I guess in the back of my mind I imagined I might find my uncle Joe, but the truth is, I never really started out to do that. I just wanted to hurt my folks like they had hurt me."

"Never did I dream I would meet you and fall head over heels. And we did, didn't we?"

We giggled silly-like, and we walked hand-in-hand around the farm, just looking and thinking. We went back to the house in time for a big noon dinner of fried chicken and gravy and mashed potatoes and finished off with homemade ice cream.

By the time the day had ended and dusk settled in, we were all talked out. We just got quiet, listening to the katydids in the trees. One by one, we drifted up to our rooms, dressed for bed, said our good-nights, sleep-tights, and we could only hear the lonely call of the whippoorwills as we drifted off to sleep.

61

New Beginnings

I was on a bucking horse, and I was about to be thrown and trampled by a herd of Longhorns and the old black bull was coming closer and closer to me. I tried to reach out and grab the saddle as Lady Midnight ran past me but I missed and I felt myself falling, falling, falling, and trampling hooves were right on top of me…

And then I dimly heard the voice of my grandmother Farmer, shaking me and saying, "Rowdy, Rowdy, wake up. You are having a bad dream."

I opened my eyes. I was still seeing that massive herd of cattle stampeding and about to run over me and the old black bull was just about to gore me.

But then I rubbed my eyes, looked up from my bed and saw my grandmother's gentle face hovering over me. "That was a mighty lively dream you were in, Rowdy. You were yelling for help about a bull after you and you were about to get trampled to death by a thundering herd."

"Oh, I was really having a deep nightmare, wasn't I. I see you clear as daylight, but it is so strange. I can still see the stampede I was caught up in."

"Breakfast is almost ready, son. Your dad wants you to get up and eat so you can go help with the calves."

And so she left me to dress and use the bathroom. I glanced out the window and saw the milk cows coming up the lane toward the barn. They stopped to drink at the water tank, then hurried on into the big dairy barn where two men were getting ready for them.

I thought what a difference it was to live on a farm in Missouri, compared to a ranch in Texas. Here, the cows had to be teased into the stanchions that held them while they were being milked, and the calves had to be fed from a bottle with giant nipples.

But in Texas, the cows ran loose in the pastures and the calves did the milking. I must confess that although I was in love with my little Jersey calves, and enjoyed the thrill of showing them in competition at the local fair and the state fair as well, my choice was beef cows and calves.

"Don't be lazy Rowdy," I remembered my grandfather telling me before he died, "There is a place for both kinds of cattle. You can have both kinds when you grow up, if that is what you want. But you must learn to handle both kinds."

From my upstairs bedroom, I could hear voices downstairs, and one of them woke me up right quick. It was the voice of Olivia.

I just couldn't hardly believe my good fortune. Here I was back at my home where I was born, I had spent the summer in Texas on a cattle ranch, I had had all kinds of adventures and learned things I never would have learned if I hadn't been a "bad boy." And yet, I had found the most important treasure anyone could ever have.

I had found the girl of my dreams. And here she was, in my very own home, where I had been born, and where I fully expected to live the rest of my life.

I rushed down the stairs, remembering that I used to slide down the railing, but now realized that was kid stuff, and I just walked into the kitchen. There sat Olivia, her mother and Miss Sally. Stellama was already dishing stacks of hotcakes, bacon, eggs, and gravy into great bowls.

"Well, Mr. Sleepy Head," Olivia teased. "Have you planned to sleep all day?"

I sat down beside her, but refrained from giving her a peck on the cheek and settled for a squeeze on her hand under the table. "No, I just overslept so I could relive my greatest adventure – running away from Old Blacky, the Longhorn bull."

That, of course, started up the story of my trip to Texas and I didn't have to say another words as I ate, for Olivia, Maybell and Sally talked about the things I had done and said, until breakfast was over and the women folks were washing the dishes.

When I asked where mother and Booger Joe were, Stellama said, "They went to have breakfast with your grandmother McLin. It's been a long time since they were together. They deserve and need some privacy until they recover from the shock of having Joe back home. I hope he stays."

That brought Sally up out of her chair. "But he cannot stay. He's my man. I've got to have him – even if he is worthless as teats on a boar hog."

That brought tears of laughter to everyone except Sally. Stellama said, "Miss Sally, you are as welcome as rain, if you want to stay here, too, with Joe and the rest of our family."

Sally's face got red. "I'm sorry. But just the thought of not having that worthless cowpuncher around to aggravate me scared me to death."

Dad and Ollie stepped into the kitchen. "Well, didn't save anything for us, huh?" dad said. "Have you got any pancake batter left? I see plenty of syrup left."

"Have a seat, Ollie. Mother will whomp up a feed of cakes and eggs before you get up to the table," dad smiled.

As we all sat there, quiet and grateful for a good breakfast and our blessings, Joe, my mother, my Aunt Winnie, and my beloved Ellama drove up.

They got out, admired the new comers to our livestock. Then, around the corner came several someone's that we had seemingly over looked and forgotten about in all of our excitement.

It was Dolly and her seven puppies, and daddy Moochie happily escorting them.

Olivia and I were sitting in the middle of all this, hugging each other. It was just a fraction of the many, many years of joy and blessings that were to come.

My reverie was evidently longer than I had anticipated, for my youngest grandchild, sitting at my feet said, "Go on gram'pa. Don't stop now. You just got to the exciting part, I bet."

I bent over and picked her up and sat her on my lap. "But little 'Livia, your gramps is weary from talking so much. Now you all must permit me to stop for a rest. But tomorrow night, I promise – I will tell you more of the story of our lives – and how you all came to be. Is that fair?"

Little 'Livia started to pout, but when grandmother Olivia picked her up and carried her to the door and took the puppy from her arms she puckered up. "'Livia wants baby Moochie to sleep with her."

And so her grandmother Olivia carried her around the room where the rest of our large family had so patiently endured the story of our life and times.

It seemed our children would never tire of the story of our lives, how mother Olivia and I met and married so young and had accumulated seven children of our own. And now, how the family had grown by ten more children – and plenty of the time for that number to increase, if the desire was to be ordained.

Yes, our golden moments were untarnished as I looked around the spacious living room of the large colonial house my grandparents had built long before even I was born. Even so, our memories were so enriched and love so deep that our faith kept us all together.

We had long since come to believe in the Life Everlasting. Living and loving and working as we had these many years had taught us there was no such thing as eternal death, but to the contrary, eternal life existed in another dimension of this vast universe we call our home.

I was never far away from the words of my beloved wife, Olivia, that day in Texas when we together discovered the litter of puppies from Olivia's dog, Dolly. We had found them in a barn on the Oliver Ranch, seven of them, and we were overjoyed.

And Olivia, then my best girl and later to be my wife, saw a vision of our lives together.

"Oh, look," she had exclaimed. "Seven puppies. Seven is a lucky number. Oh Rowdy, does this mean we will have seven babies?"

And so her happy moment had come to pass and we did, indeed, have seven babies – two sets of twins, and the last ones a single, each named after their parents, or maternal or paternal grandparents.

And now the requisite number of seven had stretched to ten, in grandchildren.

And I had not the slightest doubt that in time, our Creator who had found and kept us together all of these years would bring about the second "magic number" of babies and we would attain a total of fourteen grandchildren in due time.

Our parents had by now all joined our ancestors in the "life beyond life," and their physical remains rested in graves near where they were born. But there was never a day in the lives of those of us still on this earth that they were not with us in memory and were sharing our lives in spirit form.

Life never ends, we have taught our children. It just changes form. The spirit is still intact, and it will always be so.

Thus, our old friends, the cowboys that had lived and worked all their lives on our ranches in both Texas and Missouri were "with us" on special occasions such as our Christmas and New Year's days, and on special occasions when we were troubled and needed spiritual support, and always our troubles vanished and we knew we were being cared for.

I often thought of my old boyhood friend, JJ, and the triplets, Ruby, Tina and May. They had lived tough lives but they were always happy to the end. Aunt Mary was accorded a special honor when a burial place for her was found in the very center of our church cemetery. It was the white folks' way of honoring her for the truth and courage this one-time slave had given to all of us.

JJ's mother and father, Mary and Sherman, had moved to the big city where life was easier for them, and the future brighter. They, too, were sleeping the long sleep but I am certain their calls were among the highest in honor.

Olivia's brothers, the wild young scamps, had settled down and married hometown Texas girls and each had large families and they were still living, boasting they were, "Too tough to die," but I always kidded them, "You are too mean to die and even the devil doesn't have any place to keep you."

But in truth, they were honored and respected in Texas as the most honest and capable stockmen of all, as well as overseers of the oil fields of the home ranch. My time, and Olivia's was divided between our Missouri cattle operations and helping my brothers-in-law manage the Texas holdings.

Fuss and Boy, our cowboy friends, hold special places in the cowboy cemetery on the ranch, and my uncle, Booger Joe, and his incomparable wife, Salt River Sally, still live on their beloved ranch on her home place.

What will be next? That's a question Olivia and I have asked ourselves thousands of times, but can never find a satisfactory answer.

We finally decided that our futures were to remain secret, even as we draw our last breaths on this old earth.

But those days after our hearts have ceased to beat, our guardian angels will pluck the living spirits from our useless physical bodies and in some fashion we are not capable of understanding, present the record of our lives to the Council On High.

There, we will be born again in different form, but with personalities intact, and hopefully honored for our work in our short lives on earth, and then prepared for new assignments somewhere in the never-beginning, never-ending universe.

And now, I must stop dreaming. All the family has left grandma's living room and gone to sleep, as Olivia and I remain, in loving embrace.

Peace.

www.ingramcontent.com/pod-product-compliance
Lightning Source LLC
LaVergne TN
LVHW050923080826
845145LV00001B/194

* 9 7 8 0 5 7 8 0 3 0 0 5 0 *